Life of Death

by Philip Lewis

FICTION
COLLECTIVE
T W O

Boulder • Normal

Published by Fiction Collective Two with support given by the English
Department Publications Unit of Illinois State University, the English
Department Publications Center of the University of Colorado at Boul-
der, the Illinois Arts Council, and the National Endowment for the Arts

Address all inquiries to: Fiction Collective Two, c/o English Department,
Publications Center, College Box 494, University of Colorado at Boulder, Boulder, CO 80309-0494

Life of Death
Philip Lewis

ISBN: Cloth, 0-932511-74-0, $18.95
ISBN: Paper, 0-932511-75-9, $8.95

Produced and printed in the United States of America
Distributed by the Talman Company

Cover/Jacket Design: Dave LaFleur

"See them clamor, these nimble apes! They clamor over one another, and thus scuffle into the mud and the abyss."

—Nietzsche

LIFE OF DEATH

1

PEOPLE, IN AMERICA, when they read this, will automatically call for its destruction. To them, it will be an object of the utmost evil, an outright pack of lies, some sickly piece of insanity thrown together by some psycho nigger. Well, I hope they think that way—and besides, what's more, I really don't give a damn one way or the other what they think of it. I've had it with those pricks anyhow. The only reason why those sons-of-bitches would call it a piece, call it outlandish and improbable is because it is true, every last bit of it; even the lies here and there have a hell of a lot more truth than the truths because whatever happens to be a lie on my part is the truth to so many others like me who have been laughed right out of society because "they couldn't fit". A likely story. It happens every time. This is all part and parcel of the cancer and the sickness of the nation at large, but at best it is merely an extension. Nevertheless I have done my best to piece together the fragments of this vicious past; but in doing so I came to the likely conclusion that there is no piecing together into any coherent whole any life, or any previous life, which does not make any good sense whatsoever. Things hover in the air, hang together flimsily, but all is fragmented and incoherent and nothing comes together. What we feel is cut away from what we think; and what we think is cut away from what we say, and so on. This is what is known as chaos, and this is why the book is as crazy and fucked-up as it is. People who call this a piece of "lunacy" are merely covering up for the fact that they are just as much a part of that "lunacy" as all the people in America and elsewhere that I have known and the streets that I have walked.

But, in the meantime, I had to get out. I felt like there just wasn't any other choice; I couldn't really decide or figure out just who I was and what I was and where I was going. I wrote, but it meant nothing; I laughed, I sang, I wept, I screwed, I ate and drank and danced, but it was all nothing; it sounded like nothing; it felt like nothing. What I really wanted deep down was to pay back the impossible for all those long years and months and weeks and days and nights of pure insanity, chaos, hopelessness and despair. What I wanted was to destroy, destroy the monsters and the leeches who had made my life a hell, who made the world a hell, who were talking through my mouth and other mouths. If I hadn't gotten away from those goddamn, financial billionaire vampires from Frisco to Cairo from sucking my blood and strumming my vocal chords then all of my past, all of my future, all of my joy and hate and despair and misery and struggles towards some kind of peace of mind would have gone for nothing.

2

I WAS A MEMBER of the black bourgeois, but I tried my damnedest to make like it wasn't so. Really, emotionally, I wasn't, so it wasn't too hard to hide: it always showed itself in the contempt I had for everyone in college. I dropped out at eighteen from Coon State University. The explanation for my dropping out—and my not returning—is a long, long story. It all began when I was very young. I had wanted to be an artist when I was a child. But my mother, Ida Phillips, used to take my crayons away from me every time I even attempted to put something to paper. No matter—I drew on the mirrors with soap. Whenever I did this, she would beat me. "You little turd," she would say, the dumb white Portuguese Jew of a bitch that she was, "I don't want you to grow up doodling. You've got better things to do...I want you to go into business. So you'd better stop fucking around in school and get your damn math—you'll be using that, and not no goddamn paint-brushes, you hear?" And that was just for starters. For when my father came home, from his bookshop he ran in Dupont Circle during the day, he had to give me a few slaps, too.

My father was a failed businessman—that was all. He didn't make much money at his Third-World bookshop once the eighties came around. No one was interested. Besides, there were always better bookshops around than the one he had running, which was known as, simply, the Third-World

Bookstore. High rent, low customer turn out, books going yellow, leaks in the ceiling—he was fading out. He talked endlessly of filing for bankruptcy protection or welfare. He kept bad books, and it was easy for him to get ripped off. Especially by those other book-runners next door to him, young white hippies and ganja-smokers who, apart from selling Gaddafi's Green Book, took heed and stocked *The Closing of the American Mind.*

And he had, since the 1960s, long since stopped believing in the shit that he was selling. He just jumped on the bandwagon at that time, that's all, just being out of Vietnam, where he had contracted tropical syphilis, and couldn't find himself a job. But that wagon had long since burnt up...My mother didn't stick up for him, though. She had her own life to live, she wasn't the least bit concerned about him. Besides, she was lazy like he was. But what really wrecked my father was that Vietnamese hooker he had fallen for and then murdered by the demands of his lieutenant. (Afterwards, he had murdered *him,* too.) Well...the girl was gone, but the syphilis remained. And nothing availed to stop this strong strain of tropical madness—it was too powerful. By now it was eating up his brain, and he on the whole was an incompetent, foolish, stuttering, nervous, neurotic and emotionally twisted type of man who kept his entire personal life to himself. At least around me—he told a few things to his wife, Ida. But again, that was but a few—the rest she figured out for herself—which was why he and she almost never slept together anymore.

My mother was very white—in contrast to my father. A Portuguese Jew born in New Jersey. Don't ask me how they met—they never told me. (My father was very black.) She had her own career, too—as a check-out clerk in the Ace Supermarket in downtown Belford. To her the job was absolute humiliation; she suffered from severe neuroses and guilt pangs which she took all out on me. She wanted me to grow up and become a success and model myself on the

Lumbford's—my father's family. They were rich, whereas we were poor. (My father had been disinherited.) One of the Lumbford's, a big, hulking, jive-ass cocksucker called Terell, used to come around in his BMW and drop by and see how us lowly petit-bourgeois were doing. They were the envy of all of us four—my older brother was off at Ohio State studying physics. My mother went through pains to try and imitate their lifestyle—wearing the most expensive clothes, etc. But she was only a quasi-psychotic who, once she got off work, began running around with all the white women and men in town she could get her hands on. She had personals running in the newspapers; boys and girls came over while I was at school and father at work. She always demanded money for her services; she was an attractive woman—she really was—who demanded a "generous" friend to keep her "comfy" while her husband was "out of town." She was always successful—Pops never caught her. Except one time—and that was where she had the nick across her cadaverous forehead, where he slashed her with the kitchen knife after being caught with another woman. (And ruined her white silk pillows what with all of the blood.)

And me? I sucked up most of it—but I went on through school, elementary, junior high, high, and finally through my first year of college, trying to make believe that I really was going into business. But in reality, damn if I was. As for the crayons and the soap, I always found them and used them again, and again they were snatched from my hands, and I was slapped in the face by my mom and pop. I also had a violent streak in me—because I wasn't talkative; I didn't like to see people or didn't want to speak to them, unless they came to my level of understanding...meaning, they couldn't like what everyone else liked. They had to be rebels like me.

My mother and father destroyed everything I drew—so I was obliged to hide it all at school. As for that, a little incident in the third grade set the tone for everything else that was to happen to me later. Up till that time I was like a parrot popping

13

out all the stuff they fed me. I told the few friends I had I was going to be rich once I got to be thirty, because I would be a successful businessman. But I was to realize sooner or later what Mom and Pops really felt about me. One time I got beat up by a bunch of little hooligans who then hung me on the fence by my underwear. Once they did this they had a ball pelting me all over with sticks and their fists. When this was over with, the teachers caught them and called my mother because I was unconscious. The way it was told to me, after I was awakened, was that every time they tried to call the house, the phone simply clicked off. So they made me call the number. I called it. All I remember was the tone coming on and then the thing shutting off, and the tone coming back on. This happened twice. I told them it was nothing doing. The teachers were perplexed, and out of their own kindness they decided to send me home. Well...when they got home, and knocked on the door in a teddy and yanked me inside before I could even open my mouth. "You little faggot," she screamed, "was that you who was disturbing me when I was busy? Huh?" The teachers were shocked to find out what kind of a mother I had, so they quietly slipped away. It was a public school, anyway—they didn't want to claim responsibility when I got killed. I didn't die, but since I couldn't speak about what happened, all she did was slap me around with her big wide fists and scream: "You skipped school! You skipped school! You did it, right? Isn't that right?"

"Honey, what's wrong?" yelled a man's voice from way over in the bedroom. "Mom," I said, quaking with fear and anticipating a blow to my face and starting to cry, my chest beginning to swell and heave with sobs. "Who's that strange man inna bedroom? Dat ain't Pop!"

She pushed me on my shoulder... "You ain't supposed to say AIN'T. Now get the fuck upstairs, you little bastard. What happened, got beat up? Huh? What's this scar—"

"Honey, is the kid home? Maybe I oughta leave..." says the voice, again. Who in the hell was this, I thought. "No, baby, stay, stay, I'm getting him out of harm's way…" she then turned to me. "Go upstairs, you shit. Maybe you did get your ass kicked. It's not going to be as bad as when I get my motherfucking hands on your dirty black ass. Go up the fuckin' stairs!" CRACK!—she slapped me. I cried. Soon coming up the hallway was the man in the bedroom—he was white. And nude. And had a hard-on. I departed, seeing him embrace my "mom" and take her back into the bedroom.

And I spent the rest of the night listening to them make love and grunt and fart and rustle around on the bed. Pop didn't return. I didn't know—had he died?

Yet—I grew to hate him, too.

I needed help, I needed someone to reach out to. But there was no one. The Lumbfords were snobs. In high school I finally had a number of friends, but once you've gotten friendship, sometimes you can see through that it's just a bunch of bullshit, that, fundamentally, you can't trust anyone these days. How many times I gave guys money—ten dollars, sometimes, which I stole out of my mom's pocketbook—and then never had it paid back. How many times did my "friends" become enemies the next day, sometimes tying me, during drunken parties, to the hood of the car and racing me around town…and then, the next day, giving a half-assed apology. (I had few real friends—among them, Roddy MacInness, whom I was later to run across at just the right time.) But, at least, in high school, they had the decency to apologize. For when I got to college, when they bashed you in the face, when they threw you off balconies, when they denied you a job, or gave you a bad grade for kicks, there WAS no goddamn apology.

I lived in Belford, Maryland—a tacky suburb which, in the wake of a wave of immigrants, grew into a slum. Perhaps not a massive slum—not yet. The "spics" are still pouring in, filling up the rooming houses, sometimes six or seven to a room, and that story has yet to be written. When I was growing to manhood I watched it rot. Bit by bit, day by day, I watched as the shutters fell off, the trash men stopped coming by and henceforth the garbage piled up, the stoops fell off, and finally all these execrable restaurants selling all this—to me—lousy food such as ox-tail...and nothing in your ears could be heard but Spanish—on our end. There used to be just one "Belford" until it grew a North, a South, a Southwest, an East, a West, etc. In spite of the encroaching rot, and the humiliating experiences with the police as well as in school, I did reasonably well in school—and rarely did my grades drop. In high school, I got no D's or E's. (I **couldn't.**)

Art is a damn expensive hobby, or profession, but that's what I had decided upon eons ago. Soon I went from crayons to pencil. By high school I was using oils—all in class, I didn't want to get caught. But soon I got up enough nerve to send my things home, because my art teachers were strongly encouraging, thank goodness, and saw good potential. They told me there was no reason for me to be ashamed of my artistic skill—I was better than most of them, they said. So I took my oil paintings home and painted there—and found them in the trash, slashed up. Mom did it.

That was that—I hated her guts; I hadn't forgotten her and her honky lover—and I stole one hundred dollars from her purse and headed for the art store. But then I began thinking...I needed more than just supplies. I had to LEAVE home—there was no way I could stay. I was being used just to bring more money into this no good disorganized family household. I remembered the days, in the fifth grade, when I didn't even have lunch, because this was always going to someone else. So I went back and stole more—six hundred, in all. And with it, I went to Riggs National and opened up my first bank account. Then I came back and fucked up the house—totaled it. I hadn't forgotten. I was just keeping it all in. Went to work on the stereo systems with a hatchet, chopping them up so good they didn't even resemble anything like a stereo anymore. The last speaker I saved because I needed that to throw into the television screen. With this done, I felt I had gotten tit for tat—and I was ecstatic with a shitty kind of joy. It was almost as if I had committed a solemn gesture, a religious act. It was beautiful. And the real beautiful thing about it was that they never knew who really did it, because I left right afterwards. They would never have suspected me of committing such a heinous crime, and I prided myself on it, because I got right back at their foolishness and greed in my own little way.

My hate for them never lessened. It grew as time went on. Finally it was decided, before I could even open my mouth, that I was going to Coon State University and major in business. When I heard those words I was jolted—but I was expecting it, somewhat. I just didn't know that I was going to Coon State, that old bastion of Negro education where we all go to get as white as ice cream, and just as cold, too. I knew how to handle this shit, I thought...And so I just followed along with school for a couple semesters until something really bad happened. I was taking more art courses, but still...nobody was encouraging me. Teachers told me I couldn't make it. My colors were too strong, one would say; another would keep his damn mouth shut; and the third would say, too many cool colors, or too Venetian, or I wasn't creative enough—all kinds of crap. I decided—fuck it. Not even in art was I going to cut it. I decided I wasn't going to succeed in America; I wasn't going to assimilate. But I wasn't going to live in the goddamn ghetto, either—least of all Belford, which was worse than the ghetto. I was going to get a plane ticket the fuck out. To Istanbul. Or Amsterdam—which I finally decided upon, because it was so close and the cheapest fare. I didn't dare go for England—I knew about Brits, I thought.

Here's my last day in college. I went in the classroom for French class. Then I stepped out for the bathroom—and never returned. I didn't even go for my books. I couldn't even get registered because the lines were too long, the red tape too tangled up, the cashiers too lazy and obnoxious and rude, the students (children) too nasty and rude, and so I simply tore up my registration materials. If I wasn't going to have a future, it was my choice. I could see that everyone else around me was fucked out mentally, and I decided that I didn't want to be one of them. I didn't care. I slipped away...that's all I remembered. Kapooff.

I got to the bus stop. This part I well remembered. I left EVERYTHING behind—even my art work. I felt I couldn't do anything anymore. I just wanted to leave the country and get my head in order to figure out just what it was I really wanted to do. Later on I retrieved my briefcase, but I knew it was over, and left my locker untouched. Just some damn books which meant nothing to me either which way. The bus pulled up...it was packed, rattling like an old wooden box on top of a washing machine...I took off, squeezed in with the rest of 'em. I looked at their hacked-up faces. Who the hell ever created you, I thought to myself, looking out the window. These men and women with their skin gone gray, their teeth falling out, swaggering and swaggering, ripping at each other's guts, but backing down and down if they dared try to stand up for their human dignity and burn the city down, all of it, from top to bottom. But was I that damn different? Ten minutes later I was in a peep show jerking off to fake moans and groans. A rather nice warm spot to jack off. The pimps made good profits off my balls...

3

A PERIOD OF DRIFTING SET IN. I was kicked from door to door by all the hotels and restaurants in the city because they didn't see me fit to work in their hovels. It didn't matter how well dressed and articulate I was—I just simply couldn't crack it. What was it? Surplus? Too many foreigners? Too much competition amongst the niggers? I didn't know.

Now I WAS desperate. I began thinking of suicide because I began to see that there was no way out. In everything I kept ruling out the Dummheit Cafe unconsciously; I had already drawn an "X" through that with my mind from the outset. But that Dummheit was just about the only solution I saw at that point. I knew it had to boil down to that—my whole life was about boiling down. I was familiar with all these establishments—Dummheit Cafe, as I already knew, was a staunchly conservative organization which did big business with South Africa, even as most of the other joint stockers pulled out at the time. But big shit, I thought to myself when I stepped on the bus heading out to Pocohontas, Maryland, where the Mall was located (an upper-upper-upper-income bracket area), and where Dummheit was sitting in anticipation of my application form. I knew all the routines by then: be neat, conservative, well-dressed, etc. Anyway, no problem. I got off and went up to the big Pocohontas Mall. It was one of the fanciest and most stylish at the time. It had, as a directory sign posted on a little hill, a sexy Indian girl in profile spitting out the words "Pocohontas" in fancy and suggestive script. Actually it originally attracted a blue-collar crowd mostly in the beginning, but with the onslaught of the yuppies who were pouring on everywhere, even in Belford, the whole joint was "re-designed" so it would fit the needs of a wealthier clientele. But just the same, it looked so pale to me, so empty and lifeless, a nothingness nothing if there ever was one, trying in vain to be classy amid a great deal of sloth. The uniform, as I saw approaching the joint, for men, was that of an overseas cap, a black one or a white one, a short sleeve shirt, a small black bow tie, black shiny shoes, and black pants with a maroon stripe going down the side. They were also notorious, as I well knew, for hiring very beautiful bus girls and cashiers, for they always came on the commercials grinning those big fat sex grins as usual. Unless, of course, they were regulars, or stool pigeons. It didn't matter what race. At the outset, I took this for equality between the races and lack of all racial discrimination. I was to know better later, of course, why they had this policy...The place was also patronized by bourgeois Jews, negroes, Chinamen, even Arabs, all of them cynical, hard-nosed, self-indulgent, like those I saw on the street: there was no difference whatsoever, except for the worse. And all eating like a pack of hysterical wolves, slopping their shit everywhere—but it didn't stop me from marching right up to the slop-den in my double-breasted business suit and demanding to see the manager. I was confronted by a snotty little Chink lady who was extremely attractive, and I noticed on her name tag she had "Pu Sei" stamped in on it—a pure coincidence to me, though I figured she wasn't a good lay one way or the other. The manager came right out. "I'd like a job," I told him. "Perfect!" he said, just like that. I was jolted. "I'm Mr. Quackenbros. We need lots of people here. You could try for busboy or dishwasher—we need lots and lots. Gimme your application, we'll take a look at it." Then he heads towards the back, and something loud crashes onto the ground, followed by raucous screams. He comes back. "Oh yeah, by the way, you're hired," he says again, suddenly. I braced for some rough stuff as I remembered what people told me about this joint. I tried to keep a straight face, and apparently I was successful, for he didn't waver once in his rambles. "Yeah, we'll give you a shot and see how you are. Forget this"—he says, waving the application— "unless there's a serious problem and I don't think there is since you're obviously a college student and I think you'll be good at it. So let's give it a shot." He gave me my uniform: two white shirts and two black pants and two bow ties and two caps—the two caps I later began to know as the "cunt" cap and the "gook" cap because the overseas cap resembled a cunt and the gook cap was one of those bellboy like caps which I could see Chinamen wearing in those old photographs in Manchu China. That out of the way, I went downtown, sat in a nearby shopping mall, at which time I'd usually be home, having convinced my parents I had gone to school. But—who in hell was the "stupid white boy" from Georgetown?

4

THEY SHOVED ME INSTANTLY into uniform and had me working like a madman. Christ, how fast and quick did the bloom of work rub off! Why, it was even worse than college, the shit I had left behind. It was worse because it was the very core of the germ itself. The Mecca of Learning, even though it was rotten and sick to the core, was really just the outer garments, as it were, of a disgusting, hideous, loathsome farce of a corpse kept alive by a few billionaire vampires who wanted to suck out every last drop of juice in the motherfucking thing. You might as well been home masturbating...And the customers! Why even try to make them happy? They were all criminals, as I could see clearly enough. Criminals, rogues, cutthroats to the bone, and yet held up by all society as the "backbone" of America. Well...if someone had a brain in his head, he'd figure it out sooner or later that someone, somehow had to break her damn back, or else America'll suck the whole planet down into the nether regions. And reading pamphlets about Steinway was further depressing. They were a worldwide, yet all-American institution. WORLD-WIDE! I could just see them now, the poor lice-ridden urchins of Bombay and the starving Turks and refugee Cambodians in the swill and muck of Ankara or Jakarta or Bangkok, or those poor black boys behind the dishwashing machines in the blistering heat of Conakry or Capetown, bursting their brains, wrenching their necks to make a hamburger, on an empty stomach to boot, that some pig-faced white bourgeois bastard will take a few nibbles out of and toss into the garbage. Does that hungry busboy get even a modicum, just one crumb of the bloody wasted hamburger? **No!** He slaves away making food to be wasted by the ton—and the bastard goes home exhausted on an empty stomach!

Fortunately it wasn't like that for me—they fed me all the food I wished to eat. But as time went on I discovered that this tasty food could be so utterly nauseating, if one kept eating the same things day after day, that one could just as well *not* eat. For the whole joy of eating was lost on me. Food became fuel, oil to slick up the human machine, coal to shove in the furnace of my mouth. Eating was no longer of any other importance, but I had to eat, for if I hadn't eaten I would have dropped out on the spot. My first job was to "merchandise"—that is, keep the food looking juicy and tasty in the eyes of the customers as they passed along. It was the highest paid job on the line upstairs: but I longed for a break from the heat of the ovens, the stink of the food, the ugly-looking customers, and a snotty little old white cunt who seemed hell-bent on pestering the life out of me. My clothes were dirty with beet-stains within seconds. The guy who directed me around was a squirt with curly hair and a pointy nose and a red face who was known as the "Food Production Manager": Mr. Carlin. He was right out of a shoot-em-up Clint Eastwood movie flick, always trying to play bad when handling either the customers or the workers. Personally I didn't mind when he got on the customers: they were animals anyway. But whenever one of the lady workers goofed up he'd say something like, "Hey, stupid, watch what you're doin'! You're gettin' this shit mixed up with that shit!" The shit being the broccoli and the corn. The customers wouldn't have that...and as for the customers, they had to make their decisions on whatever plate they wanted, for if they took too long, Carlin jumped out and squeaked, "Hey, you, what the hell do ya want, you been sittin' there for twenty-years already?!" And the customer, usually an old bloke, would just sit there in amazement. Yes, the tension ran high throughout the whole joint. Damn, I thought, what kind of a place is this, where the fuckin' workers shout at the patrons like that? When I shoveled the haddock around on the juicy side I had the sudden hallucination of the entire environment being a chow line in a prison, and I began to imagine the whole pack, the workers and the customers, as prisoners stuffing slop into other prisoner's mouths. After this hallucination I heard someone call in from the hole that was in the wall behind me; this was where the short-order cooks stuck out the haddock, or the fried chicken, or the mashed potatoes when they had them fully cooked and when the other stuff sitting out in the display cases ran out. If the other food in the display cases didn't run out in time, then they grabbed it and shoved it in a kind of storage "room" built into the wall and consisting of three compartments for "Vegetables," "Meat," and again "Vegetables". When the food there in the cases ran out I just reached around and pulled out the food from the "fridge". But the smell of the food once I took off the steam-soaked plastic wrapping hit me right in the nose; it was strong and overpowering; if I had been hungry before or during the job, handling the merchandising position killed any desire I had to eat, for the time being. It was hard to keep up; people just kept moving on, more and more of them every time. Occasionally I would peer up to look at a bunch of stereotyped cartoon figures seemingly passing for humans, faces and gestures which told me I didn't have to speak to them to know whether or not they lacked brains and decency. At four o'clock the Jew left, with a bunch of other Jews who worked in the kitchen. Two minutes later I looked around me. There were almost no English-speaking people then. Some skinny, wiry, wild-haired tart of a wetback took the place of my pestering Jewish mommy and began pestering me no less, perhaps because she saw that I was new at the joint and that gave her ample opportunity to jump on my back and start shooting the shit. Carlin had ducked out by then; and then I ran, all at once, smack into one big, plump, wide-assed *señorita* from South America with the ugliest hands I had ever seen—atrocious burn marks, I assumed, from the type of work they gave her to do at this place. Some more walked in, giving half-assed hellos or none at all, their uniforms on or half on or not yet on, their hair bound up, their bow ties fixed on or lost, their name tags stuck on their breasts. The señorita kept staring hungrily at me and licking her lips in obvious anticipation of something from me. I had a rumbling in my pants looking at the painted face with the wide cheekbones and the big black eyes with yellowed whites, the teeth with golden caps, and in particular that big wide ass she threw around like a burlesque queen. I knew I had to cop her, I kept thinking. She said hello, and I responded weakly; yet, before I could have proper access to this delicious piece of ass, suddenly HE walked in, HE being none other than the stupid-assed white boy from Georgetown: Mr. Albino. I never did learn his first name, but I didn't even need to once I sized him up. I noticed a pint-sized runt of a muscular build and with his sleeves rolled up, a mane of blond hair on his head and a thick mustache and a heavily protruding jaw-bone, almost like an ape. But the one thing I noticed was the queer glare in his steely-blue eyes which bore some insidious societal disease lurking underneath; I knew he was thinking, "ah—another one for the meat racks!" And so it was, as I found out immediately. He was in such a frenzy he had me moving about without even a thought for the Spanish lady. He spat out order after order. He didn't discriminate. Maybe that's what they mean when they say "equal opportunities" these days— everyone's got an equal opportunity to get his ass kicked high and wide...When the break came I wanted to leave; it was so useless and degrading that I would rather drift forever than fritter my life away making food looking tastier for fat-assed patrons to chew up. I spotted at the counter an older, thickset Jewish lady coming in with some odd-looking glasses and taking her seat at the cash register. Another one for the meat racks—again. I ate, but I didn't taste the food; I tasted only my nerves and the butterflies doing a war-dance on my belly. I cut out for the Pocohontas Mall, but the very sight of the mall was murder to me; the utter impersonality, the boredom, the brutality, and hate lurking underneath the grand luxury and affluence and elegance, and above all the ennui, the terrible ennui and want for something more rewarding, the want to escape forever where there is a world more open and more free and where life is meaningful and simple and where it is not so sophisticated as to make even the slightest wrinkle in the pants look like a heinous crime. I felt the eyes of the mall inhabitants looking at me and through me, denouncing me for being (so they thought) an "underclassman."

I was already marked off for ridicule and betrayal by the world. I saw a couple of beggars pass—and this was too much. I went back to the restaurant. I still had over forty minutes left. I went into the kitchen and there they all were, the "merry" crew, most off duty, like me, all waiting to devour me. I saw no Americans here, save two cracker women and the blacks, of course. There was Clyde Wong, a native of Da Nang, Vietnam, but of half-Chinese ancestry; he was the only one I really liked at the start. Then there were other Chinese: Gu Fi, a part-time bus girl who looked like she was in a perpetual opium haze (yet had a juicy body); the same went for the gorgeous Toi Pu Sei, who was a little flirt and a snot from Penang Malaysia, whom I had seen before and recognized instantly. She was studying in London, I discovered from Clyde, who "liked" her. Suk Ming, a "throw-in" (meaning a fifth-wheel-on-the-wagon as far as the general work-force is concerned), was boring, and worked in a nearby pantry selling exotic "tropical" fruits and minded her own business; Ling-Chow couldn't speak a word of English, but was stupid in any language anyhow; Mary Chiao was nervous, fidgety and quick-eyed, curt and abrupt, yet kept staring at my cock all the time. Ding Bat was the one with the juicy ass, one of the mainstays—but she had the face of a circus clown, it was so hideous; the eyes drooped and gave the appearance that they were hollow; from a distance, if you'd have seen her, I swear you couldn't even see her eyeballs. Above all, she was a perfect dolt. Her buck teeth stuck out a mile, her voice was sharp and knife-like, she mixed up her r's and l's, like all the rest—and every consonant was punctuated with an F or a TH because her teeth kept interfering with her tongue, just like in the cartoons. All she needs is to wear one of those straw hats to make it complete, I thought. And there were more Chinks to come, as I learned later; there was Yo-Yo the physicist, who was always in a good mood even when he was upset, and looked very distinguished with his horn-rimmed glasses. He was one of the mainstays, as was Clyde and Ding Bat and Toi Pu Sei—the last one of the "main" lackeys. In addition there was another part-timer named Tramsokong Louangphuck, from Laos, but speaking with a French and a Mississippi twang of the boat people who were pushed from Marseille to Biloxi. In all likelihood she was probably illegal, like many of the Spanish were known to be. Then there was Barnaby, the Jamaican pot-washer with six-fingers, silly, noisy, foolish, often drunk, docile, gossipy and lecherous, and always blinking his eyes; there was Sal Moustafa, from Libya, a quiet type who stared you right in the eye yet never said a word. He was the janitor who kept the bathrooms clean from time to time. There was always a big weekly or bi-weekly turnover at the joint. There were a bunch of others I never got to meet because of the turnover. In the first few days, several of the El Salvadorans were gone and many Jamaicans, about four, had cut out. A Jew also split. (The snotty one who kept pestering me, as it turned out.) In two days that added up to eight; in four days it would make sixteen; in eight thirty-two; in sixteen only God knows, maybe the whole damn shop would cut out. Carlos Bamba, a short-order cook, as it turned out, was related to three El Salvadoran twats who, in the long run, were to make life hell for me. One of them I already knew: the big fat one with the burnt hands and the big ass, was named Rosa Montemar. I'd met her the first day, apparently, and it seemed already she wanted a piece of me, though I could see she was beginning to change her attitude towards me, for reasons I didn't understand at first. Rosa was single, naturally; there was no way she could have been married. The second, much younger, and far noisier, was a tart named Lolita Barabbas, Barabbas being the family name for Rosa and the rest of them, including the second cook downstairs, Mario Barabbas, who seemed to have quite a bit on his mind. I met her before, also. Lolita was a hyped-up oversophisticated doll-baby—I originally thought she was from the Philippines. I'd seen her just as I had seen Concha, the fourteen year old—no, actually thirteen, but going on fourteen. She wasn't even allowed to work without a permit, but Mr. Quackenbros just hired her right off, as they said. The three sisters—Rosa, Lolita and Concha. The Barabbas sisters. That wasn't the last I would hear from them...as for the Spanish girls there was another, as I heard, sitting in the dining room on break one afternoon. I was eating—and then I heard banging and clashing and the sputtering of heated Spanish filling the air. I went in and looked for myself at the spectacle. I was suddenly confronted by a pair of hard, grey-brown eyes, a sharp twisted mouth and sinister, arched, pointy thin brows which moved with the rapidity of a roller coaster, a rather flat face and short cut hair to the neck. It was Maria Lopez, the head dishwasher from Guatemala. Side by side with her was another character, thin as a rail, with a mop of greasy hair and a long fleshy nose and thin eyebrows above deeply sunken black eyes; he wore a mustache now and then when he felt like it, and he had very sharp cheekbones. The first time I met him he spoke no English; when he confronted me he switched to another language I discerned to be either Italian or Romanian. He didn't tell me his name, he was in such a fury, for reasons I didn't know at the start. Maria called him "Gusepaya," or sometimes "Jorge," in Spanish; I didn't know what she meant until, when I went to punch out at night on the time clock, I checked out the names and out of curiosity looked at his. His real name was Giuseppe, Giuseppe Montevecchia, from Naples, Italy. He lived most of his life in America, yet he could never get rid of his accent just right. In the end he wound up speaking some kind of weird patois which, to my ears, sounded like Afro-American-Puerto-Rican dialect, from New York or New Jersey. Anyhow, it was just him. One would, just from his speech, assume offhand that he was an octaroon, since he was swarthy like a Persian or an Arab. Nevertheless he wasn't too kind to me at first, yet it was always very funny what he did, no matter whether he was on the plus side or the minus side. But that Carlin character....he was so nasty, so vicious to just about everybody in the whole restaurant, snorting, whining, pushing and cursing, kicking the workers around, that even Albino had to tell him to stop it. He was, as I saw clearly now, a hooligan of the basest kind. But at the same time he could be an absolute lackey, absolutely servile and stoop himself to anyone, no matter what his, or even her, color. He could obey all commands—when Albino told him to stop pushing Lolita around, then he obeyed. Personally I couldn't make heads or tails out of the guy—the only likely conclusion that I could come to was that he was an animal.

As for the rest, they hadn't yet come in. They had to throw out the nameless, colorless bunch of no-name faces first. But last of all there was Elsie, another background character, who had a perpetual toothache and made a career out of wrapping silverware, from Belfast and then Biloxi, ending up with an almost unintelligible accent and a bleeding hot temper, and a brain that had been looted through and through by being stuck too long on the grinding wheel. The slaughterhouse had done in poor Elsie Malone.

Nevertheless, all that's neither here or there—just talk, shit, inconsequential facts. After about a week I quarreled with Lolita and Concha; they were just getting into my hair with their goddamn greasy asses. So they switched me to busboy at my request. Johnny-Boy Carlin (that was his nickname, or perhaps even his real actual name) was relieved that he wouldn't have to put up with my "ineptitude" at the chow line, merchandising the food. As a busboy I was given usually one section of the vast dining room to clean. And everyday I got to see those upwardly-mobile transients from nearby who claimed to be "starving" after a hard day at the office. I had no desire to return to their type of life, but mine I hated even worse than theirs. How degrading it all seemed seeing myself in this lackey bow tie with my cunt cap on my head and wiping the tables for these handsome upwardly mobile transients in their worsteds and Bluchers and cosmetics and wacky slick hair-dos! It was the height of degradation. If only my mother could see me now...It was hard to believe I had gone down this far already—and the thought of it was rankling, that this was really only the beginning of something infinitely worse, and to think that there really was no way out of it. You just do or die. And that's what I did. When a tray lay before me, I put it together neatly and shoved it on the rack at the entrance to the dishroom, and someone, usually Giuseppe, wheeled it into the kitchen. I did this for a full eight hours. I had an hour to rest my back and if it hurt in between, it was tough shit. After all, I was getting spoon-fed, shut up by thirty dollars a day. I had the workers to gossip to about how some other workers personal lives were fucking up royally. At least—not yet—I didn't have to deal with any bills and taxes.

I got off every day now at nine-thirty, and usually arrived home by ten-thirty, depending upon the traffic. Before I went home I got down to the locker rooms and stepped out of my uniform and folded it up and placed it in my briefcase. There were no longer any books in that case; they were all stinking of beets and carrots and pork ribs and Chinese rice.

5

YOU HEAR ABOUT PEOPLE, you see them and hear their names—you could do it just like that for a good thirty years and remember absolutely nothing about them. That's the way things happen in this country—no one trusts the stranger, nor anyone closer, for that matter—not even their mothers. For instance, I'd see someone like Mary Chiao, who lost her job in the great turnover, or Ding Bat, or Elsie Malone, just about daily but recalled nothing except their appearances. Everything was all surface. Indeed, if one had ever asked anything more of them, other than what he was supposed to have known for mere practical purposes, other than washing dishes and scrubbing floors and punching cash-register buttons, he'd have been rapped across the face for what it was worth.

The excuses I had to invent to make it look like I wasn't out scrubbing dishes to my mother! I told her that I was going to parties, but she found this improbable—how could I go out to parties if I didn't have any friends at Coon State? "Bachelor parties," I lied to her. My mother responded dryly; when I tried to get into the kitchen in order to get my dinner she backed me off, and leaned up against the doorway and looked at me icily. "Dishwashers don't eat here, Louie," she smirked.

I was so blindingly angry I wanted to stave her goddamn head in with one of those heavy wooden beams which were always laying around that old broken-down, half-finished excuse for a house. I walked out of that excuse to get a snack at a nearby restaurant. The fucking status-mongering honky bitch, I thought.

To top it off, she didn't even speak to me after that. She'd only drop an icy line or two. She really didn't even consider me a part of the family. My father was almost never home, even when he was supposed to be. He was at his "bookshop," as he said—but many times he was at a VD clinic looking for a cure for that tropical shit he had or even, sometimes, in the hospital when the pain got to be too intense. That gave my mother ample opportunity to go after all the men she wished. Her health was failing her; it wasn't AIDS: nobody knew what it was. She got fatigued so easily. And then there were the fucking bouts; they were getting worse and worse. She was even going for blacks—of all people. She was fond of bringing home those idiots who worked with her at the Ace Supermarket. She was at it for hours...sometimes she had two or three. I couldn't blame her for that—after all my father was diseased. There was no other way around that...But Ida just took off, just like a fucking freak. Before long, in between the icy stares and cold-shouldering she threw my way, she became a complete sex-addict.

No problem for me: from now on, I shut the bitch out of my life—and concentrated on my work at the Dummheit Cafe.

I began wondering whether or not she was really my mother. I would look at her and notice almost no physical resemblance between her and myself. She was just about completely different. Quite frankly, I don't even think she was my mother; I think she was just a white-assed intruder picking off the apples on my already rotted-up family tree.

There it was...old Belford. Good old Belford, the neighborhood in which I lived for over fifteen years. It was through here that I walked every day in order to get up to the bus stop which would take me straight into Pocohontas Mall. In between home and the bus stop, there loomed, from the outset, on my street, West Belford, relatively affluent, of course, but only a little clean corner of what came out to be a filthy, scum-ridden maggot hatch of a borough lying in between. Where I lived was upper-middle-class with deceptively nice fat two-story houses spread far apart and allowing breathing space for backyards, fences, trees and bushes, the whole lot. Cut off my street, and the backyards get smaller; go down the little hill leading up to the Boys' Club and you're walking right into the real Belford. There is an actual dividing line between the affluent and the poor. Walking up past the football field connected in conjunction with the Boys' Club, you run smack into tenement buildings; you've just moved to the North section where you'll see legions of Hispanics. No bus line passes through this section because they hadn't the good sense to put one out there, that's all. North-North Belford, as I liked to think of it, was the classic kind of ghetto, almost an island of its own. Some of the streets in between, like Panama Street, were mixed up with a bunch of Africans and Indians and Jamaicans and Nicaraguans and Vietnamese and Cambodians, but these were rare. These were those rare streets in which the foreigners actually brought something of their old culture that they left behind them and put it into the life of that street, or so my myopic eyes had led me to believe in the beginning. It was a treat at first to see this weird form of polyglot United Nations with Arabic and Quechua being spoken side by side. But later, I began to see it differently, of course. When the children played they always remained within the sphere of their own little ethnic group; I noticed how the Nigerians played on one side of the street and the Chinese on the other; I noticed how the groups managed to remain functioning and well within the confines of those decrepit old corridors yet perfectly separate, everybody not even really interacting but merely putting up with each other in the quest for survival. And come to think of it, it was just like that at the Dummheit Cafe. Furthermore, outside or inside the corridors, the streets were infernal. Drug peddlers did it right under your nose. Little girls desperate for money peddled their syphilitic twats right out to you for only a quarter. People waited in the bushes to jump you—first it was knives, and now it was guns—real ones, automatics. The Latins huddled around in corners on the broken up sidewalks with the grass sprouting out of the cracks; they pulled chunks out of the potholes and threw them at each other; they trampled on the broken glass and the yellowed newspapers and dead crushed squirrels with their intestines strewn dried all along the street; they sat everywhere staring at you from the back alleys where they sat guzzling scotch and gossiping—from the lice-ridden old moldy couches they threw out on the streets when they got evicted, from the boarded-up windows which they kicked out in order to go squatting in some of the abandoned buildings...Sometimes you think to yourself that you won't even make it down a particular street alive. But South Belford was where the Asians lived, and although it was just as nasty and shacky as the North section, with the same kind of tenement buildings, there was an obvious difference. First of all, you noticed the shutters still on the buildings; you noticed that the environment was at a whole more orderly and less dumpy than the other hole you walked out of. And the Asians were also doing big business—at least in comparison to the Jamaicans and the El Salvadorans, who either did nothing or got by peddling drugs. Louangphuck's parents, for instance, were running a fish market which was very success-ful in the area; in fact they were trumpeted by the Asian community as being one of the great All-American success stories. (If they only knew what *their* daughter was selling!) The Asians—at least a number of them—were very successful entrepreneurs in Belford and they set up all the stores and markets in which the blacks and the Latins shopped to buy their shit. Plus there were other places that only the Orientals would shop at, such as the place where they sold Vietnamese food and spoke only Vietnamese. But even there, there was talk of gang rivalry and extortion in the South Belford area. Yet all in all with the ethnic diversity and the hodge-podge of different cultures and lifestyles, power was in question, of course; it was all a matter of who would get power and who would rise up economically and get on a par with the whites or the third-generation immigrants who had already "made it". But the power, once accumulated, was wasted; everything came down time and again to sugar-coated, wasted whiteness. Whiteness, the fashions, the hairstyles, the speech, the language, the culture—that was the trend-setter, the measuring-rod of all existence. In a few years I began seeing fewer and fewer saris around the place and more and more Brooks Brothers overcoats. The Vietnamese put away their straw hats—that was out. The assimilation nightmare could be seen on every street. The kids were soon sent off to learn English, the language of hatred; and once they learned it, another generation of gook-lackey robots was thus created. And come to think of it, it was just like that at the Dummheit Cafe. But as disgusting as the whole scheme of white-washing was, I could do nothing to stop it. In fact, I didn't even have time to worry about stopping it. There were always worse things to contemplate, naturally. First was the utter, complete loss of privacy. Even when I went back to my room in the evening they, the slaves of the Third-World, the bus riders, the subway-riders, the whole lot, were still there, dancing in my head, and I became the prisoner outside the prison as well as inside, of the famous and fabulous financial empire known as Steinway Corporations.

Steinway (who was himself long dead), the great White Anglo-Saxon Protestant father of the world, owned seemingly everything from dishwashing machines to knives to airplanes to ships to vast land tracts in India, South Africa, Malaysia, Gabon, Nicaragua and Costa Rica, the Philippines, Argentina and Egypt, skyscrapers, discos, whorehouses in Cairo and Kuala Lampur, opium fields and oil rigs in the Middle East.

That taken into consideration, who was I? And who were we, compared to the vast interstellar money-making ectoplasm stretched from wall to wall?

Look...let's just pick a day, any day, and start from there. Monday. 10:00 a.m. I wake up. Everything looks the same to me—the bed, with its pink sheets and blue blanket and green pillowcase, the bedroom with the girlie magazines scattered everywhere. I tell my mother, who doesn't like that, that it's my love-life; I don't have any other choice, unless it's her. On my bookcase I have a stack of books by various authors which betrays my intellectual inclinations. If things get too hot at the Dummheit, I can always cool off with some fine intellectualizations of my own pain and humiliation. I've started that already, to make sure I don't go off my rocker. I've marked off page 35 of the *Time of the Assassins*. I think of the passage because I was just reminding myself of the filthy tables which were lying in wait for me, what was waiting for me there. Those filthy yuppies and coffee-shop Jews...I didn't think of my mother—she was gone, right off to work. I was all alone in the house. I get up and look around the room at the disorder one more time and get down to the bathroom to wash under my arms and between my legs; I don't even bother to wash the rest of my body. Doesn't matter—everyone stinks inside, too, don't they? Smelly like me...Mom leaves no note, no nothing. Just splits. There's a taste still left in my mouth—the pasteurized Steinway milk of the last midnight snack. I have to get some food into my mouth—I'm due at the joint by eleven and it's now ten and the bus-ride takes forty-five minutes getting through the traffic, bad any damn time of the day. I didn't have time for a good, healthy, nutritious meal, so how's about a quick one? I take two slices of bread and coat them with whipped butter and eat them; I gulp milk out of a carton. Steinway again, of course—the butter included. At this time, I'd be off to school—but who needs school now that you know already what would have been waiting for you at the end of the educational line?

I get out. I walk through the neighborhood. How quiet and plaintive it all is. The beautiful brownstone slums. An elephantine serenity. Yet it seems like the whole place is laughing at me, like I am alone, naked, unwanted, being taunted at all sides, though all their mouths are shut and there isn't a peep out of them. Yet they stare—and how!—I know that stare anywhere—it seems to say to me, the eyes, "What the hell are you doing here, nigger? weirdo? fuckface?"—or, worse yet, "Gee, you're sick." Perhaps they're right. Forget it—move on, time to work, don't think about the pain. Some guys have it worse, you know...

I get on the bus. There they are, my dispensable, irresistible, unreliable, irrefundable, non-depositable, non-returnable factory chums. I can already smell the dishes and the dishwater, the rancid butter, the shitty toilets and the stink of the customers. It reads right into their ugly hacked-up worn-out faces. All of them melted right into the gray background. All a terrible cliché of poverty, need, want, boredom, despair, hope, failure. I sit back in the seat; there's grease on the window. I turn to the back of me and there's gossipy old Barnaby with the six fingers on each hand; he hasn't washed his uniform in years. Here he looks half-crazed; he also needs a haircut because his hair is growing out of all bounds. Drunk, obviously, because he keeps laughing. He wants to tell us about Mario's home life, and he tells it to Sal at his request. Then there's a new guy wearing a uniform that I don't know; he isn't talking. The rest are. We pass through North Belford and now the chili-chokers get on. Maria gets on, neck stuck out like a goose, and sinister as usual; Rosa, reasonably well-dressed, perfumed, the mouth hanging loose, the eyes droopy and dazed, Lolita tagging along, also hot and ready to roll for a night of mopping floors and washing dishes and barking at the customers. As I recall, it was this very bus ride which revealed to me many things which were to become a central element in what was to be the course of the soap-opera existence between certain workers at the slaughterhouse.

With all the foreigners on, including a few Vietcong and some Indians, we took off out of Belford and down a narrow strip of a Boulevard leading ultimately up into a Georgia Avenue. Along this way, on that certain day, certain things, as I said, were revealed to me. One of them was the amount of pay. Clyde Wong had explained to me that we were both being paid a hefty $4.50 an hour. When explaining things to me, I recall that he was always very mellow, cool and confident, and almost never in a hurry. As he said to me he tried to work as slow as possible come night so he could get paid overtime. "Four-fifty an hour," he said. "Very high pay for cleaning jop, do you know? Do you understand?" he said, always interjecting with "do you understand" to make sure I knew what he was trying to make out in English. "See, if I make 4.50 for one hour—"

"No, you wrong, Chinese," Rose suddenly butted in. Rosa and her sisters always called Clyde "Chinese" because they didn't know, and didn't want to know, his real name. In all likelihood, however, they did know his real name, but just wanted to call him "Chinese" for kicks. "Chinese, you wrong, you no 4.50, *3.50!*—dat's you: 3.50!" That, of course, was when I discovered that I had been cheated out of one dollar per hour, and that I wasn't to get a raise for the next five months. "3.50, Chinese! Rice-picker! 3.50!" they taunted him. Clyde, however, shrugged it off. "Very stupid," he said. "They have no way of acting the right way. They are very bad. Some Spanish people are very good. But some other very bad—and Rosa very bad," he explained, and then laughed. He took out a pack of cigarettes, Gauloises Bleues, and began puffing away, not realizing that smoking was forbidden. Nobody realized it—least of all Lolita, who was smoking frantically, with cigarette holder, of course. A red one. That was her favorite color, as I recall. And this is where it all began—at least with me—the flap with the Barabbas sisters. Rosa asked me... "Ey, stupi', you fuck?" "Yeah, I fuck, you wanna get laid?" Clyde nudged me and chuckled. Rosa then went up to him

about it. She began whispering dirty words in Clyde's ear—
right under Miguel's nose—her brother, I think. I asked Basil,
the new guy from Jamaica who came in for work yesterday.
"Brodder? I dunno...wait, mon." He asks Giuseppe, who's
planning on skipping the first few hours to go buy himself an
overcoat at Lippy's downtown, and Giuseppe says: "No, man,
you know who dat is? Is her hosband! I'm serious...but keep
it down, 'cause I gots somethin' goin' wid her, too. Especially
you, Louie," he said, pointing to me. "Keep you mout' shut,
you talkin' too mach. You wanna gets everybody in troubol
causa you big mouth?" Giuseppe didn't like me all that much
then. My presence to him was annoying and irritating. I always
laughed over it. I told him, starting to laugh, "You gonna skip
work again to go down to the peep shows downtown again?
You dig wackin' your beef inna booth?" Barnaby laughed at
that one.

"Jus' wait, man, I'm gonna sock you onea dese days!"

"Good enough. Don't worry—it was a gag..."

"But don't say nothin' to nobody where I'm goin, awright?
I gots dis, dis coat I gotsa buy cause its goin outta stock an' I
wanna get it," he explained.

"How will you palm it off with Mr. Albino?"

"I'm gonna senda note from my doctor. An' don't you say
shit either!" I noticed that he was composing a faked letter in
an exaggerated script in a notepad in his lap. I forgot about it
and my mind passed to Rosa again. "Mon, das crazy, wot is
wrong wid Rosa, mon! Clyde, you hear dat?" Clyde doesn't
hear it, because Rosa is wrestling with Clyde and she's all over
him. He just keeps laughing; he doesn't budge. Rosa tells him
to feel up her fat ass, and he just pats there lightly, then he
grabs a bit of it. I know what Rosa wants because she's giving
off a scent which is so strong we've got to open the windows
to get it out. On top of this, she's getting wet in the crotch.
Clyde sees all this and he laughs so hard he weeps; but, just
the same, he'd probably want to knock a good piece off if they
were alone. But he just keeps laughing. In all likelihood he's

a married man, since he's twenty-nine years old and going on thirty. Then Lolita winks to me and sticks her middle finger in her mouth and runs it back and fourth to indicate what she wants; then Ding Bat cracks up and roars with laughter, and Sal waves his hand at them. Yo-Yo grins.

"She want to go *chinga*, little guy," Lolita said, laughing. "You go *chinga* with her, okay?"

"Tonight, ten o'clock. At my place," I said, thinking my mother would be out getting screwed by niggers herself. "No! Now!" Rosa yelled, however, caressing her pussy through the uniform pants.

"Not with all these people," I told her. "Just gimmie your address—or we'll tear it off in the bathroom when we get to work—"

"Now, I know wha' he is. You a faggot, right? You *maricón, sí?* You dunno how to do i', yes?" Then she jerks back to her sister, yelping in Spanish, saying that I was a faggot, and Rosa says in Spanish that Clyde and all the Chinks are faggots. "Faggot, you, you faggot," Rosa said, walking up to me and stinking like a dead dog on the side of the road. "You no how to fuck. Chinese no fuck. How you?"

"Tonight, ten o'clock. I'm ready if you want."

"Wha?"

"If you want you can call me tonight for a fuck," I insisted.

"No!—you a faggot, Chinese a faggot, so all you can beat it! Gedadah heah, *negro!*"

"Up yours, banana breath!" I retorted. "Fat-ass greaser. Go shovea banana up your taco twat. Or get Lolita to suck you off." After that I lay back and relaxed by the window. Clyde stopped laughing and sat down in another seat. It went on like this for about six minutes and then Rosa began jerking herself off in the back—I could smell that pissy-fishy smell of pussies in the air and I knew just who was up to it. Rosa's sex problems were even worse than I thought. Was Miguel a fag? Or impotent, perhaps? I could hear her screaming at Miguel to eat it, that she was going to kill him, or dump him on the side of the road. Finally the Chinese girls caught wind of the smell and all, and they got up and ran up to the back of the bus to see what was going on. Rosa had forced Concha into jerking her off; Moy Ling stood there with her mouth dropped, yelled over and over, "NO GOOD! NO GOOD!" Finally the situation got so much out of hand the bus stopped, half-way to Dummheit; the bus driver couldn't put up with us foreigners anymore. Besides, he's a foreigner himself—an Indian Sikh from Delhi: "Adioz!" he screams in his Indian-accented Spanish. We all get off. Clyde wakes up, doesn't know what's happening. Rosa is stinking like a fish and panting like a dog. Concha just the same. Lolita struts. Sal and Mario lift Maria onto their shoulders and cart her out; she can't wake up, she's been slaving all day and all night...by the time the next bus comes we're beating up a breeze. It's already late. We get on the bus, the bus hesitates and then gets whiplashed by another car. No matter, the bus gets to Pocohontas, we get up to the joint and the manager is screaming his head off because we're all thirty minutes late. "Bus break down," Ding Bat explained. But Toi Pu Sei's there, having drove up in her nice little Porche she got with her "savings". She's in there setting up the tables and getting everything in order, the food, the salt and pepper, the cash registers, the toilets—everything, so that the mob which is waiting outside to storm on in can come in and fuck everything up.

I got to the locker room. Clyde keeps staring at me, then he walks over to me. "What happened on the last bus, do you know?"

"Rosa was caught playing with herself, that's what," I said.

Clyde frowns. "I don' understand. How could she play alone?" I see that he didn't catch the meaning of it. I motion in my crotch and then he raises his brows, nodding. "Ahhhhhhh—I see, I see. Spanish no good! Rosa no good! Sal okay. Rosa no good!" He laughs, and leaves after putting on his uniform, with the vaginal cap, brushing back his hair lightly. "I see," he says, winking and laughing still. I was only

half-way into my uniform when Mr. Albino popped in as Clyde
and Basil were chattering with the cook and the second cook
and a few others who were in the toilet. He's steaming—
though we don't know why, really. He's just a jerk... "Ey—no
more shit from the resta ya or I'm sendin you all to the fuckin'
welfare house!" He jerks around. "You—Basil, dining room!—
Clyde, dining room! You get to your jobs, you know what they
are, you shits!—move it! Yo-Yo, mop the floors! Clean the
bathrooms! And YOU"—motions to me—"I want you to help
Maria wash the dishes. I need three people there. The dishes
are piled up all over the damn floor and in the sink. It's total
hell up there. *You*"—motions out of doors to Mario—"we
don't need you cooking, so help Maria, you know? Señor?
You-know-what-I-to-do? Right? Sí?" he snorts, condescendingly. "Now—get in there and work your fucking asses or get
the hell outta my joint!" He runs out, hysterical, pop-eyed,
muttering, waving his hands, cursing. "Oh, yeah. Why can't
you be like the Chinamen? They do nothing but work! That's
all they think about—work! work! work! Now *scat!*"

I put on my plastic apron and went up to the dish room.
Barnaby is at the pots already—it's a second home to him.
Maria was waiting for me. "Well, *muchacho*, get goin'!" I got
to the other end. Mario, a genuine toughie, began banging his
fists on the machine every time he stacked the dishes. He was
intentionally starting up a disturbance. After a while I could
understand why. The whole thing, from start to finish, as I saw
for the first time that day, worked just like an assembly line.
Clyde dragged in a full cart of dishes taking the thing by the
handles on the end, the cart full of dirty dishes and forks and
knives and spoons and bowls and glasses. Everything had to
be done in order—yet with lightning speed. I was in charge of
pulling out the trays and taking the glasses and putting them
in gray carts; the coffee cups had to be put in brown carts
which were stacked behind me according to the doorway
which led out into the dining room and where the busboys
carted in the dirty dishes from the dining room. Out in the

dining room, plush and with wall-to-wall carpeting, the tables round and uncovered, some square and leaning up against the wall with seats that were built into the wall; here the classy patrons or the fat ugly patrons sat and ate—and never tipped. They were too greedy to tip. They talked too loud, most of them didn't know how to dress, they were hideously impolite, most of them were honkies, they were racist, they had no manners, they were all old and decrepit shits, they were bastards, suburbanites, Jews, negroes, gooks, apes, Yuppies from the city nearby...what more disgusting things could I say? The carpet could never be clean, because the goddamn no-account kids kept throwing their food on the ground and getting into food fights; the Jews kept coming in every night to smoke pack after pack of cigarettes and throw the butts on the floor, to throw chicken bones on the floor along with the melon scraps and the watermelon scraps and orange peels and peas and rice and mashed potatoes and salt and pepper and French bread and Carefree sugarless gum, because there was no trash can and they were so nasty and dirty and vicious and ill-mannered and so unmotivated and inconsiderate they couldn't even motivate themselves to put the damn scraps on the tray or the plate—where they belonged. The result was that the tables were always filthy and couldn't be cleaned in time for the next customers. And in the hours between eleven and eight, when the joint closed, they were always full, the tables always taken. The busers, Basil and Clyde, cleaned up the scraps and the junk on the floor and the food that was never half-way eaten and set everything in order on the tray: scraps on the top, the big dishes stacked under the medium-sized dishes and the large bowls on top of the medium sized dishes and the small bowls on top of the large bowls and the glasses next to the scraps and the forks and knives and spoons next to the coffee cups which were next to the glasses; the napkins were left to blow on the floor, or shoved in the coffee cups. Nobody ever drank the tea because it was poison, it tasted like nothing, besides, it kept getting cold. So they threw it on the floor to make like they drank it—providing they had a guilty conscience for buying something they didn't really want...The trays sat neatly in order, they were set on their cart racks on tiers and the carts, of which there were four, were wheeled into the dishroom. The doors in the dishroom had been busted down two months ago because, as Maria said to Mario, she kept slamming the doors in Gu Fi's face. The dishes carted in, I unloaded them and put in the glasses; I then passed the tray onto Mario, who took out the forks; and then further on to Maria, who stacked the dishes. Giuseppe showed up at twelve with a faked note from the "doc"; with his uniform already on he punched in and went right in with his paper pussy cap on and he got on the end of the dishwashing machine and began stacking them in, face up, on plastic bars which wheeled the dishes through hot soap and water in conveyor-belt sequence. He pressed the green "GO" button and the machine came on—after pressing it four times. The button wouldn't press right most of the time. Maria then left her plate post and went onto taking out the clean dishes which passed out through the other end. The machine sounded almost like music and we seemed to gandy-dance to the rhythm of the machine. At about this time Lolita would come around and bark, and wonder if we would bringa' mo' pleetes for me, pleeeese?—we sure would. Maria isn't fast enough. She's had six months at the joint and she's already near fed up. I can't help that shit...The dishes keep coming out and she yanks them out in a frenzy, gritting her teeth and shaking her hair and cursing and frowning. The fork cartons full, Elsie comes by to set them in the machine where she will come back to take them all to her corner and where she will wrap them and set them in a box and wheel them into the top kitchen, where they will be set onto the line outside wherein the customers would pick them up, unwrap them, dirty them up, throw them all over the table and the floor, and then some. Elsie keeps up yet, wrapping and sorting in that little corner where she has been for the last six years. Elsie also has a toothache because tooth decay is coming on, so she curses from time to time in a brogue, and stamps her foot on the ground. She also buses when there isn't enough to go around out in the dining room—and there always isn't enough. The dishes keep coming in faster and faster; the minute we think they've been cleaned and ready, Lolita comes in barking for more and then Clyde brings in more and more, then Ling brings them in, then Basil, then Gu Fi. There has to be a bunch out in the dining room because they don't want it looking too dirty and there's always too many people coming in to eat. Why they don't go anywhere else, I don't know. To them, this must be Heaven, the very center of the universe.

The dishes having been cleaned, they were wheeled out onto the line and set into cunt-like springs under the counter, where Lolita, jumping up and down and dancing and barking with "joy" to make the customers feel at home—just like an airline stewardess or a cockroach—would put on the latest menu: pork ribs and Chinese rice. Always "Chinese" rice. Along with this came pimentos and parsley; on the side were string beans and corn and spinach and broccoli and mashed potatoes. Also, came the cookies, the chocolate cake Rosa made, along with the Jell-O and the fresh rolls. If you didn't want spare ribs why maybe you wanted fried chicken or Salisbury steak, or liver and onions; if you wanted neither why then just take a salad and a batch of sugar cookies. There's everything you would want, and always a little bit more, as they would say on the telly. At the stove in the top kitchen a tall mulatto kid is cooking the fish and shrimp; that's what's on at this hour. The next hour, the fish and chips, and the fried chicken and the ham and always those motherfucking liver 'n' onions. Thus, the top part of our little universe is complete; the fried chicken and string beans having been put into the pots and taken out of the pots, making them dirty and therefore ripe for Barnaby's scrubbing with his six-fingered hands. They get sent down with the left-over pieces after the fried chicken hour is up, just as when the fish hour is up. Next, the haddock hour and the spinach hour, so the corn must go. They send it down the elevator shaft to Barnaby who eats it to keep from starving, then dumps the rest down the dishwashing disposal machine. When this happens the machine gets jammed and then he must take out the plunger and work over it like a demon, but he must be fast, nevertheless, because if he isn't, the pots will pile up and Sal will be caught without pots to put in the corn and the rice he cooks, and upstairs, Ding Bat is preparing the pastries; they don't even need her today but she wants the cash, so she makes coconut cakes when the chocolates run out. The second cook makes the pork ribs; he's Tito Velasquez and he's always in a perpetual state of frustration; sometimes he gets so worked up he spits in the ribs and pounds his hands on them in disgust, or throws them across the kitchen for kicks. Tito cooks the ribs, because the chef, Jonas, can't cook them himself. Across the way is the stock room where Basil gets the salt when the shakers run out, and the pepper and the napkins and the straws, and there are also toilet seat covers for over all the bathrooms and on the walls are posters proclaiming the spread of the AIDS germ and telling the customers not to eat each other's food. And once more, up in the line, stands Lolita doing her joyful airline-cum-cockroach dance, smiling at the customers with a good evening sir— "Whaa you waa?"—and pouring on the ribs soaked with Tito's spit. The rib hour, no doubt. The customer passes on where he will get his coconut cake from Ding Bat and the rolls from Elsie Malone, and gets wrung up on the cash register by Louangphuck, and forks over his money to the Jewish mommy, Ruby Rubenstein, also the company stool pigeon and a host of other nice things. This done, he eats, thinking only of his food and not who made it, belches a trifle, throws the napkin on the ground, dirties up the plate and hands it back to Clyde Wong, who hands it back to us—and thus the cycle of our life is complete, our whole lives up until the seven-thirty fade out—when the crowds taper down.

By seven-thirty the crowds started to file out. I noticed the faces of the workers; they seemed relieved, but a handful seemed not to be affected in the least. I found it surprising that a few could get somewhat of a kick out of it—particularly the blacks and the Chinese. Not the Spanish—except Lolita the insect. Tito was jumping up and down and huffing and puffing and banging on just about anything he could get his hands on. There was a rumor that he even socked Mr. Carlin in the jaw. Not only that, it was apparently his last day—for when I went downstairs to check up on the billboard the hours and days in which I'd be working throughout the week I noticed that Tito was designated as such: TITO MENDEZ—OUT ON HIS GREASY ASS!!!!!—and that was that for Tito. Apparently the cogs weren't meshing right with his anger, for there had to be docile servility and stupid blind obedience or bitter last minute desperation, or just simple insanity or just plain naivete, the better to lash them along with the cattle-prods. But, in the meantime, Albino came out huffing and puffing again for he had since gone down to the office to check up on what was to be served the following morning for the Brunch, and he was counting the cash as well, but now he was up on our necks huffing and puffing; he always did this when things were drawing to a close—"Now look, Lolita, quit yappin'," he would say, over and over, "I want everything put out there just right! Don't take the food! Don't dirty up the goddamn floors!"—sometimes the workers took home some of the food with them and this was not permitted—"You gotta eat all that here. Don't forget that...get the carts back in order!" he says, pointing to the kitchenettes; then he goes back into the dish room—but only for a second; he's rarely there in the dishroom, probably because he fears Maria because Maria hates Albino with a passion and she's a pretty big strong girl, but anyway he still keeps on ranting and screaming that we must do this and that, and then this and then that, and then once more for the umpteenth time, which is to say, break down the dishes which would make it easier for Lolita to plop them into the mechanical cunt-like springboards inside the counter where the dishes are pulled out to be served and then the food bins and the entire aluminum set-up is cleaned out with the utmost meticulousness because Albino is known to come snooping around with his goddamn magnifying glass checking for germs; he's scared to death of germs, because he knows they're all from Costa Rica somewhere and he thinks they're all full of venereal diseases and he knows that each and every potential customer, including him on his own little breaks in between, has got to eat off those so-called infected plates, which is why he proposes that they use disinfectant spray in order to get all the germs out, and even then, sometimes, when Lolita thinks she's wiped it down good and clean, Albino comes snooping around for germs with his magnifying glass, saying all the while, looking it up and down, snorting: "Look, this shit is filthy! You didn't get all that fuck off the goddamn thing! C'mon, we gotta work as a team...faster! I wanna go home..." Very true indeed, for Albino can't go home unless we've got everything set right in order for, just remember, Mr. Quackenbros goes around at night checking up on what his slaves, including Mr. Albino, have done for him and if the slaves have done a nasty job at it then Quackenbros gets it in the ass from Mr. Red-Dot himself, Mr. Najib, the boss boss, and when Albino gets it in the ass he goes around and buggers all of us in return, because, like everywhere else in this world, the blind lead the blind, and, as always, one never leaves too early, by the way, because, even by nine o'clock, one hour after the joint closes, there's always a few patrons lying around with their babies slopping peas and carrots all over the tables, and apparently the patrons show no sympathy for the poor headless animals who will have to clean up their baby-dribbles and their melon scraps and cigarettes in the ash trays, which must be cleaned out and properly set back on the tables, which, in themselves, must be properly cleaned and wiped down with perfection and then moved out so that Gu Fi or Ding Bat can vacuum the junk off the floors with the ten-year old vacuum cleaners which, unfortunately, keep break-

ing down and catching on fire, and not only that, but sometimes, about once a week or so, the dishwasher catches on fire
even, but there's not much to be done with that problem since
the dishwashing machine costs all the way up in the hundreds
of thousands and they "don't have the money" to replace the
damn thing but the truth is, they don't have the time (besides
the electricians would be out of business across the board),
because the busboys must cart in all the dishes from off the
tables to give to the dishwashers who will then scrape the
melon off the platters and set them down in the machine and
have them passed through with everything else and set down
properly in order in the carts, of which Lolita takes care of, and
sometimes Lolita cuts back to clean all the forks and cutting
knives and dipping spoons with liquid Ajax in the sink, and
often these get mixed up with the containers and ash trays
which are then thrown in the drawer or shoved under the
stove posthaste by someone apparently not giving a good
goddamn, the food then lifted out and sent down to be thrown
out, by Barnaby, and then the Barabbas sisters are free; they
go home, and that's that for them but it takes longer for
busboys because the dining room must be properly fixed up
and set in order; the dishwashers take the longest of all
because, once the dishes are cleaned and set in the cunt-like
springboards out there, the glasses put in the racks and set up
alongside the wall next to the microwave, we've got to
dismantle the machine, bit by bit—on the inside and outside,
the cleaning pipes, the filters which all come out reeking and
clotted with a nasty hash of butter wrappings, peas, rice,
onions, meatballs, lemon pieces, ice-cubes, pancakes, tomatoes, cookies, lettuce gone soggy, chicken and chicken-bones,
spare-rib bones, mash potatoes, spinach and corned beef
hash and Jell-O and straws and newspapers and candy
wrappings and baby puke, lima beans, blood, string beans,
broken plates, a few rotten teeth...you get the fucking idea,
don't you?

It was all nauseating...the whole thing, all of it, from start

49

to finish. The most dreadful thing was to get up in the morning thinking that I'd have to go through another day of it. Worse yet was the shit netted out to me from my mother. That's why I stopped hanging around the house almost all the time now. I even vowed one day I would never come back, in a fit of anger and depression. She didn't even speak to me anyway, didn't say a word—that was the shit. When I wanted to discuss something she would turn her head away. Sometimes Pops would come around and say, "She doesn't think you're her son anymore. Quite frankly I feel just about the same."

So, I thought to myself, judging by the way she always thought of me, the way she treated me, I felt just about the same, too. "Well fuck you then," I said after the thought. I still didn't mention my plans for my flight. "I got my own life to lead, even if it does suck shit. You think what you want!"

Mom jerked up at this quip. "How could a businessman ever become so stupid as to take on a job as *dishwasher?*"

Now this was new to me...Businessman? "I was never in the least interested in business. Where in the hell did you get that shit from?" She looked even more surprised. "I—you were so damn stupid—you still are!—you didn't even know my major. Why, it's art...you didn't know that? Damn, you're dumb!"

Her eyes were hysterical; and I began to feel a little hysterical and jittery myself. "Well I've gotta get out of here," I said, finally. My father went off to flop on the bed in silence. He himself was highly disoriented; the argument really meant nothing to him—just more words floating in the air. I felt threatened when she attacked my money-making scheme; what it meant was that I would be tied down to Belford's horrors forever. And the fucking neighborhood, as I well knew myself, was getting worse and worse with each passing month—bit by teeny tiny bit. "Quit the job," she finally demanded, flopping on the couch. That's where I always saw her—on the couch. In a few hours she would be in the bed—with somebody, and that somebody wasn't going to be my father. "Up yours," I said to her, walking out of the house. "LOUIE! YOU AND YOUR FILTHY FUCKING MOUTH!! GET THE HELL OVER HERE—YOU FORGET I'M YOUR MOTHER!!" she screamed out the door at the top of her lungs, so that even the "neighbors"(!) could hear it.

I didn't even eat breakfast because I woke up nowadays around ten-thirty and had to be at work by twelve. Twelve to nine—that was my working schedule. Twelve to nine on the front line jerking sodas or tea or coffee!

My position was changed quickly, even before I got my first check. Three days into my stay at the Dummheit I was officially switched over to busboy and some-time dishwasher, but as the weeks passed I became a general knock-around, a kind of fifth-wheel they kept on hand for "floating" whenever they needed an extra monkey. The dishwashing I felt was the best because I didn't have to look at those shit-ass monkey bastards throwing their scraps on the floors and slobbering all over the table, like that old fool who used to come in ordering oatmeal every time, only to sit and begin talking in a girl's voice and then a child's voice, and then his wife's. Sometimes he came in with his wife, but he didn't do the voice then, of course. Another was a precinct officer and his slant-eyed whore wife shipped in F.O.B. from the Orient. I began to find out a lot of interestingly cruel and exploitative ways of dealing with human or semi-human beings quite often by overhearing conversations on both sides of the fence; they did not necessarily have to deal with the Dummheit, either. Americans in particular enjoy this kind of rubbish. I heard about this system by eavesdropping on Albino when he was sitting in a seat watching me in his nice beautiful Italian silk tie and Brazilian dago shoes wipe the tables off. He was talking about something involving the Orientals and the mail order service. They sure had a big laugh over it...especially the part where they actually shipped their whores to their "husbands" by way of a box in the shape of a coffin. That's how in the hell Toi Pu Sei, the sexy gook over there, got here to begin with. That way they could all get automatic American passports! "Man, did you hear about those Oriental dating services especially that Hong Kong thing where, you know, the new mail order system which they ship those Chink bitches in to you from the Orient by way of a fuckin' coffin?"

"No way!" Albino said, surprised. I wiped closer and closer towards them so I could hear the conversation because the word "Chink" caught my ears.

"Well—what they really do is, like they put them in a fuckin' box and they ship 'em off to fuckin San Diego in a *box!* I don't believe that..."

"They'll do anything nowadays."

"Oh yeah—anything goes. Say...there goes that Ding Bat..."

Ding Bat's all through for the night; she's been hard at it all day and all night and she walks out with a grin like it never even happened to her. That's what I saw from her every day—pure unmitigated Chinaman happy-go-luckiness. In fact I could see it on most of the Chinese. They seemed naturally content, like nothing was hurting them. I'd ask Clyde what he felt about it and he'd say that nothing was wrong, absolutely nothing. He said everything was a-ok. But you'd have to be a stupid man to believe it, of course, to believe that they were all happy-go-lucky and content to break their backs over the forge. You'd have to be stupid like Albino when he said, right after she left, shaking his head in bewilderment at her strength, "Goddamn! That Ding Bat's been here since eleven inna morning and she just comes right out singing! Can you believe that? It's ridiculous! A woman at her age working for thirteen hours a day!"

"She's a Chinaman," Johnny-boy said. "They dig it; it's their thing..."

"I think you mean China*woman*. Not man—you think she's gotta dick or something?"

"Well...who knows what the fuck those Chinks have? I dunno...probably even got fuckin tails," Johnny-Boy laughs.

"If they can have slanted eyes they can have fuckin tails

too."

"No kidding."

"Dey goddamn fucking coolie labor, man," Barnaby said, approaching the two, just like that, all of a sudden, walking out the door. He seems all ready to snooze all happily after slaving his fat dirty ass off on those pots. Albino looked up at him. "Got it all straightened out, buddy? Everything just fine and dandy, isn't it? Good—that's my boy. Here's your check. See you tomorrow!..." He walks out the joint. Albino looks hard at him. "Carlin, look...am I seein' what I think I'm seein'—six fingers on that kid?"

"NAW! Uh-uh—no way. It's not genetically possible."

"I kinda swore I did. He ought to wash his ass, I can smell 'im all the way back here. Now, about those Chinese..."

"You think he's got six fingers?"

"Fuck his ass. I could care less. Now, about those Chinese..." I wanted to listen harder because the dishwashing machine was making noises, so I stopped working and listened directly to them, but he saw me when he turned around. "Say, what the hell are you doin', you bastard? Eavesdroppin' on us? eh? What? Get those tables in order!" I kept working with one ear open. "Well those Chinese—you see that guy back there, Louie? Hell! What the hell's he? He's for business! So he thinks!"

"Bisness? Are you fuckin' serious?..."

"That's what Quackenbros told me. Yeah, he wants **tuition** for college!"

"College? What for? He's already got his native occupation! Ha ha! You know...stepin fetchit??"

"Naw, the blacks make too much noise and they're always out drunk. The Spanish—"

"Well what about Ethel, she comes in on time..."

"Yeah, right, she's like that old bandana wearin' motherfucker you see on Warner Brothers an' shit. Yeah, right. The Spanish, those goddamn greasy bastards just get into my fuckin hair. We oughta fire the whole pack!..."

"An ship 'em back to El Salvador!"

"Ey—do you know if somea those people are illegal?"

"Which ones? There's a bunch of 'em here!"

"The Spanish people."

"Sure...Quackenbros did that shit. Reverse racist. **Affirmative Action Man!**"

"Naw, but the gooks are all right. They work hard. Unlike the Jews...I can't stand these fucking Jews. Did you see all these Jews who came in here today? And the mess they make. Why do they keep doing this? What in hell is this place to them—Israel?"

"And the workers..."

"Jesus," Albino interjected. "Really, we oughta fire this United Nations charity welfare club an' just hire all Chinese. Make it all Chinese—"

"Then the whole joint would get slanted downwards an' you wouldn't know what the fuck they'd be sayin'."

"Stop talkin' like a nigger, Carlin...I like 'em, though, the Chinese," he said, grinning and nodding, eying Gu Fi in the back vacuuming her section of the dining room. "They're my kinda people."

"They stay shut."

"They never fuss. Day in and day out. They make good old Mr. Albino feel like a real man," he said, chuckling and rubbing his hands. Shitass! What a bunch of savages I was working for! I knew what I went through in the last two and a half weeks was only the start of it; I hadn't yet provoked myself into getting my brains smashed...that was for later times. But it could come up just right now if I did the wrong thing. How in the hell could someone like Barnaby work for those beasts and walk out grinning? Maybe he was one himself, who knows? Or the Spanish? Or the Chinese? Didn't they know what the animals had stashed up their assholes?...I would sit on the bus and look on their faces and see how many of them were laughing and giggling and cracking jokes, but I felt that they were trying not to get at something, they were hiding something. The real thing came out when they had nothing to say to each other. Then they were just like the people I would see in the ads, indeed they were even like the ads themselves—just a part of the background. I could only keep aloof in little ways. I turned back to the books I was reading. I even turned to music—jazz music. It was old, a music of another epoch, and I could keep calm by humming Louis Armstrong melodies from the old 78s that I heard in the library one time before I went to work at this place. I was glad I made that little experiment.

I used the music and the books as a shield against the rotted and moldy glittering backdrop of disco, the ultimate spiritual stupefaction of the people I knew around me. The disco wasn't just about dancing—it was an entire world, a whole heaven and a cosmos, a cosmos built up from money pickpocketed from the innocent, the unknowing and the oppressed, a cosmos of broken refrigerators and dirty tap water and fleas and tainted meat and the homeless and needle-marks in the veins. Walkman radios kept some of them around me from freaking off and blasting out their brains. That's why some lame-brain like Lolita could say, when I questioned her about what she felt about her work, with her earphones perched down beneath the grease in her hair, "Aw, who cares, go wey frahm her', stupi'!" I asked Giuseppe and he didn't even answer—he just waved his hand in the air wearily. I asked Basil and he gave this answer: "I'm gonnuh qwit, mon. I 'ate eeet dere even dough I been dere onlee one week. Albino getten on mah nerves!" And he said this over and over again as the months passed—but I never saw him quit. It was bad enough for me to be working at the joint, but the fact that the others showed not the slightest air of resentment made the whole bus around me seem like a steel funerary coffin pushing us back into that fiery furnace of death and cocaine and broken bones and noses—*Belford*.

Drones don't communicate. They keep everything on a dead even level, and you got to level with them. I did that, but at the same time I could wear my gook cap instead of my cunt cap because it would set me apart from the bunch in one way. Luckily, though, all was not content in the dishwasher's garden of Eden. Tito wasn't the only one in the joint who was pissed—if you looked deeper, you'd see quite clearly that everyone was pissed, of course—but the real angry young chili-choker was Mario. Good old Mario Barabbas. I heard this one from Basil who told it to me on the way to work. Today was the day, he said to Maria that day when we got there, and when I was washing dishes with them again, that he was going to get what was coming to him. He had to pay his dues; he was a poor Spanish-speaking wage slave from El Salvador living in a hell-hole in the wall in the worst section of North Belford. Every night he had rats running across the bedroom floor and mice coming out of the sinks; every day the water was filthy and good neither for drinking or washing, so he had to buy the water, which was complicated and expensive. The area in which he lived was not even fit for rat inhabitation; it was so dangerous he had to have ten locks put on the doors to keep the muggers and the freaks out; he was forced to nail up his window after a break-in which cost him his television, his clothes, his suitcase, his toiletry, and 600 dollars to boot. Yet even that was useless because it was getting hot out—it was May—and there was no air-conditioning, the electricity wasn't even working in most of the sockets and therefore the fan he had couldn't be put to use, and he couldn't sell the fan—nobody would have it. He tried to get the electricity fixed—he did, but at such an exorbitant sum he was forced to go on welfare to help pay for the bills. And even then the electricity failed again because the repairmen weren't any good—they hadn't done a good enough job pasting up all the wires. Apropos of the electricity the roof leaked everywhere when it rained; in the very center of the apartment the water ran in so much he needed an umbrella to go in the fucking living room. To solve this problem he always put a bucket on the tea table...but roaches were running out of the sink. The walls were weak; when Carlos was snoozing in the room he shared with Miguel and Mario—the three always slept together, often in the same bed—the ceiling collapsed right on him. Fortunately he had the pillow on his face...In the living room the paint kept peeling off, the lime fell off, the wood and nothing but brick remained. When the toilet broke down he was unable to do anything about it—it was too expensive. He was already loaded with bills, and the fucking landlady kept raising the rent every month, it seemed, by fifty more dollars. When he couldn't pay his telephone bills the guys from the company knocked on his door in the middle of the night and ripped the phone right out of his wall, smiling all the while. He never paid the bill, so they turned off the water—besides, it wasn't worth a shit at any rate. He only had the electricity. He couldn't make repairs on the apartment. And when he took his complaints to the landlady she took him into a back room, and took out a pair of pliers and broke his nose wrenching it around, tying his hands to the bedpost, and kicking him in the balls. (That's the time when I saw him come in all hyped up with bandages all over his face and arms.) Afterwards she turned him loose after punching him around and making threats. He took his complaints to the police; they neither showed up nor filed a report. (There were too many incidences like that going on anyway—they were bored to tears, poor things!) Soon they took his car away. That was even worse—it meant now he actually had to walk through the hell of inner-North Belford. On every corner there were kids dealing drugs; they carried huge guns, machine guns; the place reeked of piss everywhere, old newspapers abounded, broken glass, old thrown-out rotten food—it was all of a piece. He had been mugged countless times—it was the most dangerous place in the borough, or one of them. And last, but not least, were the fucking nieces, the three Barabbas sisters—especially Lolita. She threw away the Welfare money like nothing; she spent it all on clothes and fancy jewelry instead of the bills which needed to be paid. And to top it off she had a baby—at thirteen. And it was retarded. Lolita wanted to throw the baby out but the mother wouldn't hear of it. So they kept it—another mouth to feed. That's why Mario kept stealing food from the slaughterhouse, because he could no longer afford to buy it. And then there was Concha, with her promiscuity, her predilection for white boys, and then Rosa...his list of problems seemed endless. Actually, when I heard about them from Basil that day, I broke out laughing, because it was so grossly absurd. He had brought the problem to the managers with this rebuff: do your work or get the fuck out. So he felt he had to get even with those sons-of-bitches who were killing him, or trying to kill him. Today he was waiting for the manager; he was molding his hands as I worked the dishes into the machine. He turned on the hot water in the sink and began preparing for something drastic. So Mr. Albino, arms akimbo and strutting like a Nazi, steps in, and glares at him with the utmost viciousness. He'd been drinking, I could tell. "Ey, don't turn this shit on—what the hell are you doin'? You big ape, look, you got the whole goddamn floor flooded over so you better get a mop and mop that shit up or else you're goin' outta here faster than you can say shit—"

"A—hem!" Mario snorted. Mr. Albino stood suddenly erect and looked dead in his eyes. "Ey—what's the ahem for, huh? Answer me! Is that something they say in Nicaragua when they get pissed off? Huh? Answer me! C'mon, shitass!" I could tell he'd been drinking... I could smell him. He was wobbling around with his factory chart..."Stupid prick fuck-head! Pussy breath! C'mon! Look"—Mario stared him dead in the eyes, not moving a muscle—"Look, I no eat savages! Okay?—I know you no speaka English well. Hey...look!...wanna banana? Eh, motherfuck..."—and at that point he grabbed hold of Mr. Albino and dunked his head in. Mr. Albino began flapping his arms wildly as Mario banged down on him and tried to strangle him on the edge of the sink. Giuseppe began to shout with joy, and so did Maria, and so did I—inside. The rest came to a complete halt as people rushed in to pry Mario off, but it was no use; he kept butting them off. Finally he took Mr.

Albino out and Mr. Albino recovered faster than he thought he would. He was deep red through and through... "I'll get you, you snot-sucking spick!" Albino shrieked, and began to throw punches at Mario, who threw bigger punches. Giuseppe jumped in by tossing plates on the ground; Maria kicked Albino all over and spat on him, shouting, "*Gringo! Idiota! Cabeza de mierda!*" over and over, plus a lot of fancy cuss words to boot. Clyde popped in—and ducked out. The Chinese girls shouted over and over, "No good! No good! Spaneesh no good!"—though more was in store for them up ahead...but here comes Johnny-Boy, in with his leather jacket and chains and spikes and whatnot, plus the tattoos; he comes for his paycheck. He comes to the rescue, sees the danger, pulls out a gun and fires into the ceiling. Everything stops dead, full stop. Maria faces him, as does Giuseppe and Mario and I. I wonder what the hell he's going to do... "Stop it right now!! All of you bastards!!" I see him in the back jumping up and down and shifting from side to side like he's having convulsions..."I'll break your stupid spick necks, you jerk-offs!!" And with that he ran over to Giuseppe first, but Giuseppe grabbed up a plate and defended himself. No matter: Johnny-Boy forced him to put the plate down, and he does—and pistol-whips him. Mario then drove his fists into Johnny-Boy's back—he hated Johnny-Boy the worst of all. But Johnny-Boy was too tough even for Mario. He pulled Mario through the kitchen slapping him and kicking him in the balls. He rapped his head up against the wall, socking him in the back with his pistol and putting a big fat juicy knot right there, and then he put the gun to his head and dragged him up to the hot stove while everyone screamed and backed off and stuck his face on the hot grill and burned him. Lolita wasn't there— she was in the toilet taking a piss. Rosa was giving head to Barnaby the pot-washer and Sal Moustafa the janitor at the same time. Concha was there, though—she took up the ice shovel to beat Johnny-Boy, but Albino kicked her in the stomach and held her down trying to get his fingers up her ass, held her as Johnny-Boy beat the shit out of Mario Barabbas, and fired him without pay...they shoved him in the elevator; he was still half-conscious after the burns...Johnny-Boy rushed to the basement threatening the whole crew with his gun and then he yanked Mario out and threw him out through the back alley emergency exit...he collapsed, got up, and staggered out, crying like a fool—and Johnny-Boy and Albino laughed their heads off. The whole crew was outraged. We worked through the whole afternoon and evening and night with the thought of murder—at least some of us, because Barnaby was his giggly old happy self and so was Gu Fi and Ding Bat. But when the word got around some heated words spilled out and Johnny-Boy went up to Maria and threatened to kill her if she opened her motherfucking *cucaracha* lips again. Maria let out a curse word and Johnny-Boy fired at the ceiling. I stumbled around in rage, peeped outside at the smug self-satisfied faces just sitting there munching away without a ripple in their calm dead sea of smugness and I rapped my fist on the walls, wondering why did I have to come down to this and wondering what it would take to kill those animals, thinking perhaps that I could burn the joint down if possible because the gas equipment in the restaurant was weak and they needed all the money they could get for repairs. But I pushed it out of my mind, and went home in the dark thinking about nothing but killing those apes. But that wasn't the last because when we walked in the joint one Sunday morning ready for a rough-and-tumble day, the entire joint had been wrecked; the dishwashing machine had holes in it, the dishes were all broken, the stove broken up and the parts melted down, the grease thrown on the steps and the floor—someone had tripped up and fell while he or she was making his or her way down. As it turns out, the one who tripped up was Mrs. Steinberg, one of the extra food managers they had on hand for women tokens, who was lying on the ground, conscious, but writhing and weeping and muttering to herself that she had a broken neck. Well...so much the better. Wish it could have been Albino or Johnny-Boy. They got downstairs after mopping it for half-an-hour and found the situation even worse. The managers office was ransacked; the safe broken open and everything taken out of it; plus all the food had been stolen, the glass shattered, and the stove had paint thrown all in it, as had the floor all around. The doors were broken off the latches and the latches were so broken up that they had to buy new ones from way across town. The storage room was cleaned out fair and square...When we got to the bathrooms and near another flight of stairs, Mr. Quackenbros was there, lying on his back and muttering to himself, but this time in regret that he had ever chosen to manage an insane asylum, or a hoosegow, rather than going into the housing business as he intended. The toilet bowls, by the way, had been smashed out so thoroughly, with the water all over the ground and flooding up every place, along with the mirrors and the facebowls and the scuffed-up and crushed and hacked-up tiles, that they'd have to build an entirely new bathroom.

So with that crisis in mind, after they filed a police report and sealed off the area, we were given two weeks off on the "dole" for "good behavior" until the entire joint was refixed. But the mob did a lot of damage, especially to the gas pipes; and it was those gas pipes that never got wholly repaired just right because they were old and poorly installed due to such haste: they had to be done within a two-week period.

Mario himself was gone; he hadn't hung himself—no, he had gone back to El Salvador through Mexico, where he had taken the nearest flight to Mexico City on the stolen $6,650. The other half he gave to the Barabbas family—and the money was gone in a day. Lolita and Concha, of course, were to blame for buying up sixteen pairs of hand-woven Italian five inch pumps!

Things began happening. Soon Mrs. Steinberg, of whom I

remember nothing, because she was out most of the time because she was four months pregnant, disappeared on account of a set-up rigged by Johnny-Boy and Albino in their attempt to push higher in the Dummheit ranks. Johnny-Boy was the short-order prep-cook, but showed "good managing skills" according to Albino. That was good reason—or excuse—for making him the Food Production Manager—still insignificant, but it was hell for everyone else. So, there were, all in all, five managers running the place, many of whom rarely showed up. Mrs. Steinberg went out completely on account of "possession of cocaine," but it was Carlin who had stuffed it into her apron after getting some of it from Maggie Constable, the part-time cashier and full-time coconut-head. She was a thick-set butch of a girl from New Jersey who had more power than most of the managers—even Quackenbros, because she had been working there for seven years. There had been another relief manager there who was black, but Mr. Quackenbros had him "shifted" to another branch of Dummheit. After all, Mr. Quackenbros wasn't the boss boss. The Boss Boss only came in once a month to see how his slaves, including Mr. Quackenbros and Mr. Albino and Mr. Carlin and Mrs. Steinberg, were working out. And, of course, the Boss Boss wasn't even the Boss Boss Boss, who had his headquarters in Washington, D.C., and even then, he wasn't The King, who had his in Chicago, in the Sears and Roebuck building, and still yet, he wasn't the ruler of all the Dummheit branches, who was based in New York City, in the jungle of Wall Street. This, still insignificant, led up past co-rulers and vice-rulers and co-presidents and vice-presidents to presidents to presidents-in-chiefs up to God's agents, the first agent of God in London, the second in Bönn, the third in Paris, the fourth in Brussels, the fifth in Cairo, the sixth in Tokyo, the seventh in Manila, and the eighth and the ninth shuttling between Bangkok, Singapore, Hong-Kong and Taipei. But the agent didn't mean God, not even the great great God of Johannesburg, South Africa, the king of the gold mines and the favelas and the shanties and the diamond fields and the big show-palaces—that great God lay between the skyscrapers in none other than Lacklove, Maryland, the suburbo-urbanized money jungle where God the pool-shark played out all his debts and wheeled all his dealings with his divine fried-chicken wisdom. Indeed, he was so much God, that images of him could not be made or circulated, and surely we had seen nothing of his likes, just as the nothings of East London, Berlin, Paris, Istanbul, Cairo, Cape Town, Brussels, Manila, Yokohama, Peking, Ulanbatar, Lagos, Abidjian, Tunis, Budapest, Fez, Harlem, East L.A., Moscow, Bengasi, Athens, Lusaka and Ankara had seen nothing of this divine peanut planter from afar yet from which they were condemned for life to slaving away on his world-wide plantation.

Somewhere along the line I got involved with a beautiful and sexy young bus girl at the Dummheit slaughterhouse. Her name was Penny McDonald, from Kentucky, of all places. She was only seventeen years old at the time and I was nineteen. She was a brunette with sharp cheekbones and harsh almond green eyes, a rather large and wide mouth with full lips—and a ripe, ripe body. It still gives me a hard-on thinking about her, much less writing about her. Her ass was round and stuck out, yes—but her tits were terrific. When I overheard her in a conversation she had about her breasts with Giuseppe who was ogling her while Rosa was out, she mentioned that she had a bust size of forty. Forty...*and seventeen!* She also had wide hips and rather plump thighs and legs—to say nothing of that big round ass. When I bused alongside her one day I took an interest in her right off. The minute I spotted her, or when she spotted me, busing alongside each other, we began to chat a while. And this is where this big kinky trip around the worker's world had its origins. Penny initiated everything—though, at first, I thought she was just another flirtatious, half-lesbian, sexless, cuntless American white woman. But it just wasn't like that at all. I saw where she was at clearly when, as I was cleaning the bathrooms, she just walked right in without excusing herself or asking me to leave. She went in and closed the door. She stood in there but soon I forgot she was in there since I was in a rush to clean everything—and I opened the door. She was on the stool taking a piss and her pants were down around her ankles; as she lifted up a slight trickle of urine dripped down from her crotch into the toilet. She had jerked up out of surprise and I closed the door remembering just how she looked on the toilet. All I needed was to get blasted by a white Southerner, I thought to myself, and a female to boot. But when she got out she had a grin on her face, and walked very slowly. "You sly bastard," she said to me, "you wanted ta see me piss, didn't you?" Her Southern accent had been muffled after living in the North for many years. She was only seventeen, like I said, but I thought her good enough still. I hadn't gotten anything sexually since high school! A year and a half of sexual frustration was beginning to show very strongly. I sprouted an erection by mistake—I tried to cover it up. But Penny didn't want me to cover it up. "Lemme see what it looks like," she drooled. I pulled my hand away and she looked at it. That only made it harder knowing that she was getting off on looking at my cock. "Say, you ever done it before?" she said to me. "Yeah, but not much. Only three times," I said. Her mouth dropped in slight surprise. "You poor man. THREE TIMES?? Shit—Louie, you need help. I ain't a virgin—hell naw. I been at it since I was thirteen. I love it—I gotta admit!...you gettin hot unner the collar, I bet, you ain't had it but three fuckin' times. You gotta girlfriend?"

"No."

Mockingly she turned down her lips. "What about ME, Louie?" I looked into her juicy lips and hazel eyes. "Other than you, no," I said, breathing deeply. "That's what I meant."

She got up into my face, staring me right in the eyes. I was really hysterical now and she could see it; I knew she was half-

crazy herself…"That damn work sure makes yuh horny…"
She felt my arm, up in my armpit, then on my face, then on
my hip and ran her finger along my dick. My heart leaped. I
expected it to happen. "How big? Show me."
"Not right now, people are still comin' in."
"Fuck them—they're a buncha bastards," she said. I couldn't
have agreed more. Then she began smiling and grinning, and
shook the hair out of her eyes. She had a big wide idiot's grin
which I found just as exciting as her body, perhaps even more.
She ran her tongue along her teeth and directed me into the
latrine and locked the door behind her. She was breathing
hysterically. "I haven't had anything in a month," she added
somewhere along the line. Once in the toilet we went right up
into each others faces and she wound her arms around my
neck, smooching me so frantically she almost lost herself. I
clutched her ass and ran my hands all around the cheeks and
I began to get a real headache because I was so excited feeling
that juicy ass. "Take it out," she whispered in my ear—and
right here Maggie Constable steps in. I knew because I could
hear her running her fat jowls. "Aw shit, Louey, it's Maggie—
that black girl, she's a *stool!*" she whispered in my ear the last
word. We were doomed anyhow because we were in the toilet
with the door locked. Maggie wanted to come in. "Comon, I
gotta use da stool…who in heah? Hope it ain't you, Louie—"
"It's me, Penny," Penny yelled. "I'm takin' a douche! Use da
men's toilet. Nobody in there anyhow," she lied.
"Where da hell Louey den? Huh?"
"He's cleanin' the other bathrooms, Maggie! That's all."
"Well lemme see—"
"Will you just get the hell outta here, Maggie!" she roared.
Maggie leaves. "Goddamn stupid bitch…she wantsa pry into
yer fuckin' life, Louey—"
"Aha!" she roared, catching us off guard. "Fuckin' inna
bathrooms again! You always do dat shit, Penny! You a freak!
Open the damn door—"
"Eh? What's goin on?" Aw, hell—the other stool pigeon—

Ruby Rubenstein. "Whatsa matta, dey joikin' eeech odder awfa sumtin? Wha?" Maggie tells her. "We oughta go tell de meanughah," she croons. "She could be spreadin' AIDS to da men woikas!" We get out, our pants on. Penny explains everything. "At least I ain't a fuckin' dyker like you-all," she snorts, and grabs my hand and leads the both of us out. We went up to get back to work because it was nearing the end of our breaktime. But we were still in heat—Penny knew from the look in my eyes and I knew from the look in hers. But as I was wiping off the tables; Johnny-Boy came up and confronted us two.

"Say, what in hell were you two doin' in the bathrooms just a while ago?" he snapped. We were bewildered at how the information suddenly got around like that.

"Well??" he said, impatient, wobbling around on his shoes. "I heard you were doin' something that you were not supposed to—"

"Carlin, it ain't nonea your business, so why don't you just piss off, faggot," Penny snapped at him with a dead pan air. I was jolted at how brazen she was toward the managers. "You'd never get up the courage to make it even if you tried!"

Johnny-Boy was incensed—impulsively he gave her a resounding slap across the jaw—right in front of the patrons in the middle of the dining room. "LISSEN TO ME, YOU BITCH! YOU WANNA GET FIRED, HUH?? YOU LISSEN TO YOUR BOSS SOME TIME YOU STINKIN' WHORE COCKSUCKER!!" Penny threw the tray on the ground and dashed off into the mall crying. One of the girls in the back, Chloe, saw what was happening, and rushed over and confronted Carlin, but Carlin told her to fuck off. Then I ran away from him too, seeing what an obvious asshole he was. I ran right with Penny onto the mall, hearing him scream, and wondering why in the hell I didn't listen to Rodney MacInness..."COME BACK, YOU MOTHERFUCKERS!! COME BACK!! YOU GODDAMN NIGGER MOTHERFUCKERS!! NIGGER-LOVIN' WHITE-TRASH BITCH!! GODDAMN NIGGER MOTHERFUCKERS!!! COCKSUCKERS!!!!!!

I'LL LYNCH YOU!! SNOTNOSES!!" A handful of patrons got up and confronted Carlin personally: "Now look sir, that was totally uncalled for! Ridiculous! You didn't have to—"

"Shutup, sit down and eat or get the hell out of this place," he snapped. "They were dealing drugs, don't you understand..." I heard him as I dashed out way away from the joint—vowing never to return—the first time I made that vow. "...they were dealing drugs!..."

The following night Carlin wasn't there. I went to pick up my check from Mr. Albino.

"Say—Louie," Albino said as he handed me the check, "you feelin' fine, huh?"

"Sure, everything's just fine."

"Carlin not a problem, is he?"

"Oh no...not at all," I said, feeling an urge to jump up and down and scream.

"Good. I just want you to know...I want you to know that if I ever hear of any other incident in the bathrooms OR out in the mall, Louie, like what happened yesterday, you're gonna find yourself working some other place." Smiles. "Got that, buddy?"

"Sure."

"Thanks for coming by."

I walked away knowing that there was just no fucking way out one way or the other. Back to Belford...

When I got out that Friday night it was deserted and I knew well that meant that my workaholic compadres had gone off to live it up in the bars and discos downtown—or the streets shooting up and snorting, like some of the Barabbases would do. If coke wasn't business, then it was pleasure. It was an inextricable part of life, just like your own right hand. It didn't matter where you went or what you did: coke was always there. I also knew that a lot of those fat juicy sums I saw lying there in Albino's safe was blood money, drug money. It was helping them personally, and they hadn't been caught yet. The stool pigeons—Tramsokong Louangphuck (well, not actually a stool pigeon but a major figure in the drug operation ring in the Dummheit), Ruby Rubenstein, and Maggie Constable were the top agents. Number one and three lived right there in Belford, so they were getting it hot off the streets—not to mention ganja, which was for "relaxation" purposes. In the disco they went to they did it all the time—meaning drugs, of course. The young people hung out there mostly. Several times people like Giuseppe, who was beginning to change his attitude towards me gradually, tried to coax me into coming along with them, but I avoided all persuasions like the plague. The joint, in my mind, was a free for all—absolutely anything goes once you step into the Copacabana disco, which is what it was known as. It was in Dupont Circle, smack in the so-called "bohemian" environment of Third-World bookstores and ganja-smokers and graffiti-artists. But we weren't radicals; we didn't read books (except I...); and all we were interested in was getting ourselves soused up in just about any fashion in order to forget that we were being brutalized in the way we were. But to get back to the disco—it was a lousy affair. You went in at your own risk. Just recently someone had his head bashed open with a wine bottle by some drunken queen. And not only that, there was screwing and snorting and just about anything going on in the bathrooms and the locker rooms. It was a cancer germ—and only a guy or anything else with a whole lot of money was ever allowed inside the prison. I'd heard about it from Lolita. She was only fifteen, yet she looked very much like an adult, even with her size, so she got herself a fake ID card and managed to slip into the joint. There she, at least according to her stories, scored every time. AN ID CARD TO FUCK! It was one of the most asinine and silly things I ever heard. Pretty soon, I thought, you'd need a blue card in order to have the right to piss, because fucking was just another ordinary activity—at least in my mind, if not in the minds of other so-called Americans. But the big shits didn't see things that way, of course. You needed to have a permit for everything. You couldn't be underage—

young kids were supposed to stay chaste. Indulgence in sin, apparently, would mess up their minds. Oh, no, to mess up your mind, to soil and sully it, was something only for us adults to engage in, because when you're an adult, you can, like all "mature" individuals should, choose whether you want to be a freak or not. If you're a good red-blooded man from the Americas, you can do it—it's your choice, no one is stopping you. The only problem is is that people here can't make any judgments, which is why they have fake ID cards to begin with. Morality is for the books, like the high school reading list; it was like homework—people ignored it, unless their honor was at stake. The world of sex was almost like an inaccessible empire, a kind of military junta forbidden to certain persons at a certain age or a certain wage. You needed a passport to do it—and that passport was the ID card.

Perhaps, if the reality were too sour, if it could only be stomached for a moment or so, maybe one could drift off into a world of stark fantasy once he got off from work. But, naturally, this sweet land of coke dreams could be razed with the slightest din of the outside world. Yet to me the inner world was the only one that mattered; it was the world which was threatened on all sides by the nine-to-five get-the-fuck-up-and-get-your-ass-on-the-ball pattern of existence. Inside, in my own little fantasy world, there were no barriers between wanting and doing, for all the walls between those two entities had been broken down. In this world I was not just plain Louie Phillips but also King Carlos leading his nation into the golden age of prosperity; I was Don Juan in Bangkok or Baghdad or Alexandria or Manila with a billion addresses and fully confident of the fact that no matter where and when I wished to turn in and hit the sack, there would always be a bunch of 'em waiting for me, mouths agape, all colors, shapes and sizes. I was also the sailor on the high seas, the ships docking off at Hong Kong, and me walking up the docks, a slut under my arms, bell-bottomed and money pouring out of my pockets, my skin gone blue and red with the Chinese neon. I was teaching English to the Japs in Osaka and screwing the geishas, tossing Yen out the window gaily and recklessly to all the poor Koreans; I was the stock broker in New York and Bönn and Paris, yet always there when the gold dropped in at London at eight hundred points. I was Sinbad sailing up the Volga and the Rhine and the Mekong, or I was Buddha enlightened, a burning piece of live human ore sitting in peace under the coconut tree. Or Isaiah, back in the swampy muckheaps of the Biblical lands, amidst the epic life of death and decadence, writing the book never to be forgotten, never to be passed up, even by the lowest of the low. A book...perhaps it was that, most of all, that I already had swimming in my mind and wished most of all to create? Why was I working, anyway? Surely it just wasn't for the fun of it— I needed to get out and be me...But—if I ever took it into my head to write a book, it would unquestionably be about the inner private life I dwelled in and not this death life of plexiglass and daily body counts. That was nothing; you can't set that shit to poetry, just as you can't set the Dummheit Cafe to good literature, good books. Sometimes, when it was useless trying to read girlie magazines, or escape in any fashion, I would take off to the bathroom while the house was deserted. There, I would shut the door—and be confronted, always with great horror, at the reflection of myself in the mirror. By now, I was getting genuinely afraid to see my reflection; I put my hand in front of my face so as not to be confronted directly with that beast staring back at me on the other side of the fence. It seemed as if, standing in front of the mirror, my hand now taken away and standing face to face with the beast, I was actually confronting another self who was my enemy; I was looking dead at The Devil, a monster who had taken possession of my whole body and soul at an early age and I had forgotten just when and where it happened—but I knew that that bastard, even though it had my face, my clothes, my features, my hair, my complexion—was *not* me: it was all that The Others, which is to say, mother, father, brother, sister, family, friends, lovers, bosses, books, television, music, and whatnot, made of me. The reflection was a straw dummy made up of a fatras of pure cultural shit, handed down from the years, and nothing but a stumbling block in my path to find myself, to find a way out of this mess. For here, in the jungle in which my mother made the cardinal mistake of giving birth, I must not stop and rest, even if I would surely die by a policeman's bullet on the run from the madhouse. All being calculated into status symbols, and me being, no matter what, forever at the bottom, even at the tippy top, why must I even *breathe*, for God's sake, if the very act of breathing makes no sense, if it all runs to money, to success and power-play, or taxes, or Sugar-corn Pops; why must I eat if the food had been robbed of its nutrients, if it bloats my body out of all shape, if it clouds my mind and breaks my health? Or, for that matter, talk? Sing? Laugh? Dance? Write? There is nothing to talk of except the latest coup or revolution, half-way round the freaking earth (there'll never be one here, surely), or the latest prison riot. No use singing still, because the songs are all meaningless, and just yet, there isn't even a fucking melody at all. Worse still, as I learned later, when the computer finally took my soul for good, that there is the right time to laugh, and that's when the comedy hour is on; and there's the **right** time to cry, when the tear-jerkers, the poor soap-opera eunuchs, come on sputtering in all their castrated heat. Everything, in short, must be done in its proper time and place—all apropos of what you feel to the contrary. You've got to fly with the flies—or get stuck on the sweet flypaper of life.

And now, my friends, it is time to take leave—of the world. The earth to me is nauseating; I have already seen all, heard all, felt all. I know it's true: the world from here to Manila is all of a piece, because the prime-time news gives me updates on everything down to the last pee-drop. Henceforth I shall shut myself up in the closet and forget that I am alive, that I am human, that I am a coon, or a mule, which is more truthful. Again—who am I? I've heard that before. And, I'll honestly tell you—I don't know. I don't know a fucking thing.

Who could forget the day I finally got a "job"! Just as the day logically began with dirty dishes and screams and complaints and sick leaves and stale food, so it logically ended with broken dishes and curses and screams, the boss jumping up and down, the kitchen too hot, the ammonia causing those poor Chinks to nod off in the mop pail...everything got fouled up every time. That's enough of that. What more could I say? Every night it was the same for me. It was always a kind of special treat to look around the joint when everybody had cleared out. Look...millions of chicken bones, rice, carrots, peas, Coca-Cola glasses overturned and marked up with lipstick, grease from the lips and fingers, bubble-gum stains in the seats and carpet, sometimes vomit, sometimes a whole drumstick or even a whole dinner left untouched. In fact, half of the slop they never ate. The peas nobody liked;—same for the cauliflower and the lentil soup. People always left it sitting there on the plate. Cut into the back room...every night I was witness to this ghastly spectacle of an ultra-rich institution tossing loaf after loaf of bread right into the garbage. I looked around—the cans were full of tossed-out, perfectly good bread. What one child in Ethiopia, or Calcutta, I thought, would do for just ONE roll, ONE eeeny weeny goddamned roll lying beneath the scrap heap in the Dummheit Cafe garbage pails! The truth is, of course, Americans don't know how to starve— perhaps because, just the same, they don't know how to eat, either. When one eats anywhere else in the world he licks the platter clean: food is food. In America you take two bites and toss the rest in the garbage pail—or throw up. They eat too much, the Americans—that's well known. But it's junk food— *jungle* food—even less healty than the rubbish they feed their own pets. Maybe, then, the buggers had a reason for tossing the bread out. Well...after a few weeks passed at the joint, I joined in with wasting the damned bread. It was poison, absolute poison. If I could only step back in time with some loaves of Turkish bread! I wonder what they would make of it now that I'm over here. Or Arab bread, or French bread. Perhaps they would dispose of **those,** too. I never knew what real food was for many a goddamn year. I had many memories of the horrors of eating fast food, the food going fast to the bottom of the belly and boring a hole right there with every bite—and in the end, the food made you writhe, the grease made you either fall to the floor in a delirium or jump up frenetically and DO something, anything, just so long as it was action. The food began to fill me with horror as the weeks passed; my heart and nerves sank to my stomach, bitter, eternally dissatisfied, jaded, wanting more, more, more. The food tasted not of chicken, or rice, or salt or pepper but of despair or desperation or a frenzied anxiety of what was in store for me next. It was as if, through all the television commercials slammed in my face like a ton of ice, that I was being force-fed, like a mule, or, worse yet, I was being *raped* —raped by pork chops, Chinese rice, fat hamburgers, milk shakes, etc. My body was being molested and defiled by all the unhealthy and unnutritious elements in the food which only seemed to make me even more into a writhing mass of emotional monstrosity. Indeed I was just finishing one good old poisonous all-American ham sandwich with potato chips when I shut myself up in the closet. And I shut myself in there because I know, truly, that I am alone, lost, out in the wilderness, for my intestines are roaring with discontent; because, as I said to myself so many times in the past and even now—**I am a man in shackles!** And I cry. Yes, I weep and weep, just like a fool. And I know not why.

And neither did Basil, just the following morning, when he was suddenly forced by Carlin and Albino to get rid of his long hair.

73

"It doesn't fit our image," Quackenbros quacked. "Too off-beat." "Looks like shit to me," muttered Albino. Well...guess there was simply no choice but to get rid of them. His locks, which he bound up in a rubber band when he worked, were clipped off, one by one, while Carlin watched and giggled. It was downstairs in the kitchen where this happened. Jonas looked and had a great laugh out of it as well. Lolita was dying. "I gla' he ga' ridda dat ahgly hair," she drooled, laughing—"He look likea mohnsterr!" Basil got up, humiliated, looking at all the workers around him giggling about his shorn locks, and picked up a wet rag and went back to busing tables. Later he confronted me about it. "He racist, ever' onea dem, mon. He no like de way I wear my hear. Bot, eet ees my business, you know. He teenk everbody shood wear WHITE mon hear, white mon hear to heem luk right. Quackenbros no unnerstan' black mon, Louey. He bery nice, but dat no count. He say customah complain about de haircot."

"But that's their fuckin' problem if they don't like it," I said.

"But you no say dot to Albino an' Mistah Quackenbros," he said. "Eet dosant mattah, Quackenbros an' Carlin' an' Albino all one of a kind!" Around this time Penny walked by. "They did it, huh?" she said. "Sure," Basil nodded, angry. "Dey do it ever time." "I know it—I was tellin' Louey about 'em. Always on your case. Remember last week, when Carlin freaked off? Well...it happens every time an' there ain't a damn thing you can do about it, either. You caint even complain. See, they got me on three weeks notice already for what happened. They almost had you fired for walkin' out on them. But who gives! See, I been here for four years. They hired me at *thirteen*. You know how I feel about 'em. The customers don't even give a shit—in fact, they enjoy it. That's prubably why it keeps happenin'. You see these tight pants? You know why they gamme dis size to wear? 'Cause my ass sticks out an' they can see it better that way. An' I'm only seventeen! Damn—you know what, Louey, here you're justa goddamn number like the rest. You ain't nothin—nothin' at all. It don't mater who or what the hell you are—if ya work properly, then they'll fit you right in on the machine." Basil then cut out to bus the tables. "Shit, I hate it. He's got me makin' drinks 'cause that other snot, Toi, she ain't in right now. She gettin' a vacation. Me? They *never* gave me none. Say, you think she's a lil snob, Pu Seey, but once you get up close to her, you better watch yer step. She a maneater—an she eats 'em WHOLE. I swear! She a slut."

Then she switched the subject: "What you doin' tonight?"

"Nothing," I said, feeling a movement in my drawers.

"Good," she whispered, and pulled out a piece of paper. "Here's my address. I live alone—naw, my roommate's on vacation."

She left, winking, and went back to work. Albino came up and I quickly stashed it away. Right there a whole pattern began to make itself felt; it was to go on like that, with many other workers, for six solid months or more. All female, of course—I wasn't like Johnny-Boy was reputed to be. And, again, all beautiful and voluptuous and very, very young. I was being crunched into nothing, and as I was being crunched I had to seek out stronger and stronger antidotes to ease the pain of my crunching bones. I was still aware of nothing—even after two months at the joint. One of the main reasons why I was so unaware of so many things was because I was so damn persistently horny. Whenever I got up to get to work, I was always pooped out from masturbating. I had at least a dozen magazines shoved under the bed. I had many more pictures torn out of magazines and pasted on the walls. I always awoke after a wet dream and with an erection. When I came down to breakfast a sudden, compulsive, overpowering urge to jerk off seized me suddenly. I had to whank it off, no questions asked. When I couldn't find a room in the house to beat it off, then I forgot about it and locked it in— until after dark. This was just around the time Penny gave me her address. But, unfortunately, I soon realized my dream-pussy came with strings attached. Everyone wanted her: Giuseppe,

Barnaby, Jonas, Carlos—all of them. I also saw she would not have cared if she slipped a bit of it to each man waiting his turn. A real freebie, because there was no pay involved. I had never met a girl quite like her in my life. Nothing but her body kept her employed—that was obvious from the way she kept fucking things up. That's why she never got fired... But at first, when she gave me the address, I balked, since I wasn't too sex-mad like most everyone working there. She kept wondering when I would stop over. Well, I was a calm sort of guy...at least that's what I thought I was. Besides, there were plenty of diseases going around. I continued to think that way about it until...well, until I really needed it badly. Then I rushed out of the house one night thinking about her. I was in such a frantic mood sexually that I could have raped my own mother if she allowed me to. I could hardly breathe; my whole body all over was aching for release, and it was painful. I got out to South Belford on foot, walking all through the sordid neighborhood just to get a little lay from some teenage white girl. She was living there in an apartment complex as usual and I got into the apartment building and walked right up to the third floor where she was situated. I noticed absolutely nothing in the grimy building at the outset, which was dirty and filthy and smelling of piss and was noisy and had music booming right out in the open and the sounds of wives being strangled with lampcords. I thought of nothing but pussy, pussy, pussy. PUSSY!...I got up to the third floor. From way down the dark corridor I saw her leaning in the doorway, but couldn't make out what she had on because the light was streaming out from inside her apartment. I walked up the hallway. She stood in the doorway half-naked, like a whore, leaning up against the frame, a man's shirt on—that's all I could see, other than her thick creamy thighs and her bare feet, and her face obviously swollen with desire. I was trying obviously to see through what she had on, for she interrupted me: "Yes, Louie? What do you want?" I told her I came to meet her. She didn't seem surprised—though I knew she was. I hadn't shown up and she hadn't expected me to. She just kept staring and then told me to "come on in." I went in. As I followed her I could spot nothing underneath—I could see the crack of her fat ass. I felt like exploding—in my pants, especially. She was all alone. The place was bare—that's all I remember, other than the fact that there was a couch onto which she threw me in her drunken heat of a rut. She leaned on me, her boobs squashed on my collar-bone, then our faces met. We kissed. She opened her mouth and I stuck my tongue inside; she did the same, and my cock sprang alive. Instantly she felt it up and her blood began to boil. "Take it off," she said, getting up and unbuttoning her shirt. She was naked underneath. I wondered how many nights she had been sitting in the doorway like that, dressed only in a man's shirt! "Everything—NOW!" Her voice had such a violent urgency in it that I was jolted. I took off my clothes quickly and stood there with my cock dangling around in the air. That only made it more exciting. Her pussy was dripping like a faucet already; I could tell from the wet-stains in her inner thighs and the stream of juice pouring down her leg. She grabbed at me lustfully and wrestled me onto the couch, pulling at my cock all the while. She took it in her hand and began to stroke it and then took it into her mouth, slowly, running her fingers around it. I felt, any more like that and I would go berserk. It was too much—her suction was beautiful. As I recall she was the first fuck since high school—in a year and a half. My dick was so hard and my nerves were so raw and tense, I could have exploded like a bomb and sent all my parts flying around her apartment. Then she rubbed it in her tits and sucked on it some more. I stroked her hair—then grabbed it. I always wanted a piece of white meat!—Not that I cared about them as a race…I thought about the women at Coon State University. That almost killed it thinking about those crazy whores. I forgot about them quickly…there, that's good. Then Penny stopped sucking me and stood up, her cunt wetter than ever and grinning like an idiot, breathing hard, her lips trembling, her eyes opening and closing. Then, remarking how lovely my cock was and how tasty it was in her mouth, she lowered that wet muff on my prick and wrapped her arms around my neck. Her hands slid all over my back, massaging it, pinching a little, as she raped my mouth with her tongue. She was chewing me up, the bitch...and chew and chew she can, it doesn't matter either/or! She just makes you forget who the hell you are!...I pulled out of her and told her to roll over; I was going to fuck her in the ass. She obliged, of course. Penny would have done anything. She even told me to lick up there, but I refused...then I licked up there like she said. I didn't care...she told me all kinds of things about what she did on the couch, as I remember; she kept telling me just how much she liked to suck cocks and drink sperm—and all this crazy talk, by a girl, was enough to make me jump out the window. It drove me wild with desire... I carefully slipped it up her rectum. It was like a tight mouth which slid open and closed at will and yet snugly accepted my prick in resignation. I worked on her ass as she wiggled her big buttocks in heat, giggling now and then as I pushed it up to the tip of her colon. Finally I spurted off— it felt like my balls had blown up. My crotch was aching as my cock slipped out of her ass, and I tumbled onto her bed. "Oooooooooh!" she whimpered, with that heated, cracked smile, "that was so fuckin' incredible, wasn't it? I even cleaned myself out...I love it up my ass, Louey...Won't you do it again? You want my—oh, yes! Lemme suck it! I wanna suck it!"—So she sucked my cock. She was jerking me off in her mouth and twirling her tongue around. I couldn't last that much longer...and she was laughing, too. That got me so hot, I came in her mouth, spurt after juicy sticky spurt of sperm down her throat. I really got excited as all hell. I wonder what Pu Sei must be like, then! Goddamn! She opened wide and showed me the cream inside her mouth. What a bitch!... She was drunk by that time—we'd only been at it half an hour. But it wasn't over. I never had a fuck like this—I could hardly believe it was really happening. I had to get that pussy, and I got it. She didn't grip it but it was like a tight jar of jam. No wonder they all wanted this bitch! I marvelled at those big rippling white thighs, fat as two pillars, clutching around me as I worked her cunt to the bone. She was growing violent, clutching me around the waist, scratching me; she must have come eight or nine times before she collapsed in sated giggling exhaustion, and me on top of her. I lay with my head cradled in her crotch. I looked at my prick—it was sore. Now I could say I got my end in—I could be the subject of gossip—some honor, I thought. I kissed her navel. She stroked my hair with a giggle. Goddamn, she was still hot. I had my hand up her snatch as I dozed off...What relief, after a year and a half.

I didn't think of what was in store for me the following morning. Tonight we were in our own little drunken world of pure, unadulterated, 90-proof sexual bliss. Fuck the world...

Whenever I was let off from work, in the days they picked out for me during the week—it was never the weekends because they "needed us too bad"—I found there was nothing else to do, except wait around for Penny—until she got off at nine-thirty; or, which was what I usually did, take the Metro down into Washington. The very name was a euphemism for rottenness—here, I thought, was a city dedicated to a slaver and a murderer, perhaps a faggot, who traded slaves for molasses. I found it amazing, and still do to this day—how on earth such a place could be so bad. People walked as if they were soldiers armed with bayonets, heading towards you, bumping into you and yet knowing that you're there, but doing it for kicks. Dirty beggars in soiled jackets held up "I'm Hungry" signs, a little Styrofoam cup in one hand filled with nothing, pampered rich negresses with their rich white pimp executives lunching at cafes which seem to be everywhere and never seem to end, the dreary and inane monotony of traffic lights, stop signs, plastic trash containers, gook-run hot-dog stands, empty stupid faces, hot watches for sale, alternative bookstores with their wares outside, coffeehouses filled with decorticated hippies, pointless political posters barely scratching the wall of this huge dungeon of death...and above it all, the ceaseless, murderous din of the traffic, and this hysterical, batrachian laughter only Americans are capable of, all garnished, like a bad meal peppered, with processions of police in riot gear.

The World, in short...

I hated it, hated it to my bone marrow. And yet I found it impossible to just simply get up and go. Every time the urge seized me to walk out on The World, I would cut down to 16th and M street where all the airline agencies were crammed together like pigeon-hole rows and ask about the flight to Amsterdam. It was always the same answer— "Eight hundred bucks." Goddamn their souls, if they had them! It seemed they were trying seriously to keep me in my place; it seemed as if they were closing off all borders, locking all the doors, shutting all the windowpanes just to keep me in the cage. They didn't want me to escape; they would've rather seen me die first. That made more sense: dying for your country—by leaping head first into the Potomac River.

Nothing during those empty moments of despair in an American life when one finds himself walking those filthy streets can suffice to snap one out of his fathomless pain but a piece of fresh juicy ass. I was so lucky to run across Penny— I was just thinking about her and the night when we did it. It was down by Farragut North. She waved her hand at me and I went over to her. I chatted a while with her—I don't remember just what I said for soon I found myself tagging along with her up to one of the skyscraper-brothels, a Woolworth's building. Thinking about her, my hysteria and heart palpitations calmed down. The number of times she wanted to have it, her juicy body—it would cure any emotional disease I had, better than a billion psychotherapies. It just made you want to masturbate forever. In fact my encounters with Penny were really a form of mutual masturbation. One never looked at his or her partner as he or she was; the other party was always seen through the distorted lens of one's own rutted-up vantage point. Each party became nothing more than a pork-chop. We were just cute little hotsy-totsy lollipops to each other when we caught ourselves in the elevator, oblivious to the death and ennui all around us. When it got real crowded, she began feeling me up. There were thirty stories in the building so that gave her ample time to do what she wished. I wasn't too keen on making it in public, but suddenly, when we got smashed up against each other, she began grabbing for my cock and there was little I could do to resist when she got into her stuff. I looked up and, seeing her hand working into my drawers, saw her with that heated, cracked, half-witted look in her eyes. And she unzipped my fly and yanked my cock out in the open. I was scared shitless...but she assured me everything was a-ok. Finally, to top it off, the elevator broke down. Everyone was in a frenzy. We waited for ten minutes and not a soul came—except us, of course. I slipped my hand up her skirt and along her thighs and inside and she almost shit on herself with desire. I reached up into her cunt, parted the lips and began searching around for that Grafenburg spot everybody was all bananas about. I didn't find it—but I made her snatch so wet and so hot I could feel the cooze juice dripping down my arm and splattering on the elevator floor... She grunted, trying to keep from screaming, because the elevator was filled with people. Soon I got my whole fist up her crotch and she kept whanking and whanking like a madwoman, and finally she cupped her hand around it and gathered the cream into one hand and rubbed it all over both hands. "Keeps my hands moist," she breathed after she piped down when I finished jerking her off. She licked the rest off her fingers. I did the same with her come, but it was sticky and fishy, so the first thing on my mind was to break away and find a bathroom and wash my hands.

The one thing which could break my desire for Penny was

when she mentioned now and then the kid which she had abandoned on a doorstep after it got born. Whether it lived or died was anyone's guess. "I didn't wanna put up with it no more," she said when speaking of the kid—and she never showed one ounce of remorse thinking about the foundling child. "Besides, it don't even need me. Perhaps it either—well, either someone comes along and picks it up or it dies—that's that. Babies would be just too much of a hassle." I was stunned to the floor by this revelation, which told me something about the insanity of the Dummheit workers as well as the rest of the society in which I was living. I asked her, concealing my shock, "Why didn't you want it?"

" 'Cause—I just wanted to go on with my life an' just havin' my own life to myself when I got off work. I can't handle no baby an' work at the same time, Louie...that'd drive me batty."

6

RIGHT BEFORE ME ALWAYS, at no matter what time of day, was that inescapable world of the warring genitals. There was Rosa and Miguel and the confusion and chaos in which they were embroiled. There was Johnny-Boy and his attempts to jump down Elsie's pants and everyone else's, including Clyde's; and so on and so forth. Everyone was sex-mad. It had a great deal to do with the difficulty and the nature of the work and the desire to escape, plus the unavoidable fact that sex is what makes the world go round. Everywhere I went or had been before it was the same: nothing but sex, sex, sex, and more and more of the same straight on down the line. Everything you saw, everything you tasted or felt, meant sex, meant fuck; just the same all things in the world lose their significance if this fuck is not in some way related or attached in some special way. For the elegance of a shoe is worthless if it is not to be taken off; the dress and gown are nothing if they aren't to be ripped off in the heat of rut. Even worse, the food has no value if it doesn't give you enough energy to fuck or be fucked or if it doesn't multiply the sperm count, or what have you. And, all things considered, anything could be a viable sexual object. A horseshoe could be even more thought-provoking than a dildo, providing the fuck and the horse shoe are properly interrelated. For at bottom, everything is sex in this life of death, everything leads to sex, and nothing else—unless it happens to be power—really has any more value than this fuck. Those two, of course, are interchangeable: people grab one to get to the other, and vice versa: the cycle, in this world, never ends. It often happens that way in a country like America where there live, deep down in the sex jungle, the greatest puritans and moralists in the world who are also the biggest leeches and freaks and sado-masochists and half-crazed savages who would know no better than to kill up a billion of 'em for Christ. And yes, violence played its part: sex in the world of genital warfare is also a vicious, tragic, evil passion. Nobody's got a real outlet for it: you can't go to the peep show, they've too many kooks; it's too dirty anyway. (They're also closing 'em all down.) You can't buy a dirty magazine because they've been all confiscated by the "community leaders" who are in the goddamned bathrooms jerking off over them—besides, they're too expensive. You can't go to a bar and ask for company for the night because they think you have VD and as it turns out, they have it themselves, or maybe they're just afraid of fucking or it makes them feel guilty. Above all you can't ask your girlfriend or wife; that would be a sacrilege; for the girlfriend and the wife belong to the **Love** world and not the **Fuck** world. The Love world is that sacred abode in the bourgeois purgatory, a la Harold Robbins and his maggots, where one does what the world does if he ever took unto himself a mate, that is—don't *fuck*, don't enjoy it, unless that element of Love is involved—or else it becomes instantaneously a part of the *fuck* world, belonging to *hell*, the niggers, the banana-eaters, the perverts and enemies of society. However, the fuck world is not to be discarded right offhand for it is also a kind of necessity, albeit a secret one (which gets fulfilled in the back-alleys and toilets) and one to be spoken of with an embarrassed smirk. It has been declared evil, this fuck world, and evil, sinful, horrible, disgusting it is, for it is all of a piece with stabs in the back and drugs and mafia-hit-men. It's a forbidden zone—but, and this is noteworthy— it has never been shut down entirely. As a matter of fact, it thrives like a bunch of weeds, more and more so as time goes on, no matter how sordid or filthy. Indeed, it seems almost as if the filthier it gets, the more sordid, the more tantalizing it becomes to the righteous citizen. To go there one needs a passport which, according to the mores of organized society, means a college degree and a marriage license. But in the **real** world, as opposed to the written down world of mores and ethics, which are for liars anyhow, the only necessary *carte d'identite* is an erectable dick and two balls—and a hot juicy cunt and a pair of burning ovaries. Everything else, the big brown eyes, the ruby lips, the juicy breasts, the long legs—is just an extension of the main elements—the cock and cunt. The love world is okay, yes—when one is trying to make for himself a place in the society—or so we may think. But when the lights go out the devil comes out, and all the Christians and Jews and Muslims and Buddhists and Hindus and Zoroastrians and automatons and Marxists and angels flock over across the border to the Republic of Fuckadola which, in the last two thousand years, has since been opened up as a tourist resort for the men of the jungle of Christ whose minds have been divided between good and bad, white and black, Americans and Iraqis, Englishmen and Mau Maus, French and Algerians, the chastity belt and the ben-wa balls and…and, last but not least, between faithful Elsie Malone and the half-savage Rosa Montemar.

Basil, Giuseppe, and Barnaby were those in the forefront of all the gossip about the workers—especially the female workers. Giuseppe would sit and talk about the affair he was having with Rosa under Miguel's nose; Basil was hung up on Concha. She was only thirteen, and possible jail-bait but she was so incredibly sexy no one, no matter what his age, could resist having sex with her. The same went for Lolita; she wasn't as sexy but her voice worked wonders on the groin. Basil told me a lot about what was going on with the Barabbases in general—they were a favorite topic for gossip because the whole family was so supremely disorganized—particularly the younger members like Rosa, the nympho, the other two sisters, and then Miguel, who made the cardinal mistake of marrying a Barabbas. Last I heard of the sisters, they had bought up 3,000 dollars worth of Italian-made five inch pumps and got horsewhipped by their mother, who naturally forced them to send most of them back. MOST, of course— she didn't get all of them. Lolita was sure a big spender. But the curious thing about Lolita was that, for all her elegance, she wasn't rich—far from it. No, she was POOR, poor as a church mouse. She was a product of the North Belford area of Nicaraguans and El Salvadoran refugees. They were the real thing, I found out; her sister Rosa, she had her hands burned to a near crisp by an incendiary bomb shelling in San Salvador. Better yet, I thought, if the guerillas had mopped up the whole goddamn bunch! I mean the sisters, of course. The sisters I couldn't stand; they were nothing but a bunch of stool pigeons, a pack of walking pussies. And especially that Rosa, Rosa Montemar. Rosa was married, but that didn't matter one way or the other. She was hot stuff: she was always on the prowl for a cock yet she never said it outright. She used facial and body language, which always works, even more so in her case. She walked with a twitch and a shake of her big wide ass that would have even a faggot going up a rail in a matter of milliseconds. Her eyes were half-closed, her mouth hung open lasciviously, and she always looked quite aloof and distanced yet anyone could see that prick was on her mind; anyone could smell her breath and look into her eyes and sense the sperm sloshing around through her brain cells. As I said, she was married, to a little runt named Miguel Lamartino, and they even had two pretty little girls—but this was meaningless. Rosa, the whore, had run through six or seven other husbands, in spite of her tender age (26). Most of them, I presume, were dead, or on the funny farm. And besides that she had a steady stream of male lovers of all ages, mostly one-nighters. As Giuseppe told it to me, she'd drag him right up to her dingy apartment on 14th Avenue, flop him right down on the bed under Miguel's nose and strip him down and suck him right off. He was having an affair with her, he said, right under Miguel's nose. He talked about this so-called "affair" in such glowing terms as to make me doubtful of the whole thing and think that it was just another one of his Italian sex fantasies. Besides, he was an outrageous liar, that Giuseppe. He probably had been working at the joint for no more than a year—no, that's wrong, he *had* been working there for many years. After all, nobody else would have hired him, he was too crazy, too much of that hysterical wop blood in him. He was always clowning around, even in the midst of work. It was common for me to tease him while I was carrying in the dishes from the dining room and start saying some dirty words I picked up in Italian, such as "*Putana Siciliana!*" or "*Culo Prrrrroscusito!*" and he'd get real angry, but it was always very funny because later on he'd be nicer and he'd joke around with his buddies (Barnaby, Basil, etc.) just the same. One time, during these lunch breaks, he even instigated a food fight. He started it all when he began pitching grapes at the Chink ladies—Toi Pu Sei, for one. Pu Sei was all gaga for some bullshit or other and she was sitting next to the window jabbering off to Gu Fi and Ding Bat in Cantonese gibberish. Giuseppe, sitting next to Basil and Barnaby, started making fun of them and mocking their Cantonese. Soon all four of us joined in on the mockery, since we hated their guts, they were such stupid, unintelligent, screwy, noisy, buck-toothed little bastards. Gu Fi, who couldn't speak a word of English, rolled her slit eyes at us, jumped up with a fistful of noodles and hurled them right in Giuseppe's face. That did it for him. Soon he grabbed his chocolate layer cake and laid it up aside Ding Bat's head, and took the mash potatoes and slapped it right in Gu Fi's face. Gu Fi retaliated and flung her mash potatoes at Basil; Pu Sei, aiming for me, naturally, took her jello and slapped it on my shirt—she had poor aim. But Giuseppe had better aim and caught Pu Sei right in the forehead with a greasy thigh bone. Gu Fi jumped up and shouted "fuck off," perhaps, in Cantonese, we didn't know what it meant. Apropos of this, Pu Sei was still hyped up and talking the crap and Giuseppe decided to put a lid on the bitch once and for all. "Heeeeere we gooooooo!" he howled, and pitched three more grapes at Pu Sei. The last flew in her mouth and down her throat as she talked. It didn't choke her, but it left her so stunned she shut up just the same. "Bullseye!" he roared. The rest of us roared with laughter.

In just the same stupid way he got his finger jammed up in the dishwashing machine. There was a knife stuck in the machine, a butter knife, and it wasn't too significant, but Mr. Albino, that greaseball fascist, kept raving about "his" machine and the fact that "his" machine was worth a hundred thousand dollars. A hundred thousand burned up to wash dishes!—anyhow, Giuseppe was forced into getting the knife out of the machine. When he reached his fingers in the mechanism he decided suddenly to play a little joke on Albino. He wanted to shock the shit out of him—he was always getting scared at something serious. Just a coward, no more. But Giuseppe put his finger into a tiny hole, a ring-like instrument—and locked his finger on it. It was stuck, the finger, but he didn't think it so serious. And just at this time Basil comes in and, eager to get down to washing the dishes because the dishcarts are full of dishes, he presses the button, and on goes the machine. Mr Albino sees what's happening and as usual he has shit fits. He's on the point of beating up Basil...but then, there's another problem: Giuseppe, following his stuck finger, is being sucked into the machine! He goes right into the machine, right up to the point where the soap's being sprayed on. Fortunately he didn't get to the hot water or else he would have been burned to death. But he was trapped for hours in the machine while everything ground to a dead halt and Maria Lopez stood in the doorway with Rosa blasting away in heated Spanish, wringing her fists in the air. The boss was too busy calling us jerk-offs and misfits and stupid foreigners and spics and niggers and gooks to be concerned about getting Giuseppe out of the machine. Besides, he hated Giuseppe's guts and he probably kept him inside just for the hell of it. He chewed on his own gums, he ranted and raved and jumped up and down. He was hysterical and talked endlessly of firing the whole crew. As it turns out, three were fired on the spot—Penny McDonald, who had nothing whatsoever to do with it ("I told you it was just my big tits!"), and a Jamaican and an El Salvadoran—the 10th, 11th, and 12th to be fired within the last week. And all the while Giuseppe sat in the machine face up, soaked and wet. When it was all over we pulled him out by his feet and he was unconscious. He was rushed off to the hospital where he caught double pneumonia and stayed out for a month. After he got out he became somewhat obsessed with bringing a lawsuit against Albino in order to get the money, but somehow he always backed down. But the managers, apparently, didn't give a damn whatever happened to Giuseppe or one of their dispensable human machines. Life is cheap in the states, apparently.

But then there were the lesser kids, the unknowns, whose tragedies were but a scratch on the wall of the great prison. There was a little noticed background figure named Yee Sing Hwong. She, as usual, came from the South, Guangdong Province, on the mainland of China, and spoke Cantonese just like the rest. But unlike most of them she was quite pleasant and even-tempered. She had been hired on the spot as a bus girl; she came in the following afternoon dashed out in the tight white uniform required of the cafe ladies—short-sleeve blouse with a black bow tie, and a tight black mini-skirt wrapped around the hips—and the white overseas cap cocked on a bit off. Fortunately—or unfortunately—for her, the dress was too tight, as always—and it revealed for the eyes of us rapacious male workers a very attractive shape. She was all smiles...she didn't know what the hell to do; she didn't have any experience whatsoever. Yet she got the hang of it sooner or later and obeyed every order down to the letter. She stayed and associated with the other Chinese girls—she could barely speak a word of English. She was never on the wrong side of anything, apparently. But then suddenly one day Yee was confronted by Mary Chiao and her Jamaican friend who worked together in the pastries department just adjacent to the cafeteria. Mary Chiao (she got her job back) and a host of other Chinese greeted her as usual. But then a Jamaican guy—Basil, as it happened (Barnaby was telling the story)—stepped in, saw that Yee was new to the joint, and wanted to chat with her, but she was frightened by him. Instead she was welcomed by Chloe, the Jamaican girl. Chloe welcomed her rather aloofly, talking dryly and with precision in a meaty West Indian accent—while Yee shook with fear. She always shook when confronted with black people. "Hello," she said.

"Hello," said Yee Sing.

"How are you?"

"Fine."

"What's your name?"

"Yee. Yee Sing Hwong. I'm...Chinese," she stuttered.

"Chinese, ah...I see. So—do you enjoy wohking heah Yee Sing?"

"Yes, I—fink—so—I dunno."

"You dunno? How come?"

"I—I—don't—speak good English," she stuttered.

"Don't speak good English—I see. Look," Chloe said, taking her into a corner "People here crazy, girl. People here crazy because dey desperit, dey sick. You must qwit or else."

Yee was taken aback, and laughed out loud. "Why? I like heah. Is very good foah me. Very good foah Chinees peepol—"

"No girl, you wrong," Chloe interrupted. Mary had stepped out and the others were sitting at a table, watching with puzzlement. "Dis is de jungle. You don't work in de jungle my frien'. Go—dere are betta jobs everywhea, an' dey pay much more dan hea."

"But hea dey friendly—"

"Mistah Quackenbros an' Mistah Albino no like Chinees peepol. Nobody heah like Chinees peepol or black peepol. But black peepol do no'ting to haht you. Why you afraid of us? You should be afraid of da Boss, he somet'ing to be afraid of. He would like no'ting betta dan to get de opportoonidy to get down yo' pants, girl. An' dey wood do it, because you are sexually attracteev to thees hooligans. Dey tink Chinees people chil'ren, dey tink dey coolie laybah, stupid, untinking Chinks. Dey no like you, girl. Dey want to use you. Dey work you into yo' greeve an' always smile."

Well...Yee couldn't understand much English, especially when spoken in a Jamaican dialect, but she picked up enough of it. She dismissed the warning once Chloe left and punched out for home.

And then one night she was in the locker room getting dressed when a few of the regular stool pigeons came in with something stashed up their sleeves, literally. Yee Sing thought it was candy bars, she was so naive and so unaware of the foolish dealings around the slaughterhouse. Well, as it turns out, it wasn't the candy bars they were lugging in—it was a bunch of cocaine. It must have been worth about a million dollars. Where they had gotten the money for that kind of thing nobody knew—least of all Yee Sing Hwong. Nevertheless, they laid it out and began snorting like bulls. Yee was scared shitless and wanted to break away but it wasn't so easy like that. First they badgered the shit out of her, then threatened, then flung out their knives and guns. Yee couldn't make heads or tails of the incident; it was all a farce in her eyes and she began laughing, but stopped when they fired at the ceiling. Yet Yee never took the cocaine. She tried physically to run but they caught her and beat her to a pulp and shoved the money and the dope into her pockets and split off. As expected, the cops picked her up and tried her. She pleaded in tears that she was innocent but no one would see it that way because the stool pigeons—the Jews and the Niggers—Ruby, Maggie and Tramsokong—had it worked around to make it look as if she was dealing the dope. Yet she wasn't the dealer, of course. But then Mr. Albino and Johnny-Boy and Mr. Najib called her to the desk one night to straighten things out—they were sure they knew what was wrong. Yee was sure they knew who dealt with the dope—she could always trust the management. Then they sat her down between them and discussed the case. They were all prepared for everything because Mr. Albino had brought in coffee for the four of them. Yee gladly accepted anything from these trustworthy young gents. They were white—you could always trust a handsome young American white man. And when she took three gulps the rest were still chattering, but she suddenly complained of a stomach ache, shook, dropped the coffee and fell on the ground jerking, and the three began grabbing and ripping hysterically at her clothes, licking their chops, sucking on her mouth and her tits and her belly and her ass—they took everything off. They turned her over and over...she sure had a nice ass for a Chink. She was one of those creamy ones..."C'mon, I wan't the ass...no, the pussy, that's hotter...how about some head? Stupid bitch!...suck her ass, that's sweet too!" They forced their pricks into any opening she had. They did all this for about an hour; when they finished she was full of their cream and stinking of their sweat. But Yee never regained consciousness. They threw water on her, they shook her, they slapped her—nothing. She kicked off!...the three were frightened out of their wits so they took her body to the back room, put on a bunch of plastic gear and proceeded to hack her up like beef. That was Mr. Carlin's idea. They took her parts to the meat grinder and ground it up and burnt the rest in Nitric acid in the oil barrel. They turned her into hamburger meat, and no one knew what had become of her because someone ate her...

Then there was Toi Pü Sei, the juiciest of them all. Chinese, of course—but only half-Chinese. Her mother was a Malaysian and she looked like a Malaysian, her skin golden brown and her eyes a bit larger and more liquid, the lips fuller and more sensual, the hair black and shiny, hanging in light bangs over the forehead. Like Rosa, she was hot stuff—her chest was pretty ample for her race, to say nothing of her ass, that juicy love cushion, as Giuseppe put it while talking about her—but such a snob and a tease that, whilst working alongside her, she got on the wrong side of me instantly. I first took her for a pleasant girl—until, as I bused the tables, she piled all of her shit onto my tray and walked off swinging her hips in my face. Or, when I was washing the dishes, she would bend over to "tie her shoes" whilst she was wearing her skirt instead of the pants (she even clipped the skirt shorter, the bitch!) and the skirt would run up along her ass; or, as I often served drinks, she would push me on the arm and snort in my face to keep moving meanwhile laughing all the time. Also, she wouldn't speak to me when I asked her a question. She was just seventeen and a student at Elysian Fields Institute—where all the fucking racists went, which was even worse. When we rode home on the bus she didn't hesitate, since it was always crowded, to squeeze herself up against me, face to face, and try to stare me down. She was nothing but a cocktease. She did this all the time...

Finally I got sick of her. I wanted to gouge out the cunt's fuckin' eyes after a matter of weeks. I can't fathom how she slipped into my life in such a repulsive and dictatorial way. She was always at the cash register waiting for me now; her hand was always on that fucking bell which, as a customer got his food, meant that the customer wanted his shit carried out to the table for him. If it was one of those stinking black bourgeois, then they wanted it carried out for them simply because it made them look hip. But I wouldn't have it like that, so I refused to answer the bell, and when I refused to answer it, then some of the other busers, like Basil, or Gu Fi, or Yo Yo, would pick it up. But she always called on me to do the job and it was always me she had singled out to cart the food to those idiots. To top it off, the last time she even went so far as to put all of her dishes onto my tray and then ate a banana tossing the peel right in front of me, as I was struggling to get to the dishroom, causing me to trip up and drop every one of the dishes on the floor. Most of them fell right on me—I lay there with blood pouring out of my nose like a faucet. Toi looked back and cut her eye at me coldly and haughtily and walked off. Now that was the last motherfucking straw. It was bad enough for her merely to pile all those dishes on me, but the banana peel...and the way she stared! It had been building up to that point for a long time. She always relied upon me to take the food out to the pigs in the dining room: if I didn't budge, then she would play the stool pigeon. When we were off it, at lunch, she sat at the opposite table with the other Chinese and wagged her finger at me deprecatingly and said: "You should do better, I call manager if you no do right!" Clyde smiled at this, but it was no laughing matter. There was nothing funny about it at all. She had been driving me up the fuckin' wall all the month. It always seemed that she was so well off, so protected, so innocent, so pure...I could see her, the bitch, chatting at the coffee table with her Chink friends...she never seemed to get angry. Worse yet, she never even showed any emotion. The other Chinks did—Chen was drowsy, Ding Bat was childish, Gu Fi was stupid and lethargic, etc., etc., etc. But not Pü Sei—and this is one of the things which enraged me about her—she was robotic. Even her sexy movements—she was like an automaton or, more precisely, one of these stupid Chinese dolls with a little fat head wobbling on a tenny-tiny body one could pick up in some Chink shop around Belford's way. Stinking cunt.

None of that mattered anymore after a month or so, of course, for I finally vowed revenge on her slanty-eyed ass. I knew just how to pull it off. Pu Sei was always the last to leave the joint at night. I never knew why; it was simply just that way. (And she was usually the first one here, as well.) Beautiful, for that was when I was going to pull it off—at night. So I worked overtime and after cleaning the shit-bowls I cut out at ten-thirty. I knew for sure that she wasn't cutting out any earlier than eleven, so I went to a nearby theater and sat down and watched the flick for ninety-nine cents. It was mule fare, but that's not important. In fact I don't even remember one scene from the movie; I was just anxious to lay one on Pü Sei's hot juicy ass—and her jawbone. My prick was already twitching in my black uniform slacks. I saw nothing but lovely golden brown tits and pussies with a faint tuft of hair and soft little yellow asses, and I wanted to tear off a good chunk and teach her a lesson. Finally I couldn't stand it any longer, and I left the theater. I went back to the cafe and found to my surprise that the lights were still on even after a full hour. It was now 11:36 at night. Toi Pü Sei was still there; I saw her car in the driveway. I looked in the windows; everything was cleaned, polished, set right. I got back inside, even more curious now as to what was going on. As I cut through the kitchen on tip-toe I began to have a hunch who was up to it all. I got to the basement. All the lights were on. Everything was locked up. I looked across from the stairs to see that the manager's office was still open, the lights still on. Then suddenly all the lights went out all around. Whoever was there noticed no one. Just who the hell was inside there, though? I had to take a peek...I felt my life depended on it. I got down on all fours and crawled over to the door, peered inside...aha, just as I suspected. Purehearted Pu Sei was being put to good use by those fucking managers; they had both their dicks shoved down her throat at one time—and Pu Sei was slurping on both like a madwoman. I wasn't surprised in the least bit. I always knew something was fishy about Pü Sei and her demeanor. Penny told me so. And look at her now...it seems she can suck it pretty good, can't she! And she can take it from the rear, too!...I had a hard-on like a rail. Not only did I just *think* that she was hot meat, I **knew** it. That was even better...now they're coming, I can tell...they're squirting it all over her, real hard, it goes on her face, in her mouth, up her nose...it just squirts right out like water from a hose and drips on the floor...she laps it all up, even off the floor, now it's over...they're paying her for it now…300 dollars a piece for her services. Gotta hide…I got behind the stove and crawled into the big oven. From the outside I could see that they turned the lights back on. Now I can hear the managers are leaving her; they gave her two smacking wet goodbye kisses. Perfect. She went into the dressing room; I stood outside the door. There she stayed another ten minutes before I finally decided to make my move. I walked inside, and she balked and stood up, obviously very frightened and wanting to know right away why I was barging in on her. She was half-undressed and into her undies, but I didn't listen. I told her I came to clean the ladies room, which I had already cleaned, but that didn't matter a good goddamn to me whatsoever. She was still suspicious, of course—black men always made her suspicious—but I persuaded her that I wouldn't look. I went to the sink with a rag while she stood in the back undressing; as I peeped back I noticed that she had slipped everything off. In a jiffy I switched my dick out of my underwear and into my pants to make it more noticeable and for the hell of it I switched around the other way to get the "soap". She suddenly let out a squeal as I caught her there, not naked, but with a new set of undies. She took one glance at my peter and began to wince and turn away. "Aw knock it off, I know what's on your mind," I told her, easing in. "I know what you want. But I'm sorry 'cause I'm not up to it at the moment, I'm busy…"

"Up to it? Up to what? You think I some sorta freak?" she snorted in her Chinese-British accented English.

"Yes, I do."

"Oh, yeah? I not like you. I'm a virgin. And I don't even like talking about it either!" (Well, virgins don't usually use sperm for facial cream, I thought to myself!…)

"Maybe because you do it so much."

"A bloody lie, you arse-hole!"

"Say what you wish. The trouble with you is that you're a horny-ass fucking bitch who hasn't had a good enough dicking in quite a while. You've had too much of that puny-ass ofay dick. You ought to get raped. Besides, virgins don't usually use sperm for facial cream anyway! Oh, yeah, and look"—and I noticed that her panties were wet around the bottom—"you're all wet, if you know what I mean!"

"Oh no, no is it, I pee on myself, yes! That is it," she exclaimed in mock frustration. But that was enough. My cock was in full erection and it was apparent that she was getting a kick out of it because she couldn't keep her eyes off the damn thing. She stood there for about four minutes doing nothing; she just kept staring at my cock. Finally I had to take a piss, of all things; I cut to the toilet and dropped my pants under her nose. She didn't look shocked anymore—I noticed the change in her eyes and the animal hunger which arises out of ceaseless hours of drudgery, of slaving over those old goddamn tepid sinks. She shifted into the bathroom and dropped her panties in front of me but instead of moving on to me went in the toilet and sat on the seat and began jerking herself off; I could tell from the squishy noises. I moved on inside because she never bothered to lock the door and I let my cock dangle in the air. I was all aflutter; then, looking dead at her, I moved in on her. She was in ecstasy masturbating herself and was totally unconscious of me—till her eyes met mine, and she said no, no, no, but I could tell by her hardened nipples and her drooping slack face and her sopping twat that the real answer was yes, yes, yes! "You bitch," I breathed, backing her up against the wall as she shook her head, "I'm gonna ream the shit out of you!" And without another word I got my hands around her neck and began ramming it in like a lunatic. Her head knocked against the wall—and then she pushed me off and in a ferocious heat of rut she ripped off my uniform, growling in the utter heat of estrus...like hell she was a virgin, I thought. She was born with it in her ass! And I forced a finger in her ass, then two, then three; she pushed them in on her own accord as I rammed her still harder, really raping her for what it was worth. Then I had a great idea. I slipped it out suddenly because I felt something coming on, then I pissed all over her. The crazy bitch began laughing hysterically and wiping the piss all over her naked body; when that was over, I jammed it down her throat until it reached to the balls. She was gasping, and I felt like a prince for making her into a pure and total sex object. But she sucked on it wildly just the same—like a lollipop. I knew she needed it; she had been hard at the grinding wheel all afternoon and not even the managers could quench her fire. I was so much into the blowjob that the hostility towards her was lost on me, and I actually began fucking her mouth like a pussy and she had me coming in no time, one of the biggest ejaculations I ever had; it felt as if the Nile river were getting ready to blow out through my crotch. She just kept sucking the head and driving me crazy with it. I blasted it off in her mouth and filled up her gullet and cheeks and it ran out of her lips and down her chin, she wanted to spit out all of this mess but I wouldn't have it. I wanted to see her lap up every drop. And so she did. She even began to like it and looked around for more. She made a meal of it, the whore; her eyes were glazed, the slits were tightened...her nostrils flared, she seemed to lose consciousness as she sucked out the rest of it...she sure loved the jism...

Apropos of this, there was another—well, there was a *bunch* of it going on behind the manager's backs. Even the managers were into it because, as Giuseppe told me, Albino and Johnny-Boy were butt-buddies. This I had no trouble believing since I always found them buzzing around each other when the slaughterhouse was closing down. Giuseppe and Basil took me up to the time card rack and showed me proof that the two were fags; what the time cards showed is that the two went home at the exact same time every night—11:00 and 11:12 to 11:20 for Johnny-Boy. They did it this way because, as Basil said, they didn't want to raise suspicion among Quackenbros and the Boss Boss and the Boss Boss Boss that they were sodomizing each other. At this same time, Albino and Carlin began vying for power—actually it was Carlin and Albino vying with all their might against Quackenbros. They did this with subtlety by encouraging him to stay home and mind his own business; Carlin and Albino kept saying that they could take care of all duties for him. What they were really doing was butting the "nigger-lover" Quackenbros out of the rat race by diminishing his influence over the workers and by instilling fear in everyone else. As a result the cafe grew increasingly more chaotic as time passed; it had always been chaotic, but now it was even worse than it had ever been before. A couple of fags vying for power! It was grotesque! And then Carlin's cocaine habit...he just recently picked it up after Carlos sent him some from Maggie, or maybe it was Maggie who gave it straight to him, or maybe Ruby did it or Tramsokong. No matter; drugs had a good hold on the lifestyle of the Dummheit cafe.

Then there was Giuseppe himself, on the other side of the coin. When he was out, that meant he was plopping his hot slut Rosa. He was always talking about Rosa, but he hardly said that much about Miguel. In fact, he hardly knew Miguel, because Miguel was always out drunk; he had a drinking problem. And it was easy to see why, too. He made the cardinal mistake of marrying Rosa Montemar. Rosa was big, strong-boned, strong-willed, highly temperamental, wildly sexual, with an annoying high-pitched voice which didn't fit her body-size at all. Sex pervaded her whole soul, to use the cliché. The most incongruous thing in the whole world was she and her husband, Miguel, when set side by side. Miguel was weak, whimpering, masochistic, half-starved, and with a look in his eyes that kept you guessing whether he would freak out and wreck the joint and kill everyone in it, or simply break down and cry. He was awfully thin and short, with curly hair and sharp eyebrows and a fleshy red nose and thick lips, with dead white skin as opposed to the golden brown of Rosa. He was a borderline sort of chap in this very way. Often drooled. Walked in a slumping gait and was perpetually stupefied. His only solace, not surprisingly perhaps, was God. God, that great great God of the gutters you hear from every street corner in the ghetto every Sunday morning. Miguel needed Him (providing he existed), because he lived in the gutters—not so much as the dump he was living in at the time—he had moved into a better apartment, but the bedbugs were still a problem, among other things—as the emotional dump he was stuck in with Rosa Montemar. They had been married for three years—a long time for Rosa, in her case; she had six husbands behind her when she married him at 23. The first came at 16 and ended within three months; the marriage was in El Salvador. The man couldn't take it anymore, they said; Rosa just couldn't control herself, she was a nuisance, she was ill-tempered, she was obnoxious, she was a slut, and so on and so forth. What decided the issue for him eventually was when her hands got blown up. Imagine those things on your cock! The second one said the same thing when she was living in Mexico a year later—and blew his brains out. The third one was perhaps the only one who really did like her—and Rosa only used him up, to the family's great disgust. She was still 17, and he 28. He had money; he had wanted her to become a good middle-class respectable lady. Rosa too wanted to become bourgeois, but she also wanted to fuck and fuck, and throw things around the house when the mood seized her. The guy broke himself trying to get Rosa into shape and wound up in the insane asylum...and the rest is old news: walkouts, divorce, suicide, murder attempts—usually the latter by Rosa, because she would get so violently jealous, which was crazy. She wanted to fuck all the guys in the world, yet she didn't want them fucking anybody but her. Above all, it was her sex needs which drove them crazy. Being a pathological nymphomaniac, she got hot right out in public whenever the mood struck her—and it did like a thunder-clap—and she would jam her fingers right up her hole right out

in the open. This was enough to drive all of the husbands
crazy. She kept eating bananas—she had a fetish for bananas
and other phallic objects. She spent half of her money buying
sex aids of all sorts, crazier and crazier ones every time. When
she finally left Mexico at 22 she had run through every boy in
the village. She was better than the prostitutes because it was
all free, and lasted as long as she could hold out. She would
always put up a fight at first but once it started coming on
strong she was like melted cheese. By then you could piss or
shit on her even and she'd get an orgasm right off. She had to
have it in her mouth—she would die in an hour if the world
had run out of sperm all at once. She had to feel the slime hot
in her mouth, to drink up those nasty white spurts. It drove her
bananas. She was addicted to it—she kept sperm sealed in a
jar, Giuseppe's, Miguel's, Tito's, and a bunch of others. They
were all marked, too, because there just wasn't one jar,
either—there were several jars under the bed, in the closet, in
the bathroom, in the refrigerators—everywhere. Miguel wasn't
quite ready for all this when he got acquainted with her back
in Mexico City. He thought she was just playful. Well...a hell
of a lot was in store for him once he cut out with her for
America.

And once in the States, following the horde and settling
right down in Belford with the rest of them, she began to go
on a sexual rampage. When her sister Concha came up to live,
she was forced into sharing the room with her and Miguel. And
that was a problem: for Miguel was impotent—at least by
Rosa's standards. Once Rosa started there was no stopping
her; Miguel merely wanted to do like every other man would—
take one or two rounds of fucking every three days and go the
hell to sleep—perhaps until morning—PERHAPS. But you
can't do it that way with a nymphomaniac! Rosa was simply
hot all the time—she couldn't help it, it was pathological. Then
she turned to, in her heat, of all people—*Concha*. She wanted
Concha to masturbate her, and Concha balked and flatly
refused. But Rosa, on one occasion, backed her up against the

wall with a kitchen knife and demanded that she take down her panties. She was gasping hysterically—and Concha almost fainted dead away. But Rosa threatened to kill her if she fainted—and so Concha weakly thrust her panties down while Rosa hungrily fiddled in her cunt. "C'mon, to the bedroom," she breathed—and the both of them went. Concha wept, but Rosa slapped her, again and again. "Shutup, you little twat!" she screamed. "I want you to make love to me. Look...I don't care if you're a girl or my sister, I love you. I want to make love to you. I want you inside me. I have a dildo and I am going to fuck you and you me...I can't stand it, Concha...I don't want to do this but...but...Miguel, he's...*no good!*" And Rosa dropped the knife, sobbing hysterically. She fell to the floor, weeping like a child. Concha picked up the knife and led Rosa into the room and told her to get dressed; she promised to get her a good lover. "No, no—I need more than one. Three or four! The bigger the better, especially those *morenos!* Ah! Concha! Three or four! I need it all the time," she begged, half-hysterical. "But I still love you...I find you so attractive and so sweet. I can't help myself...I'm a sex-ape, can't ya see? Huh? I went to the gynecologist and he said I was mentally and psychologically disturbed! What does he mean by that? All I know is that I can't take it. I don't care who it is, man or woman, just so long as I feel a nice, warm human body smushed up against me...it gets me off...help me, please...touch it! my clitoris! Put something up me!..." So Rosa got up on her knees still sobbing, reached in the drawer and pulled out a mini-vibrator which she then shoved up her cunt and turned on high. She began tickling her clitoris and lay back in a stupor jerking herself off...Concha sighed and shook her head. "Animal," she whispered under her breath. "I'm going to get Giuseppe for you, Rosa," Concha said, raising her voice. Rosa then came, got dressed and went out with the thing still up her. "He's good—all the girls I know say this. He's a good fuck. You'll never be dissatisfied."

And this is the point where, according to Giuseppe, he

stepped in on the scene. It was all highly implausible. "It happened like dis," he told me, while Rosa was out one day. "See, I step in Dummheit one night to to pick ohp my paycheck. Rosa was makin' da bredrolls an' she jost kep' eyein' me real hard—man, she was jus' set right on fire. I could even—I swear! I could see her pussy shake when she saw me, her whole skin color, he change, get real funny-lookin'. Well—I knew I had it inna bag, see! Perfect! Bot—you see dis, right, I want her to come to me. I don't wanna do it dat old way when da lady wait for you—naw, I wanna wait for her. An' so what happens? Da joint close down, right. So she over in da girl room, right. She grab up in my crotch an' she go, 'I wanna suck it! Lemme suck it!' She just freak off...so I take her inna backa da room...we see each odder, eye ta eye. We kiss. Den...aw, why am I tellin' dis to you? Dis private business, man!"

"Well it's too late now," said Basil, laughing. Barnaby was real excited, flexing his twelve fingers. "C'mon, man, tell us more! We wanna know."

"Naw, see, is peepul like you who go aroun' spreadin' roomors! I don't like dat...well, anyway, she got so hot, she fall over on me. She suck my dick. I fuck her inna bathroom, we squirm all over her body, right! Man...I came like all. I fill her hot pussy all the way up, she kiss me all over, she say she love me..." And, to conclude the story, they went home and fucked some more; and again and again and again and again. She couldn't help it. "I was tirin' out, but Jees, man! She just kep' comin' on an' comin' on! She couldn' control dat pussy. When she hava orgasm she scratch an' claw an' yell an' scream, she tera you inta two pieces—likea wild animul!" But apparently she was the same with Miguel, because we could see how he was branded when he walked into work. He often went down to the toilet to escape the Dummheit profligacy which was driving him batty. He couldn't bear to work around Rosa when she was there. And Rosa was further carried away by the lure of high fashion. Giuseppe, the collegiate, was always hip to fashion, and so he began buying her lavish clothes. Even on the bus he showed me the pumps he brought her for eighty dollars—real classy stuff: "Made in Brazil". But Miguel was sitting not too far away from us and he had to keep the box a secret. "Ey, don' show dis to him, man," he said, cautiously eyeing Miguel in the back seat, branded as usual and head tossing from side to side every time the bus hit a bump or a pothole. "He crazy. He'll flip right out an' kill every one of us, man."

"He ain' noting, man. He don' do noting. He dry up totally," said Basil.

"Naw—but Miguel, right," he said in a whisper, "he begin to fin' out who da hell send her dese new choes, so be careful!"

It was the truth. Miguel had begun demanding how she managed to get the kind of money to buy all those wild clothes, and she said, one day, backing him up in a corner, her hands tightened around his collar— "GIUSEPPE!! That's who! You can't fuck—you're a weakling!" And then, drooling, mumbling, he remarked about some strange jars lying under their bed. "It's come," she said dryly. "You wan't some? Yes, I have other lovers. I have *twelve* of them. Why? Because I am so passionate, and you are not a man and you do not know how to satisfy a woman! Faggot!"

Miguel retaliated: "But just the same, you are not a woman, my dear Rosa: you are a beast. You are the Devil incarnate. You are insatiable. I can do nothing for you: you are completely out of control, a woman of the streets. I don't give a shit anymore one way or the other. You are wild, an animal!" And at this Rosa slapped him, then punched him, then took his shoe off his own foot and smashed it across his face. Miguel reeled, and screamed for Almighty God to save him from this beast. Then she scratched him up with her big nails, leaving red streaks all over him. But then she was hungry—she also had a big appetite for food and drink. "Fix me some rice!" she screamed. "And some tomatoes! And some chicken—fried chicken!" Miguel didn't know how to cook fried chicken—but he tried, remembering what he did at Dummheit. He knew how to cook rice—but there was no rice, and Rosa consistently demanded that she have rice. She waited, impatiently, arms folded. Then she jumped up, yelping. "I better see my rice, you hear me, faggot!? *You hear me?!*" And she pushed him aside, bent over the pot—and saw that he was cooking peas and not rice. "Idiot!" she screamed—and threw the hot peas on him. Angrily, she snatched up the hot grease and went for him—but then stopped and laid down the pan, and stooped over him. "My poor Miguel," she said now, calmly. "I am sorry, it was my mistake, I forgot to tell you to go and buy some rice for dinner, no? Please forgive me. But anyway I will not be having dinner with you. I will eat with my lover Alfredo on 16th Avenue and stay overnight, maybe. Get up; I leave you to yourself. You are no good; you are useless to me."

"And you are useless to the world and to God," Miguel shouted, beginning to cry.

"Crybaby!" she screamed, then calmed down and became icy suddenly. She was an emotional roller-coaster. Then she stepped right on Miguel, shoved him out of the way with her heel, and gave him one cold "adios"—and didn't return for the whole night.

That incident happened the night Giuseppe bought those shoes home to Rosa. Giuseppe was lucky that he had his off day right after that incident because Miguel wanted to "talk" with Giuseppe. I met Giuseppe at the Zilch warehouse department store and he was "hiding out," as he said. I was enjoying this shit! "Man, he dangerous, I kin tell by da look on 'is eyes," he said, looking frightened. "Where's Rosa?"

"I dunno," he said.

"She planned to go out with someone last night," I said, thinking about that "Alfredo" that Basil had told me about but hesitated to slip him the information about this new clandestine lover. But Giuseppe caught that "someone" dangling from my sentence. "Who? You?" He looked real concerned about it. (Me?) "Who was Rosa goin' out with?..."

"Basil said it was someone named Alfredo..."

"Who'd he hear dat shit from?"

"Barnaby."

"Barnaby?"

"Yeah...Barnaby knows everything."

"Barnaby's a liar...she really don't like no one but me. She useta keep sperm jars under her bead an' all for safe—"

"I think she still does."

"Waita minot...you tell me she's got **more??**"

"Hell...you told me one time she needed three or four—"

"Naw, but she said she'd no need nobody else when I gotta her!"

"Well...I don't know. Barnaby and Basil gave me that information."

"Dem damn Jamaicans ees always bullshit," he said to me. "C'mon, les get to Pocohontas..."

"Why?"

" 'Cause I wanna buy somet'in for Rosa," he said. "I'm gonna buy her dis overcoat made in Italy—real spicy an' wild! three ondred dollars!"

"But what if Miguel's dere?"

"Den I beat his ass. Is dat simple, man. Fock him. E's a punk."

"Well why are you hiding from him, then?"

" 'Cause, cause he may carry some sorta nasty theeng like gons eround," he said.

Well...when we got to Pocohontas and into a high-class clothing store he picked out, instead, a leather jacket for her which she, as he said, always desired to have. I thought it rather crazy why he had to live up to the demands of a leech like her. She was sucking away everything he got. He had another job as a sales clerk selling used cars and he was on two weeks notice for clowning around on the job, so he really had only one job which he had to support both himself and Rosa's insatiable demands. She was worse than a prostitute, because, at least, a whore charged you a flat fee for her service. For Rosa's service, it could have been somewhere between two cents and two shmillion-grillion dollars!

Barnaby was dead on the scene of what was happening between Rosa and Miguel. That Sunday Rosa freaked out and tried to "seduce" the minister at the Belford Catholic Church and the whole congregation was in an uproar. She beat up the minister backstage and Miguel had a nervous breakdown; he was convalescing at St. Elizabeth's. "Perfect!" yelled Giuseppe when he heard of the good news. "Now I won haveta worry 'bout him no more! Now I gots her all to myself..." But that wasn't quite true, as Barnaby told him later on in the day. "There're others, man," he said. "Man, Giuseppe, you make it look like you the only one sticking it up Rosa's ass. You ain't—but here's another thing. She ain't like you, man—"

"Das bullshit, man!—"

"What about Alfredo?"

"Alfredo who?"

"Da one Rosa doin' it with! She got at least TWELVE, as I said," snapped Barnaby. Giuseppe tried not to believe him—but he had his suspicions since, after all, Rosa was fond of doing such crazy things as having a man jerk off in her drink and having her drink it. In fact Rosa passed right by the window arm in arm with two big guys, but when she saw Giuseppe, who didn't see her, she ducked out fast and got on the bus. Barnaby leaped up and pointed, but it was too late by then. "Man, see, you Jamaicans always fulla so much shit," he said, still hard-headed. "You gonna see whatta goot relations I gots wid her. You-all just tryin' ta spread shit eround."

We switched the subject. "Ey—what about the lawsuit?"

"Wha—naw, I can't do it, man—too moch hassle. Dummheit too big."

"That ain't true," I said. "You could sue the president if you wished," I said. Giuseppe laughed. "Man, you dunno nothin', man. You can no sue Steinway. Steinway own airplanes an' everythin'. You crazy for wantin' *me* to sue Steinway. I canno do it."

"But you need the money—don't you?"

"An' basides dot, mon, you onlee deel weed de Albino moddafucka, right? So—you get ees arse in trobol!"

"An' I loos my job hear? You know how long he take me to getta dis job? I already loos my odder one! Jos' one job!"

"You're gonna lose it anyway," I said.

"How come?"

" 'Causea your relations with Albino," I said. "You just got in a fight with him not too long ago."

"We been fightin' for years."

"But I overheard Albino talking to Carlin and he said he doesn't wanna put up with you anymore. He wants to make this whole place Chinese," I said.

"You know why?—'cause dat's all de Chinese peoples do is work, dats all dey tink about. Dey stupid."

"Clyde's allright, though."

"But Clyde Vietnamese."

"But he's still a Chinese."

Aside from that, the next morning Rosa was scheduled to come in and I made a mental note of it on the billboard downstairs. As for Penny's departure, her schedule was crossed out with a line drawn through it. It read: **"DOLLY PARTON'S OUT OF IT!!"** There was even a rumor that Johnny-Boy raped Penny. But, then, Johnny Boy was keeping his eye on just about all the girls in the whole joint—especially Rosa and Gu Fi. He especially wanted those two because the first was a whore and the second exotic. Whenever he talked with Rosa he always looked very hard and longingly at her and licked his lips when she wobbled away. In fact, he even did that when Clyde walked away because he also found Clyde sexually attractive. Every thought of what was going to happen day after day put butterflies in my stomach every morning when I woke up. I got a real kick out of it; it was better than a soap opera...I was always anxious to hear some news from Barnaby or Basil about Rosa's getting angry at all three of us because he couldn't accept the fact that Rosa was a savage nymphomaniacal harridan. But all that changed one morning when I was busing the tables alongside Basil and Yo Yo. Yo Yo was down at the other end near the door when he suddenly ran up and told us something in Chinese because he was so excited. Obviously something was wrong, because even happy-go-lucky Yo Yo was distressed at the situation. Giuseppe was washing dishes with Maria and he was coming out from time to time to clown around and run all around the seats in front of everybody in pursuit of Basil and I. He apparently didn't know that Rosa was in the downstairs kitchen. Yo Yo told us what he saw. He used his facial and hand expressions whenever his English, which was always atrocious, ran out on him. He told us that Rosa was in bad shape and Basil dashed down to the basement and I followed him and I began to hear screams and whining coming from the girl's room. Basil headed for the girl's room, but he was stopped by Quackenbros, who queried him: "Basil, why are you going in the ladies room?"

"I heara *screem*, mon! Risa een trobol, dat's why," he said.

"Lemme see," Quackenbros said, and stepped in, opening the door. "Oh my God," he exclaimed, peering inside. He immediately got inside and closed off the area. "GO BACK! GO BACK!" he yelled to Basil and Jonas, who came up to see what was happening. Toi, Ding Bat, and the rest were milling around casually and curious as to what was going on. When Rosa began sobbing and screaming inside the room suddenly Ding Bat and Toi started breaking out into really loud yelling themselves. They too were apparently upset over something. They carried it on and on with their sharp piercing Chinese voices and finally Carlin came out waving a stick in his hands, a cut-off broomstick, and Albino followed up, coming after him. "Carlin, Carlin! Cool out now...it's nothing...she just had a..." he peeped inside at his request. "Holy shit! Cummere, Carlin!—" Quackenbros stepped out and urged us all to get back to work and mind our own business. Barnaby, however, was washing the pots right next to the ladies room and he could hear everything. When break time came, and after a few hysterical howls and screams, Barnaby gave us the incident: "Alfredo beat her up, man," Barnaby said. "But look—she kep' speakin' in Spanish. She couldn't speak no English den, see. She had to hab' somebody to translate dat shit for her so dem managers could unnerstand. She was all lost; she ain' known what was goin' down in no English—"

"Well, get on with it!"

"She—I only know justa littul bitta Spanish, but she said that Giuseppe beat her up," he said—and we all jumped up in our seats. Giuseppe exploded. "GODDAMMIT!! THAT'S A FUCKIN' LIE YOU BLACK BASTARD!!" he shrieked. Basil followed up. "Waita minot, mon—meebe—"

But it was too late already. From the back we could see Quackenbros heading towards the dining room and closer and closer towards where we happened to be situated. Carlin and Albino followed, Carlin waving a stick. Quackenbros looked back at him. "Carlin, put the stick down—"

"But he's a fuckin' murderer," he said. "You should fuckin' see her, man! She's got fuckin'—"

"If you don't stop that damn language in here now you're gonna be managing somewhere else, you got me?? What in hell do you think this is, huh? The Mafia??" Well...He turned towards Giuseppe; Giuseppe says to us quickly, "Gotta go, fellas—" and ducked out of Quackenbros' grasp. "EY! STOP HIM! GET AFTER HIM! MR. PHILLIPS!" I didn't go after him, for some reason—but Carlin waved the stick over my head and said: "Get up, napps! After him!—" But Quackenbros nabbed Carlin again. Carlin was resenting it, I could tell..."I've had enough of the slurs, Carlin! If I hear it again, you're outta here. I'm sick of your crap. If you wanna work in a goddamn skinhead—"

"Quackenbros!" Albino yells, pulling Rosa up to the rear of the dining room. I looked up at her. I was shocked; she had been pulverized into near non-recognition! Both of her eyes were blackened; she had scars and purple-marks all over her face; she had her arm in a sling, and her jaw was broken. She was limping and her wrist was slashed all around her hand; perhaps she was trying to commit suicide. There was no way, I thought, Giuseppe could have done anything on that order, the way he talked about Rosa so. Or perhaps he could— judging by the way everything was just so fucking crazy around here. The patrons kept eating; only a few of them ever paid the scene any mind. Quackenbros left unfortunately because he had to be somewhere and there we were— doomed. Albino yanked the three of us up. "We're finished eating, aren't we, gents!?" he said, condescendingly, with a slight sneer. Barnaby didn't listen; he was still eating. Carlin went over to him and slapped him on his head then wiped his hand on his apron and sneered: "Hey, shit-ass! Didn't you hear? Chow-time's up—"

"Ey, Johnny, watch it—remember Charlie? Huh? You don't wanna lose your job...go take carea those idiots in the kitchen, I'll handle these three. Ey, now I don't know who beat her up, but I want some answers from you all. Rosa says Giuseppe did it. Is that right?"

"No, it isn't," I said. "Actually Barnaby knows what happened. I just heard about it."

"Okay—Barnaby. What in hell happened to Rosa last night?"

"Well...she got beat up by some kid named Alfredo."

"Who the hell's Alfredo?"

"That's the man she in love with."

"I thought she was in love with Giuseppe," Albino said quizzically.

"Naw—but she in love wid Alfredo, too," Barnaby said. I tried not to laugh.

"Does she know any other guys?"

"Ten others."

"Jeses Christ! You mean to tell me it was a gang rape??"

"Naw—nothin' like that. She jus' went ovah one night to have dinner wid dis guy name Alfredo, an' Afredo was all strung out on shit, das all, an' he beat 'er up, das all."

111

"What kinda shit?"

"Drugs, man."

"What kinda drugs—look, you gotta be more specific with me 'cause if we don't find this shit out now we—*all* of us might not be workin' in this fuckin' joint no more—including Quackenbros. He ain't the *boss* boss, see—that's that Indian guy who comes in here every month or so, see. When he sees this he'll close the whole joint down. He almost did it twice 'causea you guys. He'll think no one's got protection an' we'll be saddled with a billion fuckin' lawsuits from God-knows-where. You can't do any fuckin' thing right, can you? Now get—what really happened?"

Rosa had gone out with Alfredo three nights in a row when she got clobbered by him. As it turns out, Alfredo also raped and sodomized and beat her with his numchucks and forced her to eat shit. He wasn't even strung out on drugs at the time, though there were some traces of coke in his blood. The coke he got from none other than the Stool Pigeons—particularly Maggie. That was the girl who had sold him the stuff. At the same point Maggie went on a "vacation" to New Jersey to escape being convicted for selling Alfredo the coke. But, luckily, Alfredo didn't even remember getting anything from Maggie, so she was really safe. They tried to get him on drug intoxication but there were no drugs around after a thorough searching. A week later they took the situation to a police court in Belford and the whole scene was an uproar, as I heard it through Basil. I didn't go, neither did the other two, but Giuseppe was there—and something really bad happened in the interim, because the case was thrown out with a quick bang. "All evidence wohrs against heem, mon," Basil said, after he showed up in the last courtroom meeting as a witness. "Dey hahd de verdict—an BANG! Giuseppe wors **GUILTY!**"

I was jolted. "Guilty? How? But what about—"

"Alfredo wen' back to El Salvador!" Basil laughed. "Dere's no way dey kin' find evedence ughinst Rosa. No way, mon. Dey breeng out de exhibits, de sperm jars—

A,B,C,D,E,F,G,H,I,J,K,L,M,N,O,P...on and on and on. Dey got Miguel...but he wors no good. He crazy. So—Giuseppe get five years for assault an' battery!"

Just like that? Five years for nothing! Giuseppe went wild when this happened. He went up to one of the security guards and began to insult him, and the guard whipped him across the head. When this happened Rosa, who was glaring at him rather aloofly, began laughing with glee—and then all the defendants rose up and started a literal riot in the courtroom. The entire court was wrecked, Rosa got her ass kicked again, Giuseppe escaped in the chaos and slipped into hiding, and the whole thing was silenced only when the joint was teargassed.

Meanwhile Maggie went back to work pounding on the cash register and selling the cocaine with Ruby and Tramsokong. Giuseppe came out of hiding when Rosa suddenly dropped all the charges against her man and persuaded everyone that the real assailant was Alfredo. In the meantime the whole environment was growing increasingly chaotic due to Albino and Carlin's destined climb to the top of the managerial ladder. Johnny-Boy himself felt increasingly arrogant and chauvinistic towards all the workers. And then there was that thing he had for Rosa. He had caught wind of her sexual excesses once Albino told her that she had twelve lovers and molested her younger sister for kicks. The way he used to talk to her I felt the situation would come to a head some time. I was mopping up the floors one night. One by one, all the crew members left. I stayed extra long because I was itching to see what would happen between Rosa and Johnny-Boy. Carlin must have had something up his sleeve, for he walked up to me and grabbed the mop away from me and said, condescendingly: "Ey, bro, you can go home now, alright, man? Just punch out—your time card's right up there. Now go and get dressed like a good boy and go home and eat your chow," he said, laughing. Of course, I didn't find it humorous, and he seemed to notice it. "You seem not to have found that funny, Mr...*Phillips,*" he said, mimicking my last name by biting down on his bottom lip—the implication being I was a fool. "You really ought to laugh more. It's good for you! Makes you healthy..." In the back Rosa was still cleaning up the floors at a very slow pace because she had problems with that broken arm of hers. Johnny-Boy went in the dining room to check up on what was there. I punched out and walked out the door. Carlin didn't even bother to wave goodbye—even Albino did *that.* Anyhow, once he went into the basement, I went back inside the building and hid in the pantry. Rosa didn't see me—she was wiping off the tables slowly with that bad arm. Steady, steady...don't fall... Now she was finished and she started to mop the floor around her as her masters told her to do it. Carlin reappeared. He began hovering around her. He pretended to be "concerned" about her health. "Hey, Rosa, you alright?" She didn't answer the first time. Johnny laughs. "C'mon, Rosa...I don't mean to be mean...ha ha! wasn't that funny?" Rosa said, "I'm fine." "Nothing wrong?" "Nothing— I'm just fine." He kept staring at her and looking her up and down, then he decided to take his cue. He tells her, "Say, you think I'm sexy? Huh?" "Yeah—you sexy," she mumbles, half-assedly. "Naw...do ya *really* think so? I mean—like you *dream* about me?" "Why?" " 'Cause I love you—how's that?" "Mr. Carlin, you're fine," she said blandly, and kept mopping. But Carlin showed no signs of letting up. "Look, I just wanna talk. Don't you wanna talk to me...baby? Huh, baby? Huhhhhhh?" he said, trying to fake the softness. My stomach tightened for some rough action; I tried to keep extremely quiet as Johnny-Boy went around sizing up Rosa; my feet were perched up on the ends of the vacuum cleaners and I was liable to slip off them and put myself in a heap of trouble. Then Johnny-Boy grew even more brazen. "You fuck?" "No— I don't even know what you're talking about," Rosa said, frustrated. Johnny-Boy didn't hear. He paused, then said, "Take it off, Rosa." "Why?" "I must have it." Rosa refused; she didn't like Johnny-Boy; she knew he was a homo. "C'mon, you bitch, take it off," he demands, snorting. A bulge begins forming in his pants and that means something to Rosa and she just keeps mopping. "You filthy whore," he says, "you do it with twelve guys, don't you? You rape your sister, I hear! You really must be a perverted slut. You—you—I know you want it. I know ya want me. You like dicks, don't you? You keep come inna jar! You're a fuckin' dirty bitch! Take it off now! C'mon—look at it. I'm well hung. See, bitch, see, look at mine—" he then pulls down his pants; obviously he's showing her his cock. From way over in the kitchen I can see past the stove and his medium-sized, thick and bulky erection isn't making any impression on her. She doesn't want it, not one bit. She's been through the court case and she's fed up with men—so she thinks. Besides, she hurts too much to fool around just now. Any other time, maybe, he would have been successful. But Johnny's persistent—he doesn't pull up his pants. "Look—just put your hand on it. C'mon, I hear all about you. You do it to anyone else. Why not me?..." Rosa refuses, and then Johnny-Boy grabs the mop and throws it on the ground and confronts her face to face. "Look! Bitch! Foreigner tramp! I want it right this instant! Look—!" And here he begins to push her and insult her. I have the slight temptation to go out and help her by taking the ice shovel off the rack and whacking him across the head with it. The temptation grew as he taunted her more and more, but I couldn't get myself to get out there and save her. He starts to point the finger in her face. His dick is in full erection, pointing up at her—"I'm gonna rape your spick ass, okay? SUCK IT! SUCK IT NOW!!" Rosa refuses to talk—again. Suddenly I hear a plate smash to the ground and my nerves twitch. Suddenly she screams because she's so frustrated, and Johnny-Boy gets worked up, he leans her against the wall, he punches her in the face. He throws her on the ground, rips her clothes off, then picks up the mop water and throws it all over her, and stomps on her wildly and hysterically. He's going to rape the fat cow, and so he does. He jumps on her mangled-up hands to make sure she doesn't do anything rebellious, and he jumps wildly on her broken arm and she shrieks hysterically. Then he gets over her and plows it right in, ripping one of the lips…"**Do you like it, you fuckin' taco twat?!**" he shrieks and pants, ripping through her bloody cunt…but that's not enough; she's yelling! And he's got to do something quick about that. So he grabs a wire and wraps it around her throat and neck…it almost cuts right through…"You like it?? You like it?? You like it?? You like it?? Huh?? Say yes!! Yess!! YESS!! YESS!!!!" Rosa shrieks, rolls around bleeding and kicking on the ground. She wants to get away, but she can't and she begins crying wildly. Yet Johnny-Boy's not finished, either. He puts her head between the double-doors and squeezes the two doors tight together until she begins shrieking wildly and hysterically. The shrieks are so exciting to Johnny-Boy that he comes on himself, on the floor, over and over again—which makes him even wilder. Now he begins to swing her about. He rams her head into the dishwashing machine. He tried to shove her in there, but she was too heavy. Finally he searched frantically for something to clobber her with. I thought about running out again, but still I couldn't get myself to do it; I was paralyzed. And scared. He searched and searched…when this happened Rosa took a dish and threw it right in his face. She could hardly move because she was in so much pain. The dish almost broke his nose and he was bleeding like a pig. Then he wildly and insanely grabbed the dish and began to smash it over her head until it broke, and by then she was unconscious. Then he pulled down his pants again and squirted on her one last time and bent over her and shitted in her face and hair. Then he turned on the stove and burnt her hands on it—even when they were already burned. Then he just kept whacking away at her corpse and shoved the fucking thing in a plastic bag, which he pissed in, and tied it up, and heaved it over his shoulders and threw it in the elevator. Well! A great job finished! Something in my mind still told me, over and over, so much that it became torture: go get it, go get the shovel, kill him! No one's here! But I couldn't…I felt too weak and too frightened and too intimidated. Suppose he did the same to me? He was going both ways, anyhow...And then he puts the elevator at half-mast, then up, then down. I saw the utter demoniacal look on his face, the absolute sadism and viciousness in his expression as he toyed with the elevator, speeding it up and down, back and forth. Then he figured he had to split. He already punched out hours ago—Rosa hadn't done it yet. Then he goes over to the time card and pulls out one of the cards and scribbles a bunch of junk all over it with a ball point pen. "You're fuckin' outta here, wetback fuckin' greaser bitch," he hisses—and wipes his ass with the card, and sets it back up on the rack. I glimpsed at my watch. 11:56. Perhaps Rosa was dead—who knows. No one knows. Now Johnny-Boy went searching around the joint to make sure no one spied on what he did. He only seems to show a tinge of remorse. He only looked a bit scared, perhaps just suspicious. I didn't like Rosa, but I was strongly tempted to murder him with the shovel as a justifiable means of getting back at his murder of Rosa. After all, he was a fucking Caucasoid monkey, a descendant of a race of shit and garbage...He pulled up his pants; he had so many orgasms beating her up the place smelled like sperm all over. I wondered how I was going to get out. Johnny-Boy then went down in the basement; when he did I dashed out of the building as fast as I could—and knocked over one of the tables by mistake. Carlin came running up, but it was too late—he couldn't see me in the dark...

Morning!...it was the Sunday Brunch...I just remembered. I had nightmares about the incident the previous night. I was almost too scared to go and I kept asking myself why in the hell I kept coming to this crazy place. It was like going to jail every day and the madness was just starting. Once inside the joint I went to work at the brunch and everything was in such a hurry that they probably didn't recognize Rosa's body even if they found it in the elevator, nor the shitty time-card. I got to the elevator and looked around. Johnny-Boy was there, just as innocent as ever. I checked the elevator. Nothing. Carlin looked me up and down but he didn't say anything. Then I went into the basement and Carlin followed me there. "Hey, shit-ass, where the fuck you going? Huh? Get your ass up there to those fuckin' dishes!" He should know about shitasses, I thought. I went back up and started washing the dishes with Maria because Giuseppe was off. I didn't dare tell her what happened. I just kept up the pace. "C'mon, muchacho, keep goin', keep goin'!" she always said...but there was a bad look on my face. "Yeah. What wrong? Eh? *Qué pasa?*" Then, even from all the way up here, you could hear screams. I knew it had to be Rosa. "DONDE ESTA??" she yelled to me, looking harshly at me, then she shook me. I told her I had nothing to with any of what was happening. She kept banging her fists on the dishwashing machine and dropping dishes now and then and rambled on complaining about what kind of a nuthouse it was around her and then the screams grew louder and louder, like she was getting killed. Basil dashed inside the dishroom. "Who in da fuck dot, mon?? Who?" Barnaby ran up. "Man, I hear some screams—sound like Rosa or some—"

"ROSA?? Ah!—" Maria rambled off again and again and began asking me what had happened. Then she asked Barnaby, then Basil. She got no answers. Lolita and Concha knew who it was and so they suddenly dropped everything, right in the midst of their work, and rushed downstairs to see what was happening. Carlin disappeared. By the time the sisters got downstairs, the screaming thing was in the elevator and banging wildly on the elevator, so loud you could hear it all the way in the dining room...Quackenbros wasn't there that day. Albino was downstairs asleep—and drunk as hell—but Carlin shook him awake and told him he was needed badly upstairs. Albino then stumbled up and got put down by Lolita and Concha who cornered him and started hitting on him; he grabbed them and locked them inside his office for the time being. Maria was furious as all hell; the rest of us were running around and all the customers were screaming hysterically for their food... "...hey, what the fuck is this?...Ethel, let's get back to the Bingo!..." So go on back there, you Jew motherfuckers, I thought. I was so hysterical inside I felt the temptation to grab up a potato and throw it right at one of them—just for kicks, to hurt one of those filthy dining-room swine. But I got pushed down in the uproar. Someone, maybe Maria, pulled open the elevator door and there she was, Rosa, all covered with shit and piss, ants and roaches crawling all over her body, which was naked, and the insects she wiped off herself, shrieking wildly and crazily, totally naked, the fumes horrifying, shit in her hair...she jumped up and out. "ROSA!! Ahhhhhh!—" Maria screaming, shocked and enraged to the boiling point. Everyone was stunned to the floor. Carlin rushed up and wrestled her to the ground. Rosa punched at him, screaming in Spanish that he raped her, and Maria went wild herself...she got a wire and went for Carlin and began strangling him with the wire. Albino got up just in time and jumped on Maria and began punching her wildly and drunkenly in the face. Get the shovel! I thought to myself...get the motherfucking shovel!! It'll never get back to order! Jonas dashed up with a pipe in his hand from God-knows-where and saw what Albino was doing to Maria and Carlin to Rosa. Carlin dragged Rosa downstairs, but when he got halfway he slipped and Rosa tumbled all the way down the stairs and she hit her head, but she was still screaming wildly. The sisters saw it all and Concha smashed her way out through the glass window and tried to rescue Rosa. Goddammit and fucking hell!! What kind of a zoo was this place? I'd never seen anything like it—never. Jonas was beating up Albino with the pipe, when Carlin dashed downstairs and with a butcher knife ordered the three to break it up. Maria was there also. All the Chinese girls had gathered around and they were complaining wildly. Toi pushed a whole chocolate cake on the ground in frustration. Then Carlin pulled out a gun. "All right—Rosa, get to the trash room! Now!" The girls screamed...Carlin fired at the ceiling. "SHUT UP YOU GODDAMN SPICK

MOTHERFUCKERS! GODDAMN NIGGERS AND GOOKS! SHUT UP AND GET BACK TO WORK!! THERE WILL—" He pushed Rosa into the back, gagged her, pointing the pistol to her forehead, and locked her inside the trash room— "—NO MORE SHIT FROM YOU SAVAGES OR ELSE YOU ALL GET ON TWO FUCKIN' WEEKS NOTICE. IS THAT CLEAR??" No one answered—Carlin fired at the ceiling. "IS THAT CLEAR ASSHOLES??"

"Yes," we said—and went back to work. Lolita took up her post again and began barking at the customers a bit brashly. "What was that all about?" said the customers, who had been held up for thirteen straight minutes. But Albino was in a bloody drunken mess because of the whipping he got at the hands of Jonas; he stumbled downstairs clutching his head and sunk in his chair in agony. Carlin was stunned and demanded to know who did it, but he backed down and said— "I was fighting Rosa," instead. Jonas was the fourth most powerful figure in the restaurant and besides, he was a huge, big, ginger-colored black man who was six-foot-six and weighed 240 lbs. He was Maria's lover.

We all calmed down. We had been defeated; we were numerous, but we had no power, and we were absolutely disorganized. And we weren't armed. The managers were armed. Quackenbros presence didn't help any because he himself was a part of it—he was benign, but treacherous. Worse, we weren't even afforded the luxury of his benign hostility: he stayed home most of the time, worrying about his real estate bullshit...Rosa got out only at the promise that she'd behave like a good little girl and stop acting like a jungle spick savage and act like a real American and take a bath, as Carlin put it. Albino was so drunk, he couldn't even tell what in hell was going on, anyway...he was working with Carlin, and Carlin was a dangerous character, obviously. He couldn't afford to back down...besides, Albino had his own ambitions to take over the joint.

I went home feeling utter nausea and wondering why in the

hell didn't I quit from the outset, when Mario got insulted, rather than endure all this chaos. I didn't know...was it because it was a kind of education for me?

Worse, I just about had enough money to leave, anyway. I guess I was just emotionally intimidated by the managers...

My whole life was working in a circular pattern: work, sleep, and eat. In between, nothing mattered; it was all a part of the background music. Like Muzak...it had no significance. I read books and they didn't help: they were just a dope...When I rode home on the bus that night I couldn't even look in their faces. They themselves were waiting to get back on their streets to take a fight out on the most vulnerable among them to let out the frustrations of the day. I stood at the bus stop waiting for the bus to come. It was always late. Always about five or ten minutes off. It was now warm outside, but I didn't notice the weather or anything else. I wasn't even hungry and I rarely ate now because I didn't feel like I wanted to be raped by food anymore in order to get fattened up...When the bus pulled up I looked straight upward and out towards the mall, then at the sky. I put my money in the slot like I was taught. I sat down with the rest of them and tried to avoid their faces. I didn't even feel like talking to them; I couldn't even look them eye to eye. Everyone was silent and completely pooped. One by one, without a word spoken, their earphones secured on their ears, their heads wagging back and forth every time the bus hit a pothole, the bus itself creaking and rattling like a casket, everyone got off, right in the heart of the old neighborhood—BELFORD.

I didn't even want to see my mother now—in fact, I even spent my time wandering around the streets at night just to avoid even associating with my mother. Sleeping brought on nightmares, but once in a while I had to come home to get some sleep. Pops was there, but he didn't say anything to me; Mom said nothing just the same. Good, I thought; I didn't want to ever have to put up with her mouth. She began getting rather frail and sickly looking, and I took it for AIDS. That was another good reason for staying away from home: I was under sabotage by a syphilitic and an AIDS patient. That's just about all I needed—to get infected by my own relatives.

So I was out on the streets almost all the time. Belford, of course. Just to walk through the place, even in the daytime, made my hair stand on end. Drug dealers were right out there, under your nose. You can see them now, standing next to their cars or vans, clustering in groups, speaking in Spanish, Quechua, Vietnamese, Jamaican patois, Black American English, White Appalachian, Cambodian, Arabic, Hindi, Farsi. The whole bunch is out there. They stand on the corners, under the trees, behind the bushes. Guys walk with sticks, bandanas around their heads. If you want to take a crap or a piss, you do it on the side of the road—just like you threw all yesterday's rotten vegetables right out there with the shit. In the summertime the flies got thicker than the blacktop tar. The smell's so strong you fucking can't breathe...

Move on. Stay off the sidewalks, because one of those maniacs just might jump out of the hedges and cut off your balls, and he might not even have a legitimate reason for slashing off your balls, but he'd do it anyway, perhaps under the influence of PCP, and that's the shit you've got to watch. Move on—get over in the streets. Watch out for the construction work the goddamn workers did on the 12th Avenue stretch up along the apartments. They're always tearing up the goddamn streets for some damn reason or other. They'll give a billion excuses. They're fixing the electricity because the last storm knocked everything out of place. They're fixing the plumbing, checking the gas lines, checking the wires, filling up the concrete in the empty spots, spreading on the blacktop, pounding on those goddamned pneumatic drills like madmen. Watch it—don't knock over the cones; don't fall in the manholes. Just think: early in the morning they'll be right out there again with those big fat tractors, snorting, wheezing, tearing everything up, causing a traffic jam from here to eternity. We were always late because of these fools. They're always there all the time, working and working and working and working. A sheer, pure habit—that's all it was. There wasn't any explanation for why they had to be out there. Nobody'd ever ask them, either. Just a symptom of the common boredom and workamania. No! Don't think about work and workaholism and workamania or else you'll find yourself thinking about what happened tonight and the night before. Let's pretend there isn't such a thing as work. Let's make-believe; let's just think that every thing's just a-ok. Hey, listen...over there. There's a party going on. Spanish kids, of course. Wanna crash it?

To get to the bus stop I was obliged to trample through the sleaziest sections. Well...here I am, right in the dead of the darkness. On a certain day I would run smack into a little El Salvadoran girl offering me a blow-job for a quarter. Probably no more than fifteen, I suppose. Her face looks like a bent-up skillet with the grease still left in it. She's got herpes, or syphilis—the two worst in Belford. Let's pretend it's the daytime and she's pestering me for a suck. I pass her up; she keeps pestering me and showing me her ass which is so nice and juicy and smooth. I almost give in. She even goes so far as to show me her boobies and her cunt...it's just in the mouth, she claims...nowhere else. But I don't need it now. Pass on...nighttime.

Tenth Avenue. It happened right there, as I recall. A whore's haven. They did it mostly on the corners, usually. Sometimes they gave you some addresses—Giuseppe knew a few of them who hung around the 10th place neighborhood. Along this neighborhood stood good old Zilch Department Store, where all the foreigners bought everything at a discount, and adjacent to the Warehouse was a waste site carved out through negligent use. First it had been a playground, then an amusement park, then they shut it down after a race riot; a pharmacy then sprang up, then a grocery, then a warehouse, but nobody shopped at either of these places. A pizza parlor was there for a year, but nobody ate there; it closed up, the building was handed over to the Steinway crew who turned it into a Dummheit Cafe branch. It was a success, but they were so successful they became utterly unsanitary—and because people kept peeing on the floors and fucking in the bathrooms, and because they were caught dead using rat meat for hamburgers to "beat the costs", they were hounded out of business. After that Kentucky Fried Chicken had a go at it, but abandoned just as soon as they started; then they suggested that a pastry shop be opened, so they got into it. But the guy running the store was Jewish and the following afternoon, right after the opening they found a bunch of swastikas painted in black all over the whole joint. The owner was absolutely disgusted, so he gave up, and so the Koreans moved in on it and set up a laundry. But then the owner was tied up in the rackets; one night a bunch of creditors came along because he refused to pay his debts to the Mac. The gang broke in and burned the joint to the ground—and it's been a dump site ever since. A tombstone to the American Dream of enterprise.

On that spot, if you look hard enough, you'll find the ground littered with hypodermic needles. The gangs are congregating at night; you can hear their sputtering dialects reaching up to the dead pristine whiteness of the moon. They break into homes and clobber themselves ad nauseum. Clothes and sofas and coffee tables are all over the streets from the last evictions. And there's one more for the record every day: look at that *dead* man lying over there on the bench. *I* think he's dead. Further out, the huge parking lot which was so dangerous they almost decided to get the National Guards to keep the freaks and fags in check. But it wasn't any use because they were everywhere: in the laundry mat, in the tailor shop, in the liquor store, in the opticians office, in the clothing stores, in the supermarket nearby...corruption and decay is everywhere. Enough rhetoric already! Time to go home?

That sign!...I've seen it almost my whole life. It makes me sick, sick to the core. Probably even had it up in the 1890s: it looks old as shit. White with black lettering...sits there bent up, covered with graffiti. It's pretty large, but old. **BELFORD,** it reads, confronting you suddenly and uneasily as soon as the X-2 bus pulls into the area along the boulevard. Once you cross that line—that's that. You're out of middle-America. Just like that. It's a thin-line between have and have-not—not that the haves have anything worth having. **WELCOME TO BELFORD,** it says, and what a welcome you get! Folks, this is where all the gooks and spicks and niggers go once they've stopped making your burgers. There's a repair shop on the left-hand side for lemons. On the right is a candy store where all the Vietcong kids get their treats. It's inexpensive. The only problem is that not a one, either working or not working, speaks any English. You wonder how they ever got the job...Now then. Belford park. Alias, PCP park. Don't even go near there because there were killings over bad drug deals. Turn back! Time to go home. They're all asleep now. It's twelve in the morning. Well...back to North Belford. Everything's falling to pieces. Abandoned cars. Smashed-out windows. The buildings weren't even fit for human habitation. Move on...don't think about the pain. Keep it down. Say! I think to myself, with a sudden rush of last-minute inspiration, I wanna go buy a hat. I thought of buying a felt hat like they used to wear in the old days. Or maybe I don't really have this awful despair chewing me up like that. We'll see...

Inside the Zilch department store. I want to buy a hat. No particular reason—I just decided I wanted to buy one. Nothing in the slightest, as I make my way through the plastic doors, holds anything new or original or fresh to me. How many times I have walked in this hole-in-the-wall thinking about suicide, about cutting my own throat, or leaping out the damned window, I can't recall. Every last detail of the department store, the escalators, the phones in the porch-ways, the floor-mates with the insignia, the display windows, the mannequins, the clothes and the tags stuck on them, the rails with the dime-novels lying there with their half-naked sluts...all of it brings back a thousand, a hundred-thousand, a million, a hundred-million, a thousand-million, a million-million intricate pangs of psychic grievances, a fresh stab of pain, a recollection of the last few suicide attempts, the last time I got beat up on the job, the last time I got cheated by friend and foe and family and freak alike. I had been back there just a few weeks ago, after many years. The pain, the suffocation, the ennui and torture was the same. You can't beat it, the bedraggled environment...the graffiti on the walls...the hypodermic needles lying on the ground in the 'rest-rooms', swimming in the piss puddles...the dope-rackets going on under your nose...the freaks waiting in the bushes for provender...the death you feel all around you in those people, those Belford tics who have gone for nothing washing dishes and mopping floors and laying bricks, pulling the streets apart, clogging up the drainpipes, blasting the drills, punching the cards, pushing the computer buttons. You see all this, you feel it, you walk here, you put yourself into your old persona again which you thought beforehand was just a husk, some time-worn detritus you just thought you left on the banks of the Nile years and years ago. And what are you, then? Nothing. You are nothing again. You are a man in harness again. You are a mule and a lecher and a masturbator again. You are just a nigger, just a busboy, a slave. And you want to die.

You walk on. You feel as if you're walking in a damn sleeping bag, in a death womb. No one deserves to live or feel this way, no matter what anyone says.

I don't want to buy the hat; I don't have any need for it. There's no point in buying it; there's no point in buying anything because, just the same, one's in the shit up to his neck; one only fits right in with the other cogs in a machine, like the other buttons on a computer and like the other cliches on the Harcourt and Brace textbook; and when one can only keep to the bloody wheel of work, sleep and eat, one can only look to God, if there ever was a God, to cut to the church along the road and pray, pray that some damn fool across the seas will take it into his head to sneak attack us, bomb us, kill us, because, if the damn fool ever did kill us we'd all go up in the ashes and smoke and the flames of incendiarism and therefore there'd be no despair, we'd all be relieved of it all; and one would rejoice in the death of us all, all of us who are nothing in ourselves, who never did anything of any account nor would ever do something with our lives since, as always—*there's no goddamn point in living anymore!!*

7

I ARRIVED AT THE SLAUGHTERHOUSE, prepared to take a good whacking from my masters.

There was work to be done—they wanted me in the dining room tonight. So they gave me my good old cunt cap, which they found lying in the trash. I hated it—I preferred to wear the gook cap because the cunt cap had DUMMHEIT embroidered all across in black, in an elegant cursive, really swanky and stylish. No matter, I hated every last bit of it, swank or no swank. They reminded me: "You can't afford to be losing these things, keep them with you at all times. They are very important in case you must return them if you decide to leave…" Blah, blah, blou, blip, de, dum, and v.v., I knew the whole yarn from start to finish. I grabbed a paper towel, but then went downstairs to the locker room for I had to take a piss. I punched in on the time clock. The other insects were waiting with their cards. I cut out to the basement. There's Barnaby over the sink, squinting like a fool and scrubbing and scrubbing, just like he's been doing for the last four years. The flies are eating him right up; they're swarming around him frantically. But he doesn't care. He's like a mule. I ask him what he thinks of washing pots…

"Don't you ever get tired of washing the pots?"

"Oh, no—not at all…I never get tired…"

"You're satisfied?"

128

"Satisfied."

"Completely?"

"Completely."

That's that...time for work. I go into the locker room. I already forgot about pissing. Basil's there; he's got some unpleasant news for me. "Yee Sing, she been kidnapped," he said in earnest. Sure..."Yeah, mon. Not onlee dat, but Penny, she been fired. She also having an affair wid Johnny-Boy. Or...dat's what Johnny-Boy tink. Really, she no like him. But Johnny-Boy want to marry her, but he no marry her. Say, Louey, you see dot guy out dere—Barnaby? Ain't he seeck, mon? He Jamaican!...wot? You deedn't know dot? Yeah, mon...he make Jamaican peepul look like shit! You see da flies, he eat 'um for hees breakfohst! He no wash himself—no getta fokin' haircot. He look like de jungle up in hees bush!—"

Suddenly there was a commotion upstairs. "What da hell going on, mon?" he mumbled—and beat it upstairs. I followed him. Then I heard loud, piercing screams and then SMASH!—a car wreck...glass got smashed...I ran up. What the hell was it? Albino was asleep, Quackenbros out for the day...I looked at the scenario. A Trans-Am Pontiac had crashed right into the nearby ice cream parlor. The whole thing was upside down, the windows broken out, splintered. Wait...something's moving inside. Like a German shepherd. A pit bull. No—it's human. No! wrong again, it's Johnny-Boy Carlin. He spins around in a daze...he's pooped...totally lost...not a scratch on him, but he's on acid, I can tell. The cops come. One car pulls up. Then two more. Then six more. Then an ambulance, then three more ambulances, a fire engine, an army tank, a battleship—the whole shenanigans. The guards come on tough, patrolling the area with their bayonets. The crowd is in a frenzy. They gather all around, waving their hands, knocking each other down. Fights break out, gunshots ring through the air...one dies..."Attaboy, baby!" the mob screams. "Go for it! Wowee, baby! Lookin' guuuuuuuuud! Allright! Allright! Allright! Outtasight! Hot shit! Wowee! Bravo!

Magnifico! Grandioso!" They get a shove with the bayonets...No one lets up. Carlin was just coming in for his paycheck, that's all—he just got the damn thing out of control—and his brain, too, or what was left of it—if he ever had one.

It took two hours to get the mess cleaned up. Finally they hauled Johnny-Boy off. Albino was still snoozing away—he didn't care, for he had laid all responsibility in the hands of good old Ruby Rubenstein and Maggie Constable, the stool pigeons. "Get movin', Louis," Ruby whined, perched upon her stool. Maggie stood at the cash register, the fucking animal... "You got tables ta clean, 'n' ya shouldn' be stickin' ya nose inta odda people's bizness! ya hear me?"

"Go to hell!" I screamed at her, wiping off the tables as I picked up dish after dish.

"Send me da ticket, you bastard—you know it bedder dan I do," she retaliated.

"Cocksucker!" I screamed again. She thumbed her nose at me and went back to dealing the blood money. But then there was a switch—I was wanted to make "drinks." So I oblige, like the slave I am. An old fart comes up to me, a female, and what does she want? "Hot tea," she says. Not knowing how to make it I rip open the tea bag and pour the leaves in the cup. "Goddammit! No! You fool! Forget it! Why in hell did you ever hire this man? He's a jerk! He can't even fix a cup of hot tea—"

"Well, why don't you fix it yourself and shut the fuck up!" I snapped, and turned away. As I turned back into the dining room I caught Maggie: "I'll fix you latuh, boy." "Sure, you fucking negress!" I mumbled under my breath—but not too loudly. I knew all about her dealings and of course I wasn't stupid, like Yee Sing Hwong was stupid. After all, I was a nigger, not a gook...Oh, well, I've got to get to the tables because I must fill up the salt shakers outside. I cut down to the pantry. Well...look who's there, as I get down those stairs smelling of stale olive oil and rotten eggs: my Toi Pu Sei. Fixing pancake rolls for tomorrow's Sunday Brunch. Why the hell they can't fix it on Sunday I don't know. That's just them...I fish out the salt. When I do this I peep in the other room and see Jonas and Maria making out passionately. They often suck on each other. Everybody's got to have it in his or her mouth some time or other—we've all become sexual vampires—no, that's not right. We've become *leeches* —because vampires are human after all. Anyhow, with the salt in my hands I prepare to trek up the stairs to the dining room where I will fill all the salt shakers and sit and stare at the customers eating until they finish and then I will take them into the back where they will be cleaned by Maria and Giuseppe. Then Giuseppe comes downstairs. "Say, where da hell is Maria? We got dishes pile up all over! Damn. She make me sick! She wid dat stupid black kid again, eh, Jonus!" I persuade him I'll help out with the dishes until they finish. After all it's not too crowded tonight. Right down by Carlos, the little P.A. system was storming off. "Carlos, goddammit, *vamos!* I want the fuckin' rice! You bastard! Maria Jonas! where the hell are you two lovebirds? You wanna lose ya jobs?? Giuseppe!"... "See dat, man?" Giuseppe said. "Dey gotsa camura up in here some-where. Dey keeps watch on your ass, too. Hey, *Maria!* —no, you go back inna dining room. Tanight, dey got dat stupid black bitch, Maggie, she a bitch, a fuckin' nigga, you know? An' dat fat Jew—what's her name—Ruby Rubenstein!"

"Ssssssh! Not so loud—Albino's sleeping still!"

"Oh yeah—dat's right. Less beat it. Da hell wid Maria—get Bessie, da Chinese girl."

"But she's stupid. Dumb-ass Chink—what does she know, with her crooked-ass English?"

"Giuseppe!" Maggie screamed.

"Allright! ah, damn! I don' wanna wake dat sonovabitch!" So we go back up. Pu Sei's up first. She gets right in front of me and waddles her ass, showing how short she's clipped her skirt. Nobody complains of this short-short skirt she wears wherein you could almost see her cunt buried in the panties. She sees me in the back and so she begins to shake her ass and hikes up her skirt and "scratches" her ass. "I know what it's all about," I mumbled. "What?" she said. "You're just a fucking Toi Pu Sei, that's all!" "I don't get it," she said. "You will after hours, if you keep it up," I replied.

I made it up to the dining room and began busing. I reached for a tray sitting on one of the tables. A white couple was sitting there and they seemed to roll their eyes in disgust every time I stacked the dishes onto the tray. Obviously they didn't like my presence—and they eased up when I departed breathing sighs of relief. Well... I go on to the next table. These ones just look and grin, watching my every move as I stack up their plates. They enjoy it, as I can see by the sheepish grin on that certain bald-pated bastard with his spectacles cocked over his nose and his eyeballs going in time to the dishes. My whole presence on this planet is a joke; I was just born to serve and make others feel good, like all niggers. And then I go on to the next one, and the next and the next. The humiliation increases, increases, increases. It gets worse every minute, every hour, every day. One's such a bastard she doesn't even like the way I look; she won't even let me take away her food. A Jew, of course, with a big, blown-out pompadour and big, clammy-gray eye lids, lips like a prolapsed asshole..."Go away," she mumbles with those asshole lips, grabbing her trash away from me. "Who do you think you are, you saucy bastard?" she snorts, the fuck-head. I was jolted and angered, but the really bad thing was that I couldn't retaliate—at least not at that point. I went back to the better ones—the ones who kept grinning all the time. That's just something to forget...well, all of it is...every bit...

I wiped off the table by the window. Right next to me a Yuppie couple was mumbling about us. "Those workers really get all into it, don't they?" a female voice rung out. "Sure," replied a male voice, smug and contented, "it's really exciting when—well, when they get to fighting and kicking and smashing cars into the side of ice cream parlors, it's a gas...it sure beats the movies!" The both of them howl with laughter. They think they're in the fuckin' theater, it seems. Outside, the scene had cleared out by now... it wasn't funny anymore. I looked at Ruby dealing the blood money. She had her granny glasses down on the tip of her nose. She looked like Santa Claus in drag... "Won meel?" she snorts. "Three feefty widdout der rowls. Ah hot pataydoe? Dass all? Eiddy cents pleese..." I looked at the money in the cash box. Blood money! A prostitution scheme. Look at all of it...it's oodles...two thousand, three thousand...all in a day...Big fat bills, just tossed here and there...Casino money...

But then, I saw there was puke on my table, because I got my hands in it by mistake. Somebody didn't like something— I didn't know what it was. Something had gotten into the food for sure, because Clyde came dashing up to me. "Somebody, ah! too many people in da bathroom downstairs. Too many! Must have da shits—you know? What is wrong with da food— why are you laughing? What so funny?...Upstairs? Where?" Basil came rushing over to me. "Come—you must see dis, mon." He pulled me by the arm. "What? What now? This is a madhouse!" I walked over to the scenario...It was worse than I had expected. Some old man kept puking blood, all over the floor. His wife was having fits... "Oh, God! Help him please! Cawl da ahmbulance! Help! Help! Oh, my Lawd!..." She begins to weep. The rest turn around and stare dead at him...it's entertainment. The security comes in again. He keeps puking up his blood. Finally a piece of his body comes out...a real chunk...she throws a fit and collapses...nobody knows what the hell is happening...they ship another off— two in a row. Johnny-Boy and the old ex-rabbi from the nearby Jewish neighborhood. But he'll be back—like Johnny-Boy will. They always sew him back up, so they say, some kind of way, and it always breaks loose again. His days are numbered...

Many people were throwing up and becoming sick in the Dummheit. This happened because a fluke got loose somehow—salmonella was going rampant. I didn't eat the food. I bagged my own lunches—or just starved. I was sick of it anyway...The bathrooms were loaded with diarrhea. Finally one day the toilets broke down, mainly because the pipes froze over. Both the male and female toilets. Albino was wide awake then!... he grabbed me and Clyde and set us to work in the toilets. He got Louangphuck and Bessie Chong, a newcomer replacing Penny, to bus the tables. Having been forced to do the toilets, for the first time I could see Clyde's anger showing through. Before then he hardly said a thing in regards to the work. "I hate this bery much," he said, through his teeth. He could barely force out an English word when he spoke; he kept lapsing back into Cantonese. Albino saw how angry he was and threatened to call Carlin, but he shouted back at Albino, and Albino said to him, pushing him into the toilets; "Look, you either get this shit done or you're lookin' to get fired, buddy. Don't you ever get hot under the collar with me 'cause I'm the last sonofabitch you'd want to get hot about. Just you wait..." And then he went on clomping back up the stairs. "... Chink!..." he whispered to himself as he got up on the top stairs. Then Johnny-Boy rushed down in a whirlwind just as I went in the back. "Ey, what the fuck you starin' at, you shit!?" he yelled out to me. "An' you—Chinaboy—git your fuckin ass to work!" he pushes Clyde and begins to insult him. He even grabs his ass, over and over. Clyde goes crazy when this happens, but Johnny-Boy flicks out a switch-blade on him and forces him to work, standing over him like an overseer. I gritted my teeth in anger and decided to get a knife from Jonas. But Jonas didn't have a knife. I went back to the scene. Clyde got the mop pails and put on rubber gloves, as I did also, because as good old Mr. Albino says we should not risk catching AIDS for the life of us. Sure enough...but hell!! The ladies room is a mess...they fucked it all to hell. There was blood all in the sinks, in the shitbowls. They did their damn monthlies right there on the floor. And I had to clean the lot of it up. Just then, thinking about monthlies, I thought about Barnaby who munched out a woman on her period. His whole face, so he says, was covered with blood...just like a volcano. I couldn't believe he could do such a stupid thing. I always thought he was a fool like the rest, but not that bad...aw, shit! more blood! a fucking bloody-assed mess!— it's splattered up everywhere. The old tampons are littered all over the floor. I ran back to get another mop pail...until I stopped, dead in my tracks. I turned around. I saw some dark-brown, fungus-like mess crawling all over one toilet. The door was closed. I closed my eyes. I opened the door, then my eyes...it was pure hell. The whole toilet running with diarrhea. And dark, too. And smelly as all hell, a strong gaseous reek. It was winter at the time, but the stuff was so hot it didn't freeze over. The whole toilet was black. I lifted the seat cover...blood! No! A fetus!...a tiny one, unbroken...I dashed out of the bathroom; in my haste I tipped over the mop pail. It splattered all over the blood on the floor, and washed it up...but I wasn't conscious of it. Before I could get to a sink I broke out in bumps, my lips became numb, I began to chill over, I sweated like hell, I shook, my stomach heaved—and I puked all over the floor. Albino caught me in the act. "Goddammit to hell!" he screamed. Then, with a false show of concern, he put his arm around me and said: "What was it? The food? Salmonella? What?"

"Check the t-toilets," I said, heaving. Then he got on his nerve again. "So—you haven't been cleaning the toilets, eh? What's wrong now? Not—"

"Just check, goddammit," I snapped at him. He stared hard at me, then went in to see for himself. I stopped throwing up and then put my ear to the hall. Nothing from him. He walked back in. "Well..." he said, shaking his head in disgust, "somebody's gonna havta clean that shit up, it can't stay there. It's all a part of the game. And this puke—someone might slip on it. Get a mop an' mop it up *now*. Quit the goddamn clowning—"

"But I was sick—"

"You're fulla shit. Getta mop—here, take two pails. I'm

gonna get Maggie to help you out with this. She's been doing this stuff for years. Get a hose, something!..." he runs up in hysteria because the P.A. system is sounding off about "rice." "Don't leave that slop laying there!...C'mon!...Move! Move! Move!" He's back upstairs, the prick...he went to bawl out some others. I can hear him going after Giuseppe now. He hadn't an ounce of pity. Then Maggie showed up. She was eyeing me cautiously. She was coming to get hers, too, the slime. I remembered the initial encounter with that negress, at the counter. This was when I had designs of breaking away and running off. I knew she had to come quick with her overstuffed hippopotamus ass... "Say, you—wha da fuck you doin' standin' eroun'? Huh? HUH??" She snorted, in an obnoxious Bronx accent louder and louder in 35 fucking keys. "Well why don't you just stop screaming and let's... *work,*" I drooled. "Who you talkin' back to punk-ass?" I knew it had to come to this! "You," I said. "If you're gonna be an asshole—" "Asshole WHO??" She said, flicking out a small object. A blade popped out of the little object. I was aghast. No one was even looking. She led me on down the hallway pointing to my back. "Now, niggie, I hurd what you been doin' wif what's her name an' what's her name. If you want yo' dick cut off you just try to make a pass at me, you unnahstand?"

"I wouldn't want to," I snorted—and at this she gave me a slap in the mouth. "I don' wanna hear yo' shit! Get movin'!" she screamed, pushing me into the room. I held my aching jaw. I could have disemboweled her ugly ass right there. How I hated them all right then, how I hated the whole human race for being the filthy bastards that they were!—but she seemed no less soft when she got an eyeful of the toilets. In the background I could hear Clyde yelling and screaming now and then through the closed door and thumps and thuds on the floor and grunts from Johnny-Boy to keep working in a nasty bear-like tone. But Maggie wasn't going to do any of the work. She just wanted to get back at me. Then she put away the knife and pulled out a gun. Then she leaned up against the doorway, trapping me in with the menstrual blood and the fetus and the black shit...Basil popped in. "What da hell goin' on!" "Basil, shut ya goddamn mouth, an' git back ta werk, stupi' ass Jamaycun bamma! Move it! Now!" He split, snorting up a breeze. Maggie fired at the ceiling. "Shut up, black-ass fool! Shut the shit or I'll plug yo' Caribbean faggot-ass, punk!" She turned toward me. "An' you—I don' wanna see a fuckin' thing on dis damn groun' ya hear me, boy?"

"Yeah..." It was weak...

"YA HEAR ME?!?" She screamed, running up to me and poking the pistol in my face. She smashed it across my mouth and rammed it in there. Blood squirted out...it felt as if she loosened a tooth—I didn't know. Oh, sure! I heard...I went along with my chores, but with half a heart. I began to break down as I lifted the fetus out...it was all slimy...perhaps it would have made a good child, a great individual. Perhaps it would have been another Christ—or another Hitler, or a Ku Kluxer, or, worse, just another damn dishwasher...I tossed it into the wastebasket. "Is that yours?" She said, laughing. "No, it's not," I said, half-heartedly. "Looks like it," she said, laughing again, the whore...I pulled out the rest of the umbilical cord and wiped out the rest of the placenta. My finger met at the point of something. I looked...there was a mess of hypodermic needles all filled with rotten blood. I couldn't hold back anymore, I just kept looking at the fetus, and Maggie just kept screaming and waving the pistol, and I heard the screams of Clyde and Johnny-Boy wrestling in the background...I shook, then I began to cry, just like a complete fool. Then I became violently angry and continued crying ever harder and harder, and Maggie's ire was raised, but I didn't care. All the sickness and waste was just too much for my stomach, but to have a lackey standing over you like that, like in a prison, of your own race, abiding by the rules of the Enemy, that just makes you want to throw the fuck up. I lunged at her and she pushed me to the ground. She tried to put my head in the shit and I kept holding back. She held the

gun over me. "You gon' work, you gon' work, motherfucker??
Huh?? You gon' do what Mr. Albino says? Huh?"

"I'm not gonna do it," I said. She got up and jumped on my
stomach, and it was like being run over by a streetcar. I agreed
to work as she kicked me and punched me in the face and
rammed me around like a toy. I got the mop like a good slave
and mopped up the slop. But she just kept kicking me up
around my legs trying to get the balls, and I jerked around and,
with all the air in my chest, shrieked at her: "WILL YOU JUST
CUT THE SHIT, YOU APE!!" She was so shaken by this that she
fired in the ceiling, threatening to kill me. I didn't care if she
shot me or not. I didn't have a life; never had one, so what did
it matter? She pointed the gun towards me, and I broke the
broom handle and brandished it at her. I know it was useless,
but I wanted to hurt someone before I died. "Peek-a-boo,
muthafucka!" she bellowed haughtily, and then fired...I closed
my eyes and yelled aloud...it was nothing. Nothing was
inside! "Shit! How'd dat happen?" I went for her with the stick
ruthlessly and she began shrieking wildly, in an utterly blood-
curdling fashion, and she was probably trying to yell "rape"
but I caught her across the shoulder-blade before Carlin
rushed out. "Maggie, what's wrong?" Then he got pulled back
and pulverized or hit by someone because I heard dull
thumping in the back. Maggie pushed me violently to the
ground and I hurt my shoulder; she fell right afterwards; Carlin
was in the hallways groaning when he got pulled back and into
a little room where he got locked inside; I looked up to see who
the culprit was. It was Clyde Wong! He broke off the broom
handle and attacked her. "Basil, help me," he said, puffing
with near-hysteria, sputtering in Cantonese. He gets out his
own pocket knife and tells her to leave. "Fuck you, you Chink,"
she growls. Clyde gives her a good crack in the face several
times, and she conks out. He lays her down. Thinking only of
work, I get up with the other mop, but he grabs it right from
me quickly, and throws it on the ground. "No! No mo' work!
You rest!" He pulls me up, straightens me out. "Dees peepul

hea no good to no one. Dey make me clean bathloom, but bathloom very dahty. Dey think we are stupid. No, but some are nice, do you know? Yet—not all. Maggie. Constable, she is very—mean! She—is—*shit!*—do you know? No good at all!" He hardens, in that freezing position he gets into when he gets angry. "Don't clean. Let it go to hell." Then Maggie began to come to. We began to run. "The mop pails," I said—I just remembered about upstairs. "Oh, shit," he cried. "Wheel dem out now! Hurry! Fast! Like American!" We were in such a hurry we crammed ourselves into the elevator with the mop pails. We got up slowly to the top kitchen, and then someone opened it for us. We heard, at the bottom, Maggie's hysterical screams, accusations, and what-not. Then he faced the door...it was Giuseppe. "What da hell is dis? I swears! Dis is such a fuckin' madhouse aroun' hear! Firs' da toilets break—"

"Giuseppe, shut up! Get to work!" Albino stormed in. He was all red. "Say! What the hell are you two fuckers doin' in that goddamn elevator?? Get the fuck outta there!" We got out with the mop pails. "This is not goddamn Ringling Brothers, okay." We go into the dining room outside where the slop got spilled. Then he asked us, deadpan: "Did you fix those bathrooms, fellas?" he said. "Yes, everything all right," Clyde said, nodding. "Lemme check. If it's not you're dead meat," he replied, huffing and puffing. We gulped, but I shrugged my shoulders at the same time, as if I cared and didn't simultaneously. I cared for my personal safety, but not the job; I didn't care about the job anymore. I just didn't know anymore how to quit without being intimidated..."C'mon, let's get this place in order! Louangphuck! Rosa! Lolita, quit runnin' ya fuckin' mouths! Clyde! Louie! Do the floors!..." He ran downstairs, then slipped and tumbled down, screaming. He didn't conk out, because he landed on his back..."WHO IN THE FUCK LEFT THIS SHIT LYING ON THE GODDAMN STAIRCASE?? I COULDA BROKEN MY FUCKIN' NECK YOU ANIMALS!!—"

Someone said: "I din't mean it—it slipped out of the garbage can when I was carrying it down—"

"AAAAAAAAAAAAAAAAAAAAAAHHHHH!!!!!—**YOU MOTHERFUCKERS!!!**" he ranted, then clutched his head, and held his hands up in the air. Praying to Allah for help, perhaps? Who knows? Now he leaps around laughing. He's having a nervous breakdown, he needs help—we all needed it—we didn't have an ounce of hope. Just "the frightful laughter of the idiot"! We mopped the floors. Johnny-Boy had broken out—what a shock. He was furious, as I could see. Or Albino had gotten him out. He was fiddling around with his switchblade and waiting in the seats for trouble. Barely a comment from the dining pigs. "Hey shit-ass, stop fuckin' around," he said, pushing Clyde. "Hey—why da fuck you lock me up, huh, bitch?" He pushes Clyde and pushes and pushes him. The patrons look and laugh; some stand on end waiting for the fucking Grand Guignol. "Don't push me—who do you think you are, crazy?" Johnny-Boy kept calm and pushed him some more. Then Clyde broke loose with a cascade of heated Cantonese words which stunned all the patrons. This was happening right in the middle of the dining room. The dish rack was sitting there because Basil didn't move it, or perhaps me or Clyde, but people were coming to get their food and bumping right into the dish rack. "Move that goddamn thing 'fore somebody gets killed!" Ruby whined. Maggie rushed up, but she ducked back down and settled back into her old job without a peep. I guess that shit was settled…Everyone was in such a frenzy that Ruby had to move the dishrack all by herself. When this happened they had people waiting—at least ten of them—to be seated at the tables. Ruby stumbled back: everyone was perplexed as hell. "What kinda place is this?" one of them said. Beats me…I've been here for ten months and I don't know myself!…

The fight between Clyde and Carlin never got under way. Instead Carlin vowed "revenge" on Clyde for insulting him in his "gook language". Of course, Clyde was too strong to be taken lightly, and he found that out when Clyde locked him up in the janitor's room downstairs. He was beginning to crack up...now, I suspected, watching him mop the floors, trying to keep content, almost anything was possible with Clyde once you tipped the barrel with him.

The patrons filed out, the glass doors were locked, the glass wiped down, everything looked sparkling clean. They wanted us to clean them twice, but I wouldn't have it any damn way. I left—and so did all the rest of us.

I punched out. It was ten o'clock. I left for the bus station, glimpsing the empty cafe sitting there in all its swankiness and trendiness, yet harboring the hell of all the earth. Dante's Hell was heaven compared to this joint. In fact, I was thinking of him as I was passing along. Not that he meant anything...I was just curious as to when Rosa, a month ago already, had popped out of a bag filled with shit, piss and cockroaches—something beyond even his petty medieval mind, totally inconceivable and yet it reminded me of what I had read of Dante. You could have written a better Inferno yourself, if you so dared. But you couldn't sing about it—no, that was impossible in such a circumstance. In order to sing well and clear again, to think, talk and act rightly again after you've been caught like that, deep down in the undertow, you had to kill first, to get your money's worth. Rebellion just wasn't enough. It wasn't enough to go out and get pissed; it wasn't enough to walk out on your own family. You had to walk out on ALL of it—period. You had to feel strong enough to look them right in the eyes and deny them, draw the fucking line once and for all. You had to give them a piece of your mind—and clear out, forever, without regret, without guilt, without remorse or pity or even compassion. You musn't give in once, not to the slightest nostalgic temptation to crawl back into the manhole once you're out of it. You musn't even go back for the others because the only way they'll ever get out is with their own two hands. And so it was with me. I was dead, yes—but it was only a false corpse within me all the while. This corpse was dead, as I said—but it was alive washing dishes and raping waitresses just the same. A lively corpse...a life of death. Nothing could have explained it better.

I had often wondered, when alone, how The Devil had *really* come about. What had happened, of course, was that "The Devil" had wanted to be *like* God. For that they threw him down to Hell. The problem with Lucifer was that he was different; he wasn't evil. Lucifer was a whole man, but also a questioning man and itching with an insatiable curiosity. That's how I think about him now that I no longer live in America. He was real shit, not an angel like the rest in the heavens, for the angels were all fags, all dishwashers, fools, cowards, bourgeois, legislators, pimps, mountebanks, hookers, junkies, computer salesman, what-not. The angels were the little snots who were content to be all alike and flutter their goddamn wings either in contentment or for that poor-assed God, that God of contentment, of money, of wealth, fame, fancy cars, refrigerators, dishwashing machines, warehouses and munition plants. But in reality God had nothing to do with any of this crap the angels read into him—in fact, there wasn't even such a thing as God, it was only a name they slapped on an abstract idea. Some of the angels hinted at it, for they had pretenses of being spiritual, too: some went so far as to declare that God was in man, that God was an integral part of the universe, etc., etc., etc.—all without getting knocked off their goddamned pedestals or offending the heavenly censors. But Lucifer! No, he was a doozy. He wanted to go too far. He wanted to get to the bottom of this God business. He wasn't contented to sit on his ass and praise this abstract shit the whole flock of angels were busy pouring out libations to. Lucifer wanted to be like God—no, in fact, he wanted to *be God*, because he knew instinctively that this was the only way to go. Lucifer was really a Taoist in disguise—he believed in having it all and he was determined to have all, to be at one with God. But the stupid angels wouldn't call for it, it was evil, immoral, they said. God was for worship...you could sit and admire God, but you couldn't be like him. But the truth was that the angels, being as stupid, filthy, cowardly, racist, ignorant, backward and overloaded as they were, were simply too unmotivated to find out anything for themselves. They wanted life dished out to them on a silver platter. That's why they created Heaven—because they were lazy and lacked all moral discipline and responsibility. If someone had asked them to shift for themselves, they'd balk and throw a billion excuses—like the Black bourgeoisie. In fact, the whole idea of a bourgeoisie was carved out of the equally inane idea of a "heaven"—a flophouse where people could go and do what they wished, providing they sucked some fool's ass all their lives! It sounded like America to me, reading the Bible about Heaven. It sounded like the shit-hole precisely because the two inseparable poles of existence, Heaven and Hell, Yin and Yang, Light and Dark, Honkie and Nigger, were bent right in two, having been declared unmixable. And, heaven and hell, white men and black men, male and female thus being unmixable, Lucifer, the symbol of all the most feared and pernicious evil in all capitalist civilization and communist and Confucianist and Islamic civilization, had to be tossed down into that other slime pit called Hell by the bourgeois white world but really being all that these swanky, overloaded angelic bastards had so strongly feared. For it was the angels, and not God, who threw Lucifer into the can and fried him. They tossed him into hell just as they starved and killed off all their artists and musicians and poets, just like they went on their weekly nigger-lynching spree in the guise of "fighting crime", just as they were always getting their arsenals ready to fuck over the Iraqis or the Vietnamese—and just like they had me cleaning the shitbowls and tossing goddamn aborted fetuses into the trash cans. And it was not only that—but a good deal of it had to do with my curiosity and hypersensitivity to so many things, despite the outward appearance of being steel-skinned. One day I actually told them these things which were on my mind and begging to be expressed. "You know," I said to them, sitting down at a table during lunch break and dwelling on the chaos and the murder running rampant in our country—not to mention the slaughterhouse—"it's crazy when you consider the fact that the insects live and act a lot better than a lot of the fuckers here in this place," I said. "I mean, considering it, we might as well be fucking insects, or lower."

"Wow," said Giuseppe.

"Really?" said Basil, at least half-interested.

"Yeah—and another thing. I was just reading today—it is more dangerous here in America for many people than—especially in hazardous places like these—than in Beirut, and..."

"Uh huh, yeah," said Barnaby, getting up, putting his tray on the rack, and taking off with the filthy rubber gloves hanging out his back pockets.

"It's like—they—uh, there was this guy, this guy—forget it," I said, hanging up on them. They weren't in the least interested. I should have left my intellectual interests where they belonged—back home—and render unto them what was Philip Steinway's and his dishwashing Philistines. Worse, Johnny-Boy was hanging around, and he was listening. Basil looked at me. "Man, he been drinkin'," he said. "Why you say dat stoof heah, mon? You see dot ohnnimal ovah deah? You know what he like when he get high?" He was whispering. "He listen to ever'ting!"

Barnaby came back with a glass of water. "He think you weird, man," Barnaby said. "He don't like it when you be doin' somethin' funny. Ey, whass dis you readin' man?"

Johnny-Boy wobbles over when he sees the book. "You again," he snorts. He snatches the book out of my hands and drunkenly goes over it. For some queer reason he seems enraged. "Some more bullshit from the fuckin' classrooms, eh?" Johnny-Boy screams. "Get up, you...you talk too much."

"Is it really your business? Can I talk for myself?" He pushed me, and I felt a surge of wild anger. "You wanna get fired? Why don't you put a fuckin lid on it, shitface? Look...time's up," he said, and it was only twenty-five minutes into my break period, "get back to work an' don't open your trap again, you sonofabitch." He kept the book—for the record, of course. That was another thing—those books I kept bringing in to read. I went to my fathers shop and picked out a book by Knut Hamsun and sat down and read it. And when I did this THEY walked up to me and THEY gave me a time of it, *they* being the Stool Pigeons, because it didn't make sense to them one way or the other why anyone would be foolish enough to read such a stupid book about a man going hungry. The stupid honkies and Jew bastards!—they thought even worse of me when I got my hands on a book by W.E.B. DuBois—*The World and Africa*. They wanted me fired immediately when they flicked through the book after snatching it out of my hands. It was pure foolishness, they whined, like stupid goats. I wasn't concentrating on my work. I was beginning to get stupefied and wander off in thought. I wasn't supposed to think anyhow. I should be better off, perhaps, like they, a bunch of brick-headed murderers and savages killing time in the discos and back-alleys and silly clothing stores for silly elegant bastards. But WHOA! I says to myself—never mind those shits. Don't flick off. You know what the scene is now, my friend—from top to bottom, all of a motherfucking piece! You can't change the world, you can't put flesh on a heart of steel!—and so I simmer down. I says to myself again, Look! man, that book is your life, your life is in your hands. Not the dishes!—that doesn't mean anything. That has no purpose. This is just a momentary transition—don't worry about the pain. You are Dante going through the shit-heaps and discos and luxury-hotels of Hell to get to "Paradise," not "Heaven," which is really a re-wording of Hell. No—you want to get to the point where the past dies, rots in the Hell of Heaven with the heavenly angelic corpses. You want to get to the point where Heaven and Hell become one; and where the transition from dishwasher to Selfhood has been complete—and you are one with your destiny, whatever that may be.

❖

Johnny-Boy's in the hospital, I hear. He just got an overdose of cocaine. I saw the blood all over the floor, after they'd mopped it up—but the stains remained and bore testimony to it all. It was all passing over my ass as I heard it. Another one happened to do with Lolita—she dumped her old boyfriend, some guy named Jose—for a Vietnamese kid named Ding Dong. On top of that, she's having an affair with Sal Moustafa, of all people. It was all very confusing when I heard it through Basil. Jose had leaped into the Potomac River and killed himself, I heard. But Sal Moustafa, too, was dead. Ding Dong and Lolita got into a car crash not long ago and Lolita broke her neck; she also had a miscarriage with Sal's baby—the one I picked up, I discovered. They were driving home from the Tropicana disco in Holiday Inn downtown when Ding Dong, drunk as usual, crashed his car, a beautiful Rolls Royce, right into a tree. A Rolls Royce! What a fool... "Gooks can't drive, man," Barnaby said to me. He was another one giving me news of the goings-on. "Look—you know Sal Moustafa, Lolita's man? Well, Lolita was hot for him until she met Ding Dong. Then she got tireda *him,* too. Then, he went after Concha. Concha fell for him, the handsome young Libyan dude. Well, she used to give him good blowjobs, real good, until—well, no, Lolita and Sal never broke up—"

"What the hell is this?" I butted in, shocked by the news of Sal's death. "I don't givea shit about Concha's beautiful blowjobs. I'll find out for myself...Tell me just how this guy got killed. That I want to know."

"Well...Concha was going out with Sal, too. Sal had the botha dem, see. But Concha an' Sal were alone, going to a movie when they began speeding, real real fast, about 100 miles per hour, an' da car skidded outta control, 'cause it was raining—an' crushed into da telephone pole. They were inna police chase, too, see. Concha fell out— the door flew open. She got K.O.ed and broke a leg...but Sal! Hell, he got smushed...his face was on the letter box, in the compartment—torn right off his head! It was that—an' his nuts. The only two things they had lef'! The nuts flew out an' landed on the ground, that's where they found 'em. They buried 'im three days ago in a box...the mother got so hysterical she fell inna grave, you know, they Arabs, dey cain' help themselves..."

Death...I couldn't get used to it. The death of Sal didn't seem real. It was a tidal wave getting ready to engulf this entire country, it seemed to me now. The statistics I read in the paper day after day scared me and I could almost see myself in there with the rest of the dead black kids who had their brains blown out over trifles. I didn't know him, but it was frightening and painful just the same to hear of his death. He always seemed so very quiet, so innocent. How I could have wished that Concha AND Lolita, whom he died for in all his Arabian foolishness, had been smushed instead of poor Moustafa!

The coke racket. How I well remembered it. It was rampant. Lolita and Ding Dong were well in it. One time she walked in the joint with blood on her dress. It was from all the damn holes she had in her nose, by far. She snorted like a bull. You could even hear her in the back with Maggie and Ruby, who were the two centerpieces in the dope racket. They got their shit from Louangphuck, who got the coke from a Cuban dealer operating from an El Salvadoran agent in Belford, who in turn operated in Miami, and further into Colombia—and also opium from a friend she knew in Laos, and not to mention marijuana, of which she had plenty. She even grew marijuana plants in her house. All in all it kept her quite well off—but she wasn't showy with her money. She got the dope from the agents, she sold it to the stool pigeons, and the stool pigeons sold it to anyone they could hook up to. We knew it was drugs because strange people absolutely unconnected to the Dummheit franchises would pop up asking for "Tramie," "Connie," or "Ruby"—those names spoke for themselves. Extreme tactics were used outside the premises; these girls and their lackeys took up turf, they even blew up tenement houses and threatened all the dealers and the other agents.

The dope came in innumerable forms—for one, it came in between the two sides of a record they pieced together. The record was in Lao—as was all the packages I found lying in the trash, marked "Vientiane" and shipped out as fast as possible through absolutely secretive means. Her agents had unlimited access to the poppies. They took part in that Golden Triangle operation. As for the coke, it came from Bogota—but these were burnt, because of the Spanish-speakers in the joint. Tramsokong Louangphuck was the only Laotian working there at the time, so the weird Lao scribbling was seen as just another one of her letters from overseas friends and relatives. And Lolita, too, was buying it regularly. Even Basil had some from a girlfriend of his. Ding Dong had plenty. And not only that, but Lolita was drinking with her boyfriends quite hard—gin, brandy, whisky—that strong stuff. Indeed one day she turned up dead drunk, after getting soused up in a nearby pub with Ding Dong. Watching her wobble around like that, I knew I could pull it off. I was on break to boot. I led her downstairs carefully and she began fussing. "Whadda you do, you fool! Ge' offa me, stupi'! Leeme alone! Gedadah heah, now...oooooooooh! Dat feel so nice! Wha' you do to me?" I felt up in her crotch. She forgot to put on her panties. She probably had another brat coming for all I knew, for I could tell that she had been screwing with Ding Dong just then, because I could feel the spunk...she wrapped her arms around my neck, giggling, me dragging her along to the ladies room. Barnaby wasn't washing the pots—Yo Yo was, since Barnaby was off. Yo Yo didn't notice—his eyes were dead set upon the pots. Good. I clutched Lolita's bony ass and led her inside. She began to strip...she was drunk as all hell...she lifted up her skirts. Quite a pleasant surprise—she was well-made, one of the delicate ones, if only a bit small at the hips. Lolita looked up at me..."C'mon, stupi', fuck me! No—eat it, lick i', touch i'!...Put you' mouf on it...c'mon, he nice, he no bite you..." So I ate it. It wasn't too bad—I held my nose...She fell into one of those sexual comatose states. Then I felt her jerk—she had a little orgasm. And another little orgasm. And another. And another. I looked at my watch. 40 minutes to go. More than enough, I thought. She got up, sat upright; she didn't know who I was. "C'mon, stupi', lemme feel yo' bawls!... mmmmmm!...dey very good..." She went for the balls, sucked on each one, and stroked the shaft just the same. Penny could've eaten her damned heart out for this one. She sure knew how to suck for a fifteen year old. I heard Concha was better...I almost blew off in Lolita's mouth thinking about Concha. I had copped her ass one time, but she hadn't blown me. A thirteen year old sucking you off, a fifteen year old licking your nuts...and from a Banana Republic...I had to cool off. I took it out but she grabbed for it again. "No, no, more, more, I show you trick...lookie!" She took it all the way down...to the balls...she almost swallowed those, too. But it was taking me a long time to come. So much the better. I was sick of those fast ones. I liked it good and slow. I had half a damn hour, so it didn't matter much. The blowjob went on for fifteen minutes, because I kept holding back so skillfully. But not only that, Lolita's weird get-up put me off too much and coming was difficult. But her voice got me horny; that spicy Latin voice and those slurping noises she made were sexy as all hell. Finally I thought of fucking her in the ass. I turned her over and used the grease from the fried chicken bones lying on the plate to oil up her ass. But it slid right in just the same. She'd been buggered so many times she could open her rectum up like her own mouth when she relaxed her asshole. It was a nice, snug fit up in there, and the rhythm was good and rolling. But still, I couldn't come. Then I thought of Concha. Thirteen years old...I came in no time. I almost cried her name out loud. Whew! That was a long one...

I left her on her back. She got up and threw down her skirts. She was still completely drunk. I went upstairs for my "dinner"—my chocolate cake with cream and fried chicken for the belly ache and the tea which was always lukewarm. But then, BOOM! CRASH! Something's rolling down the stairs...I look...it's Lolita! She tried to get up the stairs. But she laughs still. Blood runs out of her mouth. She knocked out her front teeth. She wrenched her back so badly—she's like a pretzel—she'll have to get an operation for that one. Fool bitch! And she was flunking out of school, too, I heard. Wasting money. She wants it all too soon...she's just making a mess of her life.

Then there was Concha. I thought of her all day. I was lucky to have been chosen to clean the bathroom again for Concha was in there douching herself in the toilet. For the hell of it, I dropped my pants and opened the toilet door—then closed it. She squealed. "Oooops! My mistake," I lied—and went back to cleaning. She got out. "Whaaa you wan', fool? Whaaa?...Hey," she said, her voice heaving in obvious anticipation, "you fuck, yeah? You like fucking?"

"Oh, no, I can't stand it," I lied. "It's filth!"

"You wan' to fuck me? Free! No charge," she squealed in lust. Her squealing was driving me hysterical. Thirteen..."C'mon—I suck you. I give goo' head!"

I sprouted a gigantic hard-on and went to the door and locked it. "Okay—go ahead!"

"Wai', stupi'! You ga' pay monee first!"

"You lied!"

"No, dat was for fuck. For suck, monee! Gimme one dollah!"

I pulled out a dollar and gave it to her. She unzipped it and pulled it out and smacked those juicy red lips and went to work right away, jewels, blown-out dyed red hair, long earrings, red high pumps, tight skirt, plump juicy ass, midriff and all. It was excellent. She was a master—and thirteen! And she kept grunting when she did it...I suddenly felt something the size of a bowling ball deep in my crotch, rising and growing ever harder and harder and harder, until it finally exploded in torrents of jism everywhere...it was a gallon of it, all over her face, all in her mouth! Probably the biggest of all. It even hurt it was so good. It was all over the floor. Her face and mouth were all white inside...she let some dribble down...I spurted one last right there...it was too much...she was a hot piece of tail...just like a porn flick. But it wasn't over. I got it back up and took her cunt from the rear. She began giggling, then I jammed it in her soft behind, and as I pushed it between the plump cheeks of her ass I heard her swallowing the juice from my balls...thirteen and from the South American jungles! A pagan! Loose! Hot! Dirty! A savage pussy! A steaming vagina! Twat of the tropics!...All that kept popping up in my head, I switched from her ass to her cunt again, she kept yelping in Spanish, clenching her twat muscles—and I ended it all with one good, agonizing blast of sauce for all it was worth!

And the soda jerker was hot stuff, too. I pursued her—but failed. She was one of those stuck-up puritanical Chinese. Yet I did something incredible the same night. I succeeded with Rosa in the back of a Belford movie theater I visited with Giuseppe and her. Giuseppe wanted me to come along with him and Rosa on this one to make sure that I knew that he was really having an affair with her. I believed him by then—but he wanted to make a point. Rosa had shock treatment and got over the catastrophes which befell her a few months ago, and apparently her genitals were back in working order and as hot and randy as ever. When we got in the theater and settled down he was sitting beside Rosa and Rosa beside me. Good old Rosa—squashed right in the middle. She began getting hot after a few minutes into the film. "I want it in my mouth," she cried for the umpteenth time. So Giuseppe unzipped his fly and Rosa was so eager she pulled out his dick and sank her molars into it and began sucking on it. Giuseppe sank back, eased up against the chair. I looked at the smug contentment on his face—he ought to be peed on. The bastard...and I go on like this without getting a piece myself. But not just yet...for I notice that Rosa's fat ass is sticking right under my nose; I also notice she's wearing a long thin blouse, which is perfect because it's more manageable. I know she doesn't care what happens to her, so I stick my hand up her blouse. She isn't wearing any panties. Still more perfect. I get my ass over the arm of the chair, pull out my dick and shove it up her pussy. It feels wonderful—just like putting a hot burrito on my shaft. She moves herself to the rhythm. All the while I face the movie screen; Giuseppe's in such an ecstasy he thinks I'm sitting and minding my own business. I think and then wipe off my cock and bugger her real fast, taking a risk because she might still have shit up her ass for all I knew. But she was real good and tight up there, also. But then... "Fuck me, Giuseppe!—no!—eat me, lick me first! I like it!" I sink down. Now she turns the other way around and Giuseppe begins to eat her. Her face is right over my dick. She says nothing—she just takes it and puts it in her mouth. I'm sitting down, watching the film, minding my own business. They seem to hear our grunts but nobody pays any mind. Nobody gave a damn—because it was the good old Belford theater near the 10th street "honky-tonk" district. Rosa was a big disappointment this way. She hadn't much skill, at least in comparison to some of the others—she was overrated. I didn't see what Giuseppe was getting all excited about. She kept biting it and gnawing the wrong way, just like a little girl. That was wrong. She obviously didn't know much better, anyway. She was just all heat—period. Her sisters knew better, especially Concha. They had more control.

Going to work the following morning more news hit me through Basil. He told me Barnaby, who was off, was falling in love with Louangphuck. LOUANGPHUCK? Of all people—a snotty little hophead like Tramsokong! "He wants to marry her," he said. "He's seek, mon—he dunno what de world is all erbout. Ey, Louey mon, wanta tell you som'ting. You know yestahday, I FOCK Poosy. Toi Poosy! She a slot, mon! She want eet in her mout', like awl de odder girls! I got Rosa, too, mon—when I go out wid Giuseppe. She fuck an' suck me in de bat'ruum, you know?"

"How about Lolita?"

"Lolita??—yeech! She da woodpecker, mon! Me no fock wid de woodpecker! Da hell—"

The bus suddenly stopped over in South Belford, and the Chinese and the Vietcong got on. I noticed a battered face in the crowd. It was Gu Fi. She sure had been clobbered, who ever had done it. Jonas then leaned over to explain, since the both of us looked puzzled. "You know dat damn Johnny-Boy, Basil? He da one who did it. He *raped* her, man—an' he got away wid all of it," he said, with an angry whisper.

"Shit, he raped Rosa, didn't you hear—"

"Yeah, I heard dat from Maria," he said, shaking his head. "Dat nigga even wanna get down **her** pants, but if he do, I'm a chop his nuts off...Look, I been here eight years an' I ain't had to put up with as much shit den, in de old days, as I got to now. Really, dough, it was morea less da same ol' shit. Ain' nuffin' changed, 'cept for da worse. Nuffin'. Dere were niggers like Carlin back when I started—but this muthafucka is gotta be da worst! It's dat Carlin sonovabitch...You know what, man? He ain't even a manager!"

This was impossible to believe. "No way! He's got a tag on saying that—"

"Nuh-uh, man, he's only in trainin, see. Quackenbros don't want him to be a manager, 'cause he ain't got no responsibility for shit. Really, ain' nonof 'em do, but Carlin is sick, real sick. All he do is go aroun' beatin' peepul's asses!"

"Hell, mon, so do Albino, he no different! You see dot fight between Mario an' Albino?"

"Yeah, but...look." I thought, then and there, uh-oh, now Jonas is going to be the next one who's going to be occupying our motherfucking conversations and mental gossip columns! "Look. Albino actually had to hold Carlin's ass back 'cause he was gon' KILL onea dem damn workers. In fact, he DID kill one. You know dat Chinese girl Yee Sing Hwong? She was KILLED, man—"

"Nuh-uh, she kidnap—"

"Kidnap SHIT. She was killed, doncha see, man?—see, yall don' know nothin' do ya?"

"Now what in hell are her parents gonna do about it?"

"Dey dunno 'cause dey done made it look like she—ahem!—got kidnapped by onea da muthafuckin' turnovers! Dass flimsy as fuck, I kin see right thu dat shit. An' all da blood...DEY TURN DAT BITCH INTO SOME FOOD YOU DONE ATE, MUTHAFUCKA!!!!"

Everyone was dead silent—why not? What was there to say in the face of such exploitation?

"Rosa's suing them, isn't she?"

"Yeah, but da' ain' gon' do nuthin' 'cause millions o' niggahs 'round da country suin' dem apes. I gotta lawsuit again' them fo' tryin' to fuck wid my money. Stealin' fo'hunerd dollahs from me—what dey ows me from two weeks back somewhere. Dey ain' shit..."

"Can't anyone fight back?" I suggested, seeing how passive everyone was. "You know—if not sue them, since they're always getting away with the shit, but perhaps blowing up the joint or something—"

At this suggestion everybody began to grow talkative and disagreeing. They couldn't do that, they suggested—they had to survive, to feed their families. Besides, it was hard getting jobs these days—the times, even though it's supposedly a boom time for most of the Americans, aren't too swell for us, for more reasons than one. "Why, mon, if Rosa qwit, what oppen to her? She get her fat arse ebicted!—" Jonas shook his head. "Ain't it a bitch," he added. "Dem niggas goin' round usin' dope, puttin' Spanish fly in some Chinese girl food, her coffee—yeah! you know, dass another thing 'bout dem foreigners, why dey get their ass kicked. Dey donno dem whiteys like we do." Basil looked at him and laughed. "Serious! How da hell else is some stupid ass Chinese girl gon' trust some crazy ass whiteys who only thinkin' about her ass? She shulda known betta, 'cause she was hot." He chuckles. "I mean, she was gooood, for a Chinese chick. Gooooood! But dumb. Won't no American..."

"They're simple-minded chumps," I interjected.

"Yeah, they simple all right, but dey ain' no chumps—"

"Nuh-uh, mon! How erbout Lolita! Ees dot a bohstahd or what?"

"Well—dem damn Spanish is fulla shit."

"But you like Maria, dough."

"SO?—Maria different. Rosa's a fat whore...she caint hardly fuck, neither—ey, Giuseppe around?"

"Naw, he says he's 'sick'," I said. "It's a trick. Rosa's off, too—it's her day off as well."

"He's always sick whenever Rosa off."

"Rosa ain' shit, man...she ain' had no real experience—"

"BULLSHIT! mon—damn! Dat ees bullshit! She keep sperm—"

"SO!!! Dat don' mean shit, neither! Look—it don't matter how long she been doin' it—an' I know from my owwwwwwwwwwn experience!!—*she jus' cain' make it in bed!*"

"I know from experience, too," I said. "Say—what does Giuseppe see in her, anyway?"

He didn't answer back; he dwelled upon the thought of it, as did Basil, and all of us slumped back after the initial bursts of laughter. We grew silent, and drifted back into our own little melancholy worlds. It continued that way, more or less, for the rest of the trip. I pulled a book out of my briefcase—now I was safe—and began reading it. I had to remember what my mission was, and that was to get away from these fuckers, not to have orgies with them. I didn't want to think of what was happening between each crew member and the other; it was hardly any solace to me now except as some sort of ridiculous soap opera, my interest in it being almost solely an analytical one. In other words they were just a joke to me...when we ever going to be free of this plague?, I thought desperately now and then, lapsing into the most violent anguish in between laughs and giggles about the silly orgies between you-know-who and you-know-what. I had myself become so fragmented and confused that I could laugh wildly and joyously and inside still be sabotaged with fathomless anguish and despair. I thought alone and to myself as I read my little books on existential philosophy, one out of dozens and dozens of books I was swiping day after day from my father, whose business was, by the way, drying up rapidly—not that I cared—and as I read, their laughter and my laughter, as raucous and uninhibited as it may have seemed, terrorized me to the bone, for my laughter could not be distinguished in the least from theirs.

I kept reading and reading so much that all my thoughts were taken up by these books now and then. Sometimes I would be thinking totally of philosophical matters while reading and chattering about garbage just the same. I had become two-toned; I loved the cafe life with my lips, but with my mind I despised it, and because of this everyone thought, especially Jonas, Giuseppe, Barnaby and Basil, that I was getting a kick out of the dishwashing lifestyle. It wasn't true— but I was so unwilling to make the move to leave and go to where I intended to go in the beginning, or to reveal my true feelings about the joint, that I rarely or never talked about what was on my mind. And yet, in spite of all this, in spite of all the intensive book reading, the persistent devouring of book after book after book in search of answers which would make me understand my purpose for having been born unto this baleful and malicious womb of death, I was sucked up totally, in the end, by the cafe life. Nothing, not even Ramakrishna, could have intervened to help swerve me out of that radioactive rat race. It was too late already. For the words and the books and the little decent music that I could get my hands onto had become a hideous racket which was no less foul, disorderly, horrid and stultifying than the Steinway plantation onto which I was chained—**permanently.** For it was not my expectation to find, once I had come home from work one night, all the furniture from my home thrown out on the lawn—and then vandalized with the utmost ruthlessness. It was jolting. How could all of this had happened? Then I thought—*mother.* She had done it again. My mother's extravagant spending had gotten so much out of hand they couldn't even afford to keep up payments even on the rinky-dink cabin we were living in at the time. I walked into the house and was surprised to find the whole shenanigans torn right up and out: the phone was gone, the bed was gone, the couch was gone, all the paintings and all the coffee tables and chinaware were gone—and when I went upstairs I wasn't surprised to find that MY own bed was gone. I was disturbed. What the hell's going on? I thought. Then I beat it downstairs and found a note lying on the ground. I picked it up. It was from my father. It read:

Son—
PLEASE CALL THIS NUMBER AS SOON AS YOU GET THE CHANCE. THIS IS VERY SERIOUS.
Your Father.

Well...I called the number. And this is what they told me:
"What's going on?" I said, starting out matters.
"Well, uh...I guess you can see, can't you?" my father drooled idiotically. I was so furious I wanted to rip out the public phone. As a matter of fact I decided to hang up the phone. But then, all of a sudden my mother came on the phone booming. "Where the hell are you, Louie? What's your problem?"
"What do you mean MY problem? Who got us kicked out of here anyhow?"
She paused for a few seconds. "Well?..."
"Who?...well???..."
"Forget it, Louie," she said. "We're staying at a hotel downtown for the time being until we can sort things out...we're movin' into an apartment in four weeks—"
"FOUR WEEKS???"
"Yes...now don't you raise your voice at me, young man: I'm your mother, don't you realize, you little snot?...now look. We just...had a little trouble paying the bills, that's all—"
"Looks like more than a little," I groaned.

"What we want you to do is loan us eight hundred dollars out of your account to—"

I was so outraged at the very word "loan" that I hung up the phone promptly. No way, ofay!

After this I rushed over to the bus stop to await the bus that would take me to the slaugherhouse. The same old crew was there. But this time Giuseppe was here and we couldn't talk about him today. He was laughing. "Man, you won' bulieve dis, man—Albino an' Carlin are lovers!" he says, laughing. Not surprisingly people wave their hands at him. "It's old news," I said. "Remember the time cards?"

"Man, you niggahs lyin'," said Barnaby. Well, Barnaby was never too bright. "Naw man—is da truth," Giuseppe said, still laughing. "You know why? Cause I finna dis out from Jonus who spy on 'em one day, y'know. Ain' day' right, Jonus—"

"Hell yea, man," he said, giggling and slapping Giuseppe some skin, to which Giuseppe responded by snatching his hand away and brushing back his hair, giggling. "Silly muthafucka," Jonus said. "Well, look man—naw, I shudun say dis, it's live. For real—I saw some sick shit, right? Carlin get his ass..." he broke up laughing...

"Man, I don' wanna eben hear dis," he said. Lolita gets on the bus. She's early today. She goes toward me. "Ey, stupi'! What you waa, fool—"

"Awwww, siddan an' shaddap, bitch! Ain' nobody wanna heah dat shit! Goddamn Mexicans...ha! ha! well! Carlin got his ass butted, see," he said, with a laughing drawl. Lolita frowned. "Whaa you ahgly fool tawk about eeny-way?"

"Nonea your goddamn business, Woodie Woodpecker!" I snorted.

"Fuck you, ugly! Feo!"

"Your mother, woodpecker head—"

"Will you stop call me woo'pecker head!"

"Das cause you look like it, bitch, now shutup an' lissen to what I gotta say. Look...Albino was fuckin' Carlin up da ass!"

Lolita grew silent, her slitty eyes widened, and she leaned

forward to hear more. "You serious, mahn? He really FOCK him in his *ahss?*"

"Yup—an' I see every damn bit of it."

Lolita broke out laughing hysterically. "Ey," she interjected, "you proba'ly enjoy mossa it, deedun' you, eh? He feel good for you!"

"Well...I dunno what'chall be doin' wid Concha an' dem. Hey!"

Now Gu Fi gets on the bus again. She's been beaten even more. Both her eyes are swelling. There's no way she can work—they'll have to lay her off for the time being. "Man, she can't speak English," I said, because Jonas was thinking about going over there to comfort her. "She'll never take it from you—"

"Man, she been beat up a lot by her husband. But somea you people workin' at the dumb-ass Dummheit cop her ass, too. You-all try ta seduce her...naw, don' gimmie dat shit. We all in dis together. Same old shit. Well...da las' time, Gu Fi was vacuumin' da rug, at night, y'know, when Johnny-Boy conked her onna head wid a broom handle he sawed off, right? an' then, he left, the cops came over, but she was zonked, you know! What could she do? Nothin'. Not a fuckin' thing. See man...de peepul here is slaves, man. But you know man—I wanna quit. I don' wanna work here no more. I just wanna get my back pay—"

"Dummheit neva give back no back pay, mon, dey a buncha fuckin' crooks," Basil interrupted with a warning.

"Dey will when I ask for it," he insisted.

"What about Johnny-Boy?"

"Johnny-who? I whip his ass!"

"Or Maggie, the stool pigeon?"

"Fuck her!" he shouted. "Dat fat-ass monkey bitch—she ain't a parta dat shit at all. If she start some shit—"

"She treat Looey an' me wid a gon, mon—she real bad!"

"Fuck—I get my own gun. See, man—you-all is scared. I ain't scareda nobody in dis joint. See—*don't let dem niggers kick you in your ass!* An' you, Louey, you smarter dan dey are. You a college kid—you workin' your way through. Go head, read dem books. See, dey don' like it if you read 'em, cause they want you t' stay stupid like dey is. When you stupid, dey can fuck you over. When you gots brains, then they useless, see. Then, dey gotta KILL you—dat's de only solution dey think up. See, Louey, dey don want you t' dream **BIG** dreams. Dey want you t' think about they fuckin' dishes. Fuck that— once you get out, *break 'em!* Why the fuck not? Do you know anyafum which is wortha fuck? Not one...hardly. Da women all sluts..."

"Who you calla slut, you fool!" snorted Lolita. I recalled I diddled her when she was all crocked and whatnot. "You— whore! Lookit her...fiddteen year old an' shit, an' you sniffin' COCAINE!!" he screams. "Man! What inna fuck is dis worl' comin to? It won't even dat bad twenny thirdy years ago."

Giuseppe interjected: "Das because you wern' born."

"Don't matter—my muvva tol' me so.These bitches is da scuma da earth." He laughs. "But sometimes dat works bof' ways, if I wan' somea dat thang, ha ha! They think they so cute..."

"You crazy, you beeg blockhead," Lolita said, grinning and smirking and waving her hand at him. "Keep it up, whore— you ain' shit. Like I said, dey think they cute, but dat works bof' ways in my favor if I want dat *thang,* seewhatI'msayin...I hate that. Like that Concha bitch."

"Why yoo talka bout my seester?"

"Why, 'cause I popped her." Lolita's eyes lit up with surprise. "Yeah, I popped her. So what if I'm thirty-three yers old? Hell—pussy is pussy!

"Now look—if dose people knew better, dey do somethin' erbout dose drugs goin' round. But, y'see, DEY DON WANT TO. An' ya know why?"

" 'Cause it keeps 'em stupefied," I butted in.

"Yeah—an' dey makin' too much money. Inne end, dey so HIGH dey cain't sue nobody for da damage dem crackers done done. Dey cain' *fight*. An ya GOTTA keep fightin' it, if ya wanna survive. You cain' be no savage like da resuf 'em. Den you just wastin' you energy fightin' WIF' em, see. Just fight dem da fuck OFF, ya dig?: dats' de only way."

I kept those words in mind—but hardly when, one night, I stepped into the rest room of the Zilch to take a piss. I was on my way home to take a light nap because I had to rest up in order to get over to the Hotel Mierdalino downtown in Washington to give my mother the promised three-hundred-dollars which I had scaled down dramatically from the eight-hundred she wished. She was sore as all hell, and I was intimidated to meet her, but I had nowhere to stay, since the house wasn't ours anymore, and I really had no right to sleep in the house but I had been staying there for the last three days since they got booted out. Well, by that time, all the furniture had been stolen and I was obliged to stop by the Levitz furniture store up near Zilch but I was seized with vertigo because one of those terrible piss-pains you get after many an hour was coming on strong. I had to relieve it fast. So I trekked up to the bathroom and found Giuseppe and Pu Sei fucking on the ground. Goddammit, I couldn't even take a piss in peace. Pu Sei saw me and jerked herself up. "Pee on me," she cried. I didn't have time for it—but she made her own time. She was so sexually hysterical it was frightening. She pulled it out and I just pissed it on her; it was too bad for her if she didn't like how I degraded her. But she loved it...she had a violent orgasm when the spray hit the roof of her mouth. That signaled me to jump into the action. She enjoyed urine, as I could see. Giuseppe was boggled at what I just did. "Well shit...I gave her what the fuck she wanted! Why the hell do you think I came, anyway? What the fuck's a toilet for in the first place? PISSING AND SHITTING!!"

"Forget it, man," he said. "She love it. She wild. Wait—I take her mouth. You get on de odder enda her mouth. She gonna suck us together." My head was trying to piece things together, trying to make sense of all this crazy crap...me? and Toi Pu

Sei?—in the bathroom of a warehouse? In an orgy? What about the furniture? "C'mon, man, hurry it up!" Well...Giuseppe got that old dick of his ready, giving it a few good strokes till it was good and red and thick just like a fat sausage, the end swelling up like a gigantic acorn—and Pu Sei leaped for it hungrily and eagerly, jerking herself off as he rammed it in her mouth. Then he eased up, and made space for me. Her mouth was incredibly elastic, like her cunt. I stuck it in and she sucked on the both of us. Both our cocks were mashed up against each other—she did that herself and slurped greedily and ravenously on the two heads. You'd've never thought she was like this if you saw her working! Now it was time to really let loose. We pumped our cream into her mouth; when we finished, Pu Sei lay right out before us and spread her legs wide open. She signaled for me to take her cunt; I did without delay. Giuseppe got underneath to her ass at her beckoning— and the both of us turned her into a sandwich. In the end she was filled with our seed—which was a problem, because she ended up pregnant. She said it was my child, but Giuseppe had taken her cunt and blasted there, too. Maybe it was both of ours just the same. Anyhow, we were in deep shit—for she was engaged to a white boy on the campus of Georgetown U. She had to get rid of that thing before it started growing—for the white gorilla thought she was a virgin. He hadn't copped her at all and his assumption was that no one else had. (Pu Sei—a virgin!) On top of this he was a pure American type of cracker, because he was in the ROTC and, according to Giuseppe, belonged to the John Birch Society. That's just what we needed—another cracker like Carlin on our backs!

I made it to the hotel by way of the metrorail, but when I got there it was deserted. May I hasten to add that this was one of the worst places I have ever seen before or since. The place was so indescribably squalid, dangerous, desolate, cold, smelly and wretched, with screams in the other rooms, a hint that there may be murder running amok everywhere in all these filthy rooms; it was hard to believe that such a place could be allowed to exist in this country. Well, there was Belford, wasn't there?...I looked all around the hotel room. My face was dirty from Toi's pussy, but the water was even dirtier, and cold to boot... There were three big suitcases lying there unopened and there was a wine bottle there which had been smashed and some blood and a few teeth. **Teeth?!?!** It must have been Pops...he must have been high to shack up in this shithole. If I'm thinking rightly he tripped up and knocked out his teeth on the way to the bookstore. The bookstore...I made it over to one of the trunks. I opened one of them: I was stunned to the floor. No wonder they got bottled out of the house! The suitcase was filled with jewels and furs and expensive perfumes. And she wanted me to lend her some money...the whore! I'd teach her a lesson. I swiped a few good bracelets and stuck them inside of my overcoat and made out quickly. As I did rats scampered past me in lightning speed—one had a hamburger in his mouth... Perhaps I'd get about four-hundred dollars for each of the six bracelets. I couldn't believe it! I was still enraged at her utter insolence. Louie, please give me eight hundred dollars! In a horse's ass!

It had to be the first night in my life in which I was obliged to sleep on a park bench—for about two hours. I was absolutely terrified—but it was safer than the Hotel Mierdando. At least I wouldn't be eating rat shit... I had the bracelets in my pockets and I had to keep careful lest someone steal them and make off with them. I eventually checked into a hotel for fifty dollars a night, cashing in my precious check in order to get some sleep. But I couldn't sleep, because I couldn't help thinking about what had happened just the other day before when Penny, of all people, showed up with a bunch of black eyes and claimed Johnny-Boy had beat her up because she wasn't "faithful". A likely story. He was hounding her, she squealed, and she ranted and raved so much she had to be threatened with the butcher knife to shut up because they didn't want to scare off the customers again like they did in the past. They threw her out through the emergency exit, bribing her with two hundred dollars to keep her big titted ass to herself. Barnaby surprised me because he managed to get down Bessie Ching's pants—the puritanical soda jerker! That I found amazing...but just the same it was probably a ridiculous lie. I was thinking about all this all night and wondering how in the hell Edgar Cayce and Krishnamurti were going to help guide me back to the light of everlasting truth—what in hell were they, side by side with this colossal nonsense? A few days later I went to the pawn shop and pawned in the bracelets, but the man would only give me six hundred for all six bracelets. One hundred per bracelet...I wouldn't accept at first, but since I had nothing to lose, I quickly accepted the offer. Not long after this I began having my problems, too, like everyone else in the joint—I began thinking that I was becoming a bit "perverted." I saw Gu Fi drinking her iced tea one afternoon and suddenly I saw her rush over to get something from somewhere. No big deal...I went into the ice box maker to get some ice out for a soda and I found a bottle of brandy in the ice box. I decided to take a quick gamble. While no one was aware of it, I poured another glass of ice tea and poured just a fraction of brandy in the tea, and switched glasses. Gu Fi came back. She drank the tea. Perfect. She began reeling crazily. Now I've got it...and that day I pulled it off fine. She was way better than Rosa and she had only one man, too. The brandy really hit her hard. Those big tits and juicy ass were all mine...I called Rosa a nympho, but had I been a female, I doubt if I could have controlled my cunt even better because I, as a male, couldn't control my balls, so it was all of a piece—like I had been saying for the last fucking hour or so.

When it was finished I got up and brushed myself back up to make it look inconspicuous. I slid back on Gu Fi's clothes as she got into her hangover. She got back to her senses, wondering just what in the hell had happened—maybe she felt something funny in her cunt, but she made no obvious remark about it, she just looked around, puzzled, and got back up and got back to work. I was busing the tables as usual. It was a fast night. The bell kept ringing and the dishes piled higher and higher on the tables because the line got bigger and bigger. Why? Who knows? Why would anyone want to spend half his life coming in to eat at the same place and to watch us suffer? Perhaps it was entertainment to them?...never mind. I carted out three trays into the dish room and flopped them into Giuseppe's hands, and Giuseppe himself was busy with dishes piled all around the kitchen floor which he often walked over by accident. He was sore at this. "Ey, stop bringin' dat shit in, man," he said, frustrated. "Stop it!"

"Giuseppe," Maria chided. "Stohp! Leeve alone, leeve alone! Ah, *mierda!*" she ranted, putting the cups into the trays. Food gets on the floor and she almost begins to pull her hair out. "NO! MIRA! MIRA!" she yells... "See dat, man?" Giuseppe says, facing me. "She don't want you comin' in here cause you makea mess, see. Go away!"

"Up yours," I jested, and Giuseppe lunged at me as I sailed out of the dish room, laughing. Time passes. Soon it's all over again and Maria and Giuseppe find themselves going for the slop in the machine with all might and main, like wading through a vomit jungle. Water's flooding up the floor. "Ahhhhhh!" she screams, and rambles off in Spanish about the flooding floor. "Goddammit!—LOUIE!" Giuseppe calls me. "Hehr! You feenished, right?" I had just come in with one last tray of dishes and he near freaked off—then he calmed down. "Look,"he said, "here's a trick. See, you do dis—"—he takes the dishes and shoves them under the stove. "See dat? Now, you blame sumbody like Carlos! He a fool! Get his ass in trobol, see!"

"Giuseppe! No! No!—"

"Maria, *te chinga!* I go home. Elsie! You help, okay?—"

"You crezy," she says, twisting her mouth and fiddling with her front teeth. "'Tain mah goddamn werk! Ahm gewin' hewme mahself!" She rarely opened her mouth for anything, Elsie...

I had to give word to Mr. Albino that I was finished, but I was well tempted not to do so. Besides, I had to make it to the bank. I decided to make it to the bank instead. I punched out, sneaked into the locker room and pulled out my clothes and fled downtown to deposit my money from the bracelets and the check. But when I got there, pulled out my ID's and made a deposit, I was startled to find out that all that remained of my account of 4750 dollars was merely six hundred dollars. Now this was utterly insane. "Someone's stolen my money!" I howled to them in disbelief. The clerk in front of me shrugged her shoulders, twisted her glasses and adjusted her sweater and said: "We haven't heard of anything like that, sir."

"But someone's been into my account without my permission," I said.

"When did this happen?"

"I don't know."

"Well...we can't find out who—"

"Forget it," I said, thinking about my mother suddenly. I rushed out of the bank and down across near Dupont Circle and whereabouts where the hotel was located. I got into the hotel and with a hairpin forced my way into the door. No one was there—again. I looked all around for my money—in the suitcases, under the beds, in the refrigerator—everywhere. I found nothing. Maybe my mother was spending it down-town—I didn't know where. There was absolutely nothing I could do now—except steal all the rest of her jewels, and I couldn't do that without her getting me into trouble with the law. Six bracelets were bad enough...I sat down on the bed and began to sob. "No, no, they gotta be here, the money's gotta be here," I said. I looked harder and harder—under the rugs, in between the wretched chair covers...nothing, nothing, nothing. Except rat shit...I was finally urged to swipe the suitcase, but then there was a catch. Before I could do that I would then have to tear open the suitcase because that particular suitcase just so happened to be locked up. There-fore, in order to steal the jewels, I had to get my hands on the key and I could only do that by getting up my mother's cooze because, as I always knew, it was typical of her to be so secretive about her jewelry. I was so absolutely disgusted that I walked out of the hotel with the suitcase. The same rat came back with a drumstick this time. I didn't give a damn; I was going to smash open the Samsonite once I got over to the abandoned home. On my way back to my old home I began worrying about how Albino would treat me because I had left the tables filthy and nasty in the rush to get over to the bank. I could see Carlin giving me a head whipping and I got knots in my stomach. I also shifted my thoughts to the stolen suitcase. I knew sooner or later they would discover that it was me who broke into their hotel room because of the finger-prints on the doorknob. Perhaps I ought to go back to the hotel to wipe off the fingerprints?...

The door's locked on the house. Now the only way to get in is through the bottom basement window. When I do this I began to be wary of the neighbors swarming around nearby who might think I'm trying to break into the joint. Anyhow I get inside—but without the suitcase. Now that's ridiculous. I squeeze myself back out again and get the suitcase. There's someone looking in my direction...he turns away. Just in time...I almost got busted. Then I search frantically around the entire house looking around for a hammer to bust open the suitcase. Nothing, absolutely nothing. I've got to buy a hammer to bust the suitcase open!...Exhausted, I stick the suitcase into the attic and lock the doors. While I'm going through this procedure I jerk my head up and conk myself out for the night; when I wake up I'm already due at the Dummheit. A real bad headache's coming on; clutching my head I make it down to the joint. Albino's there and he's really pissed. "Look, about last night...why did you run off without my permission? Huh?" Carlin comes up. "What happened, Pete?..."

"He didn't clean his tables last night, it seems," Albino smirked. Carlin backed me into a corner, his eyes glazed. "Now look man, we ain't gonna hurt nobody, we ain't gonna hurt nobody. We're just gonna let it slide, 'cause we all know just how hard you-all've been working here now"—and at this, he punches me in the stomach with all his might— "Get to work on those goddamn dishes you shitfuck!" I doubled over clutching my stomach and Lolita broke out laughing. I was furious. Why me? "Shutup, Lolita!" Albino screamed. "It could happen to you," he says, and the both of them go downstairs. Fags...

Giuseppe wasn't in—Saturday was his off-day this time around. I took the place of Giuseppe working alongside Maria. We got to work right away. Then something bad happened. The dishwasher ran out of soap and so I had to go downstairs, what with all the dishes piling up, to get some more soap to put in the machine. "Get goin', muchacho!" she yelled to me with a grisly laugh. But then something worried her, as usual. "Luis!—ven!" I ran back to her. "Where Jonas? Eh? He no here for two days!" "I don't know," I said, heading downstairs to get the soap. I ran into Barnaby washing the pots and shaking his head; when he saw me he signaled me to come near. "Look man—here some really bad news," he said. "Jonus in jail, man—he gettin' his ass kicked in there, too!" I couldn't believe this one! "Nuh-uh! Hold it! I got enough of the bullshit—"

"No, man!" he said, louder. He put down his pans. "Look— ask Carlos, my friend here. He'll tell you." Carlos explained, cooking the rice. "Man, Jonus—well, Concha, you know Concha?"

"Yeah," I said. Uh-oh, I thought, maybe it happened this time.

"Well, Concha get Jonus arrestid."

"For what—"

"Guess, man."

"You aren't serious? Was he doin' it to her?"

"Dass right, man," Barnaby said, shaking his head. "Concha called da cops. Da rumor was dat he got killed by da police—"

"Naw man, no rumor, man," Carlos said. "Carlin set dis ting

up, see. Carlin wanna get power, man. Carlin set it up so Concha get Jonus arrestid. Concha ain' got no money nohow, she need monee to do da stupid shit she do, right? She alway' need money. So she take her shit to da polees about Jonus fuckin' her, right? An' Lolita get some kinda reward money for bustin' Jonus. Like six tousand dollahs. So Jonus get busted for molestation. When dis happen...da police, well..." he sighed, and shook his head, frightened out of his wits already, "d-da police...Ah! *Jonas se ha muerto!*" I forgot my Spanish in the heat of the moment. Barnaby didn't bother to tip me in on it. Carlos tried to hold himself together, but he couldn't and began crying, his tears beginning to gush. He threw a slight sob. "Dey beat him up—" he gasped, and walked off to the public bathroom, leaving the rice uncooked. I worried about the rice like a fool—my eyes were glued upon the pot of rice. "Fuck the food, man!" Barnaby exclaimed in horror. "Look—you know whut dis means, man? She gon' git us ALL in trobol! She wan' dat money. You fucked her—I know you did. Don' say nuffin! I did, too—Jonus—he been doin' it so many times—twenny or therrdy—it's ridiculous!"

"But didn' he have Maria—oh no. Maria's coming. I gotta get back to work. Don't tell her! Nothing!—" I ran in the back and began searching about for the soap. The focus of my mind inevitably shifted towards what was happening in the bottom kitchen. I listened..."...Carlos..."

"...Barnaby...where Jonus?...he seeck?..."

Silence.

"...where Jonus?...where Jonus?..." she said, louder and more frantically. I could hear the Terrible Two coming out to haunt the crew again... "...Maria!...what the fuck's goin' on?...huh?...get upstairs to those dishes!..."

"Carlos!..." I find the soap. "Soap, soap...*Luis! Ven! Ven! La jabón!...donde está Jonus?...***eh??**" Silence from Carlos; Carlin goes wild. "...stop the chattering an' get upstairs! You think this is Mexico, you assholes..."

"...I oughta sue you onea dese days..." says Carlos,

sobbing. I can't bear it. My heart is racing. Albino's going up the stairs; I hear his feet clomping on the stairs. He's in the kitchen. "Louey!" I hear him yelling. I can't take the pressure...my hands are shaking wildly. "...Louey!...where the hell are you?...dese damn dishes are filled to the rim!...all four carts are filled up!..."

"...aaaaaaaaaaaahhhhhhhhh!!!!!!..." a woman's scream—it's Maria. I rush out. She's got her hands in her face. She rushes upstairs. Carlin goes after her. "Wait!...what the hell is it?...wait a sec!..." I go upstairs and to the dishwashing machine. Maria's there. "Nada, nada," she says. "Nossing wrong! Nossing wrong!" Albino and Carlin were confronting her. She'd frozen up and had become a catatonic. She went to handling the dishes while Albino and Carlin looked at and through her. Albino said: "Everything okay now? Isn't it? You okay? You wanna go home? We been too hard?..." he leans forward and puts his hand on her shoulder; right before my eyes, Maria snaps. There was a knife lying there on the sink; she grabbed it. "No, no, Albino! Albino! Look out! She's gonna kill you! The bitch! No!! Watch!! Wooooo!!! Woooooo!!!—" She lunged at them, her eyes widened and she slashed into the both of them, screaming like a maniac. The two keeled over in fright and she broke up dishes on their heads and whatever else on the floor she could find. People tried to restrain her...but it was no use. She seemed to lose all control of her limbs. She just flailed at anything and everything; she hit me in the face by mistake and I fell backward, glimpsing the blood streaked faces of Carlin and Albino and the blood on their natty white shirts and red bow ties as they rolled on the ground. Then she rushed downstairs into the men's room—she no longer knew which was which—and just screamed her head off. I followed, clutching my head. I forgot about my headache for the time being. Carlos was trying to restrain her, then Barnaby rushed over, then Toi Pu Sei, then Ding Bat, then Basil came downstairs. Her hair was all over her head; her eyes were popping; her forehead was nicked by the sharp

knife. Suddenly a fire alarm went off as Maria broke away.
Carlin did this in order to save the business; he wanted to
pretend than an arsonist had threatened to set the building on
fire, but Albino gave the final lie and told the customers,
rushing out and stating that a "fire drill" was in operation. The
customers sped out, obeying the rules. Maria rushed into the
bathroom head first, knocking the door away with her skull.
She smashed her hand into the mirror and cut herself up. She
smashed up the furniture, bent up the lockers, tore off her
clothes and burned them with her matches, and what the hell
not. She shitted on the floor and rubbed her face in the shit,
laughing and crying at the same time. I hid in the pantry, then
came out, looking ahead at the men's room, with the rest of
the crew-members looking on in amazement and anger and
bafflement or in excitement, as was the case of Maggie and
Tramsokong. Upstairs, I heard the ambulance roar and shriek
and the shuffling of feet through the upstairs kitchen and
through the byways and down the stairs, with a stretcher and
a strait-jacket in their hands. Carlin was directing them. "That-
a-way," he said, panting like an ape, "She's goin' crazy in
there!" But when they broke in and found her there was no
noise. I peeped around the doorway and found her with her
head in the toilet. It was like a dream to me...the whole thing
seemed unreal. She was babbling in the toilet when they took
her head out by the neck, grunting and fumigating..."C'mon!
C'mon! this way..." She threw another tantrum right before all
of our eyes. We couldn't believe it. The Chinese girls—two of
them—got into a fierce argument which was silenced just as
fast once one of them mentioned about the "gun". They gaped
at Maria getting kicked and choked, grabbed by the crotch like
some kind of mule, fondled, manhandled like an animal as
they bound her up in the jacket, or tried to. In the end they just
handcuffed her as well as her feet, and held her down with
sticks; they were trying to do drug tests on her. She screamed
over and over... "Jonas! Jonas! Jonas! Jonas! Jonas! *Te quiero!
Te quiero! Te quiero!...*" Some white woman sticks a needle

in her arm...she freaks completely "aaaaaaaaaa
aahhhhhhhhh!!!!!!...aaaaaaaaaaaaaaaaaaaaaaahhhh
hhhhh!!!!!!aaaaaiiiiiaaaaaauuhhhhhhhh!!!!!waaaaaa
auuuuuuhhhhhh!!!!!" She shrieked louder and louder, her face
turning purple, like she was being branded with a hot iron...they
unloaded some shit into her from the syringe...Everyone was
dead silent...

   "...**aaaahhhhh!!!!!...aaaaahhhhhhh!!!!!...**" louder and
louder every time. Soon I rushed out; I couldn't bear it. I ran
out through the emergency exit. Maybe it was just a bad
dream...my headache from this morning came back on in full
force. I almost had to throw up. No, it was real, all real! I rushed
back. I was somehow tempted like a sado-masochist to watch
more, to view more degradation. I came in and saw them
gagging her and punching her to keep her calm; finally they
were giving her the fucking third-degree. Everyone was still
stunned and aghast. She gradually grew drowsier and drowsier,
and this enabled them to bind her up in a strait-jacket and haul
her off on the stretcher. I had half a mind to actually go back
to work. Don't do it, I thought. Nobody cared for Maria.
Nobody cared for anyone else. It was all a jungle, a steel,
plastic, short-order prep abattoir! And we were all responsible
for it, all of us, all of us jerks, all of us assholes! That was the
bad thing about all these motherfucking breakdowns—they
were so goddamn *unnecessary*. I thought about the blowjob
Concha gave me. Every last bit of blood had drained out of my
crotch and my prick was about as numb as a dead eel. She
was into the whole thing; I knew she had something to do with
it, the whore! But she wasn't the only one, Concha. I knew
who the real culprit was. It was every last sonofabitch in the
joint who felt content frying pancakes and eggs and baking
bread rolls and sausages and scrubbing and cleaning and
washing for a bunch of barbarians who didn't know the
meaning of human kindness and consideration. And I was so
fed up with these contented bastards that I abruptly grabbed
the fork out of Lolita's hands while she was cutting the beef for

the customers she assumed would be coming back in. "Stop
it! Stop the shit right now—" I grabbed the broom out of Gu
Fi's hands— "Stop this bullshit an' go home! Everybody!"
"FOCK *you! Preeck!*" Lolita yelled. "Wanna get fucked again,
you tramp?" I dashed out of the building. I just remembered
those jewels in the suitcase. I got back to the house. This time
I could open the door with a hairpin; the other night I didn't
think of it that way. I got inside and up to the attic. Then I
thought: Goddammit to hell. The hammer! I rushed outside to
the nearby hardware store to get a hammer. But when I got
there I forgot I didn't have the money for a hammer, and the
banks were now closed. Shit! I went back home and tried to
break it by jumping on it, throwing it down the stairs, ramming
it up against the wall...nothing doing. I searched harder for a
hammer or a mallet or a hatchet this time. Still the same
answer—*nada*. What could I do about this madness? What?
What was the point of it all?...Guess there was nothing left to
do except return the case to the hotel. I had received word that
they weren't even staying in that slop-den anymore—it was a
different one. I went to the old one and my suspicions were
confirmed. But I did get the card of a certain Hotel Contra. I
went to it. As I snuck into the hotel I was caught off guard by
the hotel receptionist. "Yes, sir, what do you want?" "Yes—do
you have any vacancies?" He took one good look at me and
said: "No sir, I'm afraid we don't." "Okay, sir," I said, with
derision, stepping out of the hotel. I hadn't washed in seven
days—a full week. I must have smelled awful. The only way
I could wash was in the toilet because they cut the water off
from the house and not only that, I couldn't even make access
to the hotel room in a proper fashion. Weary unto death of the
motherfucking suitcase, I hurled it into a river as I passed by
Rock Creek park. The hell with it—let some crook steal it! That
oughta teach her!

Maria stayed in the looney bin for a solid month. She
needed "therapy" to get her back in touch with herself and get
over Jonas's death. By that time I had reconciled myself to my

parents when they got the apartment building. No more sleeping on benches and in rest rooms!...but I thought of Maria almost all the time. I worried about her—she wasn't one of them, really. She was different. There was something about her. I could see her now going through all that therapeutic shit, with that old Freudian-fuck trying to soften her up by shoving that pseudo-self-awareness rot up her poor ass. Maybe that wasn't the only thing he wished to shove up her poor ass...(Her face wasn't too nice, but she did have a hot ass, that's for sure—it always stuck out no matter where she went. It was living jewelry...) But lucky for her, she shrugged it off, pretending she was okay. So she went back to work. By this time they moved Giuseppe up a notch to short-order-prep-cook, so he worked on the line now. I saw her as she worked. She was broken. It was horrible—I had just witnessed the birth of an automaton. She didn't speak—suddenly, she turned toward me and began jabbering wildly in Spanish. I caught snatches here and there, I couldn't understand most of it. I tried stepping away but she shook her head. "Eeet's okay," she said. "You stay. Ees alright." Then I thought of something. I knew my testicles were getting in the way again, for I suggested to her that I take her home because she had to go home alone all the time now. "No, no," she said. "Well, look— you have no one. I won't do anything. Just calm down—I hate every bastard in this fucking flophouse. How's that? *Es mierda! Es todo!* See? Me too...Er, uh, *tu y yo...*er, *tu y yo vamos a tu casa!* okay?"

"Okay," she nodded, picking up my broken Spanish.

So I went with her. And the next night. And the next. I forgot about the apartment and the jewelry scare already. The first night she sulked, apathetic, as if she were in a drug withdrawal state. The next few days she warmed up to me and saw that I wanted to take her under my wing. But Maria was a tough type of lady and she took me under *her* wing; I'd needed to be a big dude like Jonas to take her along like he did. She began calling me *muchacho* affectionately. Thank God she hadn't been robotized like the rest. It was only a gesture, I felt. She took me home to her house. I ate dinner with her—she was alone. She had been living with her family, she told me, up until her breakdown, but then she wished to be alone so she moved into a hovel on 10th street, near the theater. Her eyes met mine and I turned mine down. She stared at me and through me. Then I got up. "What?" she said. I sat down, my heart pounding in anticipation of what was going to happen next. She stared into my eyes. "No," she said then. I was let down—but I got up, and walked over to her. "No," she repeated. I didn't listen. I forced myself on her. She was tough, as I could see—but I felt her power succumbing to mine quickly—and then she clutched me frantically. She sobbed... "Jonas!" she cried. "Ah, muchacho—"

"Yes, I'm your muchacho," I told her, not knowing whether she saw me or Jonas. Anyhow, I played along with the fantasy. Our lips met softly and we kissed, again and again. We got rough and hot. We almost fell out of the chair. I took her up. "To the bedroom," I said—like Rosa to Concha. I got her into the bedroom. She told me, in Spanish, will you be my Jonas? and I said Yes, baby, I am your Jonas, do whatever the hell you will. And she did it. She lay down and stripped naked before me. She lay down in the bed and spread her legs wide open, stroking her cunt. "Fuck me, Jonas...I want you inside me," she moaned, beginning to sob again. "Don't worry about it, baby," I mumbled—and mounted her and slipped it in good and easy. And it was just like that the whole night through. A nice, beautiful, unexploitative, warm, loving fuck...I was her Jonas and she was my saucy impudent cracked-up Maria...I really pulled it off that time..."Ohhhhh, Jonas, fuck me! fuck me! Oooooooooh, baby, it's so beautiful...I'm gonna explode..."

"Te quiero, baby," I whispered in her ear as I fucked her...

"Te quiero," she whispered to me, over and over, "te quiero."

8

BACK ONCE AGAIN to the monotony, the drudgery and the speed and fast-paced life of Steinway Corporations. And now that we're all back there's no hiding and the only thing to do is get down to The Business at hand. Maria is in the dishroom flopping the dishes in the machine in a fury, yelping in Spanish; the chow line is getting bigger because all the shoppers are pouring in for a little bite—a little, because they never half-way eat their food anyhow. The dining room gets noisier and noisier and ever more filthy. The yuppie crowd's sitting in at this hour. Everyone's just beautiful…gabardine, silk, 24-karat cuff-buttons and all. Everyone got either a newspaper or a scandal sheet. Everyone smokes, even in the non-smoking sections. From out in the dining room you can sit and listen to the clashing of dishes and Maria's endless complaints about her fucked-up life. Gu Fi is out on break and sitting in with Ding Bat, who isn't on break but is trying to make like she is. The both of them chat on in Cantonese, as do Clyde and Yo Yo, who are cleaning the tables, but without much enthusiasm. Clyde is also puffing on a pack of Gauloises, even though he isn't supposed to do it. The Jews are beating up a breeze and snorting at the customers, though they're off duty and lounging in the dining room before going home, Carlos is in the cellar cooking the rice without a peep, quietly, content-edly, as is Yo Yo, now washing the pots, because Barnaby with his six fingers is out today, perhaps getting drunk for all one knows, or worse. Anyway, Yo Yo takes his place at the pots and does a pretty good job at it. He's a physicist, he claims. *A physicist washing the pots!* It sounds so silly that I burst out laughing every time I pass him on my way up and down the stairs. They already got too many cleaning the tables—it's about four or five, but it doesn't matter a damn because they'll always have a spare to clean the bathrooms. Bessie Ching is pouring on the drinks; Maggie Constable banging on the bell and driving Clyde crazy since he's got his hands full with three loaded trays full of dirty dishes. Basil doesn't know what he's doing; neither does Miguel, who cuts out from time to time to the bathrooms and dips his head in the toilet and sobs for dear Rosa. Rosa's out on break—in Giuseppe's bed, with Giuseppe, since the both of them are out today. What the day is in general I haven't the slightest idea; it could be Christmas as far as anyone's concerned. A fat black kid is frying ham steaks but also humming the latest pop tunes to keep from going bananas. The replacement chef is pulling the chickens out on spits of six or seven. He talks over and over of quitting and going to Barbados, but he couldn't even get up the nerve to get himself a travel brochure of his home town if they had it. Elsie is wrapping the silverware, smirking, because she had two teeth pulled out and six more are on their way out. Albino, the turd, is sitting in his office and dreaming about what he would ream if he became vice president of Steinway Corporations— all the while nibbling on a bunch of Doritos and counting the blood money. Mr. Quackenbros is out, as usual. But Lolita is in, every day of the week. She almost never asks for an off-day. The more and more confused the scene gets, the more hyped-up, the more enthusiastic and excited she gets, the more she gets a kick out of it. She seems to just fit right in, at all times. And she isn't getting paid much for it, either. No matter, it's what she likes to do—bark at the customers. It gives her a feeling of power. She does it with an astonishing grace for a fifteen-year-old. It doesn't matter whether she's an illegal immigrant, which she is, or knocked up again, which she is, but only this matters, the ease, the mechanized grace with which she barks at the customers, demanding to hear exactly what they want and give it right to them. Just like a telex machine, the whore, but, too, like the cockroach on the floor of a funerary parlor, like the ants scampering at the bottom of the barrel. With six hands full myself, I eyed her with a kind of awed disbelief; she wasn't human. Nobody was. There were so many like her, gutless, fleshless, brainless; there must have been billions and billions more of Lolitas, of every discernible color and caste and creed and country, a mechanical not-quite-human thingamajig lying at the bottom of the maggot heap of humanity, at the center of all things, in the newspaper ads, on top of the soda cans, between the magazine covers, forever in front of your eyes yet always completely inaccessible, as everyone is to each other—so close and yet so apart, like stars. There must have been a billion cunts whose only aim in life was to slash balls, to cut throats, to run the machines, to steal, blackmail, rip-off, cheat, swindle, get high, hustle, and yet smile all the while so as to pretend it really wasn't anything much. And just the same the whole town, the whole city, indeed the whole world was built for the Lolita. She was everything; she was the gold dropping in at 535, the Bull Market and the fat pounds and pence; she was the bus crashing off the Potomac River bridge and all its children and the driver and the bus itself; she was the interballistic missile, she was Miss America, Miss World, Miss Universe, the toothpaste and the popcorn machine and the telephone booth, the KGB and the CIA, the army, the navy, the air force, the marines, the coast guard, the police, the pimps, the burglars, the cutthroats, the vigilantes, the hoodlums and hooligans, the gunmen, the cokies, the junkies, the dirty little brats and the spoiled child. She was also hair curlers and French beer and fried chicken sandwiches and instant breakfast and walkman radios and suspenders and plastic garbage cans and Topolino comic books; she was all this and a little bit more, including the washing machine and the Safeway Superstore. It was only that Lolita was the kind of high-tech muscle-toned freak everyone in The World dreams of nightly and daily, lying on their backs in the beds or slumped over in their office chairs or over filthy kitchen sinks. She, her sex, her aura, was unmistakable, unavoidable—it was a world-wide plague. The moment I laid eyes on her, now fully dressed and rising up from the locker rooms, the time card anxiously in my hands and awaiting the second of doom in which I would have to punch in another indication of my continuing presence in that funny farm, as she stood to my right, up front at the counter top over the roast beef, knife in one hand and fork in the other, barking like a ballsy little female parrot, leading the whole pack around yet only a mere five and ten, her black hair streaked and wild, her eyes thick and dripping with mascara, her cheekbones drooling yet again with rouge, her lips wetter than the backhouse waters, her manner easy yet abrupt, violent, curt with the casual animal grace of a genuine toughie, and above all the voice, the voice deep and thick and throaty, strong as wine, smooth as cream and sharp as a razor blade, crackling and popping in that rambling Spanish, I knew, for once, that I had found *it*, IT being the unavoidable and inescapable aura of the Modern Woman. The very essence, I thought. Perfection, everything perfect right down to a T. To begin with, she always showed up for work walking in style. We knew it was her when, all of a sudden, peeping through the windows, the roar and sudden appearance of a Lambourghini or a Rolls Royce or a Limo or a Ferrari drowned out the din of all the fool bastards slobbering over their plates and clanging their knives and talking. With precision and perfection, she would step out of the car—I don't remember which one, there were a billion!—cock the shades over her head, puff on a cigarette and part her lips to let out a vapor of smoke forming an "O", peel off the fur if it was too hot and show, written across a long, elegant, white streamlined dress, **N'EST CE PAS!**—and it was true! *N'est ce pas la putain!* —nothing passes. Even the air doesn't pass: it hangs in the air like a turd dangling from a string. The world comes to a standstill. The chattering stops, the chewing stops, the shouting in the backroom stops, the dishwashing machine stops, the silverware lays unwrapped, the food stops cooking, the porters quit yelling, the cashiers quit banging on their registers, the bell stops ringing, the boss quits snorting and hemming and hawing, the lights dim all around except around the one little girl for whom the slightest movement of an eyelash constitutes a gesture of the highest sacredness in this world where the genitals are in a perpetual state of war.

Every moment is a sob story to us poor half-wits condemned to death at birth. The whole world is an enormous Dummheit Cafe; half of the people in this world who are born never get out of this cube alive; a still larger portion don't know if there is any other reality than just this microscopic nothingness to which they are condemned, as they all think, by Fate. Meanwhile we all work away like termites carving out "a living," oblivious to the piles of corpses which lay beneath our feet from the mass slaughter it took to build such a hideous civilization which we are now trapped in by our balls. But it is all a part of life, like the cappuccino, the worm at the bottom of the soup and the taxi-cab and the Japanese chopsticks; they, too, the dead niggers and spick trash beneath our feet, deserve recognition as an integral part of the universe. The Dummheit, too, let us not forget, also has its place. You may hate it—and what does it matter, really, whether you hate it or not! One man's meat is another man's poison. Look at Johnny-Boy: it's his meat, the cafe. He digs every moment of it. He thrives on meanness and pettiness—just like the others, and in turn like the ants, like the waterbugs and the cockroaches. Louie, my friend, welcome yourself, if you haven't already been welcomed just yet and it's a bit bloody odd that you haven't after a year-and-a-half at the joint, welcome yourself, at any rate, if you will, to the wonderful, blissful world of the ants and cockroaches. As I said, it's a fact of life: when in Rome, do as the Romans do. Just the same, in the ant colony, do as the ants do, as the cockroaches and the tics and the waterbugs: it's the proper thing to do. And so I do it, no questions asked. I act like the rest of the roaches and the ants. I wash dishes and scrub floors. I take out garbage and clear the tables, I help cook the food, I wrap the silverware, I prepare the pastries, I do this, I do that. I am a fifth wheel on the wagon, but perpetually in use because the other wheels keep falling off. Now I am keeping perfect time. I shoot higher and higher up on their books as the months' pass. They begin raising my pay. They think a hell of a lot of me, the Management. But I don't think the same, of course. I just want my money, my paychecks. But wait…what am I gonna do with 'em once I get 'em?

Seems like there was an answer to everything in the world that happened to me. Not my answers, of course—The Others provided them again. And one of them was Giuseppe— he stopped me on the way down to the lockers after I had punched out. Boy, was I pissed off! I had gotten paid, but what the hell…I had been cheated out of fifty solid bucks. Worse still, my mother took three hundred dollars out of my bank account again. And to top it off, it was an especially lousy day—for me, of course. For them, it was beautiful—they made ten-thousand fat ones. For me, I had to put up with the snorting and whining of six-hundred fat overloaded degenerates barking for the chow. They had me doing everything from cleaning bathrooms to washing dishes to wrapping silverware—they must have sensed I had some reserve of energy within me somewhere and they were trying to grab as much of it as possible. By night, everything was a total mess. There had been dishes lying all over the floors because there were too many customers and then too many dishes for the carts themselves and then a bunch of them ended up broken; besides, half of them never got washed, for the goddamn machine kept getting overloaded and breaking down and running out of soap, then even water. The floor had flooded

over, to top it off. It took an hour to mop it all up. I had shoved
the rest of the dishes under the stove when I heard someone
stepping inside the kitchen. I stiffened. Then there was a hand
on my shoulder and then I tried to break out; I knew just who
the hell it was…"C'mon, man, is me, Giuseppe," the man said,
and then I cooled down. He seemed to notice how pissed I
was so he tried to make the best of it. "Say, you get paid?" he
asked, leaning forward. "Not really—the bastards ripped me
off. They still didn't give me my back pay for the first week they
promised and the other shit for the time they claimed I walked
out on them…it's all horseshit! I'm just an all-around lackey—
and ya know what? I don't have to stay in this shit…really, I
don't. This isn't my native occupation…I got enough money
for what I want!"

"Stay, man, here, you go higher, you makin' monnee here.
They put you up onna books."

"But look at you, though."

"Yeah, what about me?"

"You got stuck up in the machine and you caught pneumonia. You—shit, if I were you I woulda quit years ago. This is an
asylum—they'll kill your ass here. Why stay? I'm outta here in
two weeks."

"Naw, don' do dat. Look, everywhere else—you can no
finna job in those fucking places, dey all bastards. Dey, dey
onlee hire stoodens an' yoppies. Man, dey prejudis. Fuck
dem—is too hard. Stay here. Look, after all dey put you
higher." Here he paused; I didn't know what to say. I remembered all too clearly the drifting from street to street in sheer
desperation and totally broke, a sheer bum, and I didn't want
to go through any of that again. Looks like I was stuck…then
Giuseppe motioned to me. "Cummere, I gots sumtin' to say,"
he said, taking me out into the empty dining room. "No, not
here, we gotta get sumting to eat. Say, get da milks, from
downstairs, dey got some pork-ribs and French bred lef' over
from today. Watch out dough—Mr. Quackenbros is down
dere. No, you stay here, I get it." Giuseppe ran downstairs to

steal the ribs and milk and rice; within two minutes he was back in the dining room with two containers filled with ribs, rice and four milks, two chocolate and two white. "C'mon, eat it," he urged, dey, dem no allow you to get no meal. Dey radder see you starve. You see, I lose my job at de odder place, so dis de only one." We ate; the food was half-cold from sitting in the freezer, but good enough still. We did this almost every night now—not just Giuseppe and I, but everyone else, especially the Chinese. Then Giuseppe had a brilliant idea.

"Look, you need to get all dat outta your system. You need to get cleaned out, I mean, *real* good. I mean, what's da use worryin' about dat little shit Mr. Albino? Nobody likes 'im. C'mon—you just gotta finda way to handle it. You ain't gonna finda nodder job here—not inna next thirdy fuckin' years. Look, I knowa great place where da crew likesta hang out— da **Copacabana**. Sound savvy, huh?—Look, tomorrow night, you get your paycheck an' cash it and let's head downtown. Tomorrow Saturday, right? Perfect! Say, fuck dat, you got monnee, don't you? Den why not lees go NOW, den? Hey, Lolita dere tonight, too. Wid her boyfriend—or one of 'em. I can' keep track of dem too good. But you oughta takea look around. An' you ain't seen nobody dance tell you seen dat Lolita Barabbas. I mean man, dat bitch can *strut*. C'mon, is only ten dollars. Just right up dis street, an' you turn off three blocks—about twenny miles. You stay here, we takea da bus, okay? my car, he's inna shop, hada car accident. Bu' is notta problem, he let you in. Copacabana let you in with no delay. He no afraida nobody, Copacabana."

"Copacabana?"

"Yeah, hesa manager!"

"The manager...?"

"Yeah, Copacabana own Copacabana. It's his shit, das all. C'mon," he says, getting up and putting on his jacket, "les get outta dis dump. No, don' t'row da bones away, make it look like dem Chinks was eatin' here, get dem in trobol. I hate dem, dose Chinks. Dey no frienda nobody. Clyde, he's alright. But

Pussy Toy, she a fuckin' whore. I hate da motherfucker...she oughta get raped by her fodder, stupid bitch. Ey, you know what she did to me once? She pour hot greece all over my uniform an' ruin' it. Den she trow shit at me. She say I'm a stupid foreigner. Shit, lookit her, she can't even speak no English, dumb gook! An' one day, I fucked da shit outta her. You was dere, too. You enjoyed it? Won't she a fuckin whore?...Naw, but I done dat many times. Many times. She a big fat whore—dass it. I screwed da daylights outta her—an she never say a word. An you know where she like ta hang around? Huh? The Copacabana! Hell...dere, she jus' lets all hell hang loose, man...say, you know dat Johnny-Boy? Dat dopie? He been on it since he was fuckin' six year old. I'm serious! An' Gu Fi, too—she on it—OPIUM, get it? Man, the whole bunch is stoned to da fuckin' gills. C'mon, less split."

We got to the bus stop, still talking. "Look, me an' Mr. Albino—we hate each odder's guts. We even got into a fight at once time, you know. Real hate...real hate. Ey! Look man, can you keep dis a secret? You know Pussy, right? You know about her an' Mr. Albino?—dere havin' an affair—"

"I know that one already," I assured him.

"Naw, he's somesing else. She PREGNANT from Mr. Albino, no shit. Man, Mr. Albino, h-he's done it wit' alla da girls inna joint. Except da old ones—he don'e like da old ones. Say—you know Maria? You know her? She do it wit' *anybody*. I swear—*anybody*. Ask da chef. She been like dat ever since Jonus go to jail. She wild now. She do it wit' girls, boys— *anybody*. Ask da new chef. Shit, at one time, I had 'er. Say, you give her fifty bocks or somesing, she your fucking slave—"

"I know that one too," I said again. "She's hot for me too. I've been all up her...she's hot stuff...she'll do anything, you're right. She's a spermulator, worse than Rosa! It's orange juice to her..."

"Bullshit, man, she tol' me odderwise. But—you probalee gave her da monee, das all. She greedy for monee. But she liked to get pumped dough. You could eben piss on her...an'

Concha! Thirteen years old! an' hot as shit—"
"An' fuckin' jail bait, motherfucker."
"How?"
"Jonas went to jail for fuckin' her."
"Shit—he did? How?"
"Child molestation. Statutory rape—that's how."
"But still—I don' care. Pussy is pussy," he insisted.
"That's what Jonas said just before he died."
"DIED??? How dat happon?"
"He was fighting off the cops, resisting arrest, and the cops claimed he had a knife and threatened them, and they shot him in the chest...and that was that."
"So *das* whut happon! Is crazy! But—dat Concha, she still hot, no matter what anyone say—"
"She won't be for long because Maria's put a bounty on her head personally."
"Whadda you mean?"
"Maria's gonna kill Concha, that's what."
"But she go to jail, den...b'sides, no one will ever let Maria kash Concha. Look, see, she can suck beddar dan Linda Lovelace...she a free-for-all. But not Rosa—Rosa's mine, o'course. But—"
"What about Miguel?"
"Miguel? Who's he? He don' mean nothin' to nobody. Shure, he's her hosband...but you see, he can not get it up in bed, see. His dick too small. B'sides, he a priest. He—you see him wid da Bibul alot, doncha? Well...dass dat. But look...I wanna tell you about da biggest slut inna joint an' that's that Toy Pussy again. She'll get your ass rollin' in no time. Not Rosa, like I hear you an' da odders say. Dassa tubba horseshit! Rosa jus' can' be satisfied by anyone else but me, dass all, see. Toy Pussy's da one. Her an' Mr. Albino, Johnny-Boy, I hate his ass. He a faggot"—we got on the bus at this point—"he also on drugs. I believe he got AIDS, Johnny-Boy. He a killer, too. You shoulda heard what he did to Gu Fi. Fuckin' tried to chop her head off—naw, he raped her, dat's what. An' he's gonna

bea new manager...man, I don' tink I wanna stay dere. But you got no choice, you know. An' dat mudderfucking Mr. Albino, he keep—he jammed me up inna goddamn dishwashing machine. Fuckin' had to go to the hospital for pnewmonia, You know what dat is? He don' like da Spanish. He so stupid, he tink I one of dem. An he say to Jack one day, 'Look, we ain't gonna hire no more spicks!' Dass what he said!...straight up...but—but look, tellin' you man, if I don' get that raise within *one week* den I'm gonna get even, I swear ta God..."

We were there already by the sight of the flashing lights and the night stalkers. We got off the bus, the talking ceased. We headed down the streets in anticipation of the great mob. The mob moved in like an ocean; it sucked us in and we were nothing against them. Suddenly we lost ourselves; we were reduced to nothing, not even a number, because even numbers have a place and have significance. In this world you are only a part of the background music which plays on in the elevator or the supermarket. People die, and when a man dies he dies anyway possible just so long as he dies. It could be a chain-saw murder, or a police-raid, or a mob-killing, or capital punishment, or a drug-overdose—at any rate, it has no significance if the same thing is happening simultaneously in forty-five different towns and cities across America. "All in a day's work!" I heard someone shout from outside in the streets—and indeed it was, the murder syndrome of the culture. Whatever happens, no matter how gruesome, is only meat for the headline gristle...at least that's how I thought of it as Giuseppe and I cut up along the streets of Washington, D.C. But we kept on. And we faded into the background like the saxophone after a couple of honks and squeals in front of the rhythm section; like the violin after a virtuoso pizzicato; like the ham actor after his scene is up. We live now only to seek, to search and destroy and devour. The workers world is far behind us. No anger, no hard feelings towards our masters now. Just marching along, just minding our own business, to get pissed and eat and drink and fuck and make merry for tomorrow all of us may die for the umpteenth time. The music shrieks and rattles the windowpanes, the bars get louder and louder, the people more hysterical and sex-ape. There is so much to do and we don't want to do anything but at the same time we want to do everything, or some things, or half-and-half, or most, or perhaps really just nothing but really we don't know what we want yet we wish we did know, yet we do and yet we don't, yet we make all sense and want to make sense and yet we do not really mean what we say when we say what we say when we make sense or not; just the same, we don't mean what we say when we say what someone said about us, that we are young, that we are restless and do not know what we want and yet we do; anyhow, just the same, we're well off, and all we need as a simple solution to life's problems is a beer and a souvlaki sandwich. Apropos of the background music, which is to say, the onions and the pickles and the lettuce and the trumpets and the saxophones, we could do anything we wanted and ask for anything we wish and have gotten it. Sure there's nowhere to flop or shack up with a bitch for the night, but the bars are all in full swing and we got our fake ID's and we can stay there if we like. We can't go to take a piss or get off the street without getting jumped, but there are record shops and movies everywhere, rated and unrated, censored and uncensored. We could ask for fried chicken and french fries, fried lamb and a gin or break some bottles for kicks, puke in the street, draw blood, scream, cry, go on a rampage, beat someone up, stab at random, shoot into the crowd, take potshots at the display windows. This is The World, our world after dark, after the engines cut off...a world in which there is no refuge.

It was far from being the first time I had set foot on that stretch between the wilderness and the ghetto gutters. In fact it seemed almost as if I owned it personally, as if I made it myself, I crossed it so many times. It was Georgia Avenue. I knew each little bit, in and out, the cracks, the markings left here and there, the grass, the stumps, the telephone polls—everything. But Georgia Avenue, besides being a link between the wilderness and the metropolis, also led up to a little place called Pocohontas and it was here that we broke our butts over the stoves and dishwashing machine for minimum wages, soaked up the despair, the humiliation, the cowardice, the fear, the emptiness, the hollow joy, the impotence and frigidity of the workers' world. Everywhere, even in the food and the drink, was nothing but the blood and spit and sweat of the headless drone who beats his brains out for bullshit minimum wages and with no insurance against his own death. Even the tastiest pork-rib plate, together with French bread and Chinese rice and dotted with parsley and pimentos, even salted into non-recognition, called instantly to mind the peculiarly recognizable taste of fried spit—the rage of the overworked and underpaid Spanish-speaking wage slave. Yet, minus the pimentos, minus the Chink rice, the frog bread, the Spanish-speaking wage slave and the spit and slaver of his fathomless despair which grabs you by the throat, there is always, as one peels back the curtains and rolls out the bright red carpet, the one and only citadel where one could, just for a moment or two, forget that he was a mere wage slave, that he lived his life either down in the depths of the ditch or three-thousand feet up in the air in a glittering crystal palace: the Copacabana, that special abode in heaven wherein anyone can find a home, regardless of age, sex, race, color, birth, breeding, religion, nationality, class or caste. It's the abode of the city, Christmas as well as Easter, Pentecost, the Mardi Gras, Lent, Mass, Halloween, Thanksgiving, the New Year, the Chinese New Year, the Vietnamese New Year, the Brooklynese New Year. This is the feast of feasts which no god of wrath may destroy, which may last forever so long as there are computer buttons and creaking cogs and empty meaningless Harold Robbins books, so long as there are pimentos and Chinese rice and pork-ribs smelling of the spit of the overworked and underpaid banana-eating wage slave.

188

Apropos of the citadel and the paradise, I can easily recall, like anyone else, in the countless times I had headed down into the city either alone or accompanied by the workers, the magnificent presence of a castle, a Carcassone of part gold, part cocaine, part pork-rib and part dime-novel. Dupont Circle, it is called, but if one chose to include the rest, let us say The Hyatt Regency and the local go-go, one might as well say it is all of a piece, from the filthiest muck of a nigger shack to the most exquisite international luxury hotels. There is always everything you would want and always a little bit more than you would want: there are always croissant egg sandwiches as well as a kilo of cocaine, a barrel of gin for the drunkard, coke for the cokie, a bunch of magazines for the masturbator, everything on earth set before your eyes in the midst of this open-air variety store of existence made in particular for one handsome group of young men and women, hipper than the hippopotami, moving up, up, up, up, and still up, forever up, up into the clouds, past the slums and ghettos, past the suburbs, past the birds, past the trees, past the airplanes, past the Manhattan skyscrapers, past the galaxies, past God, and finally past each other even in the quest and stampede for the fastest buck, the quickest fuck, the wildest sensation, the newest tweed or gabardine or herringbone, single or double breasted or even triple-breasted, from one citadel to another, from city to city, resort to resort, country to country, continent to continent, galaxy to galaxy. Here, in the midst of the jungle of leopard skin sunglasses and wall-to-wall Lambourghinis, one could do almost anything, be almost anything, try almost anything and still yet get away with it, providing he follow all directions and do as every one else does. One could be almost anything or anyone, providing he never be himself, of course. You could be the King of France or Madame Butterfly, sometimes simultaneously, sometimes in black and white, at half-tone, at quadrilateral and central and mountain time. You could be Nero or Hitler or James Brown or sit in a Parisian Cafe and smoke up a pack of *Gitanes* or *Gauloises Bleues;* you

could scale up Mount Kilimanjaro or Mount Everest at the
same time, you could screw a billion little girls, you could rape
a gook or a spook, whichever your heart desired; you could
play Al Capone, Baby-Face Nelson, Bonnie and Clyde, but
then...but then, half of it, no, all of it, all of this wild and frenetic
activity of the city is done merely to keep from nodding off in
a stupor. Everyone's bored to death, no matter how wild it all
seems, in spite of all the colors, the lights and glitter and crazed
excitement. Somehow every bit of it goes for nothing. Somehow every fucking bit, the skyscrapers, the subways, the
sewers, the Borsalinos, the Lambourghinis, the Argyle socks,
the Trojan condoms, the blaring trumpets and roaring jungle
drums and screaming saxophones and those ever-present
half-hysterical half-naked nymphomaniacs, all of it, down to
the last drop of coffee in the cup, the last spurt of the last
ejaculation, the last drop of piss hanging in the underpants, the
last ant nibbling on the last potato chip lying in the last bag
lying in the last gutter of the last street of the last borough of
the city, springs purely out of the feeling of boredom and
nothingness. Nothing, not even the slightest twitch of a
muscle, has a purpose, even though there are a million
purposes attached and even a million more explanations.
Everything is a lie—the plant is a lie, the tree is a lie, the cloud
and the sun and the sky and the Borsalino felt hat is a lie, just
like the Ferrari and the condom and the ice water and the cup
of coffee and the ever-present blond-blue-eyed nymphomaniac is a lie, like the squirrel, the rabbit, the horse, the apple,
the book, the acorn, the rock, the chair, the music and the
musical instruments, and the sun and the cloud and the trees
and even God Himself is a lie, to say nothing of the Law, since
there are no laws, and of the very Word, since there are no
words which mean any fucking thing either which way
because they are all chaos, all Babel, all a meaningless fatras.
Nevertheless, the pain and the mess of words and the spit
notwithstanding, there are still an infinite number of possibili-
ties for the bored one. Really, one could never be *too* bored;

bored as hell, yes, but never *too* bored. After all, being in a world saturated with money and money, and above that power and power and more power, one could fly to India on the back of a jet-liner, scale the seven seas from top to bottom; one could march off into a North African desert and bomb up a billion A-rabs under the influence of Mickey Mouse, or march off into the Congo or Cambodia and blast a million niggers and rape a million gooks and, if that weren't enough, cut down all the forests, kill off all the children, poison all the lakes and all the rivers and all the seven seas; one could enslave a whole people and ship them to the end of the earth; one could exterminate an Indian tribe, an animal species, a plant or insect species; one could build a billion skyscrapers, visit the moon, Mars, Pluto, Saturn and all its rings, Alpha Centauri and The Milky Way—and yet still crave for more, more, more, beyond the earth, beyond The Milky Way, beyond the universe, beyond God, Buddha, the Tao, beyond life, beyond time, beyond is-ness and not-ness and into the nethermost depths of impossibility.

Deep down in this ultra-magical kingdom of death, I sit with an uneasy complacency awaiting my boat ticket to Heaven at nine o'clock sharp. I can almost hear them sharpening their fangs. The mask parade has begun; as I slip down the streets with Giuseppe, not a peep out of me, I feel myself oozing down into the lowest low, into a death cavern from which I may never reappear. At every turn of the corner they're all there—in leather, chains, spikes, tuxes, wingtips, gowns, Brazilian g-strings, lace, pearls, belly-dancing costumes, what the hell have you. Their eyes eat through me; the eyes of the whole cold hard city eat through me. I cringe; not because of their meanness and their decadence, but because I just so happen to find myself thrown in the cruise boat with them. I'm being savored like a pork chop. It's all a glamorous nightmare turning my stomach over and over: I've become a disco vampire. With me and my "Krishnamurti," how could it have ever happened? I don't know. I don't have any answers. The freaks had no answers, and neither does the neon or the coke or the hooker on the corner with a rose in her hair. It all feels like a tight bodice crunched around me, a monkey wrench clamping my throat; I'm suffocating. Yet, outwardly, I'm happy, I'm gay, the high of the neon opiates has sent electrical charges through my balls. I'm awaiting my boat ticket to heaven at nine o'clock sharp, as I said. I'm loaded now, well-perfumed all of a sudden, sharply-dressed, but any other time, had I turned my pockets inside out I could have noticed as usual that I was broke; I was all douched up and cleaned up and the envy of the fashionplates, but just the other day, and a good deal before then, I would pinch myself at the arms and see that I was dirty and hadn't washed. Tonight, waiting for the pleasure cruise up the Anacostia River to Heaven on Earth in this sweet little nutshell universe, how glamorous and clean and immaculate do I look in my black double-breasted tuxedo with the champagne bottle lying in the ice, my gloves fitted on firmly and my silken white scarf wrapped around my neck to hide the dirt! But it meant not a thing—except the fact that I was a brilliant actor. In truth I was just like a bum—in fact, I was a bum, only I lived in a nice little boarding house on the periphery of the D.C. Belford line, shacking up with a bunch of airheaded gooks. Just the same, I was one piece of shit tossed out and not wanted by the high muck-a-mucks of the crystal palaces. They so despise me they even had a tough time of it putting me in front of the kitchen sink; they would've rather seen me starve for asking, the killers. They wouldn't let me pick out chicken ribs at the slaughterhouses, like they let the Vietcong and the other gooks do: I wasn't even good enough for that. Again, too, they wouldn't even allow me to pump out the bilge water downtown like the wetbacks did; I wasn't even good enough for *that*. Instead, however, they, the great wise men of commerce and legislature, put their great minds together in one great mass of greatness and decided with all this great greatness that, since I kept refusing to swallow this great bullshit, they should throw me in with the dirty dishes. Well...I guess that's just that. They can think what they like. Besides, I've just about had it with those shits anyhow. I don't feel an ounce of regret at having drifted to the bottom of the social barrel. In fact I'm glad. I had and have not the slightest thing in common with these hysterical anthropods. But why in the fuck am I here, then?...Giuseppe's gone, out to look for Lolita and her boyfriend and with whom we will be going to Heaven on Earth shortly. So, waiting by the alley, perpetually on the lookout for freaks, I look at the streets. A sorry sight indeed, for they look no better than dilapidated shithouses, and from on down I can't tell one from the other. And which idiot, by the way, could have ever thought up the silly idea of naming a street by number like in the goddamn coloring books! It makes it even more depressing: 9th Street, 14th Street, 20th and Connecticut, 27th and Dupont, 55th and Styx...stop! help! murder!—In Dakar, I recall now, streets are dedicated to real people, to real places, real events. Same in Istanbul, Alexandria, Marseille, Thessaloniki...the only problem here is that they're the worst streets ever to be made by man in this whole earth and only a fool, dead or alive, would want his precious name slapped on a gutter, or worse. You can't tell them apart. And yet in spite of all this individuality, you'd be killed for trying to be different. That's what's so frightening. Think and think alike. Looking at the tuxedoed termites chewing through the city life like a bunch of hungry moths, I grow impatient. Termites, all of them, all my age, already half way over the hill, all maudlin, crazy, reckless, sophisticated, unreliable, radical, chic, conservative, moderate, democratic, republican, Tory, Whig, Know-Nothing, oblique, awkward, confused, restless, vicious, hostile, white, black, Chinese, Jewish, Japanese, Ethiopian, British, French, Greek, Spanish, Italian, Belgian, Dutch, Vietnamese, Chinese, Japanese, Milanese, Brooklynese, Filipino, Egyptian, Tunisian, Libyan, Iranian, Moroccan, Waloonian, Franciscan, Dominican, Ghanian, Bahranian, Mesopotamian, all-the-same-ian. The whole world has united under the banner of "Bop Till

You Drop." And everyone's walking—not a man sitting on his ass. Where in hell are they going? Who knows? Cathay? The North Pole? Irtusk? Fez? The Mekong River? Heaven? Hell? Purgatory? Pure shit...but, not to worry, for just when I had this final relapse into the real world, Giuseppe pops back with Lolita, fresh from the slop den and babbling like a radio gone berserk and the record set on a billion revolutions per minute. There she is, in living Fujicolor, all smiles and pouts in her long black hair and her tight black dress slit up the leg to the thighs and with a burning red rose in her hair and wobbling on six-foot black high heels, side by side with her boyfriend Ding Dong from Vietnam. As I already know Lolita is from El Salvador and Giuseppe is from Naples and I'm a nigger and Ding Dong a Vietnamese gook. Everyone's a foreigner here, yet all American, American to the bone. American, because no matter where you go in the world, there is the mania for logic and the lust for the fast-tracked life: the irresistible desire of the black sheep to flock with the shepherd of Hell.

And now I'm going off to baa, with my sheepish friends, with whom I have been led out into the pasture of Astro-turf. I am going to chew it out with the termites and crawl down into the manholes. Off I go, cutting through the neon jungle with the rest. I lose my arms, my hands, my feet, my toes, my ass, my head, my balls, my chest, my spine and spleen and thighs and legs and lungs. They become part and parcel of the body of the crowd from which I can never hope to flee in refuge. So, all things considered, stamped, inspected and approved, all shut in the lockers and the keys thrown away, double-breasted Ding Dong walks into the Copacabana as he clutches his hand around Lolita's bony ass. A crowd gathered around us, and we swan in with them, following the juicy perfumed piece of ass, watching her swing her hips to the chaotic rhythm, watching Ding Dong clutch her in his frenzied ecstasy as he clamors through the hallway.

Suddenly I stopped at the doors, the swinging plexiglass doors, and listened. My heart was all aflutter. There they are;

I can hear them inside, working up a rut, the music clamoring like a billion carpenters. For a moment I hesitate. What the hell am I doing here anyhow? Should I just cut out and leave them right off?—but what would Giuseppe think of me in the morning? After all, he's doing this for me...oh, what the hell, move on in and drown. Open the swinging plexiglass doors, wind down the corridor with the multicolored ants, glimpse the flashing lights, the pounding rhythm. Now I'm inside. The rut begins. One, two, three. The buttons are pressed, the gears are shifted to moderate. Lights flash, glimmer, fade, disintegrate, blackout, flash again; the crowd jerks, twists, bumps, grinds, flings itself out like a blotch of molasses...not a hard dance after all. Not if you learn the jerks, the twitters, the cough, the hump and pump, the roll of the eyes, the shake of the shoulders, the grit of the teeth, the sniffle of the nose, the shake of the ass. Nothing to it. Look at Ding Dong and Lolita— it's not a problem for them, is it, Louie Phillips, me lad?...say, boy, I know what it is. It's the paycheck, isn't it? The check you got for one-twenty-five; they cheated you out of fifty lousy bucks! That's a lotta money for a poor guy like you. They ain't gonna pay anything, the crooks! And the way they work you...it's the power they want...they thrive on it, the vultures! Corpse-eaters! They stole it! Every bit of it! And lied to boot!...But perhaps let's say fuck it, okay, don't worry about it. Kick your shoes off and get with it. You only live once. And not only that, the Belgians really own the Congo so you can stop hemming and hawing about philosophy. You won't hear St. James Infirmary for days after you've had yourself a smashing time...who needs that old crap?...

In case you're wondering who in the hell's that, reader, that's the Devil from the other side of the mirror, goading me to get on with this funky maggot action out there. Remember him? I was beside myself, reluctant as hell to make a move in this big joint overseeing the bar where people got picked up, the bathrooms where people went to do their thing, through their noses or their assholes or pee-holes, take your choice.

And then there was "my" gang, out looking for some snatch to take home after wiggling their funky dishwater asses for a couple hours. Some life—is this the world? There was a band on stage playing the same crap we heard outside, except this time it was Latin-tinged, Cuban, in an obnoxious, hysterical, mind-fucking way: it made you think of orgies and dictatorships, or burning tanks, of cholera epidemics, of favelas full of dispossessed niggers, whole families selling themselves, Amazons hanging from coconut trees, as your mind bobbed helplessly in and out of the thundering congas...and here I was out in the middle of the big dance floor with this crazy banana music which was giving me a terrible headache. Giuseppe sensed my discomfort immediately, so he went out to fish for you know who—Toi Pu Sei, the tropical twat. "Wait here," he said, "don' move. I gotsa date an' you gonna get yours." He cut out and within a second he came back with that Pu Sei, that tart from the cafe all ready and steamed up for action. When I laid eyes on her, I forgot everything instantly. She peeled off her fur coat she was wearing and confronted me with a tight white mini-skirted dress framed around a pair of luscious golden brown legs in fishnet stockings. Her tits were sticking out like two fat bazookas pointing in my direction. What a tail! She crackled just like a live wire and shook just the same. Soon the rest came in. Barnaby startled me—he came in dressed in drag! Red high heels! A decolletage! A dress slit up the hip like Lolitas, and all the padding in between...look at the nappy hairs on his chest, it's ridiculous...he's looking for someone to dance with. A girl comes along...now I've seen everything. Maybe the girl isn't a girl. Anyhow Toi herself slips away for the time being and gets copped up by a big butch of a lesbian. The lesbian's all over her; she does it with her just like she'd do a man. Well!...my first time in here and I already know quite a bit about the inner workings of my comrades! Where's Lenin?...C'mon, jerk! Stop thinking about Lenin or you might slip back into reality again. I look around for some fresh provender and I see a hot and juicy blonde who's got her tits out and is wiggling her ass to the beat. The music is beating down on my brain; the band on stage is prancing around like a pack of overheated gazelles, and the singer is sliding and slithering around in kleptomaniac heat. I dance with the piece of ass and get a poke in the crotch and she keeps grinding up against me with that prod. She grabs my hand and puts it on— heaven of heavens, **she's got a hard-on!** I slip away and she laughs demonically. In all likelihood it may be a Dummheit girl; I couldn't tell through the dim lights. Anyhow I've got to get back to earth somehow. The rest are floating off somewhere in space. Giuseppe's laughing up a storm after what happens and so he takes the transsexual for himself; Rosa's out getting screwed and buggered in the girl's room by TWELVE guys. I turn myself back onto Pu Sei listening to the cokies snort it up in the locker rooms. The beat rolling on, we locked ourselves into position and dry-fucked for an eternity, just like everyone else, driving each other to hysteria. It's like masturbation, only you don't grow hair on your palms or catch neuroses or colds or sore throats or anorexia nervosa or tapeworms or dyspepsia or paralysis: it's the only safe sex left. A paradise of dry fucking, no doubt: all this squirming and heaving frenetically, all this wild kissing and slobbering, and yet not one cock sliding into a cunt, out of all these dazed, rutted-up maniacs. I look over my little Toi to find the whole pack of the crowd in the frantic heat of the rhythm section. Dong and Lolita are jerking like roaches on the roof, the two insects grinding closer and closer, their crazy movements going in time to the electronic epileptic rhythm, rhythms themselves which chug like trains getting ready to collide and provide more sterilized brain-fodder to feed my tired ass in the morning. I knew I had to come down to this, I kept thinking; I knew it would happen! Pretty soon I'd be right up there in the newspapers with the dead Palestinians. The whole of my murderous and rancid life polished clean, sterilized and pasteurized and edited for Good Morning America. I can't help thinking about newspapers even when I got the hottest

Oriental pussy squashed up against me like this. What a wonderful world! This shit, plus the dishwasher breaking down and catching on fire...the Chinks quarreling in the back tables, in the restaurants and the dishrooms and the chicken-factories...the niggers cleaning out honky shitbowls, aborted babies lying in the garbage pails, Koreans working the sweat-shops and massage parlors from Philly, Montreal, Belford, Detroit, Los Angeles, Boston, New York, Chicago: the whole world a machine, a Love machine of jerk and pull and spit and snort and fart and fizzle, like the bacon in the pan, like the brick crashing through the Westinghouse windowpane. The music is murder: they're doing a war dance for the Contras. It shuffles us about like popcorn and bangs like a sledgehammer against a steel poll, every strike cutting into the soul like a machete, coming down like thunderclaps over the Orinoco. It's saturated with sex, but the sex is more frigid than the Anarctic Fugue. But now the beat shifts gears; the lever has been shifted to low, which is to say *constipated*—and it IS slow, constipated, drooling and slobbering like a sickly des-perate erotomaniac on a masturbatory bender. I can't keep my head out from under the congas, they're being thrown at me...Look, goddammit, you sonofabitch! There you go again, flying off the fuckin' handle about some theosophic crap again. I thought about the fortune nooky I had plastered all over me. I suddenly grew extremely horny and found as a natural coincidence that my Toi was sucking on me like a burning leech and now she is so hot I can smell the heat of her body. We are so burned up, with nowhere to go and do it, that we feel like screaming. By this time my hard-on is like a rail, pushed to the very limits, and is quite prominent so I stay glued to her; she stays on me too because she says she can feel her pussy gaping and dripping and the juices are running down her hose. "Help me, baby," she cries in her despair of lust... "fuck me, oh God, fuck me, fuck me. Anywhere!" I loved that kind of talk from a woman; would it be that all the beautiful and sexy women in the world would say just the same to me. So I oblige. We waltz around into the girl's bathroom glued to each other like sponges, but Rosa's still in there so we go to the men's room and lock the door. We clutch each other frantically and choke ourselves jamming our tongues into our throats and then I pull down my slacks and she hikes up her dress; she isn't wearing any panties, and the stench just emanates from her. She grabs hold of my pecker in delight, strokes it, takes it in one hand and begins to slurp on it wildly, chewing on it almost. I reach my hand into her crotch and it is so wet that I feel I am sticking it in a bucket of paste. I begin to eat on her, too. I take her throbbing clit between my lips and suck no less wildly; she almost sobs for asking, the bitch. And in no time we are on the ground fucking like crazy, almost eating each other alive in our heat, she screaming wildly as I pumped her, me gasping and choking at the way her cunt gripped my cock like a hand, as if it wanted my cock and couldn't let go. She sure had some pussy talent!...she could probably smoke cigars through her cunt...cigars? Ahhhhhhh! I came like hell. What a big blast of the sauce!...it was a big one, a killer!....I could feel the slop pouring out everywhere, drowning that quim...it almost blew off my balls...everything blurred over in the frenzy. I heard the boys banging on the door, laughing, Basil, Carlos, Giuseppe, the lot of 'em, trying to break their way in. They're coming to get you, man!...I fretted and pulled up my pants and straightened out my tux and my immaculate wing-tips and 24-karat collar buttons. Then I noticed something wrong when I rolled over on my ass; the bottles in my pocket were gone. I was so horny I totally forgot I had them. I glimpsed in another direction; Toi was in a corner next to the shit-bowl guzzling the champagne and the Brandy Ouzo I had especially for Maria. The slut! She lay there with her legs open saucily. She had stripped everything off and she lay on her fur coat. Her head was reeling and she drooled and played around with a pearl necklace I didn't know she had; she probably pulled them out of her ass for the occasion...If I was ever prone to ax murder it was right then and there, sure as shit! "You fuckin' turd!" I breathed, moving in on her again. "That wasn't yours!..." But no one talks to Toi when *she* gets soused. For with her EVERYTHING comes out. She's got a billion personalities and the deeper they are the more perverted, the more they put her in tune to the core of that sex-ape succubus at the root of her being—if she could be said to have a being. "BASTARD!" she squealed, and flung the bottle at me. I ducked, it hit the mirror and smashed it. I says to myself now look boy there a crazy woman before you, she'll do anything once she gets in the mood for it. Better draw a sword!...I moved in on her still. She was totally crazy; she began to gnaw her teeth, and her eyes drooped and got real red and crazy-looking. She grabbed the puddle of sperm and tossed it at me and it splattered on my tuxedo, on my chest. That did it—I was going to kill the whore now. I moved in on her still and got my hands around her neck. She didn't say a word, or if she did it wasn't even in English. Sometimes it was French or Chinese Cantonese, or just plain Metropolitanese, but anyhow she started jabbing me in the thigh with her big spiked heels and trying to get the balls. I cracked her one across the jaw and she fell over; I cracked her again and again and again and she flopped to the ground. I stiffened; I thought, maybe she was dead. Then I softened; so much the better, I thought, as I looked over the red welts in her face and neck and then her beautiful body. I popped a hard on again and decided to rape her in the ass. I pulled down my pants and got over her, then off her, grabbing her leg and wrapping it around my neck and tearing it in with pure hate, pure bestiality. I didn't want to come to this joint anyhow; it wasn't my idea...then I felt something around my neck as I bent over near her face to press my lips to hers. It was the pearl necklace. She was strangling me. It was all an act; she hadn't been killed! She swung me around with the necklace and told me she was going to shit all over me and kill me just the same. I couldn't breathe so I kicked back up into her twat and the heel made a squishing noise which was accompanied by a shrill scream from Toi. She flipped back and clutched my dick and got a piece of the glass and tried to cut it off. I wouldn't hear of that. I cracked her across the jaw again and pushed her to the door and she slashed me across the face with the edge of the wine bottle, catching me in the forehead. I was bleeding like a stuck pig and had nothing to stop it whatsoever. She punched me in my mouth, and knocked out a tooth—and then cut out like lightning. Her hair was all over her head. The crew was wondering what in the hell went on; there was shit and come all over the floor and blood to boot. Toi ran out into the parking lot where she came to a Rolls Royce and showed herself up stark naked. She left her dress in the sink when she was rutted up the last time. The pricks gathered around her like flies: two went to her crotch, two on her tits, one snuck behind to bugger her and one crawled up on her shoulders and unzipped his fly and plopped it into her mouth. She worked away and the whole lot of them began whining. They were all immaculate and all beautiful people, but just the same, the flies did the same thing in the uptown greasy spoon, chewing away at the turds...

Luckily, I regained my marbles after the orgasm. Not before long I was drunk, however. I fell back in a daze, my arms and legs lost in the One of the great white frenzy of the night of the rutting maggots: I forgot about the Copacabana, about the world, about myself. Catatonia set in, even while flinging my crazy ass about, and the music of the murder factory had sucked me down into the great nothingness of the fat, slumbering Heaven of contentment wherein all the killers and war-makers who do not fight other nations and other peoples declare a false peace—only to rip at each other's guts instead. The beat shifts gears, the green "GO" button having been pressed, the hatches down, the levers locked, the pipes screwed down, the windows flung open, the sails unfurled. I watch, but the scene makes no sense; I look and listen, but there is no point in looking or listening because one would just as well be better off looking and listening to the goddamn washing machines. The rest of 'em is on another plane of consciousness—on another planet, to be exact, their brains screwed to the "GO" position and all screaming that incomprehensible, irresponsible language of the metropolis as it was spoken by the apes in the jungles of Neon-ia. The double-breasted maniac in the seersucker is in a frenzy, biting, clawing, licking, sucking, slurping, slobbering, coming, wetting his pants, pulling the cheeks apart. He is bursting with that sentimental lust and love of the TV sitcom and the blues of the empty bed, his patent-leather shoes clicking on the ground, the banana sucker Lolita squashed up against him like an inchworm. All glazed like donuts, slicker than goose grease, the whole crowd lit up with the magnetized cocaine spell of the slant-eyed night, jerking the jerk of the lox, the hair lice, the hamburger bun, the smashed-in skull pieces dangling from the fetid brain pan. This is the music dribbling out like snot running from the nose, the sissing of the broken-up gas pipes, of poison rattle snakes, the notes ripped from the belly of the shrieking guitars. This is the gangrened toccata for iron-lunged half-wits rotting in the back-alleys, the alarum of the vultures nibbling at the putrefacted corpses, battering the guerrillas like Swiss cheese, grinding the arms and legs down into all-beef patties, the asshole hemorrhaging, the shot-up corpses jerking on the ground, the cocaine doing flip-flops in the coccyx, the blood pumping, the eyes popping. Now and then through the inchworm dance the flash and glimmer of diamonds, the soft slush of cocaine bags falling to the floor of the precinct office, the sock in the jaw, the roar of machine guns through the alley, the brick in the window, the splash of shit and garbage in the toxic lake. A wheeze of glib enchantment farting over a teacup of maggots. An incestuous wet nightmare of Kruggerands and apple pies. An insect scream pogo-sticking it through the alleyways, dripping down to the last ultra-oscillated note, wormy with stale cheese, dripping with diamonds and deception. The crowd jerking like radioactivated rats, the beat coming on like a bad trip, arms, legs, necks and heads twisted together into a sailor's knot, sputtering like a copter, belching like a frog. The climax now clomp-clomping in on six-inch high-heel pumps, in a Grand Guignol fade-out through the Rio de Janeiro high-rise complex, now the Mekong sunset ridden with malaria and syphilis! Now the crowd stands aloof and icy as the moon, fists rolling with ease into faces, needles sliding into arms, dead empty genital talk filling the airwaves. There they are out on the dance floor, set square in the thirty-five millimeter snapshot of life, Aquacolor and Kodachrome, double-breasted and silk-lined, bell-bottomed and bow-tied, doped to the gills and still lacking for more, the perilous, reckless disco crowd heaving up and down in a robotic danse macabre on the slaughterhouse floor, the midnight din of a jangling IBM percussion pushing them up and down and back and forth like the atoms and molecules in a test tube. I can see the skyscrapers rising up in the fore-ground, rising higher and higher, swaying to the rhythm of the gutbuckets, the birds falling from the sky, the gas pipes bursting, the roofs collapsing and smoke billowing into the air. War! War!—and the roofs lain open and smashed, the build-ings gutted, the children starved, the men shot in the back and the women raped and poisoned with filthy injections. It's war out there, and it's hell, it's hell. It's a smokeless battlefield and the pricks and the cunts concealed beneath the underwear, the panties, the leather, the chastity belts, the rubber, the spikes, and the latex are the guns, the artillery, the bazookas and the flame-throwers and the dugouts and the trenches and the antiballistic missiles and the atomic land-mines. The world behind them is exploding under a cherry moon, the glass crashing to the ground, the bread-lines fattening, the billions starving day by day, the bullets crashing through the brains, the cities burning with heat and hate and the flies choking the sidewalks as the corpses pile on top of each other, and all the while through the rat-tat-tat of the machine guns the tuxedoed apes sit in the luxury of hell, throttled with the neuroses of milk chocolate and tear gas, cutting their throats and slashing into each other with their cocks and cunts to the very end with this war, this nasty little war, a war of bound and gagged genitals, a blitzkrieg of peep shows and comic books and hair curlers and dildos and condoms and sissy books and GI Joe dolls!

Tomorrow you will see the city falling once more into rush-hour chaos, and the dollar rising and falling, and the belly empty or full or half-full, the gold dropping in at London time and again, like the roller coaster, like the muck at the bottom of the sea floor. Tomorrow, more despair, more muck, more fried spit and banana-eating niggers and nobodies; tomorrow more of the pimentos and the rice and the lentils and the bursting water pipes. Tomorrow, in this jungle of inner emptiness and despair thick and greasy like the worms in a teacup, there will be nothing but the wheel which will grind us down into human pebbles and human sawdust. Day in and day out, nothing but a world soaked and saturated with the blackest despair of this great radio love which makes a man want to run off and either kill himself or gut the nearest Jew bloke. The mechanical flea music of the 254-karat pig-sty is the pasteurized produce of the pork-sausage factory, brought to you courtesy CBS. Every fifteen minutes, another pork melody for the faithful ass-kissing admirers of trash at the bottom of the barrel. Pull the switch and it is there, in Vivicolor, Technicolor, any goddamn fucking color you wish. Take it...just, for once, please leave me out of it. I am not of this this 24-karat pork-grinding machine. I do now devour these cold, processed melodic link sausages, while the faggot banshee crooners laugh their way to the bank. But all of my factory-chums and workaholic compadres, the leech included, are sausage-eating krauts, their sides bulging with the excess fat of their dietary remnants. I am just a puny little hunk of wilting flesh in the midst of this false paradise; my presence in this sink is just a dreadful mistake caused by a slight of sound judgment. I am, by way of my bookishness, one sole living beating tissue in the dead plexiglass corpse of the One of the night of frenzy; but do I know this by instinct or merely by reason? Perhaps, too, I am a sex machine and an ape and a savage like my leechy compadres; maybe my faculties are useless after all. Perhaps, I, too, am just as good and useful a part of the ejecto-world as all the rest; just a cock and balls, famous for five minutes, no more, no less, immaculate and silk-lined and polished to the bone and the veins rubbery and slippery like eels—the world of the grinding wheel and the whorehouse which is half and half of croissant egg sandwiches and the piss-soaked hypodermic needle. All wasted at the wheel, all shoved into the backhouse in a frenzy without a moment's thought for tomorrow. All turned to ape-shit and blasted by the dynamite, and not even allowed to stand but only to drift, to drift to the bottom of the barrel, to drift and fade at the bottom of the muck of the Anacostia River.

But, the roar of the tuxedoed inmates in the multi-shmillion dollar insane asylum notwithstanding, the Kraut mob clamors on and on in the bright-lit streets of neon, dazed, psychotic and degenerating into a thousand disparate fragments, thickening like concrete on the side streets, prying each other apart on a furious desperation—and leaving me torn to pieces and rotted and decayed in the plexiglass gutters, smothered to death in the plastic bag of the midnight dream, drowned to death in the sea of sperm and the maw of the Moloch devoid of all hope, all pity, all courage, all feeling, all joy—everything, every fucking thing except this hypermotorized, hypersterilized, hyperoscillated, hyperbroadcasted, hyperventilated, hypervenerated LOVE of the goddamn high muck-a-mucks which will drag me by the fucking balls time and fucking time again.

I woke up. I didn't have to, though. There wasn't any point in it now—except to keep on down the line where I was headed. Wherever that was, not even God knew for the asking...I get on my clothes and cut out for the Steinway slaughterhouse. I could already hear them licking their chops, the leeches...

I get on the bus, after passing up through the neighborhood. I saw a gang pass me. A Spanish gang. They stared dead at me, molding their hands. I thought it was the end just then. In fact The End could come any damn time now, any second—I just had to hold out my hands and wait for the kill. And I hated them for it, like I hated this sick booby hatch, and everyone in it—including myself, because I didn't have the guts to get up and shove it all behind me.

Rosa was there, too. Clamoring like an ape again, of course. Once she saw me, she said the same thing, over and over again: "Gedadah heah! Gedadah heah! *Negro!*" America had put her words in her mouth...

I was there. I didn't notice Pocahontas—or tried not to. I was completely unaware of the fact that I was going up an escalator after having walked across a nice shiny floor on which stood the clothes racks and on top of the clothes racks the latest tweed jackets for the fall sellout or the winter or the summer; I was equally unaware of the fried chicken coming in from the store cafe nearby. I didn't notice the savages I kept bumping against since there were thousands and thousands of savages coming in and thousands more would come in from the antique show or the boys' school choir for Easter celebration or what the hell have you. I just kept humming Louis Armstrong melodies to keep from going off my rocker. For there were plenty of things in my life that could just set me right off. The leeches expected a good deal out of my hide—and tough titty for me had I ever happened to run out of blood.

As I walked in I could hear Mr. Albino going through his routines. By this time I was no longer a buser—no, I had moved up a notch, depending on how you looked at it. As for myself I could safely say I hadn't gotten anywhere, at any rate. For *I* was now the banana eater, the wage-slave—and making the pork-ribs for five an hour. As if a fat salary was actually going to cure me of my illnesses. And Mr. Albino...he was worse today, a real bad mood. At once he began to bawl the shit out of me and it almost came to blows. My neck muscles tightened; my throat dried as I watched him. I began to think that I wouldn't get out of this place without killing that sonofabitch, and Johnny-Boy included. In fact, the shovel, the murder-weapon-to-be, hung right over the ice-maker; if I ever got too hot under the collar I could always snatch it up and go after the bastards in a frenzy. I kept my eye on it. In fact everyone watched it as Mr. Albino or Johnny-Boy stepped in. For they were the new managers, of course. Mr. Albino had beeen struggling for two years to be general manager of Dummheit, but Mr. Quackenbros hesitated because he felt he was too abusive to the workers. He didn't want the slaves to be whipped—and that Albino detested. Quackenbros was just a plain damn nigger-lover, he thought. He was power-hungry, he wanted too much. He was in the airplane business as well as the food business—he wanted it all. And so did Albino. He wanted to become general manager; he wanted to become ruler of all Steinway. Quackenbros, however, wouldn't hear of it; he was too young, too immature, too foolish, and besides, he was homosexual, or bisexual, which was worse. But Albino was determined to have his way—and he was going to have it. So one night he sent two henchmen to get that nigger-loving Quackenbros—but as it turns out, the henchmen were black, too—he couldn't get white ones, it seems. They were dressed very neatly, very dapper, stick pens and silk shirts and all. They showed up at his house and just as he was stepping out they let him have it with machine-gun silencers. Then they cut back, swift as lightning, and Mr. Albino paid each of them 1000 dollars for their making him the new General Manager of the Pocohontas branch of the Dummheit Cafe.

And now that he ruled the roost there was nothing to do but surrender...

Basil doesn't know what he's doing. Rosa doesn't know what she's doing either. Even Elsie's confused. The whole schedule's mixed up: Johnny-Boy had me down for dishwashing and the grill, as well as the bathroom. It's all pure hate; they're trying to kill me. Toi's suddenly gone, dropped out for good—the rumor is she's caught AIDS. I wouldn't be surprised, judging by the way she handled herself every Saturday night. She was just a free-for-all come weekends. And so was everyone else, to the point where no one else would have been surprised if they had the exact same diseases Toi Pu Sei had. Everyone's got AIDS or herpes or syphilis or crabs or clap or something. Everyone's also got quinsy, headaches, tooth decay, back problems, dyspepsia, hepatitis, respiratory infection, genitourinary tract infection, gastrointestinal infection, brain infections, tumors, abscesses, internal injuries, diarrhea, pneumonia, cancer, weak liver, coronary problems, arthritis, spermatorrhea, vasectomies, menopause, cancer of the breast, cancer of the bones, cancer of the skin, cancer of the muscles, the eyes, the balls, the cock, the vulva, the ovaries, the finger-nails, the eye-lashes, the intestines, the rib-cage, the skull, the coccyx, the lungs, the heart, the bronchial tubes, the rectum, the feet and toes, the tongue, the tonsils, the teeth, the gums, the eyeballs, the elbows and, last but not least—cancer of the brain.

Cancer of the brain...a likely plague of all of 'em, myself included. I walk in the joint after a stroll outside. I sit down in the seat, wait patiently, quietly. Then I decided to get my food. I'm on break, don't forget...I get up in line and wait—perhaps for eternity, since the line stretches from the slop-den to the outer-mall doors. It's ludicrous...listen to them, the sons-of-bitches of patrons! "Ice cream looks good...no, I want cake...I'd like butter on that, please...no, you jerk! Gimmie the pork-ribs—no, the spinach...the broccoli, the lettuce, pickles, onions...fried chicken, too..." Sure...and while you're at it, you cocksucking bastards, you can stuff it up your old raggedy asses as well, the whole lot of you!

Lolita's at the counter. "Whaa' you wan' stupi'? C'mon, jerk! Here you' fri' chicken! Here, take i'! You make i', stupi—"

"Go suck a cock, you stupid bitch!" I snorted, interrupting her tirade by pitching my bread-roll at her. She began to squeal like a mouse. "Fock you, you basterd! I get jew!" Enough of that. I moved back, for I just remembered something very important and that was to go back to the little rails and pick out the chocolate layer cake which would always give me my favorite kind of belly ache to make me fit for flopping food on the grill or dishes in the dishwasher. I do this very important little chore, but then Lolita goes back to the manager, Johnny-Boy; she's become a complete toady for that punk. And you know why? Because Carlin's threatening the whole bunch. Seems to me HE wants to be general manager, too!...I don't want to deal with that bastard, he already has me on break for just 15 minutes. He's leading me about by the balls. I think about what he would do to me if he found out, and I become a complete nervous wreck. He's done pretty nasty things in the past—and his temper's getting worse these days. But never mind this—I've got to eat. If he comes, and I doubt it if he does, he'll just have to kill me when he does. I move on because I had been sitting in the same spot for 30 seconds and everyone's getting impatient and hurling insults right and left. A grape suddenly hits me, then something splatters on my back. It's tomato sauce, and when I look I see Johnny-Boy. He threw the grapes and Lolita the sauce—but I move on still. The savages are growing more and more impatient—they must have their motherfucking Nescafe. So I gets wrung up by Tramsokong Louangphuck who, right out of the blue, says to me: "Do you smoke? I got some real good grass if you want it!" "No, I don't, thank you," I said, then passed on after she scribbles my name on the ticket. I sit down again—then get back up, because I must get sugar for my tea. "Hey, shit-ass!" Johnny-Boy screams, throwing grapes at me, which he eats as he holds his factory chart for the human robots he's programming for self-destruction today. "Cummere, right now!" And he means it, too. He pulls lightly on my collar, then says: "You are no longer on break. You have only five minutes left—you can't eat, you shithead. There's work to be done, buddy—an' I mean work!" He does this all the time—he wants me to starve to death. This morning he called me up at ten to clean out the bathrooms and get everything set up—Pu Sei was gone for good, and I had to do her jobs. When I looked on my paycheck last I saw three-thirty-five written down; before then, four dollars. They paid me according to what they felt I should have been paid..."Dreaming again, huh?" he snorts—and whacks the food tray up into the air and onto the floor. Everything breaks—it's a great scare for me. "Clean *that* shit up—that oughta keep you busy, shit! Now GET MOVIN'!" I can hear the patrons in the back, laughing their heads off. They think they're in the motherfucking theater. He pushes me into the wall and I move faster, but I'm only in the mood to kill, to destroy, to murder. I saw the shovel there and I wanted to smash his fucking face and put his lights out. I was completely blind—and he shoved me about, making sure I knew where everything was. "Now—*mop it, jerk off!*" I mopped—then I yanked up the mop and slapped the water across his face, and tipped over the mop pail. Perfect! I wasn't going to take that bullshit from anyone and I told it to his face. Then he grabbed me by the collar and pushed me up against the wall, gritting his teeth. "You shit, you fucking black bastard," he squealed, knocking my head up against the wall, "I'm gonna kill you if you don't do—"

"Carlin, cut the shit—NOW!" Johnny-Boy jerked around; I looked to see who it was. It was the chef, the replacement, Roy McNamara—wielding a butcher knife. Johnny-Boy stiffened and got plenty angry suddenly. He was the only manager in: Albino was now out almost all the time, thereby letting Johnny-Boy do whatever he wished. But that meant nothing to Roy. "Now you leave the boy alone, boy," Roy snorted. "He ain't done nothin' to you. He been here workin' his ass off for your stupid-ass restaurant while you sit in ya goddamn offis talkin' shit wid your faggot-ass butt-buddy Albino, see. An' now YOU, you think you got d'nerve to come up here, slop his food onna ground while the muthafucka han't effen don' anything to anybody—"

"That's a goddamn lie!—an' you know it! Look—I don' wanna hear one word outta your mouth, you hear me, you shit—"

But Roy persisted and waved the knife at his throat. Everything stopped in the kitchen. Lolita even came in to look. The customers began howling, some even ran in the back. "Get the fuck out, bitch!" Roy screamed and waved the knife at them. "An' for you—look. You can go 'round, rapin' an screwin' all the bitches in dis joint, you can cheat every one outta back pay, you can do dis, you can do dat—but you can only do but so much. Man, dis shit's gotta stop, you know? I don't givea fuck if you don't wanna hear it. This man haven' even eatin all fuckin' day, right, an' you gon' come up here an' throw it onna mothafuckin' groun'? You sick, man, you fuckin' Hitler. Sure, go head, hit me. You all are assholes, nonea you is worth a stinkin' damn. You an' Lolita—Lolita? Who she? She a slut like the restuf 'em. She into her shit, too. I heard da bitch callin' Louey stupi, stupi, stupi! All you goddamn Spanish peepul don' belong in dis goddamn country! We been here longern' anya yall an here you are callin us stupid! An' YOU, you gon' git yours. I'm gonna kick ya muthafuckin' ass—why? Cause I feel like it, bitch—ya hear me, ya muthafuckin' Jew-ass bamma!!"

Johnny-Boy was startled and his manhood was deeply hurt, so he began popping anything and everything at him— calling him a coon, a nigger, a jig-a-boo. Lolita, tallying behind Johnny-Boy, grabbed the shovel and went after Roy. Roy ducked away cleanly and smoothly and the shovel hit Carlin across the head—he was out. And so was Roy. He deserted the job a few seconds later—and existence, so it seemed—for we never heard from him again.

Another day. I'm sitting at the table again, eating my pork chops. Beside me, on the other side, is the old geezer who always talks to himself in a woman's voice when he eats—and then a man's and then a child's. A Jew, no doubt. A crackpot like the rest…look at the way he dribbles his oatmeal all over the plate. Maybe be needs a good wiping or a change of diapers. Behind him, the mailman with an eye-patch who always drops in for cornbread and coffee with his demented daughter. She'd be all right if you just lopped off the head. The ass was fine, and the legs were superb—I'd seen from the short-shorts she wore. But it all ended there for the face was horrid, absolute hell. And I could plainly hear from her talk that she was a complete cretin—like her father. That's why they worked in the post office to begin with…Right by the window is the white cop from The Precinct (Inner-North Belford sanctuary)and his mail-order bride from Hong Kong Incorporated, shipped C.O.D. to "Amilika" in a funerary coffin. Both of them look like they've come out of it—and like they'd want to put another one down in the ditch, the damn killers. I stop eating; I'm not a horse, I don't need to be force-fed. If I don't want the goddamn mash potatoes, then I don't want them. Big deal!

I get up. For the millionth time I take a quick look about…All I see, everywhere, bent over their plates and working their jaws like the Ostrogoths with the shits—all I see, as I said, either eating or drinking or talking or laughing or throwing up or farting or singing with "joy," are killers, murderers, apes, savages. I can't get over it—a whole nation of murder fiends, myself included. I breathe; the air is poisoned. Not with the food, but with the murder which accompanied the food: the smell of fried chicken is the smell of death, of the horror and despair of living the life of another man who is your enemy, who is not you, who does not like you or even know you. Look at them eat, the killers! Everyone's infected with the fried chicken poison: even the fucking Uzbecks in the Gobi Desert. Not far away is that old Jew turd who comes in to harass the shit out of me for a fucking hot potato. "I wan my hot pot-tay-toe," she snorts—even when I'm off duty. I don't have it, I'm not concerned about it and I says so. "I'll go tell da meahnuhgah," she says. "Okay…go right ahead!" And she walks right into the dish room..."Meahnugah! Meahnugah!" She bellows like an old Jew fool..."I wan my haht poh-tay-toe!" And she gets it—right in her motherfucking mouth. Basil threw it at her.

It was on one of these days when, Albino being out more and more, spending the dough, of course, and Johnny-Boy only half-way sober, there happened to be a Sunday brunch wherein everything got into a perfect jam. But as this jam occurred I would sit around with Basil and Barnaby who could tell me what was happening on the sex war front: Miguel is getting his ass kicked so hard he's not even working that much anymore; that's old news. But a new and startling revelation was that Pu Sei had, within the space of thirteen months, *six* abortions. Worse yet, she's pregnant again. I gulp; it's got to be me. "Nuh-uh, man, you wrong," Barnaby said, laughing as he thought of it. "You won't believe dis one—CLYDE knocked her up, man!" I was jolted. Clyde?...well, anything was possible now. After all, Clyde really was fucked, in spite of his cheery appearance and his assurance that everything was a-ok. It wasn't, because just a few minutes after we heard about what Clyde did to Toi Pu Sei, he tipped over the entire cart of dishes, just for the hell of it, and smashed up almost everything in there. Johnny-Boy heard it and rushed up and threw a tantrum, but Clyde remained calm. "No problem. Very good that I get sonofabitch off me fucking back, yes?" And he stiffened, slapped his hands together as if he had accomplished something wonderful. Johnny-Boy told him he was fired and flung out his switch blade and went for Clyde; Clyde reached around and gave him a kick in the ribs that left the whole crew stunned. Then he broke a dish across his head and pulled him downstairs, via the elevator. "Stupid man!" he snorted. "Drunkin' bastard!...Dat what he get fo' fighteen Rosa! Hah!..." He went to the slop den and pulled out a bunch of pork chops. "Da hell wid it. Everybody eat; he finished!" And outside a riot started. I went out and held my hands around my mouth. "We're closed! A fire's in the house!" I was ecstatic at this outburst of chaos. I felt omnipotent, even though I didn't do anything. Everyone rushed out at the mention of fire, and to make it look like that I went to the grill and burned up a bunch of livers to make the smoke. When this was done I went downstairs and went ankle deep into the water on the floor since the pipes, as I just discovered, had bursted again.

A week later something else happened. A hearse drove up in front of the abattoir. They soon hauled out a casket and set it on a pair of wheels. Miguel! I thought instantly. He's killed himself, for sure. He hadn't shown up for two weeks. When Albino and Johnny-Boy took control that encouraged him to do some funny shit with himself. And it all had to end in this way. Well...I didn't really know what was going on. But when I saw them wheeling that thing towards the cafe I knew for sure that it was an ex-Dummheit slave. Then they flipped open the casket. Clyde peered in and fainted dead away...it was Toi Pu Sei! She kicked off—no, wrong again. As I looked over the beautiful corpse that was her, dressed up so neatly in her Dummheit uniform (dead!), I noticed some bruises about the chin and the upper neck area. Basil dropped in and, startled, noticing the same thing, pulled back the neckline out of curiosity. "She been have her troat caht!" he exclaimed. A bunch of cops came over for investigation. They began popping us all questions. They wanted to know if we had anything to do with this murder. Well...why in hell were they wheeling the damn thing up here? "Who kill her?" asked Basil, looking at the corpse.

"Her fiancee," one cop said. "We found her tied up in a plastic Glad bag with her throat cut and her sexual organs had stab marks all over. She had probably bled to death before she had been bashed like that..."

"In the back of her head," said the second agent. He pulled back the hair on her forehead with rubber gloves and exposed a bullet hole which had pierced right through her skull, and worse, he turned her head to the back to show that the motherfucker had almost completely bashed her brains out.

It was almost a placenta back there. "Did you know anything about the assailant?"

"Nothing," I lied.

"Did you?" he said, pointing to Basil. He shook his head. Soon everyone gathered and peered into the casket. Ding Bat looked in there and began screaming. I was more interested in who she was, for I had been popping her so many times and I hardly knew anything about her. "Who was she, anyway?" I asked. Basil almost laughed. "What was—I meant, what was her profession? Who was she?"

"You've been working with her for a long time, I suppose, and you don't know?"

"She never told us," I said.

"Well, immigration had been looking for this girl for years. She was an illegal mail-order bride from Penang Malaysia, who started off as a go-go dancer. She came to Washington, so she says, to study law," he said.

"I see," I said, almost cracking up when he mentioned go-go dancer. We went into the back; I directed Basil because, unfortunately, I was getting a wild urge to laugh. I had to hold it in for another hour or so, when the cops and the FBI left; they were looking for the fiancee who had run off. As they departed I suddenly broke out into uncontrollable laughter. She was going to be a lawyer! I thought. "She woulda made a helluva lawyer," I said, trying to contain my laughter for the solemn occasion. Barnaby was also weeping, and he chastised me. "Aw, don't be so cold onna bitch, man, she dead," Barnaby said to me, then began sobbing softly. "I cain' take it...one moment, she alive an' kickin', den she *dead!*"

"Barnaby, mon, you no unnerstan', she was noting at all, man," he said. "She wors CERO! Just a sex mohsheen...too bad!" he said, almost laughing himself. He smiled and turned his head. Barnaby winced. "I disgustid at y'all," he said, then faced me. "An' you—what you thinka bout her? After all, you da philosipher around heah, so what you think? Ain' dey all supposeta be human bein's, right? Dat what you think?"

"I dunno...I was just thinking about her in the courtroom giving everybody blowjobs and free ass and pussy! She probably had AIDS—"

"Dassa ruma goin' around, man," he said. "I liked her. She was a cute girl."

"Her boyfriend was a master racist," I reminded him. "And a huge brute in the R.O.T.C. Now how's that for your nice girl, eh?"

Barnaby waved his hand at me and went back downstairs. "I ain' evun gon' talk to yall no mo," he said, and just left, down to scrub his beloved pots. Basil laughed. "Good," he giggled, "we don't wanta hear it!"

We went back to work. But soon we began to wisen up. After all, she *was* gone forever—plain fucking dead. I felt sorry for the fact that she died—and so did Basil. "No more blowjobs," he cried. "Oh, she was so byootiful..."

"Yeah...she threw that thing around real good...UhhhhHuuhhhhhh!"

"Just think...all those stab marks in her beautiful little pussy. What a waste of fresh meat," I said, shaking my head. Basil laughed. "Mon, afta awl das all she wors!"

Sitting in the cafe once more...it's heading towards the end. Maria winks at me, grabs my hand, squeezes it. She wants me; I don't know if I really want her. If I took her, what would become of me? I would remain in the shit-heap forever—speaking a language not my own. With Maria I've learned some good Spanish—I can catch everything those fucker Barabbas sisters are saying. Speaking of Barabbas, look who comes in. Good old Lolita, the anthropological airline stewardess. She's upset—she leans up against the dishwashing machine. Her face looks like a checkerboard. She sees how much Maria and I are hotsy-totsy for each other, and she almost weeps for asking. Then she barks, *"Herpes es **mierda!**"* Yes, she's got it—and a big belly to boot. She starts chattering on in wild Spanish, dazed, half-crazed, because of this dreaded disease. It's affecting her brain cells for some queer reason. I almost laugh—I suppress a titter. I can't help it. She deserved to come down with something, the bitch. She keeps talking still, tossing her hands up in the air wildly. "Whaa you whaa, stupi'? Wha'?" Me, of course. She's frowning at me. Guess it's no more blowjobs...she's cleaning the forks and knives in the kitchen sink when she suddenly feels something bad coming on. "Cusa me, I...I...gotta goh dowinstarrs, okeh? Dohn tahch nohsingk, you heara me, little guy? *Oh, Dio, chingando problema! Aii! Vamos...mierda!...vamos!...*" She dashes off with her big belly and her spinning head to the toilet. Maria and I quit yapping and continue flopping in the dishes as they pull them in. No, a mistake: nobody's pulling them in. They're too damn lazy. They don't care. I have to do it myself. I look out in the dining room. One table left—a couple of black bourgeois. I walked over to the apes and tell them the jig's up. "We're not *finished!*" they snapped, the snotty-nosed pick-a-ninnies. No problem. I waited. They eyed me curtly and snottily all the while. Finally I lost my patience and spat in the food. "You bastard!" she screamed, the black bitch. She and her imitation-white lesbian lover stormed out in a fury, snorting behind them like their species always does when it gets hyped up for some stupid shit. "Bourgeois apes! Coons! Cocksuckers!!" I screamed as they stormed out, pushing Gu Fi to one side. Gu Fi grunted, then waved her hand at them. "Shit!" she cried—the fourth English word she learned while she worked here. I went back to my job with the dishes, but when I got there Maria was sitting there, on the crates, with Elsie Malone, their hands folded. "Gahdamin musheen braoke daewn ugheein!" she spat. "Fock this—ah aeint gohn' dew noh mourea dis sheeit. Ahm gewin hewme. Guhd bye!" And she grabbed her purse and split—without punching out. "*Ah, muchacho. Es estupido.* All same. All same. Everywhere. MacDonos, Borghor Beest, Roy Rohgers...kaphew! *Mierda! Chingando mierda.* Fooleesh!" She kicks the machine. She digs in her purse and pulls out her paycheck and then begins to tell me, in Spanish, about how they kept promising a raise for the last four weeks and refused. Yes, it's bullshit...But then there's another problem. *"Donde está Lolita?...Quien? Barabbas!Ahora sabes! Donde está??"* Lolita's gone. Everybody's wondering what's going on. Maybe Johnny-Boy's fucking her. No, that's wrong, because Barnaby comes up laughing and tells us that Johnny-Boy is roaring drunk from Tennessee Whisky. Good! We got the whole joint to ourselves. But Lolita...we get downstairs and into the girl's room and there she is, jerking on the ground, breathing, clutching onto whatever's there. It's the coke...she needs it. The desire for it is so intense that she's going berserk. "Coke, coke, coke!" That's all she can say. Now she goes out to find her connection. She puts on her fur coat—backwards. She doesn't know where anything is. Finally she's so frantic and wild we've got to take her home. We walk out, too—it's only eight-thirty nine but we don't punch out. Nothing gets done anymore anyhow—not with Carlin the punk...Maria and I help Lolita into her fur coat; we're going to find her "connection"; Louangphuck, the silly Laotian runt. Or Maggie, but we don't know anything about Maggie anymore—she's been fired. Ruby's there, though, but we don't know where she lives. Yes, Louangphuck's the only one—in South Belford. We drag her onto the bus as she howls and puffs and hisses. Maria and I have none of it on us, so we're no help. The rusted, bent-up white sign passes: BELFORD. We get off. Yes, it's South. We search around for the fish market which her mother and her father own and operate, on F street. All the while we make sure her belly isn't too ostensible. I can't help but laugh; the whole thing seems like a joke to me. We go into a dark corner near a park. No freaks— not yet, at least. I look at Maria; Maria looks at me. Suddenly we're lost. I fall upon her and kiss her and clutch her frantically, dropping Lolita to the ground. And as we smooch Lolita takes off, slumping down the street in a frenzy. We grab her again, laughing, totally unaware of what she's going through. We get on a bus heading further out. We skip it, the coke connection. We're in love; we've got to make it in Maria's flat further up

North. Soon it'll wear off...

It was my day-off—and for many others. Giuseppe met me at a posh and swank mall near Dupont Circle. Savvy place, eh? he said. I got up, I didn't say a word. Giuseppe was confused. "Wha? Where you go?"

"Out," I said. "C'mon, les go the peep show." We cut out and went to the Kit Kat Jerk-Off Club where they were showing the finest imported from Scandinavia: FUCKED IN THE ASS THRICE!! I get two dollars worth of quarters from The Chinaman up at the top counter. I step forward into the sperm-soaked corridor where a little sign read: "Be careful of who you grab...it might be The Flatfoots!" Sure thing. But when we got in it was so crowded, I lost Giuseppe; instead I come tete-a-tete with another infamous *clochard*—who was apparently in need. "Say, man, which booth you goin' in, honey?" he said to me. I frowned. "None, not a fucking one," and I stepped out. The hell with it...As it turned out, Giuseppe was outside all along. "Man, don' ever go in dere, you catch AIDS 'n' things in dose places. Is a buncha shit...now, but me an' Rosa, we gettin' along real well. Say, you hear wha' happen to Lolita? She pregnant—"

"And got herpes," I added.

"Naw—das justa rash, das all, nothin' else," he assured me. "Say, les go home." We catch the bus heading into Belford. We walk up the alleyway until we reach the Zilch department store. We didn't say a word the whole time—unless it was Giuseppe winding off about Albino again. The two were getting into a real intense feud, and it even came to blows this time—from Johnny-Boy. As he charged, they were running an opium ring with the Laotians—and going scat-free from everything. I already knew that. The more I listened, the funnier it seemed. At times I even laughed in his face. Perhaps the world was coming to an end—everything was losing all control, all sense. And just as we had this spiel we walked into the public toilets where gang members had their meetings now and then. Hypodermic needles were lying all over the floor. But then Giuseppe winked. "Ey—wach dis," he said, going into the ladies room instead. He steps in—and sees someone lying on the floor. A female. A girl. Philippine. No, Spanish. No, again—it's Lolita. She's in a complete stupor. She says nothing. Blood's all over the floor. Maybe she's been stabbed to death, or dying. A coat hanger was lying right by her side; she was trying to kill herself, obviously. What the hell...Giuseppe looks all around for stabs. No stabs—but something else was wrong. Giuseppe cries out, "Where's the baby, huh?" And then my eyes fall on the toilet. The lid's closed, the rim is stained with blood. I had to look. I was all aflutter, but taken back just the same. I flipped open the lid— and there it was, the fetus...broken into several pieces and swimming with the turds in the toilet water. I nearly threw up. "Another one!" Giuseppe screamed. "Dat's da second time dat shit happon! I swear, she gonna get kill onea dese days!" But then... "Eeeeeyuuuuu! What da hell is dis?" His feet get wrapped in the umbilical cord!...Actually, as it turned out, Lolita was just on a bad cocaine trip. When she got on a better one this time she felt much better. Her hair and face were caked with the blood of the fetus. She was glad to get rid of the baby—it was Ding Dong's baby, she said. And she had dumped him. "He no good to me. I tirea heem," she said. She had a new lover who was 35, and supplied her with lots of good old nose candy and faster cars and wilder parties and sexier fucking positions—but also with the dreaded Herpes Simplex. Her eyes glazed as she talked of this wilder, headier, more jet-set lifestyle she was leading. It was everything to her. Then, as we headed up over the razor-wires on the side of the building she collapsed again, groaning in pain...An ambulance, perhaps?...The fool! She did it again. She forgot about afterbirth!

But, as always, there it was again behind my ass, even though I didn't want to be bothered, that raging ocean of frenzied Night Life; again before me always those billboards outside the glittering hovel where the pimps and whores of the hour tagged their personals on the wall. Who am I in this world, I think, as I see the personals tagged on so hastily—single black male looking to hump a half-assed white bitch over thirty? Or a slinky black fox? What do I want? A faithful fiance? Or a menage-a-trois with two bisexual females, one white and English, the other Oriental? Or a Japanese shiatsu massage? Do I need a spiritual reading? Does anybody see fit to sell me his 1978 1/2 Honda scooter? Or a Bönn alto saxophone? Should I join a rock band or a rap group? Should I purchase a round-trip ticket to Rio? Should I ship out to Bangkok and get my ashes hauled? Should I join the navy and get blown up in Bahrain? What? What?—Answer me, you shits!—You have all the answers, or at least you told me, isn't that right?

No, there were no answers. And whether I remembered anything or not after getting pissed on a wild and reckless Saturday night of love and muck and epilepsy and Westinghouse dishwashing machines was not important. I was like the rest, like Lolita, like Giuseppe, and the really horrible thing about it was that I was fully aware of the fact yet could do nothing about it anymore. It's as if we were bound together by handcuffs and latched up to the back of a speeding motor truck and dragged on down to hell. And as we follow each other we also follow the world down into the black pit of loveless love, into that netherworld of steel and chaos which will grip us all by the throat. But right now, in this purgatorial amusement park, our only creed, our only mission is this: get with it, rut with the apes in Neon-ia. So be sure to have your passports ready, you decent, respectable sons-of-bitches, when you plan to make an entrance into the Republic of Fuckadola, and if you ain't got a visa it's tough shit, 'cause the borders are patrolled from top to bottom and from left to right. The entry fee is fifty bucks and a spurt of jism in the mouth for the record. You must be 21, but if you're sixteen or younger you could always carry a falsified passport, which is what they all do since ninety per cent of 'em storming the borders of the

Fuckadola republic are mere lads and lasses. Up on the billboards for the night of music and love and golden piss-yellow happiness are all your favorite entertainers and groups. Tonight, **live** at quadrilateral, duplex, Gorgonzola and central mountain time, is Seven-Up and the Lochness Tomatoes. Also appearing simultaneously in a wave-length frequency at the Paramount Inn, on top of the oyster deck, Pinball Stripes and the fat Belgian Bastards. This hour at the Copa it will be *Dingus* and *Kitty Litter For The Faithful At The Bottom Of The Barrel;* also on the card, the Pussy-Suckers, the Oral Freaks, The Pervies, The Crazy Bastards, the Cherry Moon, I eats Ice Cream, Whadda you do?, Don't do it—It Hurts!, Ooooooooh, dat feel so nice!, the Sperm Eaters, The Racists, Hot Cream, The Lukewarm Tea and Bellyache Orchestra, the Anal-Masters, the Six Clouts Over the Noggin, Oriental Love, Dreams of Africa, Katmandu, El Salvador, Sex, Istanbul, Iskenderun, Aleppo, Assiut, Khartoum, Sfax, Benghasi, Cape Town Parade, Dead Niggers In Transkei, Latakia, Luang Prabang, Hat Yai, Mustafa Kemal Atatürk, Morganata and the Dipshits, Chaka the Zulu and The Pork Rib Stompers. The Slickster is singing his smash hit *I Want To Bang Your Box,* plus that all-time favorite *Give Me Every Inch of Your Love.* Mary Jackson appears tonight on the bill singing the tampon song in a skirt of bananas. *La Chinga* from Miami gives us their favorite hits, *Romantic Drill* and *Liberty City Stomp-off.* Next hour, the Banana-Eaters, the Chink Rice Strutters, the Wage Slave Gals, the IBM boys, The Westinghouse Crooners. If you're not there that's no problem because it's always broadcast every night from WEXP right here in this wonderful city in Washington, D.C. Or, come to think of it, it doesn't have to be Washington— it could be New York, Los Angeles, Cairo, Bangkok, Istanbul, Athens, Frankfurt, Paris, London, Ankara, Yokohama, Manila. Yes folks, from all over the world the tuxedoed inmates in this glorious international multitrillion dollar bughouse are sending you their wishes in every language in the world, right into your home at eight o'clock and central and mountain time. In

Kuala Lampur the English girls are lolling on the beaches and their sex-ape boyfriends in the Secret Service are raping the natives; in Bombay the president is residing over a mass Be-In in which all the megastars are gathered together to raise money and feed poor starving India and kill the Pakistanis. From the Hilton International in Cairo, Sheik Achmed Al-Hokkama Hahk Muk presents you with his belly dancers from the Port Said Yachting Club, belly dancing to Michael Jackson's Billie Jean played on the g-string. In Rio the banana-eaters are dancing the samba on a pair of squids; in Tokyo Michael Jordan is teaching the Prime Minister how to breakdance. In Tel Aviv there's a beauty contest wherein everything is rigged up so that Miss America wins it, along with the skull of a dead Arab, in all her blonde-and-blue-eyed Doubleminty glory. In Johannesburg the Darkey Brothers are showing their new film, *Jungle Bunnies in Heat*, which is perfectly fine because the gunshots and the bombings have been spliced out for your listening and viewing pleasure...and here, back home in Washington, D.C., standing in front of the billboard in the Republic of Fuckadola on a temporary visitor's visa which is good up until menopause, here we are, happy, contented, foolhardy, dancing a jig in pork-rib time. We are naive, hopelessly naive. We know nothing, feel nothing, comprehend nothing. We are zombies. Shits. Idiots. We are in the midst of a phosphorescent Inferno deep in the netherworld of things, of images pushed in our face to the point of utter nausea, images blasting out of the screens, strangling our senses to death. We are all gliding merrily through this blissful Hell lit up with the vibrant electro-joy of the plastic Styrofoam Utopia, smothered in the plastic bags of our dreams. This is the sound of the double-breasted back-stabbers swimming a breaststroke in the sweet coke dreams of the night. This is the noise of the future world slick with plastic and intravenous injections, surrogate sisters and the wombs laying open for rent on the installment plan. The whole of our character measured out in Dollars and Cents, pounds, Deutschemarks

223

and Drachmas. All of our hopes and dreams running to the meter and dropping in the coin slot. Hurry, my friends, my factory chums of Lenin's world of dishwater drudgery, we must get the hell out of ourselves before we slit our throats in desperation. We must soak up the madness of this city, this Washington on a Saturday night, so that we will not be dogged with philosophical reveries which just might spoil the mood.

This was just what I was waiting for. The mood of gaiety had to be broken, spoiled, ruined; the belly-dancers had to stop breakdancing, and the guitars and the saxes and the crooners had to silence themselves. You idiots, you screamers and crooners, you know not what it means, even for a moment, to be quiet, to put a lid on it, to just plain goddamn shut up. And yes, that is precisely what I would wish you to do. Shut up. Did you get that? Maybe I didn't say it loud enough—**SHUT UP!!!!** I've heard enough, seen enough, felt enough. My back is up against the wall; I can't move another inch in this rancid sugar-cube of existence. But I cannot stand still: I must not stand still. I've got goals, I've got aims—I just forget them in my haste to falsely enjoy myself in this hell. I must push forward, move on in a direction which to your myopic eyes appears backward into infancy. But what if it is? Would I not go back to the cradle just the same? Would it make any difference anyhow? I never liked this life, none of it, not a single bit of it. This had never been the proper place for me and I don't know if any other place is just as proper, but this is the worst, so help me God. For here in the midst of this great jungle of modern love and thinking I always find myself alone, unwanted, useless to the world. No matter where I go or what I do I always seem to find myself singled out; I am always made to feel like a freak, even in the midst of freaks. I feel that this will always be so, even if I had given up the route I had taken and crossed back over into the upwardly mobile world, even if I remained there till the end and attained a billion diplomas, a doctorate and an emeritus, a Lincoln Continental, a Mazda CFX, a Lambourghini, a house on the Riviera and the most beautiful children and wife in all Heaven and Hell—for the simple, undeniable fact that this is just not my world. I may not even be a man, just half a man, or three-fifths of a man, but, for Christ's sake, don't lump me in with these animals! They're all closing in on me, friend and foe alike, gnawing away at my entrails. If they ever get to the core of me, would the books help in my trying to pry off these predatory savages? Could I ever hope to find any answers in them? No, there were no answers.

Things were getting worse all around me. It wasn't just the Dummheit because the Dummheit was a reflection of what was going on all over the whole country. I've got to get out of here, I thought, before something bad happens—perhaps suicide, or murder, either by me or someone killing me. I can't allow it to happen. They'll never get me; I wouldn't allow them to get me. I would no longer allow myself to be fooled by their friendly, open vows and their warmth and their spontaneity, which apparently was just a facade covering the sub-human steel automated pleasure-hungry jaded robot heart beating in disco time. 300 million dead in a nuclear overkill wouldn't even stir them; their own death, the thought of their own deaths wouldn't stir them just the same—*for they were already dead.*

9

HERE WE ARE—all over again. I walk through Belford on to work. The apartment I share with my mother is hardly affordable and why is that? Because my mother keeps spending and spending on her lovers. As for my father, he's out of it—he's just come back home from a term in the hospital for tertiary syphilis, but the medicals say he can conk out any minute now. His bookshop has long since been closed down due to mismanagement. He keeps laughing to himself, slumping either in a chair or a corner. My mother is growing shabbier and shabbier. My presumptions were right—she *does* have AIDS. And not only that, but Louangphuck's got it, too, and Concha tested positive for the disease, though she's only fourteen. I wonder if I've got it since I haven't worn a rubber the whole time I've been humping the Dummheit bitches. More news hits me as I get on the bus with Basil and Barnaby. Miguel's not dead, since he's right here with us, but his face has been so lacerated by repeated beatings that it's hideous; a day after this he disappears forever, we don't see him anymore. Rosa disappears at the same time, as well as Giuseppe. Kaputt. Over the next few days we were panicky in a delicious way—or, at least, *they* were panicky in a delicious way. I was thinking about how I would get up the guts to quit this job and get the fuck out. But how would I quit without bringing down the wrath of my mother? Now she and I are the only ones supporting the family. I recall the days when she could have killed me for taking the job—now she doesn't want me to quit. Pop's dying of syphilis. She herself is dying of AIDS because she drank the come of a hemophiliac—but, as it turns out over the next few days, that's wrong. When she was in the hospital she was given tainted blood. TAINTED BLOOD! It was all a mistake, as they said...What would I do now that I was hemmed in? I had originally planned to go to Amsterdam. Really I was sort of just toying with the idea, kind of; it wasn't anything too serious. But now it was the only solution. I'm also hearing stories of economic failure and how it's beginning to strike at Belford residents. Suppose we had to sleep in our car—like Elsie Malone? That would fuck us up entirely. I couldn't leave the family, then. I had to keep working if I wanted to eat. I didn't know, just the same, how in hell I was going to raise the eight-hundred dollar airfare to take me to Amsterdam. I still only had *six* hundred dollars out of my whole account—thanks to you-know-who. And then there was the Samsonite case that got lost and recovered, but I had no business fucking with that after all those police investigations. As I was thinking of this I heard Basil say something about Louangphuck taking more and more PCP as a recreational drug. What for? "Dunno mohn, she johst crezy, das all," he said. "That stuff'll make you freak out," I warned, not half-way thinking about what was going on. I heard there were new drugs, even worse ones, beginning to invade the borough. And with worse drugs comes worse violence. Barnaby looked plenty worried himself. "Man, look like de whole thing onea dese days is gonna burn, it gettin' to be so bad!"

Outside, while on the bus passing through squalid Inner-North Belford, we could hear some hysterical screaming. Things were hitting the bus. What in hell was this? This sure was new. Even though there were drug wars and what-not, I never knew the violence to hit public transportations. Then suddenly, passing directly through the big windshields was a hail of machine-gun bullets, striking the driver in the face, raining and splintering slivers of glass all over everywhere. Everyone fell to the ground, screaming hysterically, like idiots! And that wasn't the end. A molotov cocktail was hurled right into the bus. Who would have known bus drivers had connections!

But this was new stuff. Barnaby began whimpering like a pig and shaking his head as the bus began to burn, and we hysterically smashed our way out the back window. We were lucky there was one because usually they weren't there. People were killing themselves to get off the fat sonofabitch...We got off in time. But Barnaby was still on the bus; he wasn't budging. The thing was going to blow up. "BARNABY, GET YOUR ASS OFF DAT DAMN T'ING, BOMBA CLOT, FOOL BAHSTAD!" Basil shouted to him—and when he did, gunmen rushed up around the bus and began firing at it. We backed off and ran away. I could feel them firing at us, because bullets were bouncing off the buildings that we were headed towards. They were black youngsters, and they had bad aim, not to mention bad judgment. This was even worse than the opium ring!

When we got around the alleyway next to the broken down movie theater and past the security guards, Barnaby had a sweater over his head and followed us. We balked—we didn't want his fat greasy ass anywhere near us. Barnaby selling drugs?!? *I've got to get out of this shit...*

"Look man," he said to us, looking around and about hysterically after he pulled the sweater off his face, "I dunno how dis happen, man—I didn' know! I didn' know!..." Basil nodded. "Don' worry, mon...justa bad deal!" He laughed nervously. I wasn't laughing—I didn't want to have anything to do with these savage Belford-Turkish cops. "Lissen—it was Maggie. She started it, da bitch."

"Why her? She's probably dead by now for all I know!"

"Maggie tried to sell me some shit."

"What was it?"

"Crack," he said. I frowned. "What in hell's that?" "Louey,

you donno, mohn?" Basil asked, frowning. "It been here for de last monff an' you could not see all de keeling?! Damn!"
"Well—what is it?"
"It's white—like cocaine—but *worse*. "That's all I needed to know. A police siren began to sound. Bullet-shots could be heard two or three blocks away where the massacre was taking place, and hysterical shouts and screams. It looked like a riot. Mobs of people waiting for their bus or who were on that bus were running and scampering around like rats escaping the wrath of the exterminators. Screams and shouts and curses filled the air. How I could have seen it all—just as another book is about to be closed, the setting for another one about this same hellhole is just beginning.

We had to get out. We deserted Barnaby; he tried to run with us with his twelve-fingered ass, but we wouldn't hear of it. "Piss off, go away," I told him. "I thought you told us you weren't gonna talk to us no more!" "Dat was just a mistake," he said, rather stupidly. It was just our luck that a carpool showed up—well, actually, it was Lolita driving a car, her first. She was sixteen and going on seventeen in a week now and so excited she was, she got out of the car and went in the drugstore, ignoring us, of course, and left it unlocked. We took a gamble, grabbed the car and jumped in it and switched up the wires, started it up and took off—without Barnaby, who ran in the store to tell Lolita we were stealing her car. We showed up halfway to the joint and parked the car on the side of Georgia Avenue. We were already late due to the massacre; what we had seen was so grim, such a foreboding of horrendous proportions to our future in that neighborhood that we didn't feel like working anytime. It was hours later when we arrived, after we, in vain, called in sick. "I don't know what in hell you can do about that now," Albino quacked. He was jumping up and down in anger and we told him very politely what had happened, that the bus driver had been shot to death for dealing drugs, etc., etc. He didn't believe a word of it and demanded that our asses be here as soon as possible.

We got there; Carlin met us at the entrance to the cafe. He was molding his hands and he grabbed the both of us and kicked us inside. Basil didn't like that and so he cracked Carlin across the face. Carlin began screaming. "NIGGER, YOU'RE FIRED! GET THE FUCK OUTTA HERE NOW!!" Basil didn't listen and went inside to work anyhow. I followed him, with butterflies in my stomach. I went to the grill, and Albino stuck his nose in the little hole over the grill area and told me that if I didn't come in like I was supposed to next time, I would find myself working somewhere else. In fact, he told me again, I was fired. He was serious, too, and so I decided to clear out and never come back. Then he called me back. "No, not now, dipshit. You're on four weeks notice. We can't get rid of you unless we can find someone with your cooking expertise to fill your position—and unfortunately we can't find anyone right now 'cause no one wants to work in this dump. You know why, don't you?" "Oh yes, of course," I said, sarcastically. So there was a crunch to keep in workers. But...if such a crunch continued on like this, would it mean that, no matter what I did, I wouldn't be fired? Well...Basil showed up the next day, fair and square; he, too, was supposedly on four weeks notice. But the fight between him and Carlin had been forgotten. I supposed that Albino's jibes at me were just mere threats then...

I think it was my last day there. Or one of them. I don't quite remember—there were many "last" days I spent anywhere in America. Barnaby was back—and his face swollen and a bandage across his nose and around his throat. Cuts were healing on his face. Anyhow...it was Roy who, when I sat down to eat with the bunch—Basil, and Carlos, and Barnaby— noticed something quite wrong with me. In fact, they all saw that something wasn't quite right—for they began coming out with it. "Get out, mon," Basil said to me. "Get outta dees place b'cause here dey goin' to keel you if you don't meka moove." Then Barnaby left. Carlos got into it. "You see heem, man," Carlos said, shaking his head and pointing to Barnaby's figure receding into the kitchen. "He mess up. Dey let heem off for drugs, dey give him his old job back. But what happon? Dey don't hava no space inna jail for heem, so why dat? He crezy! He sell drogs. Everybody know dat shit. Everybody. He mess up. Das because he not too smart anyway, den he wark hear too long. You wark hear too long, you become *loco* like Rosa, *Escuchame?"*

"Maybe you ain' lissenin' hard enough, man," Roy butted in before I could open my trap. As I recalled he was no longer a member here. He just sat in because he felt like it—he wanted to sit around with some of his buddies. "You see how everythin' fallin' to pieces? Look...half da crew on drugs, half got AIDS...Man, get out. Go back ta school! Das where you belong inna first place—"

"But I can't stand it up on campus!" I cried. "They're predators—they think of nothing except money, money, money."

"Go to sea den, mon," Basil suggested.

"I can't go to sea—I don't have any experience on board," I said. "I got it—I'll just walk out of here. Without another word. Just split. How's that?"

Carlin came rushing up to me. "What the fuck are you standin' around for, shit-ass? Get UP," he sneered, pulling me up by the collar. The other patrons sat and watched it like some sort of entertainment. Do they think they're in the movies, I thought angrily. "Now look—Barnaby's goin' home, and Yo Yo's out today. I don't know what's wrong with him—he could be drunk—but we need you to wash the pots for us. Basil, you take on these two sections, and do a good job at it or else your ass is goin' through that fuckin' window, you got it? So get downstairs fast! The shit's pilin' up down there!" I made it down to the basement. I saw clearly where the joint was headed the last time I was there. It was so chaotic I didn't know what to do anymore. I looked around. The others could hardly take it anymore themselves—but where were they going? They hadn't any future in store for them—not even

231

Concha, the youngest. None of them were going anywhere. I didn't tell anyone that I was leaving; they probably would have beat me up for it. They were getting into more and more messes with their personal lives, always complaining and talking about doing something and not doing it—a la Basil Edwards. All of it began to wear on me. I couldn't even think anymore because I had these pots in front of me I had to handle. So I grabbed up the little spray and began scrubbing the pots, pan by pan. I was a complete novice at it, but I was good because I kept watching Barnaby so many times. Then the goddamn thing got clogged up. I took out the plunger to get the crap out, but not even that would work. Then the machine began cutting off and finally the lights in the whole downstairs kitchen went off. Carlos threw up his hands. "Shit!" he cried, "you know what dat means? De water blew a fuse!" He was right. There was a massive leakage in the walls and much of the water hit the fusebox and cut off the lights. The fuse-box was in a little room right beside the bottom kitchen but I wasn't going in there. Carlin came rushing down, cursing to himself. "Shit! Shit! What the fuck is this? Goddamn fuse gets blown!" He puts his hand on the fusebox and then he screams harder than I ever heard him scream. "GODDAMMIT I COULDA KILLED MYSELF!!!…" He's gonna blame it on us now. He comes out. He's got ugly shocking red burn marks on his hands—he almost got electrocuted. "Hurry— Carlos, Louie—to the first-aid kit! Call the ambulance if poss— no, forget it! Get the bandages!" We rushed over and grabbed some bandages out of the little box that was sitting in his office. When I saw this I noticed that the safe was lying open, and that three hundred dollar bills were lying there right in front of my eyes. Johnny-Boy was way over on the other side of the room with Carlos tending his arm; I began to gamble. "Hurry, you asshole!…quick!…" I snatched up the bills and stuffed them in my back pockets and then got out the bandages, all at the same time. Perfect. Then I laid out another pair of three-hundred dollar bills, all in a second, to make it look like I hadn't stolen anything; I laid them down in the exact position. Still more perfect. I got the bandages, and he snatched them from me impulsively and grimaced when he gripped his hand. He almost began to cry, because the pain was so intense. Albino was out for that day, so he was nowhere to be found. Just at this time too the floor began flooding again, and then *all* the lights blew out in both kitchens. And there was no one there to set off the alarms and warn the people. But since it was the daytime, not one patron noticed anything. Johnny-Boy then went to work on the fusebox with his bandaged hands. He opens up the fusebox. Water pours out of it. The water pipes haven't had an inspection in at least two years—they just forgot about it entirely. What could he do?... "Louie, get a fan, quick! and get back to those pots as quick as you can, too!" I fetch a fan out of the back room. As I'm back there, I think fleetingly what it would be like if I suddenly decided to commit suicide. Then I forgot about it and got back outside. But then there's a problem: how the fuck can he plug in the fuckin' fan if there's no electricity? Now he can't dry off the fuse-box!...

Water fills up the floor. My shoes are all wet. The food stops cooking—something's going on upstairs. I hear Maria's voice just cluck-clucking away. I go upstairs... "Say, dipshit, what the fuck are you goin' upstairs for?"

"I gotta see somethin'," I told him.

"See what? There's nothin to see! Hurry up! The goddamn—"

SMASH! CRASH! PLONGGGGGGGGGG! Dishes crashed to the ground time and again. Screams followed from Maria, then Concha. Carlos went upstairs. I went up with him. Carlos got there and saw the two of them in a real brawl—but Maria had the upper hand all the way because she was strangling Concha and pounding on her belly. This was all the more bad, because Concha now had a big belly because she was pregnant. Maria pushed her off and cracked her a good one across the face. Speaking in Spanish, she said over and over that she did it for her Jonas. When it was all over, Maria went back to her post contented and Concha lay on the ground,

233

bleeding and unconscious. Lolita by that time had swooned around her fallen sister and jerked herself back up in heated anger to look at Maria in utter contempt. Maria then threw her dishes on the ground and let them break entirely; she wasn't quite right after what happened two months ago, the breakdown. She closed in on Lolita and kicked her in the jaw, and she fell over and hit her head. Then Lolita fell into convulsions, and Maria looked over her quite blandly and shook her head and walked away. Lolita was dying for the coke again—she couldn't get it out of her mind. She went up to Louangphuck and demanded some from her, but Louangphuck refused because she didn't pay for the last supply of coke she dealt her, and she wouldn't give her anything unless she gave her the money. Not only that, Tramsokong said, she was gonna kill her if she didn't cough up the money. Lolita laughed; all this was going on at the cashier's desk. Then Tramsokong leaped up wildly and hysterically, right in front of a customer, and began whacking on Lolita furiously, as if she was trying with all her might to kill her...then she threw her head into the water-pot and ran scalding hot water all over her blistered face. Lolita began screaming, and the customer began looking rather frightened, and said, rather stupidly: "Well, maybe I outta eat somewhere else!" and left, looking back time and again to see what was happening. The other patrons enjoyed it and Rubenstein joined in to do both of the jobs at once since, obviously, the brawl seemed like it would never end. It carried on into the kitchen where Maria tried to break it up and for this she got a stab in the guts and she fell over. I rushed over to Maria. "Maria!—you alright?" I yelled, looming over her. She got back up. She was alright, it was just a nick on her rib, but it was bleeding freely just the same. She held it with her hand to stop it. She nodded and kissed me on the forehead, looking rather cracked, and got up and went back to washing the dishes. Tramsokong was now freaking out completely; it had to be from the PCP she was taking. Lolita was struggling to pry herself loose from Tramsokong, and when she got from under her clutches she promised she would kill Maria for what she did to Concha, who was coming to. Damn!—what a feud: Tramsokong takes PCP, which makes her hysterical, plus she hates Lolita because Lolita is always late in coughing up the money for her cocaine habit, and plus Lolita is Concha's sister, and Lolita protects her because she is pregnant, and just the same Maria, because of Jonas's death, has put a bounty on Concha's head, ergo Maria doesn't like Lolita, either. Shit! What a joke! Then Carlin threw up his hands in despair over the fusebox and made his way upstairs. I could hear him way over in the back. "What the fuck is this shit??...Huh?...what?..." Louangphuck was totally out of control by this time. She suddenly stopped dead in her tracks and began to peel off her clothes, gritting her teeth and making funny breathing noises. Soon she was totally naked, and then she began screaming again and jerking again and she ran right out into the dining room, grabbing the chocolate cake, and splattering it all over her. She was sure a spindly thing...she didn't have an ounce of meat on her, I thought. Her tits all saggy, already...what the hell did Barnaby see in her?... "TRAM! TRAM! GET THE FUCK BACK HERE, YOU FREAK!" Carlin shouted, and tried to suppress his laughter. Everyone saw everything and the patrons broke out into wild laughter and began clapping their hands rhythmically. Lolita and Concha were there, right at the counter to see the whole scene, but Tramsokong saw no one at all; she just ran out, out. "TRAM!!..." She ran all around the dining room shrieking her goddamn head off. "Shit!" Carlin shrieked, and took a dish and threw it on the ground. Maria laughed at the scene, and his ire was jacked up to the bursting point; she was snitching a drink from the soda machine and Carlin began to punch and insult her just for kicks. He began bawling her out and said, "I don't wanna hear any morea ya *cucaracha* shit, ya hear me??" Maria said nothing to him and shrugged her shoulders; he slapped her. "I want some fuckin' answers, Taco bitch!—" Maria went wild and cracked him across the jaw and punched him; Johnny rammed his fists into her stomach several times and threw her into the dishcart and wheeled her body back down to the dishwasher where she belonged. She stopped right in front of me. She was only half-conscious, coughing; I expected her to spit out blood and kick off. I couldn't believe what I was seeing; I'd seen so much of it, I'd been totally desensitized to all brutality. But now it was worse than ever... Albino was not here and Carlin was the only guy running this place here. Louangphuck was running around in broad daylight naked and covered with a smushed chocolate layer cake. The patrons outside were hysterical with excitement; they were all young people now; most of the old people had split because they couldn't take the disorder, though the food was good that day. The quality never went down, no matter what...Carlin pushed us time and time again to keep working, because in spite of the chaos we were making good business and good time. "Hurry! We gotta keep movin'! Get five people to wash these dishes by hand!...Lolita! Tram! Stop it! Stop it now! STOP THE SHIT!!..." Lolita had rushed out to grab Tramsokong and the two fell into a wild hysterical brawl again, all right out in the dining room. Carlin was almost on the point of freaking out completely. Well...this is what he wanted!...

The situation was wild all through the afternoon and the evening and got worse and worse. One of the rowdy patrons tried to keep the chaos inside by closing off the glass doors to make sure no security ever got inside to break it up. The electricity never got fixed; we were all sitting in the dark. Finally, though, half the dining room lights flicked on. Those had dried but the others were still dripping with water. The kitchen was lit up only with candles and kerosene lamps which were put to use for the time being. With those it was pretty well-lighted, and they were set on top of the ovens and stoves, so that the clamoring crew-members wouldn't knock them over. Maria was sentenced, after recovery, to washing the dishes by hand with the help of Carlos and I and an unknown fellow. But I was also wanted to do pots; I had to do them both because the electricity wasn't working for either machine, and besides the dishwashing machine had broken down entirely. Maria and the three of us were scrubbing and scrubbing, but Maria was so nervous and angry she broke up about ten dishes which she brushed under the machine. We were far from being fast enough because Lolita kept screaming, over and over, "BREENGA ME DEM GODDAMN DEESHES!!...BREENGA MO' FOCKING PLETES!!...." Maria threw a little saucer at her and told her to shut her ass. When Carlin saw what she was doing, he whipped her across the head, over and over. I finally felt I had to do something with this fuckhead; the debating time was over inside me. Then I heard a crashing noise downstairs. That just reminded me to get to my pots. I dashed downstairs to get to them and I almost slipped and broke my neck; I held onto the railing and went down carefully. I looked; I was startled. The water pipes had burst open completely; the whole joint was flooding. Then the stove broke down, then the oven, and the corn couldn't be cooked because of the water which ruined the stove. Carlin was furious, but so was I for having to...He dashed downstairs screaming my name. "BASTARD, BASTARD, BASTARD!" he said, meaning me. He grabbed me up and started blaming me for everything. But I felt I had just about enough of Carlin's ass. I got worked up to the boiling point and sensed my cue to freak off as well. I spat in his face and threw the pot of corn at him. When the corn hit him, he went wild with rage, and I dashed upstairs for protection. When he came after me, he slipped and fell downstairs, then jerked back up and pursued me in animal savagery. He pounded on my back; he cornered me and felt he had it in the bag. He was so furious, he kept missing punches and I got the shovel off the hook; I decided this is it; if I can't get out of this muckheap, I'll kill him and go to jail for it. I swung the shovel and caught him on his back; it did nothing for him. I swung again, and he grabbed onto the end and yanked it away from me and threw it down on the ground. I took up a bottle and crashed it across his neck, not his head—I missed. Oh no, I thought; it's over. He jerked around and began attacking me. "YOU FUCKIN' NIGGER! NIGGER! NIGGER!" he shrieked hysterically. I got a crack across the face and got kicked down and punched on the face so much it felt numb; I was jerking around just like a piece of rubber, my limbs almost tore loose. Then he started strangling me, and I couldn't breathe. Maria grabbed up the shovel and tried to save me, but then Carlin snatched it from Maria and tried to hit me with it, but Maria tried to hold him back by grabbing around his waist. I saw him huffing and puffing just like a savage, a perfect beast. Then he grabbed me up after he let loose on the shovel and thrust my face onto the sink and ran hot water on my face, then turned it up full blast. I began shrieking; and when this happened Lolita rushed in and saw it and broke out into laughter, pointing,...."EY, STUPI'," she barked, "YOU LIKEA YOU DRINKA WATER, YOU *TONTO!* YOU LIKE—" She squealed, and then strangling noises and thumps and thuds issued from her body. Ruby Rubenstein continued serving up the chow, making sure that everything was a-ok, even though our unknown worker was pitching bread-rolls at the customers now and then because they were laughing at him so. They were yuppies; the whole environment to them was a wild thrill. Then the lights blew out again in the dining room, and they began howling. I ran downstairs again; Tramsokong was being restrained by Lolita and Gu Fi and Ding Bat and Chloe; the workers had all scrambled to restrain her from which she battled hysterically, spitting out animal curses and cries, calling for Lolita because Lolita owed her some money. I got yanked off, and I hit my head on the dishwashing machine: I was bleeding. I got trammeled upon, and I got up and dashed downstairs to avoid the riot. Carlin shoved Maria into the ice maker and tried to freeze her to death. All the while Ruby and Mary Chiao kept all the patrons pacified. When one of them, a younger girl, asked them just what in hell was going on, Elsie simply said: "She's jest uhpset ovur sumtin. Ah ain' know whut it iuhs. Ain' nuffin seros," and

Chiao responding accordingly, said: "Somesing...very fohnny. Dey have...pahty...yes. Nosing wiong. Go head and have nice day." And, worst of all, from Ruby Rubenstein: "Oh, they're just misbehaving. The work does that to you sometimes. They're newcomers. Well...that'll be all? Ten fifty six...yes ma'am?"

But deep down, I could sense that nothing could stop the bullshit. Sensing the end I didn't spare another moment. I thought, make a break—**NOW!!** And I did it. I picked up my old briefcase lying in the lockers; there were books inside and they were all wet and soggy from the water. I grabbed it and ran out. "HEY!" Carlin screamed... "YOU BASTARD NIGGER!! FILTHY MOTHERFUCKER!!..." Then there were shrieks. Carlin was yanking Maria out of the ice maker and Maria was all covered with ice and she threw a wild tantrum and stripped off all her clothes hastily except for her underwear, shaking the ice chips off and ran wildly all around the plaza before the guards manhandled her and stopped her. "Jonas!...Jonas!..." she kept screaming...perhaps she was screaming for me, I didn't know and didn't want to...I kept moving, out into the dark, far far far far far away from the slaughterhouse pig sty...the insanity raged on and on...Tram tried to jump through the window...she was shrieking her head off...I was gone...

I stayed away and never intended to come back. Now I was lost. I knew I had been fired, but I didn't care. I was still in my uniform, though I knew I should have left it there. Now I had to make a move, regardless of what anyone thought. I had done that before by moving into the Dummheit—but I made the wrong choice because I trusted this system too well, and I trusted America too well. Now there was nowhere else to go but out—out of the country. I couldn't fit in with the buppie generation; I couldn't fit into the working class; I fucking couldn't fit in anywhere. Now the only hope left was exile. A few days later I went down where the airline agencies were. I went into a small cut-rate agency which sold me a ticket to Amsterdam for two hundred and thirty dollars, one way, from

JFK airport. I didn't want to have to do it, but it was too late now. My plane was leaving in two days, and all I had on me was nine-hundred lousy dollars. Then I began thinking about the safe which was sometimes left open haphazardly by either Johnny-Boy or Albino. I was sitting in the living room of the apartment when I began thinking about it that way. I had only nine-hundred attached to my name after all that work, and I had the jewels to rip off from my mother, pawn them in, and then make out for JFK. Well...I debated with myself. Which came first? I needed all the cash I could get. I made it out to the bus stop and within no time found myself within the confines of the cafe again. It was eleven o'clock. They still hadn't closed yet. The mall was still open. A few guards were milling about. Lucky for me, I still had on my Dummheit uniform. I had a knife for protection against either manager. A guard glanced at me, and I told him, uneasily, that I came to pick up a check from downstairs. He nodded after he saw my uniform. No one seemed to be there when I got into the manager's office and opened up the drawers. The floors were just drying after they had repaired the pipes. Just as I had suspected, I thought. Everything went right back to normal. So it wasn't going to blow up after all. Apathy wins all the time. I peered in the drawers. There were all the checks to be paid to everyone—I took them and stuffed them in my trench-coat pocket. I opened up the safe, since it was unlocked—then closed it, and looked around. I heard a toilet flushing way over in the back. Aw shit...whatever was in the safe, I grabbed as much as I could and split, up through the elevator. I could tell by the voice that it was Albino—and he was plenty sober. I could hear him going back to work again and shutting the door behind him. I liked quitting in just this way—not giving the Steinway bunch my word. I hated them too much. People of their likes made it impossible for me to continue living in this fucking country—just like the bourgeoisie had. I decided then and there to send them to hell once and for all. I looked around in the kitchen. Everything was nice and dandy, as if nothing had ever happened. I'd fix that, I thought. I broke up the gas pipes in the stove and turned the sonofabitch on so that they would fill up the whole kitchen with gas; when I heard Albino coming, I got in the elevator and hid there. Then I loosened the stops on the gas cans and took some slick gooey stuff from underneath the stove and threw it all over the pipes—that should do it. Then I broke them up some more. I heard Albino making his way upstairs and I dashed out in record time. I had twenty-four hours until take-off time to Amsterdam. I didn't even go home to sleep that night; the following day I pawned all the jewelry my mother had. My net receipt: 2,334 dollars. Then I went back home. No one was there. No—Pops was there, I forgot. He was snoozing. Now, how to get a suitcase…I wouldn't get one. I would just get my clothes and bundle them up in a plastic bag. Yes, that's what I'd do. I got my clothes out of my drawer and split. They wouldn't hear of me again. Besides, by that time, they'd all be dead of STD's!

I bought a money belt and stuffed the money blindly inside. I kept my passport buried in my sock. What to do now? Make it to the National Airport; I had to be in New York in less than five hours. And before I knew it I was there, on the plane, at JFK, ready to take off into another world. It all happened so fast it was absurd. I could almost see the whole thing unfurling in front of me—my whole wasted life in America. I could even smell the pork-ribs still, hear them all yelling for me, yelling Louie, Louie, Louie, get your ass back here, get over here and cook our rice, cook our peas, cook our beets and pork-ribs and pimentos. And I could see it all, the dishes lying unwashed and the Chinese rice not cooking and the disco crowd still moving and shaking and squirming in maniacal heat, the knives going through their throats, their pictures popping up in the *Post,* the dope passing from hand to hand, the infections and viruses and diseases of all forms and shapes and varieties spreading and spreading, eating a hole through all the ozone layer, the grand corporational orgy wheeling more and more out of control as Love and Sex limited were swallowed up by power

in the conglomerate frenzy, Power itself finally devoured by
Maya, the god-bitch of them all. For it was Maya, the grand
force of delusion, who was the be-all and the end-all of the
whole fucking culture; it was Maya and her income tax reform
bill, Maya and the tax revolt, Maya and the stock market
rallies, Maya and the blood-sucking vampires who, time and
time again, had cut my throat and cut the throats of others and
who, even as I take myself now far away from them, would
always somehow be there, in some nasty little region in my
mind and would never go away somehow. But it was high
time I keep moving. Something in me had to die. I had to get
beyond this sugar-cube Heaven and Hell to exist in some kind
of sensible self-equilibrium, beyond the common denomina-
tor, beyond the Mecca of learning, beyond the hot stove,
beyond the dishwashing machine.

10

I HAD TAKEN UP LIFE in a small run-down hotel in the Sultan-
ahmet area of Istanbul, not very far from Santa Sophia, for
about two weeks when I suddenly ran into, of all people,
Rodney MacInness. It was a complete shock—like running
into Mr. Albino all of a sudden on the Quai Des Belges in
Marseilles. I rubbed my eyes and pinched myself to see if I was
dreaming. I wasn't. It was really him—and he had on a
uniform, too. He was in the Air Force. I was trying to get started
as a writer and living with a young woman from Egypt named
Leila. I was side my side with her, sitting on a bench, when he
discovered me. He laughed when he saw my amazement and
patted me on the shoulder. "Yeah, man, I'm for real," he said,
chuckling. "I join' the Air Force, man. Stationed at Iraklion Air
Base. Where you been all this time?"

"I was at the Dummheit," I admitted, rather embarrassed.
He sniggered. "You had to do it, didn't you," he said, shaking
his head. "But, though, you was lucky to leave, 'cause
somethin' real bad happen there. You know, they had dis
good white manager there name Quackenbros—I heard it
from some guy, his name uh, Roy, he don't work there no
more, he quit—he ain't wanna deal wid it. But here's what
happened—it's crazy—"

"May I say something?"

"Yeah—what is it?"

243

"There were never any good white managers there—Quackenbros was just slick, see."

"But he got *shot*, see. I know you know that, right? It was in the papers. But anyway, he won't as bad as Carlin' an' them, was he?"

"Hell no."

"Tol' you you shouldn' work there. That place was crazy, man." Leila listened to our American accents and broke out in a wide smile. "You two Amreekans, eh?"

"Yeah," Rodney said. "My name's Rodney. What's yours?"

"Leila," she said, smiling. "I'm—Egypteean." They shook hands, and we continued talking, as Leila listened intently.

"But again most of the other places are just about all alike," I said, thinking about the two other places where I worked.

"I know—that's why *I* quit an' joined de Air Corps," he said.

But there was another thing on his mind he wanted to tell me about. Incidentally, it happened just one week after I left the cafe.

It all began with you-know-who—Rosa, the nympho-snatch. She had at last count forty lovers. She just couldn't control that quim...And she was even going for girls...Concha claimed Rosa was sucking her off while she slept, calling her a sneak. She was the black sheep of the entire family. And all the while Miguel sat quietly, doing nothing, minding his own business. It seemed as if he had completely shoved her out of his mind and gone over to God. Well...the other half was true...but he hadn't forgotten about Rosa. He had since been kicked out on his ass—fired, right off. Rosa then went out of her way to make him look just as stupid and foolish as possible. She beat him unmercifully, sometimes got other lovers to beat him simultaneously. She was fond of jamming his head in the toilet and flushing it, kicking him in the balls and forcing him to eat shit. He was castrated, the little fool...he hadn't a ball on him...and the affair with Giuseppe was growing more and more heated ever since they reconciled after a second fight. Then a baby came in. Miguel thought it

was his baby—until, upon scrutinization, he discovered that
it wasn't his baby at all. It was Giuseppe's baby...Miguel
fretted and shitted in his pants...he didn't know what to
do...Then he began piecing everything together. He had two
other daughters they put in day care centers due to the fights
and neglect. He took out the pictures of them he had carried
around in his wallet for so long...how come he hadn't noticed
it before?...it was even worse! The two daughters weren't
even his...they didn't look anything like him. They looked like
her other lovers. Then he was struck again...he went into the
closet to check on the wedding ring he stashed in her coat
pocket and the three beautiful gowns he gave her for her
birthday. Well, the gowns were gone—but in a shoebox,
written in Spanish, "Hands off, faggot!!" he discovered thir-
teen-hundred dollars in cash...she had pawned them in!...he
couldn't fathom anything. Nothing made sense to him anymore. He felt he had only one thing in the world left to do and
he was going to pull it right off...

Rosa showed up one afternoon after collecting her pay. She
was hyped up about it. She kept talking about her new lover
Ken. "He so handsome," she kept repeating to herself, strutting like a peacock in heat like she always did. She had on a
nice white blouse and a tight brown skirt her other lover Tony
had given her. All that money being thrown around...all for
clothes...and they couldn't even afford to feed the kids
anymore...whose kids, anyway?...

Nobody was in the house. Rosa felt free to do what she
wished then. First she reached into the cupboard and brought
out a bottle of brandy and laid it down on the table. Then she
rushed off to the phone sitting on the table in the kitchen to
phone up her Giuseppe. She rung him up, the phone buzzed,
and Giuseppe answered. She almost answered back when
she was caught by surprise with an arm around her neck and
a kick in her twat. That frightened the shit out of her... She was
so frightened she froze up and weakened—she thought it was
a ghost. The phone dropped out of her hand and onto the

ground. Giuseppe kept yelling "hello" and wondering quite angrily just what in hell was going on, thinking she was playing games with him. She tried to reach him, but something strange kept pulling her back. And then a knife caught her square in her belly...again...again...she was being ripped up like a pig...you could hear her guts ripping...she puked blood, she twitched violently, throwing uncontrollable spasms, her guts hung out dripping with mush, and she was thrown to the ground, a heap of torn-up intestine...The man with the big Bowie knife was laughing, just like a madman, when Rosa, nodding off into death, noticed him pull off his black ski mask. It was Miguel. He was off his rocker. Then he began howling like an animal, doing flip-flops...he ran totally amok...after he had a swell rampage wrecking the joint, smashing her sperm-jars on the wall and breaking up the plaster, doing a beautiful piece of destruction to boot, he slipped away—nobody found him...

Rosa didn't die. For the phone was still off the hook and babbling wildly when Miguel smashed up the apartment. No one next door paid it any mind. They were already used to things happening that way. But Giuseppe knew something was wrong when he heard all the noise and gruesome sounds of Rosa struggling and then fading off. He thought it was one of her silly jokes. Then he heard banging and crashing, and then the phone was smashed up with a baseball bat. Miguel forced the baseball bat up her twat and left. Giuseppe, angry at Rosa's foolishness, headed down to the apartment, got up on the third floor and knocked on the door. No one answered. Then he banged on it. Nothing. Then he got so hysterical, he began pushing his whole weight up against it, then ramming into it. The landlady came up and told him to fuck off, literally—he had no business in the apartment and she would call the cops if anything happened. But Giuseppe wanted the cops to come, so he kept haranguing the landlady. Finally she ran off and got the police. Giuseppe mentioned about the Montemar's door being shut up, when someone was inside.

The landlady claimed no one was inside. When the police asked nearby tenants they said nothing, they didn't know what was happening. They just heard a lot of noise inside. Some said they didn't hear anything at all. Still others wouldn't even bother talking. So the police started to haul off Giuseppe when they saw blood dripping from under the door. Then they busted the doors down—and found Rosa there in a total mess, the fat end of the baseball bat shoved up her twat. Giuseppe fainted on the spot...he puked...then he conked out...he couldn't take it...

The tenants were dumbfounded. They didn't understand how it could have happened, they were just minding their own business. And Giuseppe was taken off to the hospital for shock, and Rosa had blood being pumped into her as she was rushed off to the emergency room. They had four ambulances, and they tried to make up their mind which one could go in which. Then the ambulance got lost going through town, then they got hungry and stopped over for a beer and a sandwich on the way to the Holy Roller Hospital. Giuseppe awoke in the hospital, screaming for dear Rosa, who was dying on the operating table, so he thought...he thought of nothing else but her alone...she was his life, since he was a failure, he had nothing else to live for...

Rosa was in the same hospital getting patched up the best she could. Much of the viscera had been damaged beyond repair and had to be removed. Plastic devices were put in. They were never to work just right...but her asshole was fine. It had to be for screwing. She couldn't bear to have that lost on her...The doc spent three days bent over that old hag working away on her. Miguel had ripped all around in her stomach, too, trying to get to the ovaries. That's what he wanted. He was trying to spay her. Not a too unwise idea for a snot like her.

Giuseppe's money and dough from the 42 others went into her eventual recovery. It took three whole months to get her back into shape. Three hundred twenty-five stitches...but there were problems. First of all, she was always having stomach pains. For this the doc prescribed some pills; second she was shitting blood regularly, sometimes right in the midst of things...a pure embarrassment. For this the doc prescribed some sort of strong juice which first made her so drowsy she had to take a second liquid, Puloxidin, to counteract the side-effects in her brain. But this acted as a powerful aphrodisiac and made her sexually uncontrollable, among other things: it was also very highly addictive. She went around for days looking for a bottle...it was hard to kick the habit, and she never did. She stopped shitting blood, all right (only so long as she took the addictive medicine)—but the belly-aches never went away.

Aside from these problems, Giuseppe and Rosa became totally lovesick...

A fuss came when her baby was taken into custody by the authorities who always deemed her psychopathic. She began to scream and cry...she had shit fits...she wouldn't dare part with Giuseppe's baby. And the addiction to the Puloxidin to counteract the Essetrex made her a scrounging, vicious bitch...she would actually shit blood again or go frigid if she didn't have it. She couldn't fuck that much anymore, thanks to what Miguel did...it hurt too much through the cunt now...she had to get fucked in the ass where it was more dangerous...You should've seen her belly...it looked like a smushed-in cherry-pie crust...with all those ugly scars going criss-cross! Nobody loved her anymore...they dumped her like a hot potato...one by one...they all split...Giuseppe was the only one afterwards.

To top it off Concha had to go out and get banged by two white guys at the same time...she infected them both with AIDS...and she'd also been knocked up, the bitch! All three were in the cafe working when suddenly the gas grill broke down (compliments of yours truly), along with the water pipes which threatened to burst again, and on a Sunday to boot. The whole works was in its usual frenzy, but it wasn't that bad...everything was in relative calm and order...no rebellion whatsoever...The stove was a real problem. They got Giuseppe down there immediately to fix the stove. But the bastards kept rushing by to get to the kitchen downstairs, knocking things over, getting in and out of the kitchen...Ding Bat especially. She was the clown who tipped over the gas can. The lid popped off; it sparked. The gas leaked out... "You gook! Turd!" Giuseppe shouted at her...it was delicate work he was doing. One wrong mistake and that was the end, for real.

He began unhooking the pipes while the line outside grew and grew. The U.S. Marines Jazz Band was playing here today, and everybody wanted to come and listen. People stopped in there more and more to hear the band. The customers went crazy...why don't they clean the damn tables? or the bathrooms? or the carpets with the watermelon scraps lying in the aisle-ways so people could trip up and break their necks—like one man did? He was going to sue the company...and where in hell was their liver and onions? Their shrimp? Where?...Huh?...There weren't any answers. "Wait, you shits!" Basil screamed. A busboy screaming at the customers! That was wrong...they demanded to see the manager Albino...they didn't know he was dead drunk, sucking Johnny-Boy's balls...Carlin was soused, too, though he was still oriented, at least...Albino was pooped...he was the King of the Joint, he didn't care...The customers began to rebel; they shouted in their faces for the food. Finally the grilled food was lifted from the display cases and the situation explained. Then, to top it off, the soda machine ran out of fluid. The fluid was in the basement. Louangphuck ran down to the basement and tipped over another can—that leaked out...you could hear the sissing noise...gas was everywhere...

The time was apparently four o'clock. As it happened it was Yo Yo Ying's last day at the joint. He was just a little-noticed background figure all this time. Too bad I didn't write too much up about him...He was all smiles as he let out, walking out of the building and the Pocohontas Mall—forever. He was returning to Ghanshu; the research project was complete. All he needed now was a plane ticket to Guangzhou...Lucky man!

Rosa kept up, as did Lolita and Concha with her big belly. Lolita's herpes was worsening. Her face looked like cinnamon toast now...she had to wear rubber gloves...even her jet-set lover had it, apparently.

Giuseppe sat up. He was black with soot and grime. Like a phony nigger minstrel...He winked at Rosa; Rosa laughed and licked her lips at him. She went on cutting the cake when she felt her head in a whirl. She dropped the knife. The Puloxidin...she felt her stomach heaving, she doubled over. She threw up...it was all blood...it splattered all over the table and the cake, pure, smelly purple-colored blood, just like Niagara falls...she sucked in the air weakly and collapsed...Concha cried, Lolita screamed like her throat had been cut. They all flocked around her. Giuseppe jerked up. He saw her puking all over the place, writhing on the ground, the blood running down her face, bubbling out of her mouth...he lost himself...he began banging on the stove with the hammer...he knocked a hole in the stove...more gas leaked out...it went into the dining room, all over...people ignored the smell. They thought it was from the construction workers nearby...they were woefully ignorant.

Carlin wobbled up at this point. He had a cigar he just plopped into his mouth. The whole joint was in an uproar. All business was constipated. Then Clyde tipped over an entire thing of dishes...every one broke...Johnny-Boy was absolutely off his rocker... "I oughta kill you motherfuckers!" he shrieked..."Can't you do anything right?"

Giuseppe butted in and began to prod him, pointing to Rosa, crying like a baby. "She's dying! She's dying!" he kept snorting... "Dry up the fuckin' rain, you shitface! Dry it up now! I'll jug your freakin' ass!!" Giuseppe pulls on him in a frenzy, Johnny-Boy arrogantly and snottily tosses him right into all six gas cans...they all leak out...it's all over the place...the hissing and sissing...Johnny's drunk, he can't tell...Giuseppe's unconscious...all the workers are too busy scampering about and falling up and down the stairs to be concerned...about anyone, or anything, except Rosa. They've all surrounded her. They're frantic as all hell. The customers are raising cain. They've been waiting for ten minutes! Too long!...Johnny-Boy comes over. He pushes them all out of the way. He wants to have a look..."Lemme see, lemme see..." He pulls out his cigarette-lighter; he's still got the cigar in his mouth, the arrogant turd...someone screams, "No! No! DON'T DO IT, YOU FOOL!!" Johnny-Boy plugs him with his gun! That should do it...the screams continue...he's in a daze...he doesn't know what's what...he's got the lighter again...he lights it...

KAPPOWWWW!!!!!

The whole kitchen blew up. Ditto the dining room. Carlin blew it all to hell. The idiot! He didn't know anything about the gas...he was soused...probably didn't know anyway!...The customers kill each other trying to get out. Most of them die, they look like human torches. The flame keeps spreading all over the whole building, all over the whole mall. The place is going to pot. Concha runs out screaming, a board catches her dead on the back of the skull...kaputt!!...The dishwasher turns on by itself and burns, sparking like a robot out of control...Clyde falls in the dishwasher...the suds and water are spurting out of the sides...the rest are downstairs roasting with Albino...Johnny-Boy's a crisp, burnt like a nigger...Lolita gets her head busted open, spaghetti comes out for brains...The shelf crushes Elsie to death...it all has to end this way after seven long years...Ding Bat's fried, Basil broiled, the whole crew a fucking shish-kebab...

The whole Pocohontas Mall burned down that May when I shipped out. Ten escaped with injuries. Everyone in the Dummheit died. Not a soul remained. Damn...was the past gone or not?

But after I heard it, it was hard to contain my laughter. After Roy bid us goodbye and made it to the Topkapi bus station I broke out laughing. The whole incident filled me with joy. It was a blessing from God; He had sent them all to hell where they belonged, young and old, good and bad. It was a masterpiece of arsonage and wanton destruction. All I could have wished was that all America would burn down in just this very way.

Rodney had since gone back to Iraklion Air Base. Leila was puzzled yet somewhat excited at what he and I were discussing. I explained it to her. "Don't go to America," I told her. I picked out an edition of the *Herald-Tribune* which told of widespread rioting in New York City as a result of severe racial tensions. I told her about the homeless, about the hatred of her people by the Americans, the honkies who were there, the greed and corruption, the drug and alcohol abuse, the boredom and insecurity, and so on and so fourth...She laughed. "Why all dees? Amreeka, I see, very byootiful. Bevoly Heels, eh?" I could already hear overtones of Yee Sing Hwong in her *fellaha* naivete. I explained to her more carefully, holding up the newspaper to her face. She still shook her head with a chuckle. "But zat's jost one place, you see!" she said, with a smile on her face. "Look—I want to go to Amreeka—just for short-time. Or—long-time. I dohnno. Baht—I zeenk you talk erbout ze bad zeenges an' naht good zeengs. Like—Hollywood. Or—I know. New York, ze—ze, well, Amreeka ees where ze world ees at. Ze energy. Ze excitement. Everyzeeng else dry up almost total!"

"I see," I said, shaking my head.

"Why you shake your head? Cood I jahst *see* for myself?" What could I do to convince her? It was hopeless: The Voice of America had gotten to her before I had.

And not only that, when I woke up in the morning, she wasn't there. She had departed with a note left on my pillow saying that she had gone to Ankara to obtain a work permit from the Turkish government because, as I found out upon opening the classified section of the *Tribune*, she had encircled an ad which read:

ENGLISH SPEAKERS WANTED
Be a part of the big crowd.
Join an exciting team which is also
very friendly and looks
for clean-cut energetic people
like you. Please apply

TODAY!!!
Steinway International Hotel, Istanbul,
TURKEY.
(65, Taksim square;
Ask for Mehmet)

our spirits start with a smile!

It was all unavoidable, as I could see clearly. I folded the newspaper and threw it into the trash. What would they do, those monsters and parasites? Would they make hamburgers out of *her*, too?
"Another one for the meat racks!"

Brindisi, Athens, Istanbul,
Mersin, Ankara, Alexandria,
Cairo.
September—December, 1987
March 18, 1988.